A Novel

HEARTWORM

Aaliyah Merchant

Copyright © 2022

All Rights Reserved

Table of Contents

Acknowledgements

I want to begin by thanking Nishrin and Murtuza Merchant, who believed in my potential and cared and went out of their way to help me make this dream come true. They are the kind of parents that I can only dream of having, and without them, this book would not be here.

To my uncles, Abbas and Mustufa and my kind, beautiful aunts Aiman and Ilham. I want to say a special thank you for being so supportive and helping me on my little journey to become a better writer and human.

To my friends, Noorain, Kashvi (who has claimed that this is the first book she will ever finish, other than the BFG), Prathna, Naina (the first person who actually ever read the first page), Zahra, Alefiyah, Rohail, Nikhil, Hardik, Tanvi and Fabian. Thank you for letting me pick your brains and ask questions and making me believe I could do this, and being more excited about my writing than I was myself. And Ipsita, Khusbu and Ryan for being so supportive and amazing. Ms Trotman, who will always be one of the best teachers and gave me the confidence to actually carry on writing after the first chapter. And thank you to every author's work I've ever read. It was reading that inspired me to write. Isaac Levine, who has helped me tremendously to make this happen. I also want to thank my gorgeous Tiara, who kept me company late into the night whilst I wrote, she can't read this… as she is my cat, but I know she knows.

And thank you to every author's work I've ever read. It was reading that inspired me to write.

Author's Note

I'm writing this book at the age of 18 or 19, depending on when it publishes. I'm very young but meant to be old at the same time; on the brink of adulthood, of growing up and leaving home. So know that before you read this. Know that these ideas and feelings that I relay about death and love and growing up come from an 18-year-old girl. It's an age where you know everything but haven't experienced or felt everything. I think it's an exciting perspective from a person with a lack of experience and wisdom and a sense of naivety.

Also, if you want to intensify the reading experience of this book check out the 'HEARTWORM' playlist on Spotify

Chapter 1

You're Here

She turned her head back.

She swore under her breath.

"What?" Her sister cocked her head.

"Nothing," she said as quickly as she had turned back around. She blew a breath out and tucked a piece of hair behind her ear. Why had she looked? Why had she turned? She was fine just a moment ago, and now...

She suppressed a wry laugh. This was not how she expected this night to go. She looked up at the ceiling. In all fairness, that seemed to be a trend in her life. Most things hadn't gone the way she had expected.

"Are you okay?" her sister asked.

"Yeah," she bit her lip. She couldn't help herself. Her head turned... and this time, she didn't look away. She knew she never really could.

She indulged herself with a breath. He had one hand in his pocket, smirking as the others around him laughed, he had made a joke. He raked a hand through his hair and touched the scar on his eyebrow. He had that feeling when you felt someone's eyes were on you. He lifted his own. They caught hers, as they always had. He would catch those dark eyes in any room - purposeful, soft, and sharp.

Those blue eyes took her right back. Right back to sunrises and late-night drives and early morning coffee. She didn't even try and stop herself, she knew it would never work, and maybe she didn't mind traveling back in time for a bit.

Sharp features and sharper eyes still.

They walked over, around the people whose faces all melted together now into blurriness, the sounds of chatter dimming. They met halfway. They never did that before.

"Hi," his mind was wide open in a tender smile, "You're here," he was breathless. He was rubbing at his wrist. On his left wrist were a watch and a leather bracelet with a silver clasp.

1

He looked at her like he had just found a lost piece of sentimental jewelry. Something he had been looking for for ages and given up on some time ago, and then one day, it just randomly turned up, like a gift from God. It was better to lose a lover than to have never lost at all.

"Hi," she muffled into his shoulder. They were hugging. He recognized the jasmine perfume, but it was muskier now, almost amber-like. "I mean," he pulled back, blue eyes gazing at her, and cleared his throat, "I didn't know you were back."

She forgot what it felt like to be looked at that way. "I got back the day before yesterday," there was a dazed smile on her face. She felt giddy. Even hearing his voice made her feel like her blood had been spiked. He had the same perfectly disheveled hair and the same blue eyes that captivated her vision entirely. Looking at him felt like looking at a portrait photograph with a blurred background.

"Your hair is different," she nodded. It was a little shorter. "It looks great," he couldn't take his eyes off her.

She empathized. "Thank you," she bit her lip, dark eyes gazing. "Do you want to go outside?"

"Yeah, I'd like that," he nodded. His smile only lessened slightly.

They sat outside on the wooden swing in the garden. His arm was draped behind the back of the swing, rocking them back and forth with his legs. It was the kind of heat that made you want to run around and play, as their chaotic old summer days. They were back in their hometown for the first time in a while. And everything felt the same and different. The beach was the same, and the homes were the same, but there were those little footprints of growth and change in the people that inevitably came in a year or two.

The garden wasn't completely empty, a buffet was being set up by caterers, but all the guests were still inside the house. Sitting outside, with barely anyone else around, you could still hear the sound of the waves on the beach. The noise from inside the house was actually muffled now from the closed glass doors.

"God, Anaisha," he blew a breath out. He said her name like it brought him pain and happiness at the same time. She didn't realize she even missed the smell of him, coffee and sandalwood and peppery. "What's it been? Two years?" He angled his head to face her and pressed a palm against his black pants. "I'm 21 now, so…" she pressed her lips together, "Yeah, two years."

"I know, it's the 10th," a tender smile on his face.

"Yeah," she said slowly. Memories came into her mind like waves softly hitting the shore. She wondered if he was remembering the same things.

"God, we were a…" she leaned forward, holding the edge of the swing, her summer dress floating above the ground, "Mis-match made in heaven," she said with a laugh, sharp eyes moving to face him.

"Or hell," he smirked, holding her with his eyes.

"Maybe somewhere in between?" She shrugged and leaned back again as she played with the rings on her finger, looking at him every few seconds.

Talking to him felt like reading a story from your childhood or hearing a song that you had once loved…one that you hadn't heard in a while and was slowly remembering just how good it was.

Chapter 2

So, when did it begin?

Naira and Mykal leaned back on the bed together, her hair sprawled around her head like a halo.

His hands rested on his abdomen. She was so much smaller than him that her legs dangled at the edge of the bed whilst he had to cross his over one another, for them to be at the same level.

"So, when did it begin?" she asked, tapping the little freckle on her knuckle.

Mykal took a deep breath in, drumming his fingers against his chest, "Well, we've been friends since we were kids…."

"Yeah, I swear my memories of the three of you when we were younger were always the three of you together all the time." Her tears had dried now, and she was calm. The window was slightly open and rustled the white curtains.

"Yeah, I met Ries when we were nine years old in school. He still had the same eyes, but his hair was shittier," Mykal laughed. "He had moved schools and didn't have many friends, and we were put together for this like research project thing…" suddenly, he went silent, blinking slowly. His long thick lashes were laying against his cheekbone. Naira knew he was considered good-looking, with big hazel-brown eyes and full lips, his face had chiseled out more over the year and his new short hair just accentuated it further, on top of that he was tall… but to her he would always just be, Mykal.

"and Anaisha…"I don't even remember properly meeting her" he smirked, that true smile still lingered on his face as he spoke, "she was just always there…"

"Honestly," his deep voice became quiet like he was telling her a secret. She had always thought he had a comforting voice, it had deepened with age, but it was always friendly and jokey, now comfortingly deep, like a fireplace. "I can't even remember my life before they were in it," it was almost like their lives had only truly begun when they walked into each other.

The Very Beginning:

The 'Whispering Waves' was a gorgeous neighborhood in the city. It was new and upscale with beautiful homes. The largest being seven bedrooms and the smaller townhouses being three. All the houses looked different, though, following a similar essence of a beachy, relaxing oasis. It was only a five-minute drive to the beach, about an eight-minute walk, and a fifteen-minute drive from the heart of the city. It was a small place, so twenty minutes felt long to the residents of the city. It was a beautiful place, and Mahita was grateful to now be living here. Mahita was walking on the sidewalk, holding the hand of a little five-year-old girl by her side. The perfect picture of a young mother in a sleeveless long white dress with her long, dark hair swept romantically to the side. The weather was good today, you could hear the brush of the waves in the midst, and the sky was bright blue, cloudless.

"She's adorable," said the woman in front of her, with tawny skin and black hair tied in a swinging ponytail. She was wearing sneakers, leggings and a tank top.

"Aww, thank you," Mahita smiled graciously, then tugged on her daughter's hand. "Say thank you, Ishaani."

"Thank you," the little girl peeped with a great big smile.

"You're welcome," the other woman smiled. She had a low, sweet voice.

"I'm Mahita," she held her hand out in greeting.

"Selena," she said. "You guys just moved in, right?" she pointed a few houses away. "I was actually meaning to send something over, but…."

"I totally get it, don't worry about it," she laughed, shaking off the formalities.

"I didn't realise you were about to pop!" Selena motioned to Mahita's stomach. Her stomach looked sort of comically big, considering what a small woman she was.

"Yeah, one month to go… she's going to be a September baby," she said, gently touching her stomach and looking down at her tummy.

"Two girls! Lucky," the women beamed. "I have a little boy," she touched her chest. She was absolutely beautiful, with big hazel eyes, and a toned physique. The kind of beautiful that made you think she must have been asked to model when she was younger.

"Aww, I've always wondered what it would be like to have a boy."

"Oh, well, you can borrow him some time, but I must warn you, he will drain the energy right out of you!"

She laughed, covering her mouth. "How old is he?"

"He's turning one this December," Selena said fondly, in the way that parents spoke of their children.

Mahita looked up at the sky in surprise, at the drops of water now falling over them. "Oh my, I better get going," they didn't get rain often, ever, actually.

"No, no, don't be silly. Come inside, please," Selena motioned toward her home, already stepping up to open the door. It was a gorgeous five-bedroom home made of crisp, white concrete with big glass windows and a small driveway. The garden was beautiful and intelligently designed with a barbecue, a pool, and white sofas. The interiors were beachy and earthy, all blues and whites and creams. It was a place you wanted to rest and chill out. "We can have some tea or coffee," she took a few steps forward, "or some honey cake?" she turned with a little smile. Mahita looked up at the sky, the rain was pretty heavy "I would never say no to cake…"

Chapter 3

When We Were Around Five And Six...

At this time, there were a few constants in Mykal's and Anaisha's lives. These constants included their families, going to school, and that every day after school, at around 3 or 4 in the afternoon, they would meet at the park. The games they played varied, and the activities, whether they cycled or played tag. But they would always meet. They were a part of each other's routines.

Today, the park was alive with the sound of children running around, as it always was at this time. The sun was beating down, and the water on the beach beyond glimmering silently.

Anaisha exhaled through her nose, crossing her arms over her chest as her two braids were coming slightly undone, a little sweat forming on her forehead. They were currently playing 'piggy in the middle.' Anaisha was the 'piggy,' and the poor girl just could not seem to catch the ball. In fairness, she was playing with Mykal, who was a little taller than her, and a girl who was around seven while she was five. Her now older, ten-year-old sister found the park to be 'boring' and 'for little kids'; therefore, she no longer attended.

They kept playing, and Anaisha kept running to and fro, seemingly unable to catch the ball. However, she wouldn't admit defeat. That wasn't her style. Annabel, the tall seven-year-old, threw the ball a little too hard, and Mykal missed it. The ball tumbled over to the see-saw, and Anaisha ran, she ran with all the ferocity and might she could muster and caught the ball a few seconds before Mykal jogged up behind her. As Mykal came up jogging behind her, she jumped up and down, holding the ball like a trophy above her head. He was smiling, his face broken out into a big smile, "Good job," he patted her on the back. What she didn't know was that Mykal had purposely slowed down, letting her grab that ball. He knew they wouldn't be able to go home until she had got it.

When We Were Around Eight And Nine...

The primary school teacher walked into her class, lunchtime was over, and she took insight in front of her. A room was filled with coloured tables and chairs and colourful educational posters all around the walls. There were about 20 nine-year-old students.

"Ok, quiet down, everyone..." the classroom of children did not, in fact, quiet down. The noise level of all the nine-year-olds stayed the same. The teacher took in a breath as she settled down at her desk and clapped her hands together in a sequence. Suddenly, almost like a spell was cast upon all the children that clapped back in the same sequence and the whole class was quiet, except for the chattier minority, who were still talking.

"Mykal, you can finish your conversation later," she said in a stern voice. A small boy turned around at the sound of his name.

"Sorry, Miss Thorpe," he said as he made his way toward his assigned chair at the green table with a cheeky grin on his face.

"Alrighty," she got up and strode in front of the projector, all the little eyes of the little people on her. "In my hand," she waved a piece of paper in her hands. "I have… drumroll please," she had that sweet voice of a person who had the patience and calmness to work with children all day. "Your pairs for this project!"

There was a small, collective groan at the fact that they would be in 'assigned pairs'. Although, there was another small minority that was rather relieved they wouldn't have to find a pair due to the fact that they would probably struggle to find someone. Among those few was Andries Adamos, on the blue table.

She read off the pairs, and one by one, the kids got up to sit with their pairs.

"Andries and Mykal," she read aloud. Mykal got up from his chair and walked over to sit next to the empty seat next to Andries. Even at that age, Mykal had a little swagger to his walk.

What Ms Thorpe did not foresee was that she had now created a completely mischievous and charismatic duo that would both make teachers in the future fall in love with them and curse them under their breath on the same day. She had also created a life-long friendship that they would forever be thankful for.

That weekend, their mothers had planned for the boys to meet and do their project. Nowadays, Andries could barely remember first meeting Mykal. It seemed like he was just always there, by his side. But, when Andries first walked into Mykal's home, he remembered seeing the warm face of his mother greeting him and his own at the door, carrying a little girl on her hip and the smell of cheese and the view of the ocean as soon as you walked in.

After talking to his mother, she looked down at Andries and said, "Hi, Andries. I hope you're okay with cheese quesadillas for lunch today?" she asked.

He nodded, and his mother smiled. It was his favourite food. He didn't know that she had previously spoken to his mother and found that out.

Mykal bounded down the stairs and stood next to his mother in a lime green t-shirt and black sweatpants with a hand in his pocket.

"Hi, I'm Mykal," he held his hand out to Andries's mother.

"Oh, hi!" she said, looking down at his hand with a bemused smile, and shook it, "I'm Teresa." "Mrs Adamos," his mother had said, with an eye to Mykal. "His father taught him that," she laughed at the handshake.

"Okay, why don't you boys run upstairs, and I'll call you when lunch is ready."

"It'll be 20 minutes, mam."

"Perfect," she smiled at her housekeeper, Filipa.

As they went up the stairs, they heard Selena say with a laugh, "His father taught him that, the handshake, I mean."

"It's very cute," Teresa replied.

Andries walked in, somewhat tentatively, to Mykal's room. It was a normal, smallish sized room with a great big window and a view of the ocean that made it seem larger. There was a bunk bed with a blanket of rockets and stars all over it. Glow in the dark stars on the ceiling and a clean, shiny black desk with a computer on it. A guitar lay against the desk. The floor was covered with a grey rug and a shiny black shelf along the wall filled with books.

"Do you have a brother?" Andries asked.

"No, I just wanted a bunk bed," Mykal grinned. They didn't know that in time that top bunk would basically become Andries's second place of sleep.

After lunch, they went back upstairs and worked more on their project, with Mrs Ricard walking in every so often to check up. They spoke about football and video games, nothing revolutionary, though.

In the middle of doing their project, they heard someone bounding up the stairs. Andries looked up at Mykal, who didn't seem to even realise. Suddenly, a little girl bounded through the room and sat on his bed as if it was her own.

9

"When will you be done? I want to go to the park. I got a new scooter! You have to see it, it's sooo cool," the little girl announced, she had her short dark hair in a ponytail and was wearing a purple t-shirt with a mermaid on it and shorts.

"In a bit, I think, we're not done yet," Mykal said as he cut up a piece of blue paper in a wavy pattern.

They were making a diorama of the Amazon rainforest.

"Hi, I'm Anaisha," the little girl said to Ries.

"Hey, I'm Andries," he smiled.

"You have really pretty eyes," she said, widening her own.

"Oh, uh, thanks," he said, averting his gaze to cover his 'pretty' blue eyes as he looked for the ruler.

He was blushing.

"I have to go to the bathroom," she said as she leapt off the bed.

Andries looked at her as she left and then at Mykal. "I didn't know you were friends with a girl," Andries said.

"Yeah," Mykal shrugged as he pulled out a box of markers and picked the blue ones.

"Okay, cool," Andries shrugged back. Mykal remembered thinking that was cool. Sometimes boys would make fun of him for playing with Anaisha. He didn't really care, though. He enjoyed playing with her, so he would. But it was still cool that Andries didn't care.

That day instead of going out to play, Anaisha stayed and helped them with their project. She actually had a very cool idea of bringing in a speaker with the sounds of the rainforest with them while explaining it. Andries had so much fun that evening, and even Anaisha and Mykal seemed to enjoy it just as much as if they were to go out and play.

At around six in the evening, a tall man with a now loosened tie walked in, he looked like the coolest person Andries had ever seen.

"That looks amazing," he said as he knelt down to the boys, he had a very deep voice. "Thanks, Dad," Mykal said as his father kissed him on the head. "This is my friend Andries." Something happened in Andries's chest when Mykal said he was his friend.

"Hi, I'm Andries," Andries put his hand out to shake. Mykal smiled, and so did Mr Ricard, who said, "Good handshake, Ries."

"Hey, I didn't know you got back," Selena said as she ambled into Mykal's room. Her husband bent down to kiss her on the cheek. She leaned her head on his shoulder for a second.

"Yeah, wanted to check on how their project was going," Andries didn't think that his Dad even knew about his project. He was travelling right now.

That night, Selena and Teresa spoke over the phone about the next day as the boys still had to finish up their project.

"Yes, sure. He has a guitar class right after school. So he could come to your place by 3:30… is that okay?" Selena said.

"That's perfect. Andries has tennis after school anyway," Teresa was sitting on the sofa, drinking coffee, a little too late than one should be drinking coffee.

"You know I've been meaning to put Mykal in tennis classes, where does he go…."

Chapter 4

When We Were Around Nine And Ten…

"Andries," his mother called as she put her laptop to the side and got up from the clean, grey-blue sofa to go into the kitchen. She had been reading some emails. "You're sleeping over at Mykal's today."

"Yeah, I know, Mom," Andries said as he popped a piece of popcorn into his mouth. He slept over at Mykal's every Friday after tennis. Andries grew up in a sleek duplex a little closer to the centre of town.

His mother rolled her eyes lovingly. "Alright, smartypants," she looked at her watch as she leaned on the glossy black kitchen counter. Their whole home was shiny blacks and whites and pops of dreamy livid. It was a modern haven in the sky. "Don't eat too much before your class, or you'll get sick," she said, looking at Mykal, who was currently unwrapping his third piece of chocolate. As she turned around, he quickly stuffed it into his mouth with a cheeky grin on his face. No one in the Adamos family liked Mars bars, they only kept them in the house when Mykal was coming over, and there was a carton of fruit juice, blackcurrant flavoured for Anaisha in the pantry.

"Ok, ok, time to go," Teresa tapped the counter, and soon enough, both boys swivelled off the white barstools on the kitchen counter and made their way off to tennis.

They had seen Anaisha's older cousins, who were about 14-years-old playing it.

That night after their tennis class, Anaisha had come over to Mykal's house. It was a Friday night, and all their parents were going out together, so naturally, the kids would hang out.

"No! Can we please watch the Barbie movie you promised," Anaisha wailed. "Filipa Didi, they promised!!" They were in their pyjamas, waiting for the pizza to come.

"Boys, you did promise. I remember very well," Filipa looked at them over her little rectangular glasses. She had a few greys in her hair now and was a stout, little woman with beady eyes and a loving heart.

Anaisha sat on the sofa, with her arms crossed over one another, scowling.

"Ok, kiddos, we're going to dinner now," Mykal's parents walked down the stairs, all dressed up. Their parents were now at that age in their 30s where they could still pass as young people when their children weren't around, but when they were, it made complete sense that they were parents. Their lives were filled with this lightness of having young children where the biggest problems were disciplining them over what they were eating or watching. But, still, it was, of course, a feat.

"Anaisha, what's wrong?" Mykal's father asked.

"They promised that we would watch the new Barbie movie today because we watched

Transformers last time," she pointed at the two boys, her dark eyes accusatory.

"We don't like the Barbie movies," Mykal said.

"You've never seen them!" Anaisha threw her arms in the air. "You're just saying that because they're girly, whatever that means" she rolled her eyes, looking like a little teen.

"You boys did promise last time, and Anaisha watched your movie without any complaints," Selena intervened. Anaisha nodded, happy that the adults were on her side, smiling on the inside, knowing she would now probably get her way. She was smart like that.

"Did you enjoy the movie Anaisha?" Mr Ricard said.

Anaisha nodded. "It was okay," she shrugged, "Nothing memorable, though," she blew out a breath. Selena and Marco shared a smile over the 'big word' Anaisha was using. "So, you guys might enjoy this Barbie movie," Selena said as she put her hoop earring on.

"But Mrs R, it's Barbieeeee," Andries groaned.

"Ok, so if you hate it, then you can change it in the middle, and Anaisha can watch it when she gets home," Marco shrugged.

"But then, they'll just say they hate it 5 minutes in," Anaisha leapt up.

"Ok, so watch it for 30 minutes. Filipa will time it, and if you really hate it, you can change it - fair?" he negotiated like it was a contract he was drafting. Andries and Mykal groaned, and Anaisha nodded happily.

Later on in the night, Filipa's timer went off. She walked into the TV room and announced, "Ok, 30 minutes is up," Filipa came in. "Let's change it. I can tell you hate it," Filipa said as she grabbed the remote.

"NO!" Mykal and Andries yelled in unison. They both quieted down bashfully.

Filipa pressed her lips, hiding her smile, as Anaisha smiled gleefully.

"It's not that bad…." Andries shrugged, angling his head to see around Filipa's body so he wouldn't miss a second.

"Yeah, let's keep watching," Mykal said with his big hazel eyes glued to the screen.

Filipa laughed as she walked back to the baby's room, making sure Mykal's little sister was asleep.

From then on, they would watch an array of movies, alternating, usually loving each other's choices. Actually, looking back, the boys probably enjoyed Anaisha's choices more than she enjoyed theirs.

When We Were About Ten And Eleven…

When Mahita and Zahir moved to the Whispering Waves, they never anticipated how much it would shape their future and create such a dominant part of their lives. Of course, buying a new house was important. It was the kind of house they always dreamt their children would grow up in.

A gorgeous, four-bedroom modern Mediterranean style home painted a cream colour with glamorous architecture and curved doorways, moodier lighting and plush interiors. The pool was at the very edge of the garden, so if you swam to the edge, all you saw was the ocean and beach. Three sunbeams lined the pool, and a little gazebo with a sofa and swing sat in the backyard. When they moved, they didn't foresee that they would make the kind of friends that would become like family. Nearly every weekend, they would meet up. Later, they would start planning holidays. Slowly, their adult lives started to take shape, and it was a beautiful life they all lived together, a lucky one with reliable, kind and giving friends.

It happened naturally. Mahita remembered she had only properly realised how close they had all gotten when her sister-in-law Zoya had said, "So, when are we going to meet this infamous group of yours?"

"You tell me" she shrugged.

"Next week?" Zoya said as she popped a date in a bowl on the kitchen counter into her mouth.

"Alright, I'll set it up" Mahita said, pulling her hair to the side.

"I'm excited, feels like I'm meeting the royal family… the second one that is" she winked.

Mahita had laughed and then she had realised they kind of have become like her second family. It had made her heart warm.

They would have a weekend lunch, and Zahir's sibling's family would come often. Whenever they went anywhere, whether that be the beach or a restaurant, they were the loudest, most rambunctious table. And there were usually two types of people, those that looked onwards in disdain or maybe it was envy, at this loud group of laughing young parents with children, or those that wished they would one day have something just like that.

Waiters at restaurants loved them, Mr. Ricard, with his charisma and jokes, would always befriend them, pretending it was a birthday. The ladies would purposely plan to go for coffee or drinks after Mahita was finished with work, which she always found thoughtful. And nothing made her happier than seeing her daughters find lifelong friends in the other kids. It was a blessing, they were.

It was always interesting how constants and moments in life turned into the most wonderful memories. There were some moments which you already knew while sitting at that moment would turn into a memory and others which you didn't even realise were so special that they would become a subconscious memory that started to shape who you are.

Chapter 5

When We Were Around Fourteen And Fifteen…

"What?" Anaisha said, eyeing her older cousins over her glass of juice.

Shaan, Laith, and Jai, often known as the three musketeers had been whispering and laughing ever since they sat at the table. They were sitting at breakfast in the hotel, the sun and heat seeping through the now wide-open glass doors.

"Nothing," Jai raked a hand through his long dark hair, he had grown it out to the nape of his neck. It suited his long face, "we don't want to embarrass you guys," Jai said with a smirk as he twirled the silver ring on his forefinger.

"That's good because I don't get embarrassed easily" she took a bite of her croissant and, over a mouthful, said, "spill." Eyes, intent.

"Okay, we were just talking about how you and Mykal are going to get married one day," he stuck his tongue out and pointed a fork at the two of them. The other two were snickering.

Andries's brows lifted suddenly as he bit into his toast, and Anaisha and Mykal burst out laughing. "Shut up," Mykal said as he caught his breath.

"As if, being married to her would turn me into a bloody psycho" his voice cracked on that last word. Puberty, a wonderful thing.

Anaisha rolled her eyes, "actually, I think it would be the other way around" she turned to face him, a pointed look on her face. "You'd just be playing the guitar the whole day, it would drive me crazy"

Mykal scratched his face, opening his mouth to rebuttal as she swatted his hand. "Don't do that, you'll get scars" he listened and put his hand down. Recently, Mykal had gotten some acne on his cheeks. Anaisha knew it made him insecure and he was now using a cream that a dermatologist had recommended.

"See, you even act like an old married couple" Laith added, as he leaned back on his chair with a grin.

"Stop embarrassing them, guys," Ishaani said calmly. Her hair was dark, straight and half of it was neatly pulled back. She and Anaisha were now the same height, and looked similar except for their eyes. Where Ishaani had inherited their fathers big droopy eyes, Anaisha had their

16

mothers small dark almond shape. But, Ishaani looked older and seemed it too, with her mature matter-of-fact way of speaking. Anaisha opened her mouth to say something, probably sarcastic.

"Good morning, everyone," a long limbed young girl with brown eyes sang as she came up to their table. She had very pleasant features that fit together well, very captivating but not surprisingly so. She had woken up late, unsurprisingly, and was dressed in a cute little blue summer dress and sandals and gold bangles up her right arm with little dangly silver earrings. Her wavy brown hair flowed over her bare shoulders.

Mykal stopped laughing. "Morning, Damini," he breathed as he looked up at her with big eyes. Andries sat up a little straighter and smiled. Anaisha rolled her eyes, she knew both her friends had a crush on her older cousin. It was understandable, she was very pretty.

Damini grabbed some food, ordered a coffee, and pulled up a chair next to Naira. "How was your night, babe?" Damini asked her.

"It was good," she smiled. Naira had a soft way of speaking at the time, like a shy child. Then the two of them spoke softly to each other, both laughing at random intervals. Damini always seemed to have a way with Anaisha's younger cousin, the normally quiet Naira. The four girls had been sharing a room. It was a suite with two beds, and they would all hang out in their room, but when they went to sleep, Anaisha and Ishaani would go to bed, and while she was going to sleep, she could hear Damini and Naira speaking, but never loud enough for her to actually hear what they were talking about.

Anaisha looked over at them, and they were at the other end of the table. She saw Jai and Ishaani look at each other, then over at Naira and Damini and share a smile. She made a mental note to ask Ishaani what that was about but ended up forgetting all about it.

The weather was perfect at the pool that day, the sun beaming down in the cloudless sky. Warming up all the bodies underneath it, but it wasn't hot enough to sweat uncomfortably. Damini was sitting on the edge of Mahita's sunbed as she talked to her Aunt and Uncle. "Please," she pleaded, "I promise I'll keep it small."

A young-looking waiter with dark hair in a white shirt and black shorts came up to them placing down a tray on the white cube-like table beside them, "two Diet Cokes and a Corona" he smiled, toothily.

"Thank you" Damini said as her uncle signed a paper the waiter held out.

She went back to their conversation as she rubbed suncream on her arms, "I just don't want to do it at home. I'd rather have my cool Masi and Masa chaperone, and your basement is perfect," Damini said with earnest brown eyes.

Mahita blew out a breath, raking a hand through her long black hair. "If your mom says it's okay, then sure," she smiled while shaking her head.

"But, no funny business," Zahir said with a pointed finger and a smirk as he lifted his beer.

"Yay! Thank you!" she leapt onto her aunt in a big hug. "And obviously not. I'm very well behaved," she said with a serious face, followed by a cheeky little laugh as she leaned over to get her drink.

That evening they were going zip-lining, and the next day a hot-air balloon trip was planned. The rest of the holiday was filled with days of swimming, staying up late and then maybe waking up early if there was a plan. The kids didn't realise how grateful they would be one day for these memories and experiences.

That was the summer that Anaisha had gotten into photography with the help of her Uncle Zafar. She had been taking photographs that whole holiday. In fact, she had enough pictures to fill a whole photo album. Those pictures were priceless, and whenever someone flipped through them, you could feel the beauty in those moments.

When they looked back at that holiday, what they remembered was the beautiful country acting as a backdrop, doing amazing things together. But ultimately, they could have been anywhere, and still, it would've been a time in their lives that they would have forever been grateful for. No responsibilities, just kids being kids laughing with their friends running around the country with their young parents; it was amazing. They were the kind of photos that made the people in the photos look at them and whisper, 'what a time….'

When We Were About Fifteen and Sixteen…

Mrs Perez just finished the register and shut her laptop, and looked over to the boys, "Ok, so do you guys want to quickly introduce yourselves?"

They both nodded and walked over to the front of the group. They were standing outside on the tennis courts, the sun wasn't too harsh which was good. In fact there was a breeze, which was unusual.

"Hi guys, I'm Mykal."

"I'm Andries… hello", he grinned and looked over to Mrs Perez, who walked over to him, putting a motherly hand on his shoulder and said, "They are very gifted tennis players." Both boys had shot up in the past year, growing a lot taller than Anaisha, who seemed to have stopped growing. But where Anaisha and Mykal had filled out a little more, Andries stayed fairly lanky.

Mykal looked down at his feet, grinning, and Andries smirked as she continued, "who is going to help me, help you get better at tennis," she said and smiled.

When Mrs Perez looked away, Anaisha, who was standing on her own, mouthed 'very gifted' with a lift of her brows. Mykal flipped her off, and she laughed, which turned into a cough as her teacher turned around.

"Are you alright, Anaisha?"

"Mhmm", she coughed.

"Ok, so I will put you guys into partners," she said, and a few sounds of annoyance went through the group, displeased with the fact that they could not choose their partners.

Anaisha was paired with a girl called Amy, who was a raven-haired girl. She rolled her eyes at Anaisha, crossed her arms and whispered something to the girl next to her. Anaisha gnawed at her lip as she walked over to Amy.

Anaisha tapped Amy on the shoulder with a smile and said, "So, do you want to start?"

Amy looked at her for a moment, assessing and took in a deep breath as if that was the last thing she wanted to do, then plastered on a smile, "sure."

Anaisha twirled her raquet in her hand, hardening her grip and sauntered over. "You know, if you don't want to play with me," she squinted her dark eyes "just let me know."

Amy lifted a brow and said, "No, lets play"

"Ok, then let's do it" Anaisha took in a deep breath, this happened to her often with the girls in her year group. She wished she knew why, she would have preferred it if there was a reason, if she had been rude to them and they decided to be mean to her, then it would've been fair. She once thought about speaking to Damini about it, but she didn't think she'd understand so she never did, and after a while she stopped caring.

They played for a bit and stopped for a water break. Anaisha walked over to the bench where her bottle stood. She felt like she had been holding her breath the whole game, but it went fine. She took a big gulp and tightened her ponytail, as she saw Amy walk over to her friends.

"Yeah, obviously, I would never choose her as a partner. She's so shit." Amy told her friends.

"Who's shit?" Mykal came up behind her.

"This girl, Anaisha," Amy said. Her eyes kind of lit up when she realised Mykal was behind her. Her whole demeanour changed with the thought of having a conversation with him.

"Oh, Mykal, right?" She flipped her hair and straightened her back, kind of arching her back. "My partner, this girl Anaisha," she rolled her eyes and giggled as she continued, "she's terrible and kind of a bitch, too."

Mykal cocked his head to the side. "Oh, really?" He scrunched his brows together, "I've never thought that about her"

Amy scrunched her brows, "you know her?"

"Yeah," he turned his racquet effortlessly in his hands as he straightened his back, "she's one of my best friends"

Amy's face fell.

"And I can't imagine her being a 'bitch'," he said the last word like she would regret ever even looking at Anaisha wrong.

"Yo, Ries…" Mykal called his friend who was showing a young girl how to serve.

"I'll be right back" he told the girl, as he jogged over to Mykal, who was standing by the benches.

"What's up?" The sun was coming out more now, beating down on the green floor.

Mykal held a finger up, "I just had a question, do you think Anaisha's a bitch?" He said in a tone so plain, it was almost confusing.

Ries squinted his blue eyes and started laughing, "What?"

"Amy here" He tossed his racquet from hand to hand, as he turned to face his friend and slid his tongue against his teeth. His movements were calm and loose, but Andries could tell he was on edge, "thinks she's a bitch and terrible at tennis."

Andries's eyebrows shot up as he turned to see Anaisha standing alone at the other end of the benches, bouncing her tennis ball on her racquet.

"Really?" Andries met Mykal's eyes, both matching in fury. Then he cocked his head to the side, and crossed his arms over his chest,"I mean she's definitely not the best at tennis," he said as he scratched his jaw, "but she's not a bitch" Andries turned his now steely blue eyes towards the girls and cleared his throat, "Sorry, which one of you is Amy?"

He was met with silence.

"What no answer?" His voice seemed gruffer, "that's pretty rude" he squinted.

"Cowardly, too. I mean, you were running your mouth of a minute ago," Mykal said, looking at Amy.

"Oh, it's you," Andries pointed, following Mykals gaze. "Right, well, we don't want to force you to play with Anaisha anymore, so either you can sit this out" he inclined his head to the bench, "or, play with one of us…" he pointed at himself and Mykal, "you know? considering the fact you're far superior to the rest of your class." He smiled curtly.

Amy walked over silently to the bench, she didn't say a word as she sat down.

"Okay, then" Andries said as he walked back to help the other student, a tightness in his shoulders.

"Oh, and one more thing." Mykal glared at Amy, dark eyes ablaze, voice soft and sun beating down on his back "Don't ever call her a bitch again, just keep her out of your mouth and out of your head"

Mykal was walking across the court, his heart was beating fast and felt a tap on his shoulder.

He turned around roughly to see a blue-eyed girl with curly brown hair standing behind him.

The girl stepped back slightly, a little startled.

"Sorry," he took a breath in. She was striking. They were at that age, when they now could feel attraction, and cared about that kind of thing.

"My friend and I saw what happened," she pointed behind her vaguely to the benches. She was tall and moved like her limbs were too long, it was endearing. She cleared her throat and smiled. "Anaisha can play with us if she wants. I know we're already a pair, but we can alternate turns… like the three of us," she shrugged, playing with her racquet. She had gorgeous bright blue eyes, curly hair tied up messily and some freckles across her small, buttony nose and thin bright pink lips.

21

He took a second and shook his head. "Yeah, sorry, no," he cleared his throat, "I think that's a really good idea." He recovered a little and said, "Sorry, I didn't get your name."

"I never told you what it was," she grinned; she had this soft, endearing way of talking and swung her racquet as she spoke.

"I'm Calista."

"Mykal," he said as he held his hand out to shake hers, charisma oozing out of him.

She raised her straight, thin brows at this, smiling again. It was kind of odd seeing a young boy putting his hand out to shake, it seemed so formal, but he made it feel sweet and gentlemanly. He was endearing to her, too.

"Hi", she laughed slightly as he held her eyes.

Chapter 6

Two Weeks Later

"By the way, Calista and Kiara are coming over later tonight," Anaisha announced.

Mykal looked up with sudden interest and said, "The tennis girls?" His dark brows shot up, as brown eyes widened.

He was sitting on the big beige sofa in the centre of the TV room, and his feet propped up on the oak brown table in the centre. A flat-screen in front.

Anaisha nodded, a gleam in her eye, as she leaned against the door that opened to the pool. The TV room looked out at the pool; there were two arched open doorways, letting in a breeze. The sun was still out, with its rays glistening on the water. It was the kind of room that looked cool and classic at the same time, a place that people of all ages would love to sit in and find a different kind of appreciation.

"Hmm," Mykal scratched his jaw, "hmm, okay." He took out his phone and looked at himself in the camera for a second.

Anaisha looked at Andries, who was already looking at her. A little smile on both their lips. He was sitting on one of the two brown leather spinning leather seats.

"What?" He said dropping his phone back on his lap.

"Don't what us, mister," Anaisha's hand was on her hip as she walked over to Mykal and stared him down.

Anaisha was short, petite-framed, and not the most intimidating looking person. "If you fuck this up for me, I will kill you," she pointed, but if you knew her, you would get slightly intimidated by those sharp eyes. The day after the tennis class, they had spoken to Anaisha about the girls in her year group. At first Anaisha was annoyed that they did that, saying she didn't care and she could stand up for herself. But later, she understood that was just their way of standing up for her which she appreciated, and the girls never really bothered her again and she had started hanging out with Calista and Kiara.

Andries began laughing.

"What?" Mykal asked.

She threw a pillow at him and continued with her intimidating mask, "Seriously, Myk... I want some girl friends," she rolled her eyes and blew a breath out, "I'm sick of having to hang out with you two all the time." She pointed at the two of them.

"Whatever," Mykal said, a smile in his voice.

Andries was still sniggering, sitting on the sofa with his legs over the arm, and all he said was "this is funny."

An hour later, the doorbell rung. Anaisha leapt up and went to the door. About five minutes later, they could hear footsteps and chatter as they came into the room.

"Guys," Anaisha said in her high, sweet voice "you remember Kiara and Calista," she announced, introducing them.

They were both dressed casually; Calista in sweatpants and a tank top and Kiara in shorts and a T-shirt. She wore glasses at this point, and even behind the glasses, her green eyes were luminous with straight brown hair and acne-ridden skin. Calista had her brown hair down today, still a little messy. She was the kind of girl that was beautiful, at any age, even at fifteen, with her healthy tanned skin and baby blue eyes.

"Of course, what's up?" Andries said, moving over to the lazy boy to make space for the girls on the sofa.

"Hey," Mykal said with a lift of his chin, looking at Kiara and then Calista.

"So girls," Anaisha clapped her hands together, turning everyone's attention to her as she said, "we were just about to watch a movie. Do you want anything to eat or drink?"

The movie was shitty enough to the point that it was actually entertaining.

"No, I'm telling you bad movies are awesome!" She waved an arm around, "you watch them with people because then you can make fun of it together," Calista said, with a laugh.

"That actually makes sense, its more about the people than the movie" Mykal shrugged. "I agree" Mykal nodded.

"Of course you do," Andries said an impudent look in his eye.

Mykal couldn't help but laugh lightly, "Pardon?" he mumbled as he tapped his fingers on his chin.

"Anaisha, where is the kitchen? I'm gonna get some water," Calista said as she stood up.

"No, no, I'll go get it."

"Relax," Calista laughed and said, "sit down, I'll get it… anyone else wants anything?" She looked around at rest.

"I'll get a Coke," Mykal said.

"I want one too," Andries chimed in.

"Come, I'll show you where it is," Mykal said, standing up. Anaisha rolled her eyes.

When they left, Kiara said, with a glint in her green eyes, "I'm not the only one that sees it, right?"

Andries and Anaisha shared a look, and all three of them burst out laughing.

"You're not the only one," Andries shook his head, as the laugh lingered in his throat.

Mykal was on his best behaviour that night, which only made Calista more intrigued.

After Ries and Mykal left, Calista, Kiara and Anaisha stayed up the whole night talking. The night turned into a sleepover, and Anaisha was so glad. She loved Mykal and Andries, of course, but she had never had friends that she could talk to like this. She'd had girlfriends, but whenever she was with them, there was always something in the back of her mind that wanted to leave and go hang out with Mykal and Andries. But for the first time, she was so happy hanging around with these girls. She understood all the raucous she would hear from Damini and her friends, the girly laughter and looks they would give each other. She didn't realise how much she had wanted that until now.

Around the same time, Mykal and Andries joined the football team. Looking back, that was a good idea. Though they weren't the best players on the team, Mykal was better than Ries, but they were both better at tennis. They had befriended Abel and Zade. Aki was the star player, he had that genetic disposition that made him good, but he also practised hard.

"Hey, Naira, what are you doing here?" Andries asked as he and Mykal jogged up to her, sweaty from practice. She was in a hoodie and leggings, hair open and tousled.

"I'm just here to pick up Aki." She pointed toward the pitch, "Do you guys want a ride home?" she asked politely.

"No, don't worry about it. Irfaan's coming," Andries said with a kind smile. They both chatted with her for a bit, and there was a softness that came to you when you spoke to Naira, both boys feeling like they almost needed to protect her from something.

"I like the headband, by the way," she pointed at Ries, who had started wearing headbands at practice otherwise, his hair stuck to his forehead. "You should wear them more often, it looks really good," she spoke in that soft raspy way of hers with those hazel-green eyes blinking up at him earnestly.

"You know one day, Nairu" Mykal began grinning as he saddled up to her "you're going to break so many hearts" he laughed as he bumped her shoulder.

She laughed and bumped him back, "Your so weird" and rolled her eyes.

"Hey," he held a finger up, "but if anyone gives you any shit,"

"Yeah, yeah I know I'll come to you and you've got my back et cetera" she spoke like she was reading out a shopping she had heard this countless times before.

"Hey, let's go," Aki said, walking up to the three of them.

"Hey, we've both got your back" Andries said with a hand to his chest, and wounded eyes.

"Ok, I will call both of you, at the same time. Promise." she pointed at the two of them, "can I go now?" She looked at them with wide eyes.

"Yes, run along" Mykal shooed her away, before quickly ruffling her hair.

She laughed and bounded away as Aki followed, "Good practice, guys. See you," he said with a little two-finger salute.

"See you, man," Andries said. They watched Aki put an arm around Naira's shoulder, who pushed him away, laughing.

"Your gross and sweaty, don't touch me."

Aki, who was a lot taller, smothered her in a hug.

"Are they together or something?" Mykal asked Ries as they watched them.

"No, dude, their friends," Andries said, taking a swig of water and pushing his curls that were now stuck to his forehead.

Another Two Weeks Later… When We Were About Seventeen and Eighteen…

"I hate my life," Anaisha said, picking up Andries's legs to plop herself down on the now worn, long L-shaped off-white leather sofa in the centre of Mykal's basement.

It was a big spacious room that had recently been cleaned, so now it was a lot less cluttered. In the left-hand corner of the room was all of Mykal's guitar stuff; his speakers and electric guitar hung on the wall, and across it was a fuse ball table. There was a TV opposite the sofa, and on the right side of the room was a rocking horse and little ballet slippers for Sofia. Next to that was a little bar with four silver steel chairs with high backs. It was a Saturday evening, which meant they probably had plans later that night with the rest of their friends. She was wearing a little red floral dress and sneakers. With half her hair pulled back and a few strands pulled out, it framed her face quite well.

Andries had noticed that Anaisha had started wearing dresses more often and delicate rings on her fingers.

"What happened?" Andries asked and said, "also, your skin looks really good."

He squinted with a smirk. Growing up, she had some acne, and recently it had begun clearing up, and she had started doing facials.

"I got a facial yesterday, after school."

"Ooh. A facial, very fancy," he said, tickling her. Anaisha squealed, and Mykal laughed from behind them. He was sitting on his guitar stool, with his laptop balanced on his knee and a sketch pad by his feet. Mykal had decided to start a small clothing shop where he sold his own hoodie designs, and lately he had been emailing different manufacturers. Where Andries aced at school without really trying, Mykal's talents lay elsewhere, when he wanted to do something he just… did it. Googled it, talked to his parents and just tried and figured it out.

Anaisha caught her breath as he let her go. There was a little rocking horse next to the sofa for Sofia and a fuse ball table in the corner of the room. The floors were made of light wood colour, matching the beachiness of the rest of the house.

After a few minutes, Anaisha turned to Ries and said, "Can I vent for a bit?"

She looked at Ries and slapped his knee to gauge his attention.

27

"Be my guest?" he said, laying back down and crossing his legs on her lap.

"Basically, my parents want me to invite Naira to my party, and I don't want to!"

"Why not?" Andries asked, scratching the scar on his brow.

She clicked her tongue to the roof of her mouth as she said, "I just don't want tooo… I mean, we're not that close."

"I think it would be really nice. She seems sweet," Ries said, sitting up. "And just to confirm," he pointed the finger at her, "this is why you hate your life?"

"I think you're being a bit dramatic," Mykal chimed in as he strummed the strings of his guitar. He was learning a new song.

"Are you serious?"

"I think he is," Andries said, with his eyes closed.

Oh, no, he thought. He could hear the annoyance and anger in her voice. She got angry quickly when things didn't go her way.

"Don't tell me you agree…." Anaisha said, dark almond eyes squinting.

Andries inhaled, eyelids fluttering as he thought. He could either save themselves a 'situation' as Mykal called it, or be honest with his friend. "I'm afraid I agree with Mykal," he said and opened his eyes, blue eyes shimmering with candour.

Anaisha opened her mouth to say something, and Andries held a hand up.

"Look, dude, it's your birthday, and she's your cousin. Why wouldn't she be there?" Andries said, his hair had grown out a little, curlier and longer. It looked good, Anaisha wanted to say, but she wasn't in the mood right now.

"Dude," Andries opened his eyes with the way she threw his word back at her, "it's not a family event. This is MY party, and I don't want her there." Anaisha crossed her arms over her chest.

"You're being childish, Anaisha," Andries said, but with a softness to his words.

"Yeah. Don't you feel like you're being harsh? I mean, it's not like she's your older cousin… she's nearly our age," Mykal said, still strumming away, able to multitask.

"Childish and harsh. Are you guys kidding me?" she said angrily, her voice deepened with an edge to it.

Mykal stopped strumming, the new silence making the anger louder. "Shit," Andries whispered.

Mykal was getting a little heated, too. He and Anaisha always shared a little temper. Her being the younger sibling and Mykal being the older, they always fought like siblings.

"Well, it's our job as your friends to call each other out when we're being shitty," Mykal shrugged, but his voice didn't match his cool, nonchalant gesture.

"You think I'm being shitty?" Anaisha pointed to her chest as if he had personally wounded her.

"Frankly, yeah, I do," Mykal said, jutting his chin out.

"Guys, relax," Ries said, his voice a calm echo.

"No, Ries, she's being selfish." He pointed at Anaisha, "it's our job as her friends to fucking tell her."

Anaisha was shocked. "Myk… you can be such an asshole sometimes."

"Mykal," Andries said as he sat up. There was no way he would be able to nap now. "We can tell her nicely as well."

"Anaisha look," he moved to sit closer to her, but she stopped him.

"Stop," she put a hand up.

He held his hands up and said, "Just listen to me for a minute."

She blew a breath out in exasperation and nodded as she looked straight ahead.

"We've seen Naira in tennis and stuff, and she's…" he raked his fingers through his hair, trying to find the words but struggled to do so.

"You know what, I don't care what she is!" Anaisha pushed herself off the sofa and whirled around, looking at the two boys.

"It's my party, and I'm inviting who I want. Not who you or my parents want," Anaisha said, taking her bag roughly, slamming the door shut as she left. "I'll see you guys at lunch tomorrow," she said in a huff.

The group nearly always had planned on a Sunday, the group being - their parents, them, etc.

Mykal and Ries looked at each other in shock.

"Give her time," Ries said, with a little smile on his face as Mykal came over to sit with him.

"Yeah," Mykal rolled his eyes, "I know" He nodded. His friend was right.

When Anaisha went home that day, she stood outside the door of her parent's room, expecting to argue about not inviting her cousin to her party. But, something stopped her. Her hand lingered on the door handle for a moment; she watched her own fingers not turn the handle and stepped away, walking back to her own bedroom. She went out to her balcony and dialled a number on her phone.

"Hey," Andries mumbled. It sounded like he was biting his nails.

"I'm adding Mykal, one second," she looked out at the beach in the night, all dark and mysterious but oddly comforting.

"No, don't worry, I'm still at his place actually... the parents are arguing," he laughed sardonically. "I'll put you on speaker," he said as he pressed the button before she could say anything.

"Oh, okay, good," she laughed nervously. He could hear her gulp over the phone. "Hey," Mykal said in a low, dull tone.

"Hi..." Anaisha said, her voice soft and tentative. She took a deep breath. "Okay, look, I'm sorry I was such a brat today. I-"

"It's okay, Anaisha," Mykal said, his voice has gotten deeper over the last year. It was kindly comforting.

"Yeah, we know you're not actually a brat," Ries laughed gently over the phone. "Well, she kind of is... sometimes," Mykal smirked.

"Yeah, and you can be kind of an ass, sometimes," Andries shoved Mykal. "Fair enough" Mykal tapped his leg, a little smile on his face.

"Both things are true" Anaisha nodded, looking out at the view.

They all laughed, the anger from earlier softly dissipating over the phone and waves. Andries hit Mykal, eyes wide.

Mykal scratched his jaw. "I'm sorry, Anaisha if I was a little harsh."

"It's okay, Mykie, and thank you for calling me out on my shit," she said softly as she twirled her hair. She took a breath, her voice getting louder and lighter. "I wouldn't want anyone else to do it."

"Of course, we'll never stop, especially if you keep giving us so much ammunition" she could feel Andries smirking over the phone.

Anaisha rolled her eyes but was smiling.

"Ok, now tell me, why is it shitty what I'm doing? And what was my cousin like in tennis?"

So, they told her. They told her about the way she sort of stood to the side, quiet, almost as if she was scared to talk and would have rather been anywhere but there. About how she kept clenching and unclenching her fists, rubbed her hands against her shorts or kept twirling around her racquet.

They told her that when Mykal went to talk to her, her chest kept rising up and down, and her breathing became quite heavy, and the way he could tell she was trying to stay present in their conversation but kept mumbling half-answers, almost as if she just couldn't focus or was nervous.

And they told her about how in the middle of class, she asked Mrs Perez if she could go to the bathroom and never came back to class, and how Mrs Perez went to go find her about 20 minutes later and came back saying that she wasn't coming back... and then nothing else. When they asked, she said she'd explain once class was over. And she did, and they told Anaisha what it was.

Anaisha felt guilty and sad. Guilty, as her cousin, she didn't know any of this. And guilty that she wasn't someone that she could talk to. And sad that Naira was going through this. "Thanks, guys, seriously... love you."

They stayed silent, "say it back, you dicks" she laughed. "I fucking love you," Mykal screamed over the phone.

That made them laugh and lightened the world around them. "Love you," Ries laughed.

After the phone call, she went into her parent's room. Her back was straight and a new weight on her shoulders, but a weight that she was now ready and happy to have on her back.

"Guys, are you awake?" she whispered, peeking her head through. Both her parents were in bed, and she could tell they were ready to sleep, with only one lamp on. The room was dimly lit.

"Yes, Anaisha?" she could hear the anger in her mother's voice, still upset from their fight before about inviting Naira.

She held her chin up.

31

"I came to ask you to invite Naira. Actually, I'll send her a message myself," she said, "and I'll tell her to bring her friend, Aki, too," Anaisha swallowed.

Yeah, I think it'll be nice; she nodded to herself and then said audibly to her parents, "and who knows, we might just have fun."

And then she winked.

"This is kind of you, Aish," her mom said with a smile which would've won a million hearts. Anaisha had been blessed with that same smile.

Chapter 7

That Summer

That summer was the summer when a lot of things changed.

Mykal remembered thinking that the summer would suck without Andries being there for so much of it. Usually, the holidays were split up in a way where they had at least two weeks together.

The summer was two and a half months. For a week in that time, they were together on a trip with their families. And then, after that, Andries was gone. At the end of the first month, Mykal and Anaisha went on separate holidays for just a week and then they were back. And Andries came back only a few days before school began again.

He went on a holiday with just his family, and somewhere else with his parents. Everyone knew it was a make or break holiday for his family, it wasn't really a secret that this trip planned in order for his family a trip where his parents were possibly trying to save their marriage - a trip from hell. He was gone for basically the whole summer.

So, that whole summer could be described as time spent with Anaisha. Mykal remembered thinking that the summer would suck without Andries, and it did, but at the same time, it didn't. On the weekends they spent their days on the beach ,swam and got coffee and went for dinners. They had never had a group of friends like they did now, who they basically laughed with all the time, and felt as comfortable with them as they had with each other all their lives. And when it was just the two of them, they went to musicals too. The first time Anaisha had forced him to go to one, but after the first one she didn't need to force him anymore. He was the only person who seemed to enjoy it the same way she did, and she liked sharing that time with him. Some nights they would watch movies, those nights felt like going back in time to when they were little.

She even forced him to go to musicals, which was something she never thought she'd be able to do. She had only ever gone with her family before because no one ever wanted to go, but one evening, after they had been at the beach all day they grabbed some coffee. The sun was nice and low the sky radiants pinks and purples making everything feel dreamy.

"So, how much do you love me?" She turned her head, blinking slowly as she sipped her iced coffee. She was wearing a blue cover up over her bikini. For the past couple years, she had felt a sudden self-consciousness within herself, feeling awkward when wearing a bikini and analyzing things about herself that she head never even noticed before but lately that feeling seemed to have melted away. Maybe she was getting older, or just started to give less of a fuck. But it felt good, she felt good.

He quirked a brow, "I don't".

She bumped his hip, "fuck off, your a terrible liar"

"What do you want?" He slowed down his steps. The sun was still high and beat down on his bare back.

"Not much," she looked out at the ocean as they walked on the sidewalk, "I'm pretty content and non-materialistic" she shrugged.

"You own more makeup than I can count."

"Says the guy who has like a billion hoodies" He grinned at that. "Ok, but actually" she chewed on her straw "I have two tickets to a… musical!" She sang.

"No."

"Pleaseee" she touched his shoulder.

"Aish," he groaned.

"Your a musician! You'll love it, I swear" she pleased as she tossed her hair back over her shoulder.

He gnawed at his straw, "fine."

She beamed, and stopped in her tracks, "really?"

He stopped too, "yeah" he said sheepishly. She squealed like a child and leapt on to him. "I love you, yay!"

He actually did end up enjoying it more than he expected and after that they went to a few more. Sometimes, they even went to the bad ones but Mykal still preferred concerts, they would buy cheap tickets and go with all their friends and get a little drunk before. But even just the musicals when it was just the two of them were always fun, they always had a good time together. It was a good two months, a wonderful moment in time.

That summer Anaisha had an internship with a wedding photography company, and Mykal was in music school. They always made fun of Anaisha for not having her driver's license, but Mykal stopped pestering her to get it.

It was around the middle of the summer that he realized he was happy she didn't have it. It meant he could pick her up from her internship.

At the beginning of the summer, she would get dropped there, and he would pick her up, and they would hang out either alone or with their friends. But during the middle of the summer, when her driver went on holiday, he found himself offering to drop her off.

"My classes and practice always start around 12 anyway," he shrugged as he took a sip of water in the restaurant.

"Are you sure?"

"Why are you being so formal, Aish? If I couldn't or didn't want to, I'd just say so," he smiled. She nodded and adjusted her hair, re-clipping it.

That meant his mornings would start with her, and his evenings would end with her. And during the day, he would work on his music. Every alternate day he would have guitar practice. They were working towards the summer recital, and on his days off, he would draw and sketch.

For Mykal, it was a summer of playing, drawing, and spending time with his friends and Anaisha. While for Anaisha, it was a summer of learning more about photography, taking photos, being around her friends and Mykal, and missing Andries in a way that she hadn't before.

One night they went to the market downtown; it was only ever open in the summer. The place was fresh and alive with food stalls, people selling clothes and handmade jewellery and trinkets. There were even arcade games to play. The city was the kind of place where things were open 24/7, and people liked to go to dinner late or just talk and hang out late into the night. So by 9 pm, the fair was alive.

"This is cute," Anaisha said, eyeing some necklaces in a stall. Then her phone rang.

She looked at it and mouthed to Mykal, "It's Kiara."

"Yeah, sure, we'll be there in 5," she turned off her phone and looked at Mykal.

"They are at the ice cream truck," she said. She was wearing a long white silk skirt that hit her calf, sneakers and a black halter top with her hair open.

She turned to walk, expecting Mykal to follow her. "I'll be there in a second. I need to go to the bathroom," he said.

He turned, putting a hand in his pocket; he was wearing an electric blue hoodie and long shorts and a pair of overly priced but very cool sneakers.

As he saw her walk away, he went back to the jewellery stall. He looked at the necklaces and brought a gold one that seemed the most unique.

He gave it to her the next morning when he picked her up for work.

"Hey," Anaisha said as she got into the car. She had her big, brown leather bag and two thermoses of coffee in her hand. She looked pretty tired, but her hair still looked naturally gorgeous, pinned back and wavy. They were out late the night before.

"This is for you," she said, putting the blue thermos on his side of the cupholder.

"Thanks, I have something for you too," he said as he drove out of her driveway. She looked at him, quizzical.

"Grab the white bag at the back," he said. Mykal was all smiling.

A small black box was in the bag, and she could tell it was jewellery from the packaging. Anaisha opened the box and gasped.

"Oh, it's so pretty!" She explained as the sun glistened on it.

It was a small pendant of a bouquet of daffodils. She started smiling. It was unique. The way it was a bouquet and not just the flower itself.

He slid his eyes over to her face, still smiley, one arm on the wheel and the other resting on the console.

"You like it?" He raised his brows.

"I love it," she turned to him with a huge smile. "Thank you so much."

She wrapped an arm around his free one and leaned her head on his shoulder as she put some music on.

The summer felt like a moment in time, suspended.

One night when they had tickets to a concert and decided to go to dinner before, the girls decided to get ready together so they came together. They were in a small sushi restaurant, with dim lights and black leather booths in the heart of town.

"How far are you guys?" Aki said as he spoke to Naira on the phone. Mykal had called Naira up and told them to come, at first she had said 'no'. But he knew what kind of music she liked, sent her the album and convinced her and she decided to come. He didn't know why but he felt like she was in this sort of bubble of her own making, and he felt like she needed someone to come along and pop it, he was happy to be that person.

"Were literally just walking in" Naira said as she made eye contact with Aki and turned her phone off.

Naira walked in, in a pleated mini leather skirt and small, grey stone washed t-shirt with a graphic design of a thunderstorm, that looked like it was meant for a little boy.

"I love the outfit" Mykal said as he leapt up to hug them all.

She widened her eyes, and smiled. "I thought you would, I got the shirt from that store you were telling me about, Figure 10."

"And you too, shit." Mykal looked up and down at Anaisha. She wore this short black skirt and white top with puffy sleeves that reached her elbows and tightened at her waist, with black leather boots. Half of her hair was pulled back as usual, with a few strands to frame her face.

"Really?" She smiled, he nodded, silently. Her face was glowing, and she looked quite striking.

Calista and Kiara were right behind them. Kiara had her minimal makeup on as usual, those green eyes taking up her whole face and curly brown hair. She wore dark jeans and a tight navy blue tank top, cool and casual as always. Calista was laughing at something she said. Her hair was loose and free in loose black trousers and a small red halter top. She looked gorgeous, seemingly without trying. Yet, in her own way Anaisha looked really good today, Mykal thought. As they sat and ate he couldn't help but have his eyes on her. Her features seemed even sharper than usual, and when she laughed her nose crinkled.

"Oh my god," Anaisha slammed her hands on the table "do you think Ries will be awake?"

"Mhmm" Mykal murmured as he had a sip of water, "I spoke to him today morning"

At that Anaisha grabbed her phone and video called Ries, who picked up after three rings.

"Ries!" She squealed.

"Don't you look pretty?" She started giggling, "and drunk?" He laughed over the phone.

He was lying down on a white pillow in his hotel room. The camera couldn't quite capture the glimmer of his blue eyes.

"No, more tipsy" she mumbled a little as she flipped the camera to angle it to the rest of them.

They had been standing in the crowd for about thirty minutes, it was an outdoor arena and Mykal could feel a slight sweat on his temple. Despite the chaos, his eyes caught Naira's chest sort of rising and falling quickly. He gripped her hand.

"You good?"

She nodded and tapped her foot. "When are they coming on?" She gulped.

"Probably like 15 minutes" he had to shout, it was loud, naturally.

She nodded and gulped again. He gave her the bottle of water he was holding and she took a sip and touched her chest. He bent down to her height to face her so he didn't have to shout so loud.

"They'll be here soon," she nodded, with wide green eyes "and once they start playing just enjoy it… enjoy the music and the crowd and the way everyone is here because they share this one thing" he was grinning as he spoke, a spark in his eyes.

She nodded and smiled helplessly, took an indulging breath, "that's quite poetic"

He winked, "I have my moments" she tightened her grip on his hand and he held it until she let go after the first song finished.

He kept an eye out even when she seemed okay, and Aki was always by her side, too.

"Were going to take a breather" Anaisha held on to Mykal's shoulder, as she said this.

"Let's all go together" he turned, "I don't want anyone to get lost"

"We'll be fine, idiot" she slapped his arms, "we have phones, you know and you love this music, don't miss it" she said as she walked away with Kiara arm in arm.

A moment later, the lights dropped and the stage sparked up again with low white bulbs, the screen behind the band changing to a back drop of the ocean in the night time. Mykal mellowed, "I love this song" he sighed as he wrapped his arms around Calista's shoulders who breezily leaned back on his chest. She was pretty tall and her head fell right beneath his chest.

"How do you still smell good?" She said softly.

He leaned into her ear, "it's my pheromones," he kissed her temple "your attracted to them"

38

He felt her laugh and felt the music seep into his bones, at the very base off his chest. It was always easy with her, from the moment they met they seemed to have this comfortability with each other. She quickly became one of his closest friends and her to him, and they had this wonderful understanding which no one else seemed to really understand and neither of them cared. Both similar in the sense where neither wanted anything serious. They spoke every day, and flirted often and spent nights together sometimes.

When he got in the car it felt like he had just been bathed in music and energy. Like, he had drank too many energy drinks and every nerve in his body had been spiked with something amazing, blazing and scintillating. He could never be bored of this feeling, the 'post-concert buzz' he called it. Where lights looked brighter and things sounded kind of distorted in a good way. Mykal didn't drink, he was the designated driver of the night.

"Did you have fun?" Naira asked, as they came to a stop at a traffic light. She was sat in the passenger seat.

"I had the most amazing night" he said as he drummed his fingers against the wheel. "Good music, good people, you can't ask for much more can you?" He shrugged as he turned to her with a smile.

She smirked and nodded, the street lights washing over their faces.

"Was that cringe?" He laughed.

"A little, but cringe is good. Its honest" she adjusted the air condition in front of her.

"what do you mean?" The flashlight changed to green, he hit the accelerator.

Naira smirked, "I think there's two types of cringe. The first when something is just uncomfortable" she scrunched up her face, "and it makes you want to cover your face and curl up in a ball… like watching someone try to hit on someone that is clearly uninterested or a really bad pickup line"

He laughed at that, "okay and what's the second type?"

"The second type…" she blew out a breath as she took a second to find the words, "is when something rings so honest and true, that it makes your heart sort of swell up and makes you smile awkwardly and helplessly" she laughed, as she twirled a strand of her dark hair "Like when someone talks about how much they love someone, or like what you said" she pointed at him.

"Hmm" he nodded, smiling. The rest of them were chatting in the back as Naira and Mykal continued their softer conversation in the front.

Calista pulled herself forward on Mykal's seat, leaning her head over the edge of the seat "You coming to mine after?" Her hair tickled his arm.

He grinned, "You never asked…"

"I'm asking now?" The tone of her voice shifted to something a little higher.

"Yeah, I'll come"

She pecked him quickly on the cheek.

"you guys are cute" Naira was smirking, her green eyes lit up.

Calista pinched her cheek, laughing as she sat back down.

That night, they waited as Anaisha waddled down her driveway. "Have fun you guys," she called out, "but not too much fun" she sniggered as she fiddled with the door handle. He laughed at that. As they drove away from her house he thought about Anaisha, and he felt a little buzz, alight, from the concert.

It was 12 pm on a Saturday afternoon, and Mykal had practice. It felt weird to have Anaisha walking behind him as he opened the glass doors of 'Roll with the Rhythm". This was the first place he went to learn guitar. He hadn't stopped going since.

"Hey, Mykal," the woman at the reception looked up with a delighted face as he strode in.

"Lisa!" Mykal leaned his elbow on the counter and rested his sharp chin on his knuckles. "How've you been?"

"I'm very good," she looked up from her desktop, and smiled.

He leaned over the counter, "How's the leg?" And looked down at her cast ridden left leg, crutches lay on the seat beside her.

Her eyes softened and crinkled as she smiled at the fact that he remembered, of course he did. Every year on holidays he would gift her a box of expensive chocolates which her children always got excited for.

"It's getting a lot better, actually. It should be gone in about two weeks" she was still smiling as she looked up at him.

"That's awesome! it means you can cheer us on and jump around at the recital"

She shook her head with a laugh. "Oh, I'm too old to be jumping around, with or without a cast"

"Oh, come on Lisa we both know that's not true" he smirked. "Your getting younger by the day"

She laughed, and said "you better head inside, before I start believing you"

He grinned as she motioned her head toward the door on the left behind her.

Anaisha couldn't help but roll her eyes, she also couldn't help the smile that surpassed her face.

He tapped on the counter once again and walked to the door. Lisa grinned from behind him as he leaned on the door, opening it with his shoulder.

"What's up!" Mykal announced as opened the first dark blue door on the left.

Mykal shook hands with a guy who was tuning a base that hung around his shoulders, he had longish hair tied into a bun at the back of his neck, a little scruff on his chin, wearing shorts and a big t-shirt with green eyes and tanned skin, called "Ryder."

"Hey." he smiled, as he reached his hand out to Anaisha.

Behind the drums at the back of the small room sat a girl with her short black hair and multiple piercings up her left ear and with a fox-like beauty, slanted eyes, thin lips, and tanned skin.

"This is Tatiana."

However, when she got up and hugged Anaisha, she seemed far less intimidating.

They chatted for a few minutes, as the musicians tuned their guitars and Anaisha sat on one of the small stools. They heard the click of the door and a stunning tall girl walked in. Anaisha actually looked at her for a little longer than she normally would because she was that type of stunning where you did a double-take and then just looked for a little while longer in awe.

"I have doughnuts…" she said in this raspy voice that was sort of soft and crackly at the same time.

She put down the box next to the table Anaisha was seated on. She wore straight-cut blue jeans and a black t-shirt tied at the back that accentuated her waist, with silver hoop earrings and a little diamond necklace sparkling at the base of her throat.

"Hi, you're new," she cocked her head to the side, looking at Anaisha with a little sideways smile.

"This is Anaisha," Mykal said as he tuned his guitar. Then inclined his head to Inara. "Anaisha, Inara"

"Myk, I think people can introduce themselves," Anaisha smirked.

He laughed. "Sorry, it's just like two worlds colliding," He said and brought his hands together and laughed some more.

Inara was about to hold a hand out to shake when Anaisha got up and gave her a hug. Inara smiled. "I'm so excited you're here, I've heard so much about you" she said as she let go.

"Me? I've heard so much about you!" she held her hands out, "all of you guys." Anaisha smiled as she looked around, then sat back down and stroked down the skirt of her mini yellow dress.

A few minutes later, as all of them tweaked their instruments and got ready, an older woman walked in. She wore dark skinny jeans and a polo shirt with short brown hair and black boots.

"Alright, let's do this," she clapped. She brought with her the air of authority.

She looked at Anaisha quickly and then turned her head back. "And you are?"

"I'm Anaisha. Mykal's friend," their teacher nodded as she looked at Mykal with a lifted brow.

"I wanted to see what practice looked like," she pressed her lips together, "I hope that's okay."

"Of course!" She broke into a smile, "it's perfect. We can practice with an audience now."

With that said, she then walked over to each of her students, making sure the tuning was perfect and giving them little reminders of the critiques she had made before.

She got to Mykal last and whispered with a smirk, "Your friend is very pretty."

He rolled his eyes and laughed. Fingers on the guitar.

"It's not like that."

She began walking back to the front of the room.

"It never is," she sat down on the chair next to Anaisha, "until, one day it is."

She clapped her hands again, bringing everyone's attention.

"Alright - the first song, let's go."

And they began.

They were all good, really good but you could tell Mykal and Inara were just the shining stars. And though Anaisha loved Mykal, she had to admit that Inara just slightly edged him out. She had that kind of voice that made you stop what your doing and focus, like if you listened hard enough it felt like you could hear her soul through it. Myk's fingers flew around the guitar, and there was a smile on his face as he hit each note and looked at Ryder, and they played off each other.

They had one emotional song, in which Mykal switched to acoustic... and it was like the whole room slowed down.

Inara closed her eyes while singing. And then when she opened them, she felt Mykal looking at her and leaned in. The eye contact was special.

The next song was a rock song, and Mykal switched to an electric guitar and stepped backwards as Ryder stepped in front as he began singing with Inara. He had an unexpectedly beautiful voice, which accentuated Inara's perfectly. She took the mic of its stand, and moved closer to him, raising one arm slowly as they sang, he was slightly taller than her and smiled when he sang, which made it even more enjoyable to watch. Tatiana and Mykal were just rocking in the back, and on the final chorus Mykal knelt down close to his knees in front of Tatiana. She had a smile she couldn't seem to help as she expertly played.

They looked like a proper band, a legitimate one. Anaisha felt stupid, she had known Mykal for so long but shed never actually realized how good he was. It was like shed gotten so used to hearing him play so well, that she had forgotten the level he was on and that he played with other people, who were just as skilled.

They finished, with a clash, literally. And all four had their chests slightly raising as they had undiluted smiles on their faces, looking at Anaisha and their teacher expectantly.

Their teacher was smiling as she stood up, her arms crossed across her chest.

"So, Ms Audience, thoughts?" She quirked a brow with a smug look at Anaisha.

Anaisha nodded and shook her head, looking at her lap, "you guys were," she looked up, her eyes lit up, "fucking amazing". She brought a hand up to her mouth, "sorry," she looked at the teacher, eyes like a baby's.

Ms. Cartina started laughing and said, "Sweetheart," she was holding her stomach, "that's exactly the reaction we were looking for."

Mykal looked at the rest of them, a look of pride and excitement beamed from his eyes. The look on Mykal's face after he played had the same energy as when Anaisha was looking at photographs she had taken, and they came out just exactly as she had imagined. Or when Anaisha could feel that the picture she had just taken was going to come out good, it would come out exactly as she imagined. There was nothing better.

They drove back from Kiara's house that night, after practice they went to hers for the rest of the evening, ordered pizza and listened as Anaisha boasted about her best friend. Calista, who had seen Mykal practice before had looked at him with delighted blue eyes.

Mykal pulled up at Anaisha's driveway.

"Ok, I'll see you at lunch tomorrow..." she said as she got out of the car.

He turned his head, to look at her, "Do you ever find it weird" he drummed his fingers on the wheel, "how we don't get sick of each other..."

She leaned her forehead against the open car door and stood with her ankles crossed over one another. He cleared his throat, "like, I could never get bored of hanging out with you... or Ries, and the whole group"

Anaisha twirled the ends of her hair, looking at them they couldn't look more different. Anaisha wore her little dresses and sneakers, with perfect hair and Mykal wore hoodies that you saw and wanted to get for yourself. He was the kind of person who looked like they had their life together, without trying to keep it together.

He was the kind of person that looked like they had their life together, without trying to keep it together. And the kind of guy that girls would look at, because girls appreciated more than just the way that someone looked but even the way they dressed and walked and talked. He was the kind of person that you saw and wanted to be friends with.

She took a minute to think, and he watched her, anticipatory. "I think the people we love are so intrinsically part of who we are. Where they know so much about you, and you feel at ease with them. When I'm with you guys its like breathing becomes easier..." she had a mixture of relief and fear in her eyes, that came from being completely honest. "You can never get sick of that."

44

He nodded. He knew what she meant. sometimes when Mykal felt upset, a beautiful thought would land in his mind.

"Like you being one of my best friends is a part of who I am, you know? And that might be co-dependence…" she grinned, with a life of her brows and leaned back on the door, as she bit her lip, her voice softening "but part of loving someone is being dependent on them, right? But like a healthy dependence"

"A healthy dependence" He repeated with a smile. Sometimes when Mykal felt upset, a beautiful thought would land in his mind.

The thought would be, "They're here. They're always with me" because he knew, that even if they were on the other side of the planet, or miles away. The fact that they were walking on the same planet as him, meant that he would be okay in the end.

"This.." He pointed at the space between them, "and all of us" she spoke of their best friends, "is one of the best things in my life. I don't think you can ever get sick of that kind of friendship." She smiled to him and blinked her eyes sleepily.

"I think sometimes, we can get sick of ourselves but we can never get sick of the people we love… you know nearly all there is to know about me, and you still love me… so maybe its more of a selfish reason that you don't get sick of me" She laughed.

He laughed and shook his head, "no, this…" He pointed at the space between them, with eyes so earnest that she couldn't help but smile "and all of us" he spoke of their little group, "is one of the best things in my life. I don't think you can ever get sick of that kind of friendship."

She smiled to him and blinked her eyes sleepily.

He loved these conversations with her when he felt like they were finishing each others thoughts out loud, how it felt like they were somehow connected because of how well they knew each other, but still she managed to surprise him. She felt the same way.

It was only when Andries came back that he realized.

One night, they were hanging out in Mykal's backyard, you could hear the sound of the waves and the only view of the ocean was the moons reflection on it.

Mykal had his recital the next day and had to get in some practice before. So, he headed inside for about one hour, leaving Anaisha and Andries alone together. He didn't know that much could happen in one hour.

When Andries came back that summer, Anaisha felt like she was seeing him with fresh eyes. A lot of feelings she had sort of clicked into place. He had started wearing linen shirts, which he rolled up to his biceps and shorts. He played a lot of sports, and she knew he had started working out, eating more and he had started dressing differently, linen shirts and shorts. He looked good, handsome and older. If she wanted to stay naive, she could blame it on all of that, but she was smarter than that. She knew that even a year ago, she felt herself smile whenever he looked at her. But still, he did seem more confident, self-assured than she had ever known him to be before.

When Mykal was telling this story to Naira on the bed, whilst they were lying next to each other he was painstakingly honest.

"It was the day before my recital, and I had to get in some practice before… so I headed back into the house to get in some practice for about an hour. I didn't realize so much could happen in one hour. A lot of things that I was doing sort of made sense to me."

"Like what?" Naira said softly, she didn't know why but from the way Mykal's tone had shifted she felt like this was a conversation that should be had in hushed tones.

"Like," he took a steadying breath in, "purposefully wearing a hoodie that I knew Anaisha liked and waiting for her to notice," he grinned, as he stared up at the ceiling and Naira turned her head. "Or…" he tapped the hand on his abdomen as he laughed more and turned to look at her, smiling crinkled warm brown eyes, "waking up before my alarm even went off in the mornings to pick her up, and being excited to see her the next day before I went to sleep," he grinned to her and himself, too while smiling.

"I see" Naira nodded, she was smiling as she turned her head back and watched the wooden fan move steadily on the ceiling. The way he was speaking about Anaisha was the way everyone wanted to be spoken about.

"Yeah," he turned his head back too, still smiling.

"Anyway, so I opened the door and I had a bottle of water in my hand", he cleared his throat. "I nearly dropped it when I saw them." He squinted, the fan moving fan blurring through his vision, "She was leaning her head on his shoulder, and when she turned her head up, they kissed." He said this very matter of factly.

"The thing is, when I saw it, I felt this… something was off." He laid a hand on his head, as if to calm what was going on inside it, parts of his dark hair looking white underneath the soft yellow light of the room. "My breath quickened as if I was cornered into sharing a secret with someone or lying about something… I never ended up meeting them at the beach; I just sort of walked around the neighborhood for a bit." He didn't tell Naira how he had ended up in the park that night. The Whispering Waves neighborhood park, where they would go to as kids. He never considered himself to be particularly sentimental or corny. But, without even realizing, he found himself just sitting on the grass, leaning on his elbows with headphones in his ears, music and memories unconsciously floating around the place.

"I remember Anaisha texted me, asking me when I would be done, and I texted her back that I still had to keep practising. Later that night, Andries came into the house. By that time I was back at my place, in the basement. I was playing, but my hands were so clammy that my fingers kept slipping over the strings. I couldn't even hold an E-Minor." He scratched his jaw with a laugh, "He told me what happened," Mykal had began smiling then, "now, I'm happy it did but in that moment I remember thinking, why can't I just tell him that I saw them together… but I just couldn't, and there had only been a handful of times that I had kept a secret from Ries" even as he said it, he couldn't think about even one time.

"Anyway, after that, I think they were both confused… and they're both quite prideful," Mykal smirked as Naira, and then his dark eyes softened, "and sensitive and shy with their emotions at the same time."

To put it simply, that summer Mykal realized two things… all three of them were, possibly on the cusp of falling in love, which was a wonderful thing. But one of them would land very differently than the other two.

It was both wonderful, like plunging into cold water on a hot day, when the waters too cold but you know in a few minutes it would be worth it, and it so was. Yet, it also filled him with dread as severe as waves taking you under their current. He felt like he had been swimming in the ocean, looking forward and then stopped and started treading water, turned back around to face the shore and realized he had swam far far deeper than expected.

"After that, I think they were both confused and they both have a fuck ton of pride," he smirked, as Naira laughed at that, it was true. Then he went quiet for a second… "Their also both sort of sensitive and shy with their emotions" he touched the side of his chest where his heart lay.

47

He always loved that trait they shared, because it meant that they were the kind of people who when they let you in, or cared for you it meant they truly did. "So, it took some time for them to sort their shit out."

Mykal would drive around, around the places where the offices for her internship were. Driving around there made him feel like he could relive those moments. The ones he had stolen for himself, in those drives alone. Taking the routes in which he could be in love with her without fear of anyone seeing it. Because he knew Anaisha would never be able to tell. It wasn't even a fathomable thing in her mind.

It was confusing, and he didn't really know why he did it to himself. Because it was sad, but it made him feel like of happy too. Every sign, every tree reminded him of the life he had led that and melancholic but monumental.

Chapter 8

A Month Later, When Anaisha Turned Eighteen…

Anaisha had just come back from lunch with her family and was sitting on her vanity brushing her hair out as Calista and Kiara threw open the door and yelled, "HAPPY BIRTHDAY!"

Kiara ran in and threw her arm around her friend, and the other girl was held up with an abundance of pink and white balloons, which fumbled and flew around her.

"Wait for me!" Calista said as she popped the box of cupcakes on Anaisha's bed carefully and ran up and joined the hug.

"Oh my god!" Anaisha leapt on both of them, "I thought we were meeting in the evening for dinner?" She said as she let them go.

"They wanted to come earlier," her Dad said. Her parents stood in the doorway as she cooed, "aww," and held her hands up to her face and hugged them again.

"What's all this!" She said, motioning to the balloons and box on her bed.

"Your favourite… Ocean Cakes," Calista said, opening the boxes. Her baby blue eyes lit up as she looked at her friend. Ocean Cakes' was Anaisha's favourite bakery. It was a small bakery downtown, and one bite took you straight to heaven.

"No way! You guys remembered!"

"Obviously," Kiara answered, cocking her head to the side as if it was such a silly thing to say. "Is it the German chocolate?"

"Stop!" Anaisha clapped her hands in excitement.

"You guys are literally so fucking cute," Anaisha said, then she looked at her parents and covered her mouth. She had sworn "sorry", she giggled.

"You really are getting older, aren't you," her mother said, with a smirk and a pointed finger. "Okay, we'll take our leave," her mother said as her parents headed out.

Anaisha took a bite of the cupcake. Over a mouthful, she said, "Is it the German chocolate?"

"Yes," Calista said as she took a hoodie from Anaisha's closet. The balcony door was open as usual, "but lately, I think you've preferred white chocolate."

Kiara barked a laugh, and Anaisha scrunched her eyebrows together and then put her tongue in her cheek. She got it.

"Fuck off," she rolled her eyes while unsuccessfully trying to suppress a laugh.

Anaisha couldn't remember a time when she was with Calista and Kiara, and they weren't laughing for eighty per cent of their time together. She smiled to herself at the thought.

Anaisha could hear chatter through the open door. The loud and obnoxious banter and jocularity of teenage boys.

"Stop… are they all..."

Just as she was about to finish her sentence, her door opened. "Happy birthday Anaisha!" Zade announced as he ran up to her, all gangly and loose and gave her a big hug.

"Zadeeee!" Anaisha hugged him as he said, "We came to surprise you!" He was bouncing on the balls of his feet.

"Abel!" she announced cheerfully. Abel came in all tall and muscly and gave her a one-armed hug, which was just as intense as his younger brother's big one, considering their different body compositions.

"Anaisha, you're 18 today! Man, 18's awesome... I remember when I turned 18," he said as his dark eyes held that look of his, the look of smug wisdom and superior knowledge.

"Yes, yes, we know you're older and stronger and wiser than all of us," Andries announced as he strode in with his hands loosely in his pockets, rolling his eyes. Anaisha's eyebrows shot up. She was going to say something along the lines of that. It always struck Anaisha when Andries would say nearly exactly what she was thinking.

"That's true. I am. Thanks for acknowledging the fact, Ries," Abel answered just as quickly as he put a broad arm on Andries's smaller shoulders and ruffled his hair. Andries couldn't help it, and he laughed while shoving Abel off. He strode up, one hand still cooly in his pocket and the other attempting to tame his ruffled hair. Anaisha watched them with a smile, her smile. Andries saw her watching and moved his attention toward her.

"Happy birthday, Anaisha." He said. He didn't give her a hug, just a smile and his "look", that infamous intense blue-eyed look.

"Thanks, Andries" she gulped. They had been weird ever since the beach, not really knowing what was going on. They still hung out all the time as a group or with Mykal and texted, but less than before and it just felt different.

"I like the chair," he smirked and pointed at the ivory loveseat in the corner of her room.

She laughed through her nose.

"Thanks, this fucking weird guy helped me pick it out," she twirled the ring around her forefinger.

He smiled at the fact that he was the one who helped her choose the piece of furniture. For a few seconds, they were literally just looking and smiling at each other, and Anaisha really was not sure what was going on... The awkward smiling and the awkward-looking was thankfully brought to a halt as Mykal walked around Andries, shouting "HAPPY BIRTHDAY, ANAISHA." In his hands was a speaker who was booming with a remixed and moderately inappropriate version of 'Happy Birthday'.

Mykal held the speakers up in one hand and opened his free palm up for her to hold. She gave him her hand with a smile, and he spun her around and danced with her as they all sang the song for her. Her head tilted back as she laughed at the lyrics, "I wouldn't have expected anything less."

They were all squeezed into the room, and it was filled to the brim, with not just people but with smiles and music and laughter. And just in time for the end of the song Calista already had a single cupcake ready in her hand with a small candle in the centre.

Calista stood in front of Anaisha and said, "Make a wish," as she delicately held a single cupcake in her palm with an unlit candle in the centre.

Anaisha stopped and started laughing while looking up expectantly at Calista, wondering when she'd realise.

"Fuck! Someone give me the lighter!" she shouted, and all of them burst into laughter.

Abel quickly passed her the lighter, "Okay, let me try that again," she said as she lit the candle.

"Okay, now you can make a wish," she giggled.

And with a smile, Anaisha did something else. Instead of making a wish, she made a "thanks" and 'thanked' whoever was responsible for blessing her with so much laughter in her days and friends that felt like family.

The music was still playing, and her friends lounged around her room. Anaisha began to pin half of her hair up; her hair had grown over the years. It was now long, thick and gorgeous. As she searched for a clip, there was a loud knock on the door.

Kiara went and opened it. "Hi, Naira!" Kiara said with her wide, friendly smile as she opened the door wider for a short, young girl with her black hair pulled back in a loose bun.

"Sorry, I had knocked softer, but the music-" Naira cleared her throat. "Can I come in?" She asked tentatively. "Of course! Come in!" Kiara said as she pulled her in with a laugh, half in surprise that she had asked to come into her family member's room. Anaisha was sitting on her bed now and heard everything,

"Naira, come in!" She called. "Hello, again," Naira said. They had seen each other at the family lunch a few hours before. Naira was followed by a tall boy with dark hair and slanted eyes, "Hi Aki!" Anaisha said. He strode toward her in two long strides.

"Happy birthday, Anaisha," he said with a voice cool as a breeze and a one-armed hug. "You guys really went all out," he said, gazing up at the balloons, his arm still cooly around Anaisha's shoulders. "It's Anaishas birthday!" Calista said with her sunny smile as if that was an answer enough. "Lucky girl," he said, looking down at Anaisha with an easy smile.

"Cupcake?" Kiara said, holding up the box of goodies. "No, I'm good, but thanks," he said with his easy smile. They could hear the boisterous conversation of the boys behind, and he was about to move away to talk to the guys, but his eyes drifted to Naira, who was standing still across Anaisha, her chest rising, and he moved silently to stand behind Naira.

"Happy birthday again, cousin." She said softly. "Thanks, Nairu," Anaisha said and hugged her cousin. Naira's arms hesitantly came around, and she moved away too quickly.

"Oh, I have something for you," she said as she brought out a little bag that she had hidden behind her. "It's from my parents and siblings and... Well, me… we forgot it in the car before lunch" she shrugged and cleared her throat as she passed over a shiny purple gift bag. Anaisha's eyes lit up as she opened the bag.

There were three things inside. A card, a small black box and something wrapped in a rectangular shape. First, she reached for the card and delicately opened it. Her fingers stuck under the thick envelope. It read: "Our Dear Anaisha, Happy birthday darling! Today you have turned 18, and on this special day, we wanted to gift you something special. We think this gift is as elegant and beautiful as you have grown to become. And we hope the second gift inspires you. We love you, and we miss you. Love, Chachu and Chachi."

Her eyes flicked up at Naira, who smiled at her through her green eyes. She took a quick breath to steady herself as she lifted the little box from the back. A navy blue ribbon was tied around a white box, and inside it was a small box. She could already tell what it was, and a little smile spread across her face. Carefully, she opened the box, and her eyes lit up. Inside was a delicate diamond eternity ring. It was simple and beautiful "it's stunning! Thank you!" She said as she watched the sunlight from her balcony reflect off the ring. "I love it," she said as she gave Naira a hug. "There's one more thing," Naira said quietly.

"Oh, yeah," Anaisha said as she fished out a wrapped rectangular shape. She tore off the wrapping paper and held a new book in between her hands. It was a book on photography. She squealed. "Oh my god! I love it!" She squealed, turning the book in her hands, reading the blurb.

The awkward smiling and the awkward-looking was thankfully brought to a halt as Mykal walked around Andries, shouting "HAPPY BIRTHDAY, ANAISHA." In his hands was a speaker who was booming with a remixed and moderately inappropriate version of 'Happy Birthday'.

Mykal held the speakers up in one hand and opened his free palm up for her to hold. She gave him her hand with a smile, and he spun her around and danced with her as they all sang the song for her. Her head tilted back as she laughed at the lyrics, "I wouldn't have expected anything less."

They were all squeezed into the room, and it was filled to the brim, with not just people but with smiles and music and laughter. And just in time for the end of the song Calista already had a single cupcake ready in her hand with a small candle in the centre.

Calista stood in front of Anaisha and said, "Make a wish," as she delicately held a single cupcake in her palm with an unlit candle in the centre.

Anaisha stopped and started laughing while looking up expectantly at Calista, wondering when she'd realise.

"Fuck! Someone give me the lighter!" she shouted, and all of them burst into laughter.

Abel quickly passed her the lighter, "okay, let me try that again," she said as she lit the candle "okay, now, you can make a wish," she giggled.

And with a smile, Anaisha did something else. Instead of making a wish, she made a "thanks" and 'thanked' whoever was responsible for blessing her with so much laughter in her days and friends that felt like family.

The music was still playing, and her friends lounged around her room as she finished getting ready, breakfast didn't start till a bit later, so they had some time to kill. Anaisha began to pin half of her hair up. As she searched for a clip, there was a loud knock on the door.

Kiara went and opened it. "Hi, Naira!" Kiara said with her wide, friendly smile as she opened the door wider for a short, meek young girl with her black hair pulled back in a loose bun.

"Sorry, I had knocked softer, but the music-"Naira cleared her throat. "Can I come in?" She asked tentatively. "Of course! Come in!" Kiara said as she pulled her in with a laugh, half in surprise that she had asked to come into her family member's room. Anaisha was sitting on her bed now and heard everything,

"Naira, come in!" She called. Silently, Naira walked in, followed by a tall boy with dark hair and slanted eyes, "Hi Aki!" Anaisha said. He strode toward her in two long strides.

"Happy birthday, Anaisha," he said with a voice cool as a breeze and a one-armed hug. "You guys really went all out," he said, gazing up at the balloons, his arm still cooly around Anaisha's shoulders. "It's Anaishas birthday!" Calista said with her sunny smile as if that was an answer enough. "Lucky girl," he said, looking down at Anaisha with an easy smile.

"By the way, we've cancelled the dinner reservations… you are in for a little surprise tonight. Just be ready at 8, okay?" Mykal said before they left.

The boys were in preparation mode. Andries lay down the picnic mat and put up the lights they had brought while Mykal took out the food and drinks from the picnic basket and set up the speakers for the music. Abel was barricading the part of the beach they were sitting on with the velvet rope they were given. Andries and Mykal had used their 'powers of persuasion, as Kiara often called it, and asked the neighbourhood security if they could borrow the barricade they used for events at the golf club. On their own, Andries had a winning smile and those piercing.

Blue eyes and Mykal could make anyone laugh, and everyone loved him, but together... they were unstoppable.

And Zade was running to and fro from the waves on the coast, seeing if they could catch him.

"Myk, hide the gift and flowers before the girls get here. Put them in the car." Andries said while puffing up a pillow, Andries had a good eye, but today he was determined for it to be perfect.

"Yes, chief," Mykal answered with a small salute.

"Guys, I can smell the salt and hear the waves. I know we're at the beach... and we took a ten-minute drive. Is this blindfold really necessary?" Anaisha asked. "Yes. It is. It adds to the element of surprise." Calista said with a squeeze of Anaisha's hand, she was guiding her. "Well, it feels a little kinky" Anaisha scrunched her nose.

"Well then, that means you're probably enjoying it," Kiara quipped.

Calista came behind her and fiddled with the blindfold. Anaisha could practically feel the excitement oozing off her friend. As soon as she took it off, music played out of nowhere. A fun, happy song. Anaisha blinked as her eyes adjusted, and her heart welled up as she saw what lay before her. A white picnic mat sat atop the sand, and on it was an abundance of snacks and food and pillows, a few bottles too. Around the mat were beach chairs, and all around it was fairly light. They were spread across the picnic mat and held up by poles that were pushed into the sand.

It looked like a dream.

And amidst this dream were her six closest friends, who all had bright eyes and the brightest smiles. If her family was here, and if heaven was actually real, and in moments like this, she believed it was, this is what she would have imagined it to be. Zane was dancing to the music as he put the speaker down, and Mykal felt like he couldn't control himself. He walked over to Anaisha and held a hand out, chivalrous and charming and dark eyes shining. She gave her his hand, and he twirled her around with the music. Her dark hair glowed, and her light dress flowed as the sounds of the ocean and music merged into one.

55

Now the music was in full swing, and the group were sitting around on the picnic blanket, laughing a little too much and a little too loud, and Anaisha was feeling so so happy and so so grateful.

She closed her eyes lightly and tilted her head back. She loved this feeling, the warmth that coursed through her body and the way it felt like the music was showering over her. Being played for her.

"I fucking love this song," Andries said with an insolent grin. She did too. And she showed it. She stood up and made her way over to Kiara and Calista, excitement and happiness in every movement as she stood them up and whirled them both around. Calista, carefree as ever, danced along, but Kiara laughed and shook her head. "I am not on your level," she said and pointed the finger at both of them.

"Then you better get on it..." Anaisha said with a wink while Calista poured her a shot. So Anaisha and Calista danced, without a care in the world, together, and soon enough, Kiara joined. So did Zane.

"You know, out of all of you," Calista said, pointing at all the boys with her blue glazed eyes. "Zade is my favourite," she said lazily, putting an arm around him.

"I agree." Kiara sang. "Me too," Anaisha chimed, "he's not boring," she said tauntingly, her eyes playful.

Anaisha loved the boys, they were also some of her closest friends, but sometimes she wished she could get drunk and dance with just her girls. And Zade. Her girls and Zade.

"Let's give it to her before we get wasted," Mykal said as he watched Anaisha's face scrunch up after doing a shot. Andries's face flicked up, and he nodded in agreement. In solidarity, they both got up and walked over to her. Sometimes, their movements were similar in the way that brothers did things in similar ways.

"Hi," Anaisha said with a grin as she looked up, and they both stood in front of her, the sun setting behind them. Their faces, the sun and the ocean looked so clear but dazed at the same time. She wished she had her camera.

"Can you come with us for a moment, please?" Mykal said, holding one hand out with a laugh. Andries smiled with both hands behind his back. She could see the edge of a flower arching from behind Andries's back but didn't want to ruin their surprise, so she kept quiet as she grabbed Mykal's hand. She didn't know if it was because she was slightly tipsy or the fact that Mykal had some sort of innate power that could make anyone smile, but she felt a weird sort of excitement as they led her to the car at the far side of the beach. The sun was slowly setting, kissing the ocean, the part of the ocean that looked like it was the edge of the world. Today the sky was a gradient of blues and bright orange. They saw it often, but a sunset never got old.

"Right, so we have something for you" Andries smiled and swallowed. And slowly, he moved his arms from behind his back and gave her a small black bag. From it spilt a bouquet of roses... and a bouquet of daffodils. "They're beautiful..." she said in wonder "thank you..." she said, smelling them. She cocked her head to the side "but why are there two bouquets?"

"Well, I liked the daffodils, and Ries liked the roses," Mykal said as he pointed at Ries, "and we couldn't decide, so the daffodils are from me and roses from Ries."

"What can we say? We're both equally stubborn." Andries said with a shrug. "Well, I love them both, thank you," she said with a shy smile.

"There's one more thing." Andries said. "Underneath the bouquets," Mykal finished.

"You guys really didn't have to do this," she said while giving them the bouquets to hold as she dug in the bag. A small box-like thing with a black ribbon was at the bottom of the bag.

She took a wild, uninhibited intake of breath as one hand suddenly made its way to her mouth. "No, no way... you didn't!" She said, her voice getting higher with excitement.

"We might have..." Andries winked casually, but he looked like an excited kid with the biggest smile on his face. She took the present out and blew out a breath of absolute appreciation. In her hands, she held a film camera. More specifically, a Pentax PC 700

"Sorry, we had to unbox it to add in the film. We thought you might want pictures of tonight."

Mykal said. Anaisha was holding the camera in her hand, turning it around with her careful fingers.

"It's perfect, a classic point and shoot, water-resistant-" she rattled off. She took a breath and smiled, eyes moving between the two. The sun would rise in the nighttime just to see that smile, "I fucking love it!"

"So, what's going to be your first picture?" Mykal asked, "The sunset's beautiful" he looked outward.

"It is, but I want my first picture on this to be something else" she clicked her tongue, "get together," she motioned at the two of them. And stood back, angling the camera. They both stood together, with serious faces.

Anaisha brought the camera down, "Would it kill you to smile?"

Mykal laughed, and hung an arm around Andries's shoulders as Andries bent his head down to fix his hair. When he lifted his head, Anaisha was struck with his blue eyes and a wonderful close-lipped smile. She took a step back, and blew out a breath, fuck! She thought.

She lifted her camera, winking. Through the lens, she saw them again.

Mykal hung an arm around Andries's shoulders, Andries with a loose hand in his pocket, Mykal a little taller than Ries with his infamous, perfect white smile. He had recently gotten a hair cut, and got what he told Anaisha was a 'mid-fade', and he had some light stubble across his jaw, which was definitely looking more apparent. His shoulders were looking a little bigger too. He looked like old photos of his father, but he still had those delicate, big hazel brown eyes from his mother.

"When did you guys get so good-looking?" She smirked.

"Around the same time you did" Mykal said, his smile looking more real now.

Anaisha laughed, her hearty laugh when something caught her off guard. "Fuck off," she said as she clicked the button. The camera flashed!

She brought the camera down as she walked back over to them, because it was a film camera they wouldn't be able to see it yet, but Mykal knew it would be a good photo, and he wasn't being biased he had seen nearly all her photos and when he saw some of the stuff she had done in her internship, he could see how much she had improved. And so the first picture on her film camera was off two brothers.

Soon enough, after the boys had enough of being called "boring," they joined in too.

The music was loud enough, and the waves were a background score. Andries moved smoothly, and his movements were as natural as he held Anaisha's hand and twirled her around effortlessly.

She laughed, a little flutter of something in her stomach.

Anaisha was used to dancing with her friends or at a party. She only ever experienced the freedom that accompanied the type of dancing that felt like therapy. That made you happy and free and alive and a little breathless when you were done.

But this was different, she held herself up, but her breath hitched every few seconds as he swung her around and twirled her inward to his body.

He held her hand to twirl her around, only this time he didn't; instead, he pulled her close. Holding both her hands as they danced. She gulped as she clocked his eyes, flickering towards her lips. Anaisha knew what he was doing, and she couldn't help but smile, her tongue in her cheek.

She felt this strange happiness and smugness at how he looked at her. She suddenly no longer cared that their friends were around them. This was a long time coming.

He was panting a little as she nodded lightly. His eyes lit up, and then he bent his head down as his hand held her jaw. He kissed her.

She smiled against his lips as they heard the chorus of whoops around them. She had kissed him only once before, and still it felt foreign but there was this warm happy feeling that overtook her body... Their noses touched, and for a second, she felt self-conscious but then he held her body closer to his and whatever thoughts she was thinking melted away as the moment took hold of them.

She withdrew with a laugh and hid her now warm face against his chest, as he put an arm around her. It felt good to be holding her like this, he liked being that person to her.

The waves splashed wildly along the shore, mingled with the sound of Anaisha's giggly laugh as Ries whispered something in her ear. He looked out toward the ocean, still with an arm around her as the and the stars glittered above, and Andries was smiling the kind of smile that would make a stranger who's having a bad day, look at him and smile too. And that stranger, the one who was having a bad day, would look at them with hope and realize it's a bad day… not a bad life because one day they knew they would smile like him too.

The thing is, the person looking at them wasn't a stranger at all, and it was one of the people who loved them both more than anything. And with one hand in his pocket, wearing a cool light green hoodie, with the sound of waves, music and his friends laughter in his ears, he was smiling too.

Lightning struck, not up in the sky but somewhere deep in the routes of their lives.

Two Weeks Later…

Anaisha was getting ready, and she was a bundle of nerves, but the best kind.

She held the curler away from her face, and a lock of hair twirled around the wand. She let the curl go and went over to her phone to switch the song, and her room was filled with music. Her eyes flickered to the time on her phone. Fuck, she'd have to leave in 10 minutes to pick up Naira and go to Calista's. Hurriedly she finished the last few locks of hair. She put her shoes on, a pair of strappy black heels easy enough to move around in and a mist of hair spray, a spray of perfume and another swipe of lipgloss.

She made her way out of the room... she had forgotten something... her bag.

"What the fuck! What's wrong with me?" Great, I'm talking to myself now, she thought.

Grabbing the bag, she made her way down, trying and failing to avoid her parents... "Anaisha, come to say bye..." Her mother called from the TV room. She got up from lying down on her father's lap.

Her mum's hand flew to her chest.

"You look gorgeous, babe," She peered over her reading glasses, "It's a little short, though."

"It's not. Its fine, ma," she answered in the flip of a wrist. It was a little short.

She took her glasses off and said, "Why don't you wear some earrings?"

"I can't go back up now," she said as she walked over to her parents. "I'm already late," she said and planted a kiss on both of their foreheads.

"Do you have the key?" Her dad asked, closing the A3 photography book he was reading.

"Yup," she said, hurrying off.

"Love you," they both said in unison, and Anaisha smiled as she walked away, saying 'love you too.'

She and Naira reached Calista's in the nick of time, and it turns out she wasn't ready yet.

Her housekeeper opened the door. "Hi, Wendy," the girls greeted.

After a quick exchange, she told them how Calista wasn't ready yet. Anaisha strode over to the stairs, "Calista, get your ass down here" her parents weren't there, only her siblings who she knew, so thisexchange was fairly appropriate.

"5 minutes," she shouted back. "Can you set up the drinks?"

So, Anaisha and Naira sorted what wasn't already sorted out. They heard heels clap down the stairs. "Just so you know, I'm taking these off when I start dancing. I don't care if it looks bad," Calista said as she descended, looking radiant as ever. In a silky white top and blue jeans.

"You guys look amazing!" She said as she looked at them. Naira was wearing a patent leather black skirt and a full sleeve black top. Looking cool as ever.

"Anaisha, Woah!" She said, holding her hands out in praise. She wore a short dark blue, nearly black dress. It had thick blue straps that kept falling off her shoulders, but the rest of the dress really fit her like a glove. It was tighter and shorter than what she was used to, but she felt really good in it. But to be fair, she had gotten older. She had just turned 18, and she sure was feeling it.

"You do look insane," Naira said, agreeing with Calista, a mischievous smirk on her face. "I wonder why?"

Then Calista and Naira made eye contact and started laughing at each other. "I like her," Calista said, pointing to Naira. Naira didn't usually hang out with her cousin's friends, but when Anaisha asked today, she felt pretty up to it. She had been going to therapy and feeling better, so she agreed.

Anaisha rolled her eyes with a shy smile, "Can we have a drink?" Anaisha asked, eyes sharp.

"Changing the subject, how cliche," Calista said as she poured three glasses.

About 15 minutes in, the doorbell rang, and in walked Kiara.

"Hello, sorry I'm late. I..." she stopped in her tracks, a smile spreading across her face. "Ay, Caliente... Aish, you look hot!"

"Thank you," Anaisha blushed with a laugh.

"Okay, we have time for one more drink, then we're going to be really late," Calista said. "Shit, I feel old." Calista blinked. She was the youngest of her three siblings.

The bouncer checked their IDs, and then he spread his large arm out, letting them inside. Anaisha had gone out to a club only twice before with her cousins, but they limited her to one drink, and she was wearing sneakers. Nice sneakers, but sneakers. This was her first time being 'legal', and she felt heady.

A woman led them to the table where their friends were seated. The music was reverberant, already pulsating through her body, considering she was slightly tipsy. Anaisha walked up two steps with her friends.

"Shit," Andries said and took a shot...thank god the music was so loud no one heard him.

Under the amalgamation of red and purple lights, her satin dress glowed. It was a dark royal blue, curving to her body, and sat high above her knees. She always wore little dresses, but they were looser this was a lot tighter with thick straps were showing off her collarbones. The lights glinted on her dark hair.

She was greeting Abel and Zade, and when she reached Andries, she kissed him on the cheek. He smelled like a peppery boy. She felt a fluttery feeling in her chest as she went over to sit next to Naira. He nearly touched his cheek, the remnant of the kiss. But didn't, obviously.

She was sitting with her legs gracefully crossed over one another, swaying to the music whilst having a conversation with Naira and Abel.

Andries sat with Zade and Kiara, and he was listening, but his eyes kept gliding toward her, then he'd realise he was staring and look away, but every few minutes, they would go right back like his eyes had a mind of his own.

He was seriously attracted to her, and it wasn't just the outfit or the way she looked but even the way she sat confidently. Her back was straight, and her neck tall. Even the way she talked slowly and thoughtfully, even the way she listened, listening to what the opposite person was saying, she cared.

Anaisha was feeling the same way. Andries was on a black shirt and black pants. The colour offset his skin; his eyes seemed brighter and his hair darker. And he just looked so fucking cool; you couldn't look away. He leaned his arm around the back of the sofa, the charisma and self-assuredness in every breath. Then he'd turn his ear to actually listen to what Zade or Kiara were saying, and he'd nod slowly, actually taking it in, thinking about it. Or a slow smile would spread across his face, and he'd rake one hand through his hair. She wished she had her camera.

A drink or two later, she, Abel, Naira and Calista got up to dance. Andries saw them get up.

"Fuck it," he said to himself, raking a hand through his hair as he walked with purpose toward her.

He stood behind her and whispered in her ear raspily, "Will you dance with me?"

"Come on then," she said, taking his hand and striding over to the dance floor. They danced the way they did on her birthday. There was no grinding on each other, but it was still sensual like a salsa. A sense of dignity and respect is intertwined with attraction and magnetism.

They went back over to the table and found that there were some other people at the table. Some friends of Zade's and Abel's. Introductions were made, and the conversation was had. One of the girls was very sweet. He had curly black hair and green eyes and was dressed smartly in a burgundy polo shirt.

"I love your sneakers," she complimented, tucking a strand of hair from her face. His name was Mateo, and he was funny.

Anaisha was sitting at the front of the table, so she couldn't see what was going on behind her, but she saw the faces in front of her light up and turned around,

"What's up?"

"Mykal! Finally you're here!" She yelled, getting up and enveloping him in a hug. He was wearing white trousers and a short sleeved white shirt with a black ambiguous Picasso type print on the sleeves. Aki was behind him, wired and a little drunk. She smiled up at him with her hug.

She motioned him to put his head down, "I love the shirt"

He looked up and smiled at her, his eyes looked lighter under the lights. "You like?" He lifted a brow. She looked really good, like really good.

"I love! How are you feeling?" She asked with a giggle.

"Fucking fantastic," he laughed.

"Amazing!" she introduced them to Mateo, and watched as Mykal spoke to him. Mateo laughed at something he said. She was smiling, she would never stop being impressed with Mykal's 'people skills.' She didn't realize the breath she had been holding until she let it go when he walked in, just having him there put her at ease.

"What the fuck are you doing sitting down? Let's dance!" Mykal said, pulling up Naira. She quickly placed her drink down before it spilt. She seemed a little out of her element, sipping her drink silently, fiddling with her hair. Then he motioned for the rest.

"Anaisha, would you like to dance?" Mateo asked with a confident smile.

She blinked, a little shocked, and then she laced her voice with kindness. "Actually, I'm..." she said, turning around to point at Andries, who was sitting next to her.

"No, no, it's fine, go ahead," Andries said with a small smile.

"Really? It is?" Her eyes slanted off offensively.

"Yeah," he shrugged, looking up at her.

"Okay then, sure," she said with a sugary smile at Mateo... and Andries.

And she did. The music blew through the speakers, winding through everyone there. The DJ was like some sort of snake charmer, causing everyone to lose their armour.

"Andries!"

"Anaisha, there you are," she was a blur.

"You just ditched me," she launched, hurt souring from her voice.

He was thrust. "What?" This was unjust.

"Andries, you only danced with me once..."

He glanced at her, blue eyes rapidly blinking. "You must be joking?" He was trying to wrap his head around this.

"You were dancing with Mateo, and who knows who else?" He said with a bite in his voice as he was trying to scrape the pieces together in this tumultuous weather.

"How sweet?" She said in a beat.

This was intense. "You didn't even give me a chance," he said, disappointment pouring in his voice.

"What?" She scoffed. Her eyes ablaze, she was struck. "Fuck this. I'm going back."

"Anaisha, don't go..."

"No. just leave it, Andries," and with a flip of her hair over her shoulder, she was gone. That felt like a blur.

Andries made his way back to his friends. Anaisha was already there, sitting on the opposite side of where she had been previously sitting. As further away from him as possible, he realised. She seemed fine, sipping her drink and smiling at something Aki was saying. But Calista looked at her sideways and mouthed, "You okay?"

She shrugged with her whole body. She felt tired, she had already gotten angry, and now she was just confused and a bit upset. She'd tell her in a bit, but she wouldn't be one of those girls that let a boy upset her. So she took a swig of her drink, ran her fingers through her hair, shaking it out, taking a breath for a moment and straightening her back. When she opened her eyes, she was back. The music was loud, and her friends were laughing; this was good. She was fine.

Andries sat on the other side, shaking his head from side to side as Mykal asked him, "what happened, bro?"

He explained their argument with droopy eyes.

"This is just a perfect example of miscommunication, Ries," Mykal said, slapping his arm, with a roll of his eyes.

"You are stressing for no reason." He said, looking at him solemnly.

"No..." Ries began,

"Trust me," Mykal said, cutting him off and looking at him keenly. He could fix this, and he knew exactly how.

"You guys are so dramatic," Mykal laughed as he handed a drink to Andries.

"It'll be fine, trust me. Now just enjoy the night," he said as he leaned back, one arm around the chair, a calm smile on his face.

They entered Calista's house, Andries, with his hands stuffed in his pockets, shoulders slumped and blue eyes facing the ground, and Anaisha was listening to Calista intently, her back straight, pretending everything was fine. Typical.

They were standing on either side of Mykal. He rolled his eyes and grabbed both of their hands. "Come with me, you love-struck idiots" Anaisha and Andries shared a quick, hasty look at the sound of the L-word.

"Myk-" she started, loosening her hand from his grasp as she gracefully shook her head from side to side, a resigned look on her face.

"Do you trust me?" He said, turning to face her, brows raised.

"Absolutely not," she said as she crossed her arms over her chest, but a small smile brushed her lips.

He laughed heartily, clapping his hands together, "You shouldn't," he said with a wink, putting his hand back out for her. She groaned and took it, not looking at Ries.

The rest of the group were busying themselves by taking their shoes off and chilling in the TV room. They all knew about the fight and trusted Mykal to handle it.

"Come sit." He motioned to the edge of Calista's bed. "I'm not a dog," she said with sharp eyes.

"Please, can you take a seat?" He smiled at her. She sat, crossing one knee over the other.

"Look, what happened tonight was a classic example of miscommunication," he began. His hazel brown eyes shifted between the two of them. Anaisha bent and put her elbow on her thigh, resting her chin on her knuckles as she listened to him.

"I had to take this into my hands because you," he said, pointing at Ries, "are not great at this kind of thing," he smirked.

"And you," he said, pointing at Anaisha, "you get too worked up, so I thought for your first fight, you might need some help navigating," he clapped his hands together.

"This is really bizarre," Anaisha said in a monotone voice, unmoving her chin still nonchalantly resting on her knuckles.

"Yeah, it's kind of weird, Myk," Andries admitted as he leaned back on the bed.

"But I'm used to it," Anaisha said nonchalantly, "So carry on," Anaisha waved her free hand at him.

Ries pointed a lazy finger at Anaisha, "ditto."

Quickly their eyes met. Andries's hand fell to the scar on his eyebrow as he knew what she was thinking. This was how they always connected to each other. They both seemed different but thought so similarly.

"What I brought you both here to say was that I think you guys should talk and make up quickly. Don't be stubborn about it." He said, looking at both of them. "I think you two could be something great." he shrugged, "Seriously," he whispered with a nod. "I think you could make each other really happy," he said as he gulped and looked at the two of them, running a hand through his straight black hair.

Andries pushed back on his elbows, leaning back up, "Myk -" he said.

Mykal cut him off.

"So get out of your own fucking way," he said, walking backwards toward the door, "and talk to each other properly." he scolded as he slammed the door shut.

Calista's room was the same as when they were children. There was still a boyband poster on top of the pretty pastel pink flowery wallpaper. Anaisha played with the cotton candy coloured pink canopy as they sat silently on the bed.

"Do you want to talk," he said as he fully pushed himself off his elbows. "Properly?" He nudged his foot with hers.

And she could hear the smile in his voice as he repeated Mykal's word.

"Why did you tell me to go dance with him?" She said forthrightly, letting go of the net.

"Straight to the point, I like it," he nodded. She turned her face to look at him, waiting for an answer.

"I thought you wanted to..." he shrugged. She scoffed.

"It's just... we're in this," he motioned his hands back on forth between the two of them, struggling for the words.

She helped him, "I know what you mean," she whispered, looking down at her feet. They had basically been together for ages, an unsaid relationship. But there was something about making it a 'said relationship'. He bent his head to look into her eyes. Those blue eyes gazed up at her.

"After your birthday, I thought it meant that we were like… together... properly together," a small smile spread on his face. He couldn't help but smile when he thought of them being 'properly together.'

"But then tonight, I realised we haven't actually spoken about it. So," he gulped, looking down at his feet and tentatively slowly whispered, "Do you want to be together?"

She looked up at him, for some reason not knowing what to say, her eyes moving, searching his face.

He turned around and whispered to himself as he raked a hand through his hair. "Fuck, I'm done being a pussy."

He whirled around and looked straight at her. "Lets be exclusive. I want you." He said clearly, and held her hands in his "I want to be exclusive to you. Would you want that?" with a steady voice, a blue-eyed challenge in his eyes. It felt like lightning could strike at any second.

"I don't know..." she said as she bit her lip.

He blew out a breath, still holding her eyes in his, "Not the answer I was expecting. But I'm not going to be an idiot about it this time," he voiced calmly.

"Can I ask… why not?" He said in a voice so calm and caring, she thought she might melt. She bit her lip harder, unsure.

"Aish, it's just me, you can say it." he said as he leaned back on his elbows. She blew a breath out, it was him. Ries, her best friend of years, who she had spoken to a billion times before about countless things. But this was the first time he was saying things that she had never heard from him before.

She looked at him intently as she went over to sit next to him. A small smile on her lips at the way he was handling this. "I'm scared," she groaned.

"Of?" He said, still leaning back. It felt easier to talk to him when he was doing Reis-like things. She didn't know how to explain it, but just the way he was leaning back was so… him, it put her at ease.

"I'm scared I'll fuck it up," she said in a comically agitated voice.

"Same!" He laughed. Then he looked up at the ceiling, the laugh leaving his voice "same," he whispered in his raspy voice.

They both were silent for a minute. What if it ruined their friendship? What if this was taking it a step too far?

He could feel her breathing next to him.

"You know what," he said, leaping from the bed to stand in front of her. "I am scared... fuck yeah, I am," he raked a hand through his hair, "but it's because what we already have is great. But at the same time, I didn't just kiss you that night on a whim. I meant it, I had been thinking about you all simmer" he said with resolute eyes.

"I am scared," he said, his eyes moving toward the window, looking at the moon and stars for guidance, "but I've found that things are scary when they're worth it." He turned back with a wink and a wicked smile on his face, and she couldn't help but give one back. "And if we can have something even better... I think I want to go for it."

Then he suddenly shook his head passionately.

"No," looking downwards, he looked back up, blue eyes gazing at her. "I know. I know I want to go for it," he annunciated each word clearly.

68

"do you?" He said, holding his hand out, asking her not just with his words but with his body too.

She gulped, her heart pounded against her chest. But she was enjoying it, his eyes wouldn't leave hers, and she didn't think she ever wanted them to. She took his hand and kissed him softly, gently.

Once Mykal had left them, he walked so quickly to the powder room downstairs that it felt more like a run., like he was a thief attempting to make a swift getaway. He balanced his hands on the sink while deeply breathing in air that just didn't seem to feel real anymore, he performed the simple movement of turning the sink on, letting the water run through his fingers as he splashed water onto his face, it felt good.

He did it again, he surprised himself with how aggressively he splashed it into his eyes. It had almost hurt.

And a third time. On the third splash he let his now cool hands linger on his face, as he kept his eyes shut.

This was so not him, this person that needed a moment of solitude in the powder room, and the person that splashed their face with cold water and kept their eyes shut to make themselves for

He looked in the mirror, and his wheatish skin looked pale and splotchy at the same time. His big brown eyes looked worried and foreignly sad looking back at him with an expression that felt like it had been stabbed into him. This wasn't him, he was not the person that needed a moment of solitude in the powder room, and the person that splashed their face with cold water and kept their eyes shut for a moment, because actually looking at himself felt like he was looking at a foreign person, at a friend he once knew that had betrayed him.

Andries could tell; he could tell. Of course, he could, Mykal thought. He had faltered on that last sentence.

He left the powder room and walked down the corridor, rubbing his sweaty hands along his pants. This time he made a conscious effort to *walk*.

There were two brown wooden doors, and he didn't know which one was the guest room. With a guess, he opened one door to a bedroom with a dark-haired girl sitting on the very edge of the bed, her upper body was rising up and down quickly, and he could see even in the faint light that her eyes were tightly shut, so tight it almost looked painful. And she was making this sound, that sound of when you couldn't quite catch your breath that made him feel uneasy. And despite her tightly closed eyes, even if she couldn't see it herself. In the faint light he could see her face looked wet, and glistened horribly.

It was Naira.

She didn't seem to notice him, too heavily wrapped up in the cling film that was freaking out and trying to calm herself down and going through that motion for what felt like a hellish, agonising, effort-filled eternity.

He closed the door, gently and with a careful mind walked up to her. With an even gentler hand, he touched her shoulder. She looked up, eyes darting like she had been caught committing a crime.

"What's wrong Naira?" He whispered.

She took a shallow breath, "I'm..." and then drew another, "f..." she swallowed, shut her eyes tightly and took a deep breath in. "I'm fine."

"Okay", he said, nodding slowly. It looked like she might be having a panic attack, maybe.

He raked his mind, like he was flipping through the pages of a book as he tried to figure out what to do to help her, "I'm going to get you some water, okay?"

She nodded slowly. She looked like she was counting under her breath, breathing in slowly. When Mykal left, Naira took her phone out. Her fingers were shaking, her breaths growing shallower with each one she took in as it felt like her heart might just stop from how hard it was slamming against her chest. She gasped in and held her breath, and she found the song on her phone. Her thumb shook as she tapped it and it played softly as she willed every fiber in her being to focus on the lyrics. as she sang them, hummed the melody them, and even just spoke the lyrics out loud. spoke them. She felt it wilting away, that feeling, like a monster letting her limp body go after nearly squeezing her to death. Her breath slowed, and she focused on the way it slowed. She breathed in for six seconds, and out for ten... and she kept going. Until she felt it, that sedated limp feeling of it being done.

It was gone, the sensation of trepidation and feeling frozen but like every sense was more alive than it was ever meant to be, that feeling that she could never seem to explain properly and could barely remember happening, until it happened again.

70

Mykal came back with a glass of water. She seemed calmer now. He remembered someone saying how panic attacks don't last long. But they could re-occur and feel longer. But she seemed better now, he knew she had pretty bad anxiety, but he had never been with her when she had a panic attack before.

Her were eyes still red, accompanied by a tear-stained face. But she took the glass of water with a steady hand and a wry smile on her face. She took a deep breath in and a sip. She swallowed slowly and felt it float down from her mouth to her throat to her chest. She blew a breath out as she shook her head at herself. Tears stung her eyes and her whole body felt hot and sweaty in the worst way, she felt embarrassed and almost a sense of shame that made her want to lock herself in her room and cry for hours.

But instead she looked up at the ceiling, blew a breath out and swallowed what felt like a rock in her throat and didn't let the tears drop.

"Believe it or not, that was progress for me," she laughed darkly.

Mykal's scared, sad face broke into a smile, "that's amazing." he sat down on the carpet, and leaned against the end of the bed. "Are you okay now?"

She didn't think she had been 'okay 'for some time now, but she nodded anyway.

"Do you want to talk about it?" His voice was tentative.

"No, it's okay," she said, moving her head from side to side quickly. She was clenching her fists in her hands, opening and reopening.

"Are you sure?" He said, his eyes wide and so kind, sincere and trustworthy…

She tucked a strand of hair behind her ear, sheepishly. It was hard to lie to someone who looked at you like that.

"It is just annoying. Like I'm in this clear box, watching everyone around me do all these things so effortlessly, with such ease" her big green eyes had a look of such yearning and sadness to them, he just wanted to take whatever she was feeling away.

"and I just..." she breathed out heavily, "can't. And I don't know why... my life's been great. I've not struggled, I feel like I have no reason to feel like this," she gulped, struggling to get the words out. "Like it's selfish of me," she said with a shaky breath. "I mean there are people who have lost their parents at a young age and grown up alone. They have issues, you know. I haven't been through anything so terrible."

Mykal nodded, an understanding look on his face, "Yeah, I get it. Other people have bigger fish to fry." He scratched his jaw, "but anxiety's really common, you know, and it doesn't always have something to do with what has happened in your life specifically," he squinted, as if trying to remember something.

"I think it's 25% of people... that's one in four, which means you're just one of the ones," he said softly.

She huffed a laugh. He had a very clear yet casual way of speaking.

"So I don't think it is personal, for you, it doesn't have to do with anything that happened to you... it's just one of those unfortunate things you have to deal with, by being you."

She flipped her hair back apathetically, and said under her breath, "I wish I wasn't me"

His eyes flicked up fiercely, "don't ever say that" the same gentle ferocity matched his tone, and it struck her.

He swallowed, "It sucks I get it, but" he shrugged.

"Yeah..." she breathed out heavily and lay her back on the bed.

"Sorry, they," she gulped. "I mean panic attacks," she waved a hand in the air, "they make you feel really exhausted after they happen."

He nodded "that's totally understandable."

"You go to therapy, right?" He had never spoken to her about this before.

"Yeah, on and off. It has been happening since I was... 14 ish," she took a deep breath in, "but I should go more consistently."

"Okay... can I tell you something? It might come out wrong, and I don't mean to be insensitive or unsolicited, but..." he chewed his lip.

"Go for it. Trust me, and I'll take all the advice I can get," she said in a low voice.

He spoke, facing the wall in front of them. It had wallpaper on it, and he followed the pattern with his eyes as he spoke, "Sometimes life throws curveballs our way. Ones we thought we could control but can't. The most unexpected shit that you never saw coming," he clasped his hands over his head.

"But you have to rise above it, Naira... you have to," he nodded with heavy vigour, "but, most of all, you have to want to rise above it. In every fibre of your being. Do you want to get better?"

He turned his head to see her answer. She was sitting up now, watching him as he spoke. She nodded, her eyes steady.

"Say it"

"Yes, I do. I want to get better."

"Then use that 'want'... Go to therapy on the days you don't want to, use that desire to shut your demons off, punch it out, kill that part of yourself and move forward.

It will pass if you do that, and sometimes they'll come to haunt you again, but this time you will know how to kill them. You'll know what to say and do to them."

"Don't go in with the mindset that you want to get rid of it. Go in with the mindset that you want to learn how to deal with it."

He spoke with so much passion and fervour she couldn't help but ask, "Do you have anxiety? Or just something like that?" She said, blinking.

"Not me, but my Dad does. He's better now, though." He said with a smile on his face and continued, "and we all go through shit in our head, whether there's a name for it or not," he leaned back and looked up at the ceiling, gulping down on words he couldn't say.

"Do you want to talk about it?" She said, pushing down from the bed to sit next to him. She felt better and less like a freak.

"Honestly, I'm not just saying that. I mean it," tossing his words back at him. He laughed.

The only lights turned on in the room were the lamps on the side table, a soft yellow light. It made the atmosphere seem restful and cosy. A place where he could be honest with no judgement. A place where he could fall asleep without the fear of something killing him while he slept. Maybe it was the lights or the fact that he was still tipsy. He had kept the weight on his chest for what felt like so long. This seemed like the perfect place to rest and let it go.

Or maybe it was that Naira, who was so sweet and chilled, and someone who he was sure would understand.

"It has to do with your cousin. You sure you wanna know?" He asked, looking straight ahead.

"Something bad?" She questioned.

"Depends who you're asking, I guess," a glint in his eye.

"You helped me today. Maybe I can give you some advice. She is my cousin at the end of the day."

"You have to promise you won't tell her, anyone actually," he said, turning his head to look at her.

"I promise," she nodded. "You know how Aish and I are…" she started. They were close and loved each other, but they weren't the type of close to sit up at night and talk to each other.

"Not even Aki," he said. And at that, she bit her lip, her eyes darting up to her mind as if she was wondering if she could, in fact, do that. He smiled. He understood that feeling... he would also have to think for a moment if someone asked him to keep something from Andries or Anaisha.

She settled after a few minutes of contemplation.

"Okay, not even Aki. You have my word," she said with a steady nod.

"All right then, don't say I didn't warn you," he said with a sardonic smile.

And in the soft yellow light, he told her… he just said it, casually, the way he wishes he could've been outside this room.

"I'm in love with Anaisha," He tapped his fingers on his legs and blew a breath out as he lay down on the bed, she felt the mattress sink down slowly, in the same way this information was sinking into her mind. He blew a breath out. Naira stayed silent for a second, and her green eyes slid to him.

"You are going to need to elaborate," she said as she lay down next to him. Naira and Mykal lay on the bed together, her hair sprawled around her head like a halo. His hands rested on his abdomen.

"So, when did it begin?" she asked, tapping the little freckle on her knuckle.

Mykal took a deep breath in, drumming his fingers against his chest.

"Well, we've been friends since we were kids," he began.

"Yeah, I swear my memories of the three of you when we were younger were always the three of you together all the time."

"Yeah, I met Ries when we were nine years old, in school. He still had the same eyes, but his hair was shittier," Mykal laughed. "He had moved schools and didn't have many friends, and we were put together for this like research project thing."

Suddenly, he went silent, blinking slowly. His long thick lashes were laying against his cheekbone.

"Honestly," his deep voice became quiet like he was telling her a secret. She had always thought he had a comforting voice, it had deepened with age, but it was always friendly and comfortingly deep like a fireplace.

"I can't even remember my life before they were in it" it was almost like their lives had only truly begun when they walked into each other.

And he told her everything…

She had this beautiful way of listening, of just letting him talk, and he told her everything… and while he talked he couldn't help but smile at the memories, and despite the situation he still felt that balmy, sunny feeling of pride and love and missing when he spoke of Anaisha and Andries.

"Anyway," he quickly shook his head, taking in a harried breath, "Andries really likes her, more than I do, I'm sure," he grinned sardonically.

"And even if he didn't," He held his chin up, "he's my brother, you know. I would never." A look of honourable resolution in his dark eyes.

"I always thought you could control your feelings, whenever I heard about it, you know, situations with friendships and love and feelings. I always thought how could they, how could they like the same person their best friend liked too. It just seems fucked, but I'm learning that it's not that simple." He pressed his full lips together. "Maybe this is my karma for being too judgmental," he shrugged, broad shoulders.

"No, I think it just shows your capacity to be able to love freely... a little too freely."

It was like his mouth was a dam; now that it had opened, the words wouldn't stop gushing out.

"I won't let myself turn bitter. I'll be okay. I know that it'll work itself out slowly. I'll let the feelings fade, and it'll be a distant memory..." he closed his eyes, scratching the nape of his neck.

"And someone else will walk into your life, who will make these feelings feel minuscule," Naira said, touching his shoulder gently.

"Exactly, and in the meantime, I have my friends and family..." he smiled ruefully. "I'm good," he said, turning to face her. There was a dark brown outline around his hazel eyes, Naira realised.

"You are." He was probably the easiest person to talk to she had ever met. This conversation was, oddly, one of the easiest she had ever had.

"Is this your demon?"

He nodded. "I think so," he blew a breath out.

"I'll be okay, though. I know that it'll work itself out slowly. The feelings will fade, and this will be a memory... and in the meantime, I have friends and family, more love than I can imagine... they say love is a good thing. According to J.M Barrie, 'let no one who loves be unhappy... even love unreturned has its rainbow."

He turned his head, brown eyes alight with a softness and happiness that felt peaceful, "that's cringe".

Naira laughed softly, the sound bouncing gently of the walls and soft yellow lights.

That was one of the days that marked a change in all of their little lives. Anaisha and Andries had established something between themselves about their relationship, that they cared enough about each other to be there for each other, trust and lean on each other up, and in a different way so had Mykal and Naira.

Chapter 9

That December

Ugh, I hate long flights," Andries groaned, raking a hand through his hair as they sat in the waiting area for their flight.

Anaisha leaned her head on his shoulder, "same," she said with a yawn. It was about five in the morning, and nearly everyone was exhausted though they were all awake, speaking in soft conversation. Their parents were behind them, and you could hear Mrs. Ricard keeping the excitement alive for the rest of the adults.

"I disagree, man. I mean, a flight just means that you're going somewhere, travelling!" he drummed his fingers on his knee excitedly. "That's fucking awesome and exciting, and a long flight just build up that excitement."

Damini smiled next to Mykal as she yawned "that's a good way of looking at it, Mykie."

He turned to Damini, "and it means you can watch a ton of movies or read…" he said, elbowing Naira, who was on his other side. Naira laughed, "That's very true."

"It's undisturbed time," he said as he put his arms behind the chairs. He had gotten even taller and bigger.

"Like you're suspended in it for a moment…." Naira played with the rings on her fingers. "A flight, the one place where time slows down," she said, looking at Mykal with lit-up eyes. "Exactly!" he whispered, with a spark in his eyes. They both smiled at each other.

"You guys are very odd," Anaisha said with a laugh. Mykal and Naira always related to things like this, looking at things in a different way… saying the weird thoughts on their mind.

"But fair enough, I get your point," Anaisha said. Mykal was the happiest person she knew, and it didn't go unnoticed the way he could change the mood of people or their thoughts even. She had never known someone more grateful to be alive.

"So, Soph, what movie are you going to watch?" Anaisha said as she grabbed Mykal's little sister Sofia and settled her on her lap.

That April

"Why are you yawning?" Andries said it was about 8 pm, and they were about to order dinner from their favourite burger joint. Andries already knew what their order would be, two doubles for Andries and Mykal and then Anaisha would say she wanted to try something different like some caramelized onion burger and then just end up ordering the one she knew she liked with mushrooms.

"I woke up early today, watched the sunrise…" he yawned and stretched as he took a sip of Andries's coffee on the table.

"I could never," Anaisha laughed softly, "why do you do it?" she said as she took a sip of her coffee and held a hand up, quickly swallowing. "I mean, I get it. It's gorgeous if you're already awake, but why wake up just for that?" she asked as she twirled a lock of hair.

He shrugged and stretched again, taking a deep breath and leaning forward to pick up the cup of coffee just to prolong some time so he could think of a different answer.

Andries turned his head to the side, looking at Mykal. Anaisha stayed watchful for a moment. They both sensed a difference.

Mykal turned his head, and they were both looking at him. Dark and blue eyes.

He huffed an uncharacteristically forced laugh, set the cup down and leaned back again, almost closing his eyes as he leaned back.

"Sometimes, I just get this feeling like I'm a person looking at my life from the outside like I'm a ghost of my own self, and it can be detrimental to my mental health and state of mind. And I found that doing things like meditating or watching the sunrise or playing the guitar kept me connected to something real, that the world is real and there are things like music and nature that are bigger than me, and it'll be okay. Do you know? These are like the little things I do for myself. Otherwise, I would just float away. But when I do those things, I'm back - back to me, a person I'm happy to be.

They had never heard Mykal speak like this. It was just something he didn't really do. "Then keep doing it," Anaisha said gently and walked over and sat on the arm of the sofa and held Mykal's hand. He put his other hand over hers, thanking her through touch.

"Why haven't you ever told us you felt like that before?" her voice has softened. "Yeah, why didn't you?"

Mykal opened his mouth to speak, then closed it again. He didn't know what to say. "Honestly, I don't know" if there was anyone he could talk to, he knew it was them.

Later, when Anaisha had to go to the bathroom. Andries said in a low voice. "You're my brother, and brothers can talk to each other. And if you don't want to talk about it, that's fine too. But just know I'm always there."

"I know." and he really did. "I'm sorry I never came to you before."

"You don't need to apologise" Andries scrunched his brows together, confused. "I'm glad you did now. I just need you to know that. I'm always here, and so is she," he motioned toward Anaisha, who was just coming out of the bathroom.

"What am I?" she said as she sauntered over. "A bitch." Andries's blue eyes sparkled.

"He's just so sweet to me…." Anaisha looked at Mykal "how did I ever get so lucky" As they watched their movie, Anaisha thought about what Mykal said. She looked at him silently for a minute as he laughed at some comment Andries said. Completely and fully laughed. A real laugh… it was crazy; Anaisha thought that no matter how well you thought you might know someone, the smiliest, the most social person she knew could feel like that sometimes. But she also knew that no matter what, he would come back. He would be Mykal. From that day onwards, Mykal told one of them whenever he felt that way when he felt like saying it. And they would call straight away or send a voice not, and it would usually tether him back. Andries would call, and then he would let him be. Let him get back to himself, but always with a watchful eye. Once, he even sent him a new song that he wanted him to learn on the guitar, which made him chuckle. And Anaisha's heart swelled whenever Mykal sent her a picture of the sunrise, and it seemed more beautiful to her now than it ever had before… that this thing brought someone she loved so much peace.

That June…

Andries's father's house was a lot like his own, his mother's. You could see all the touches. Teresa, even the colour palette was similar. But the livid blues were replaced with sage green. His Dad was out of town this weekend, and Andries was meant to stay at his father's that weekend anyway, so the kids decided to be a little risky. They hosted a party at the house.

"You okay, babe?" Andries said to Anaisha, who was leaning on his shoulder.

"Sweetheart, you can't even stand. Let's go upstairs," he said to her, wiping some hair off her now sweaty face. They were in that kind of love, where even when she was drunk and sweaty and eyes slightly glazed over, he still thought she was the most beautiful thing he had ever seen.

"I can!" she argued.

He laughed, "Yes, you can," he said as he led her toward the stairs.

"No! Not in that room! It's off-limits!" Andries half-shouted at people trying to get into the formal dining room.

"I'll take her, and you go deal with that," Mykal swooped in.

"Okay," Andries said as he handed over Anaisha and rushed over to lock the door of the dining room.

They reached Andries's room. It was simpler and smaller than the one at his Mom's house, with fewer personal items… a low bed with a black frame and a desk with textbooks and his laptop still open. He was working on an essay before the party. But there were a few picture frames on the bedside table. One of them was the picture that Anaisha had taken of him and Andries at the beach.

Mykal sat with her as his long fingers, calloused and scarred from years of playing the guitar, stroked her hair tentatively and gently watched her as she went to sleep. He wanted to say it now. He knew he could never say it the way he wanted to… maybe, it was only in these little moments he could steal for himself would he be able to be his only truth when she napped in the basement or in a dark room with a soft lamp on. In these calm, untouched wave-like moments where he felt like he was floating on water, just drifting away.

He would drift away for her if that's what it took. He would drift away, not knowing where he was going as long as she was next to him.

He was about to say it when she said something.

"I love you, Mykal" her eyes opened slightly as she looked at him. Dark, almond eyes were looking at him. He wanted to kiss the bump on her nose and hold her to smell more of her jasmine-scented perfume.

He stroked her hair again, and he said, "I love you, too," but he said it differently than she did and in a different way than he ever had to her before, but right now, he knew she was too drunk and too sleepy to ever realise the way the words were laid so differently.

Three Weeks Later

Mykal held his glass midway to his mouth and caught Andries's blue eyes stare. Andries cocked his head to the side, toward the entrance of the house with a raise of his brows. Mykal

80

nodded, took a gulp of his water and strode toward their parents' friends, who were standing close to Ries.

Andries joined and laughed at one of the uncle's jokes, only pretending to have heard it. Then, promptly, mid-conversation, he turned his head toward the open door of the hall and scrunched his brows together, "Oh, I think my Mum needs me for a moment."

"Oh, of course, darling... go on," one of the ladies said, with a smile that said what a sweet boy.

"Mykal, I think she wants your help too," he said, slapping his friend's shoulders.

"Can't keep auntie waiting..." he charmingly shrugged with a lazy smile.

They quickly made their way out of the hall doors, and instead of going right toward the kitchen, they took a left and walked straight through the foyer to the doorway.

Slipping through the door, barely opening it or closing it. The cool wind slapped their faces as they stepped out.

Andries threw Mykal's keys over to him as he ran over to the passenger door of his car. Mykal had already opened it by the time Andries reached, and he hopped in. Mykal started the car, reversed out, and they were off.

"Your Mum's gonna kill us, bro," he said with a small laugh as he rolled the windows down and opened the roof of the car.

"We were there for a whole hour," he said with a nonchalant shrug, "and we'll be back anyway in a bit."

"I'm connecting," Mykal said.

Automatically Andries started fidgeting with the Bluetooth settings, readying them for Mykal. "I swear to god, if you put on that fucking musical shit that you and Anaisha like..." Andries said with his stern blue eyes glaring at him.

Mykal couldn't help but laugh, "Relax, I know my audience...," he said as he entered a round-a-bout, "you know, unintellectual and unappreciative."

Andries rolled his eyes. "Fuck you," he said with a boyish grin.

Andries was drumming his long fingers on his lap as he leaned back on the seat, gently swaying his head, Mykal's eyes slipped to the side, and a smile slid on his face. He liked the music; he knew it.

Mykal had a highly eclectic taste in music and an appreciation for all of it. If it was good, it was good, was his theory. This made sense, considering that music was a passion of his.

He had started playing the guitar at eight years old and really never looked back. He could now play the drums and bass, but the guitar was what he felt the most comfortable with.

Mykal played a song about love. For some reason, it felt like every fucking song was about it; love, sex, romance. Everything was about it.

Andries hummed along to it, turning up the volume. Mykal swiftly turned his head and looked back to the road.

Something in it had resonated with him. You could see it in the blue of his eyes. That was the magic of music, Mykal thought. "What's up, brother?" Mykal asked as he switched lanes expertly.

"I really like her, man," Andries said in his gravelly voice.

"That's awesome. I'm happy for you." Andries couldn't see him in the darkness, but there was still a smile on Mykal's face as he said it.

"She's just..." he looked out the window as if only the stars could understand what he felt. Like it was that special and luminous.

"Go on, Mr Actor," Mykal prodded.

"Fuck off," Andries laughed. Ries had always had a flair for the dramatic. It wasn't necessarily intentional. I mean, with those intense blue eyes and that exceptional head of curly hair that he was constantly raking his hands through, plus the scar, it was pretty inevitable. So they had come up with 'Mr. Actor' at a pretty young age.

"Nah, man... I can't," he laughed to himself, keeping the words to himself. Usually, when Ries decided to keep his words to himself, Mykal could tell how he was feeling, but tonight it was slightly different.

Ries raked his hand through his hair. "I just feel great, you know?"

Mykal nodded. "I'm very happy to hear that."

"I mean, I have a good family, great friends," he said, placing a hand on Mykal's shoulder, "a great girl", a little smile played on his lips, "and we're going to university next year... it's gonna be fucking awesome," he said with an energetic slap on the dashboard.

"It's gonna be great," Mykal agreed with a nod.

"I want you to have the same."

"I do. I have the same great friends and a great family too. I'm chilling," Mykal said as he took a u-turn. They should probably head back now, he thought as he checked the time.

"Yeah, but what about the girl..."

Mykal laughed at that. "I have girls in my life. You don't have to worry about that," he said with a wink.

"Yeah, but I don't mean like that, man. I mean in an emotional way like "the girl," Andries said, highlighting the last part.

Mykal fell silent.

"Or perhaps guy?" Andries said cocking his head to the side.

"Still into girls," he laughed, racking his head for a way to divert this conversation.

"Stop fucking around, man," Andries said, looking out of the window, "trust me." Mykal could hear the smile in his voice.

A moment passed.

"There was someone," Mykal swallowed and blew a breath out, "but it was some time ago..." he kept his eyes straight ahead.

"What the fuck! Who?" Andries said, shocked with a hint of annoyance in his voice at the fact that Mykal had never told him.

"You don't know her," Mykal said as he took a left. They were close to the house now, thank god. Why had he said anything in the first place? He thought.

"Who do you know that I don't?" Andries questioned. His eyes darted around as he thought of every girl he had ever seen Mykal with.

"It's Calista, right?" he asked, his eyes focused on Mykal for any sign of confirmation. Mykal smirked. He knew he and Calista hung out, but he had never spoken about her like this. So he thought it was someone else. "I fucking knew it," Ries laughed.

"You know how Cal and I are. We have fun," Mykal said as he took a left. Mykal shook his head side to side, "but this is another girl, and I'm never telling," he laughed, then his laugh faltered as he drummed his fingers on the wheel too speedily. "Anyway, it would never have worked out... wasn't meant to be."

Andries didn't prod any further about exactly who this mystery woman was because he had never heard Mykal sound like this. Mykal always had the most positive answer to everything. His solution was always one of hope and chance, taking risks, laying it all out and seeing what happens.

But right now, Andries felt like their roles were reversed.

"How would you know if you never tried?" Andries said, turning his head. His blue eyes were shining with the thought of possibilities.

"Trust me, Andries." Andries blinked in mild surprise... Mykal rarely used his real name. This was just another confirmation that what he was saying was serious or different, at least. "It was," Mykal searched for the words as he parked in the driveway of Andries's house, a very delicate and complicated situation..."

He parked the car, his hand lingering on the brake, "so ultimately, not worth it," he said matter of factly now, meaning he had probably already made up his mind on this. Mykal had a lot of confidence in his emotional intelligence, rightfully so Andries felt. He barely got angry and wasn't an irrational person. He was big on communication, and he always had a very good idea of how he was feeling. And though he was indecisive as fuck in general, he was very decisive when it came to things that mattered. Decisive to the extent of stubbornness, meaning that if this was his decision, it wouldn't change.

But Ries had to try.

"Well, ultimately, I don't give a fuck," Andries said, taking his seatbelt off and turning completely to face Mykal, "how would you know if it was worth it if you never gave it a shot." He looked at Mykal incredulously.

He shook his head side to side, a sharp no.

"Trust me." Andries didn't understand why Mykal wasn't giving him more information but studying the way he was acting, Andries decided not to prod further.

"Fine," he said, putting his hands up as if he was surrendering, "live in your misery."

"What?" Mykal said, and this time he turned and looked at Andries with a confused smile on his face. "I'm not miserable. I have a pretty blessed life." he nodded to himself as he truly believed it. "I have a great family and great friends, who are all healthy and mostly happy. And I have music. And about a girl, well, there'll be someone else. It's not like she was the only girl in the world." Sometimes, it really felt like she was, but he couldn't be silly about this.

Sometimes other things are worth saving more. "It doesn't matter anymore. I have consistency, a great family and great friends, and I'm less greedy than you, you dick," he said, smacking Ries. "And that's good enough for me."

It would've been the worst and best thing to say. Just say it out loud. Tell the truth... finally. A relief. But at the same time, he would be shattering their little world.

But that wouldn't have been right. All he ever wanted, probably without even realizing it, was for Ries and Anaisha to be happy. Together or apart, that didn't matter; he just wanted them to be happy.

The way any person wants the people they love to be happy. And they were happy together. So, how could he be the person to break that happiness when he was the one who wanted it for

them the most? It was the oddest feeling to be so happy and sad at the same time. Happy for the

people you loved, and sad for yourself.

"Well, if you're having fun, that's all I care about... don't hurt Calista, though; she's awesome." Andries looked at Myk.

"Never, I love her, man." He smiled as he thought of her with her sun-kissed skin and brown hair. He could never hurt her. She was wonderful, kind and spunky. "And I know she's on the same page as me."

The Last Summer

"Damini!"

In walked a tall, slim young girl, with shiny long dark hair. She wore a pair of pink, what looked like men's trousers and a white tank top and sneakers.

She took her sunglasses off as she entered the door. "Hello, family" she boomed.

First she made her way to her grandparents and respectfully greeted them. Bending down to give them both a hug in their seats. "Why are you so late?" Her grandfather asked looking at his watch.

Before Damini could answer, her grandmother cut in "why does it matter, at least she's here" her grandmother said with a smile and took Damini's hands and giving them a kiss.

Then she was enveloped in hugs and kisses from her various family members.

"Nairu!" She hugged Naira tightly,

"I really love the hair!" She said excitedly.

"Thank you" Naira smiled, even though she couldn't see her. Damini had already seen her new hair on video calls but she hadn't seen her in real life in quite some time.

Suddenly, Damini drew back her hands on Naira's forearms and her eyes very obviously gazing up and down at Naira.

"You look very good" she complimented. Naira had put on some weight and started dressing differently she started putting together these outfits with flared pants and cute, funky little tops. She wore a lot of miniskirts and sneakers. She was working on her anxiety and feeling a lot better.

Naira tipped her head back in her laugh.

"I missed you" she said grabbing her in another hug, Damini had just graduated from university and because it was her last year she didn't come back for the spring break to travel with her friends instead.

"I missed you too." She answered with another squeeze. "by the way, I need to speak to you later."

Naira drew back with a quizzical expression on her face. "Nothing to worry about babe" she said shooing away Naira's expression. She and Anaisha hugged and then the whole family was sitting around in the living room.

"Don't stuff yourself with those" her grandmother told her cousin with a scowl. "There is a whole lunch prepared." The person she

Was scolding was Nafi, who was in his late twenties, a full on adult… but no-one argued with their grandmother and he reluctantly pulled his hand back from the bowl of salted nuts.

"Guys, come bring the food out" her aunt called from the kitchen and the kids went over to help out.

Well, they weren't necessarily 'kids 'anymore. But always would be to their family.

Their family consisted of two boys and a girl.

The girl was the oldest, Zoya and the mother of Nafi, Jai and Damini. She had a kind husband in Ifraan. Kind but very funny.

Nafi went in first, he was the oldest. A born leader type, tall and broad. His younger brother, Jai was three years younger and often got in trouble as a child. Well, he got in trouble as an adult sometimes too. In fact some of his antics at their school were still talked about even now.

The youngest from the three of them was Damini. A good mix of both her brothers.

The second brother was Zahir, who had married Mahita and they had two daughters. Ishaani and Anaisha.

Ishaani's intelligence had only grown with age and she opted for a different path from her family and did something in science. Her engagement was often a point of discussion, a discussion she often opted out of.

The youngest brother was Zafar, married to Nahla who shared the same green eyes as her youngest daughter Naira, who was also the youngest out of all her cousins. They had two older sons. Shaan and Laith. Laith and Shaan were fraternal twins, the same age as Jai. Whom was often considered their triplet.

The 'Elamin's 'had family dinners bi-weekly, usually.

The matriarch of the family was Shahidah, their grandmother who was still alive and kicking. Along with her husband, Mukhesh they had their children at a young age. So they enjoyed being part of their grandchildren's lives with lots of vitality.

87

As per there was an array of food prepared. Steam rose from some dishes as they all sat around the long dining table, specially made for all the members.

"So, Aish, Naira" she looked pointedly at both of them, "how are your friends?" Damini sat across from Anaisha, and held out her plate.

"They're good... actually I think most of them are coming tonight" Anaisha said as she placed a samosa on it.

"Is Andries coming tonight?" Damini said softly with a cheeky smile. Naira slid her eyes over to Damini, who was seated on her right, in surprise.

Anaisha instinctively looked to the left where the parents were sitting to make sure they didn't hear. "How did you know?" Anaisha whispered, her face in an expression that was between a smile and shock. And shot her eyes at Naira.

"It wasn't me, I swear" Naira said holding one ringed hand up, in defence. It really wasn't her. "Seriously, how did you know?" Naira turned her head to her older cousin.

Elegantly, Damini leaned forward on the table and with a wink she whispered back "I know everything"

Anaisha rolled her eyes.

"What do you know?" Jai said with a mouthful of rice.

"You're gross" Naira said motioning to that fact that he was talking with his mouthful.

He made a show of chewing obnoxiously, and swallowed with dramatics.

"Happy?"

"Very," Naira said with a sweet smile and went back to her own plate. Damini snickered next to her.

"Now, tell me... what does she know that I don't?" He said turning his head to face Anaisha and Damini, while twirling the ring on his middle finger. He leaned back on one leg of the chair.

"Laith, stop leaning on your chair" his grandmother called sternly from the other end of the table.

"Sorry, Ma" he said promptly and quickly stopped. "How did she see that?" He thought out loud as they all laughed.

"Apparently, Damini knows everything and Ma sees everything" Naira said, pointing her fork at the respective people.

"Very true, Nairu" he commented back. Anaisha went back to eating her food, hoping against all hope Jai had become distracted. "Now what is it that Damini knows?" He said. Anaisha let out an exasperated breath. Here's to hoping.

"Nothing" Anaisha said irritatedly.

"Her and Ries are an item apparently" Damini said.

"No their fully together" Naira said matter-of-factly.

"Naira!" Anaisha said.

"What, they already know!" Naira shrugged as she took a bite of food.

"Aww Anaisha" Damini said with a happy smile. "That's so cute!"

"Wait." Jai said, and the conversation halted. The girls 'eyes on him. "You mean Ries, as in Andries... blue eyes, curly black hair, kind of quiet but witty?"

"That's the one" Naira said.

"Oh, I had my money on Mykal" he said.

"You really need to drop that" Anaisha said incredulous.

"I mean I guessed you would end up with one of them, I just thought it would be Mykal" he shrugged.

Naira began gulping down her glass of water.

Anaisha laughed at how absurd that sounded. Then she gulped down the little flutter in her chest at the mention of Ries and started playing with her food, a shy smile on her face "but yes I and Ries are together"

Jai nodded with a grin, as he stroked a hand through his shiny, tousled hair "alright" he said with a little shared look with the rest of them, at Anaisha's awkwardness. "Well, you have my blessing" Jai said.

"Mine too" Laith chimed. "He's a good guy"

"Didn't ask for it" Anaisha cut in, yet there was a smile on her face.

Chapter 10

Damini's Graduation Party

They were in Damini's backyard. The sun was setting now, and the guests would be coming soon.

The whole family was ready.

"let's get a picture" Nahla said.

"Damini's not here yet" Naira said shooing a fly off her bare shoulder, she was wearing a cool black top made of a stiff cotton material with big, glamorous sleeves, jeans and heels. They were in Damini's garden, and the sun was setting now, the guests would be there shortly.

"Sorry, sorry I'm here" Damini said putting a diamond solitaire earring on.

"You look gorgeous, darling" her aunt Nahla said, with an admiring smile. Damini wore a short, a-line cut gorgeous silky champagne colored dress that showed off her long legs. It dipped in a, still appropriate v on her chest, always toying the line, with puffy sleeves, but due to the fabric of the dress they sort of flowed down naturally and cuffed at her wrist. Her dark hair was curled and shined under the candle lights that were put around the garden.

Everyone agreed in a chorus of compliments. "Thank you

"Beautiful" her mother said, with a proud smile, trying to meet her daughter's eyes.

"Thanks" she said with a quick smile, and didn't meet her mother's eyes.

Her mother took a deep breath in, as her husband put a comforting hand on her back.

They all came together. It was a sweet photo one that would be framed and looked back on with softened eyes.

"Anaisha," her uncle Ifraan called.

"Yeah" she turned, her floral printed dress following the movement, it hit right at her shins with little sleeved that tied at the shoulder. "Can you take a picture of us?" He said motioning to his immediate family. Anaisha had her digital camera around her neck, "why hire a photographer when we have one in our family" her father had said.

Damini overheard and caught Anaisha's eyes shaking her head vigorously with wide eyes. Everyone knew about the argument Damini was having with her parents currently. Her parents were urging her to immediately do a Masters in her degree, while she wanted to work for a year. It had caused a lot of differing opinions and arguments.

Anaisha shrugged helplessly. "Sure" she said to her uncle. Damini slumped.

Anaisha put her eye to the lens, they were all strained smiles.

Anaisha dropped the camera and let it hang around her neck "guys come on, Damini graduated!" She put her arms out, as Damini looked at her parents whose smiles were now spreading across their faces.

"Who knew it would actually end up happening?" Anaisha grinned as her aunt and uncle laughed and pulled their daughter closer. It ended up being a beautiful picture.

The music was swelling and guests were pouring in, chatter was taking up space in the air.

"Hi," Jai said with a ringed finger in the air, and a charming smile "can I get a Rum and Coke?"

"Make that two, actually do you have Diet Coke?" Naira came up placing her jewelled hands on the bar.

"How old are you again?" Jai asked with a lifted brow.

"I turned 18 last month" she said with a glint in her eyes. Actually, she would turn 18 in 3 months but he didn't need to know that. They took a sip of their drinks and stood in silence for a while, but they didn't need to talk, they were family and actually close, it was a comfortable silence. Jai, Damini and Naira had always been close sharing a similar love for books and clothes. Jai cleared his throat.

"You've changed a lot Naira" he commented. "I'm happy to see it..."

"Therapy helps" she said with a smile.

"To therapy" he held his drink up. She cheered that.

They stayed at the bar watching the party, like they were watching a movie.

"So, any goss?" Naira arched a brow with a mischievous grin.

"Not really" Jai leaned against the bar.

"You?" He took a sip of his drink.

"No" she took a sip of her drink.

He turned his head, squinting at her, "you're lying"

"What? No I'm not" she said as she played with her earring.

His face turned smug, "You're a terrible liar"

Naira scrunched up her nose, "you're a terrible person"

Jai cocked his head to the side, "sometimes, but I try not to be" he shrugged. "Now spill. I'm your blood, there's like some rule that you have to tell me"

Naira was usually harder to crack, but this was Jai and it's not like he actually cared about the love lives of a bunch of eighteen year olds.

Jai's jaw dropped as Naira finished talking. His gaze was on Anaisha who was ironically, currently taking a photograph of Mykal and Andries who were walking in through the garden gate. Laughing at something, heads bent together.

Andries was wearing a simple black shirt and crisp black trousers, his hands in his pockets. Well-tailored and well fitted. Black always suited him, standing out against his skin and matching his hair. He always stuck to similar colours and styles, never straying too far away from what was familiar, Naira realised.

Mykal wore a shirt and pants too but his was a looser fit with a black dress shirt and sneakers, but he made it work.

Anaisha greeted the two boys, hugging them both at the same time.

Naira wished she was the photographer of the family in that moment, Anaisha looked like some sort of fairy princess, her dress flowing around and both boys 'heads bent to her shoulder.

And she went to Andries's side.

She tilted her head to the side, his hair was sitting oddly, and instinctually she lifted her hand to comb it back and quickly grabbed it back. She had almost forgotten where she was for a second.

He realized, as observant as always and gave her a knowing smile as he looked down at her and ran his fingers through his hair. "All good now?" He asked.

"Perfect" she nodded.

They walked over to Naira who was standing with Jai.

Jai was grinning, "I fucking knew it"

"Shut the fuck up" Naira whispered, as the trio walked closer.

"Have you met me?" Anaisha was the type of person who would only make someone her boyfriend if it was a genuine thing, she wasn't the type to pass the time with someone.

Something deflated in Mykal. It wasn't like he thought that if Andries and Anaisha ever broke up he would swoop in or anything like that, it wasn't like he ever thought he actually had a chance. But, there was a certain feeling that came with the solid fact of it.

He blew a breath out, and smiled up at the sky. 'What had his life become? 'He thought with a little chuckle to himself, then he smiled a little smile to himself 'never mind... it would all work out the way it was meant to 'he knew that, it was more real to him than his feelings for Anaisha. The belief that this would pass and it would be okay, but right now. Fuck, it really sucked.

Soon, Zoya auntie and Nafi had also joined the conversation.

The three of them reached the little group, both boys introducing themselves to Adam. Saying "hello" to everyone else. Both of the boys lit up the conversation, Mykal jokey and charismatic. And Andries effortlessly, supplementing Mykal's jokes, in his quiet witty way. They chatted for a bit.

Mykal stood a solitary figure by one of the cocktail table's draped in black cloth. Mykal's heart began to race slightly. He took a quick breath. Watching Anaisha give Andries her undivided attention, her eyes turning to him every few minutes, as if she couldn't help herself. Without realising, his head would lift up and his eyes would drift to a girl with dark hair in a floral dress, a camera around her neck and a darkly dressed, blue eyed boy by her side. Laughing, small touches... that could be assumed as friendly, but he knew they weren't. He was watching a different movie than Naira and Jai were.

Mykal felt that thing on his chest and took deeper breaths, he swallowed. It was harder than usual. The sharp fingernail of envy lightly scratching at his mind the choking hands of desire, that quickened his heart and made him feel out of breath and like a person that needed a bath in holy water.

He took a deep breath in and put his hands behind his back, striding towards the bar. A drink of water would do him some good.

From his peripheral vision he saw Andries stand beside him.

Mykal took another sip, with more ease. Despite everything, whenever Andries was somewhere around it's like a light mist of ease came over him, a sense of real comfort. Like when you're at a party and you see someone you know/your best friend walk in and you can breathe a little more easily.

Andries stood straight and silent next to Mykal. He stuffed one hand in his pocket, raking the other through his hair.

He was quiet and watchful. This happened to Ries sometimes. Mykal followed his intense gaze,

Of course.

Ries was looking at Anaisha, who had turned now. She was taking a photo, enchanted with her other love.

Mykal smiled into the little bottle in his hand, as he took another swig. Ries clapped him on the back as he walked over to someone calling him.

He smiled, one side of his lip turning up into a little smile. His best friends were happy... how could he stay sad?

She leaned her elbow casually on the cocktail table, her champagne colored silky sleeve flowing on the cocktail table, deep set brown eyes looking straight at him. The eyes of a tiger.

"So, when did you fall for Anaisha?" Damini asked as succinctly as a strike of lightning.

Mykal blinked for a moment, he lost his footing. Then he began to laugh, even he knew it sounded forced but he had to try. "What?!" He said, incredulously. "You're crazy, Damini" he said with a laugh and a shake of his head looking back down at his phone. "Oh my god, don't even try and hide it. I can tell!" She said with a light-hearted laugh.

"You're crazy, Damini" He gulped down trying to look as 'chill 'as possible, despite the wildly, rapidly beating speed of his heart.

"i know these things Myk," she said with folded arms and a smirk. His breathing has picked up a bit. The smirk dropped from her face.

"Whoa, relax Myk" Damini said placing a manicured hand on his shoulder. "It's okay..." she said gently.

"I really don't know what you're talking about" he said, with a vigorous shake of his head.

"Oh, come on Mykal, it's really not that bad"

"They're best friends" he said looking up, a pained expression.

"Oh, honey no. You're so young, and this stuff is complicated, it will be okay I promise." She said giving him a hug.

Naira came up to them, "what are you talking about?" She sang.

Damini opened her mouth to speak, as Mykal placed a hand on her shoulder. "She knows, don't worry"

Naira turned to him, green eyes bulging, "you told her!"

"No, I figured it out" Damini smiled.

Mykal scrunched his brows together, as Naira asked how.

"Do you think I'm blind?" She said with an irritated look at Naira, "and this arena is where my expertise lie" she flipped her hair over her shoulder.

Naira's eyes flickered between the two of them. Mykal looked a lot more calm now and Damini was grinning. "Okay, so I might have done something" Naira played with the ring on her middle finger.

Damini squinted, and leaned an elbow back on the table "who did you tell?"

"Are you psychic or something?"

"Naira!" Mykal groaned and dragged a hand across his face.

"Just me" Jai strolled to them with his hands in his pockets.

"It's fine Myk, their my older cousins they won't tell anyone" she spun around to them immediately, with fiery green eyes. "Do not tell anyone. I will kill you." Then she spun back around to Mykal, eyes pleading, "I promise I'll kill them"

He took a deep breath in, "Okay. It's fine" he said putting an arm around Naira.

"Really?" She said looking up at him, she looked like she was maybe close to crying.

"Yeah, I only really care if the group finds out you know" he shrugged. Damini and Jai smiled at each other, a knowing look in their eye. Mykal was a kind boy and he was turning into a good guy.

"So, tell us? When did you realize?" Damini lifted her brows with a grin.

He shrugged "I guess it was" he looked up at the stars as if they knew, too "last summer, I started having you know feelings for her, she seemed smarter, more passionate… I thought about how pretty her laugh sounded" he scratched his jaw, grinning "I hadn't really noticed that before. Then when her and Andries were about to get together, we all knew it was inevitable even if they didn't. I realized I did really like her."

Jai nodded with a sad smile and took a sip of his drink, "have you thought of telling them?"

"No way." He almost laughed. "I mean all hell would break loose"

"I've always wanted to visit" Naira smirked, and looked at them with mischievous green eyes.

"Good one" Mykal laughed, and Naira winked back.

Damini shrugged, "It wouldn't be the worst idea… sometimes honesty is the best policy" her brown eyes looked wise as she smiled gently, "they love you Myk and they would know your not trying to hurt them."

"No way," he said, resolution in his eyes "It would ruin their happiness, I refuse to do that"

"But, what about yours?" Naira looked up at him, deep concern in those green eyes.

He took a second to think about it, "this might sound kind of weird" he started grinning, "but I get a lot of happiness from seeing them happy" he said with such a warm genuineness it could melt ice.

"Fair enough" Jai nodded, with a straightened back and square chin. "we promise we won't tell a soul" he said in a mature manner. "You better keep your mouth shut" Jai gave a pointed look to Naira.

"Trust me," Naira held her hands up "I'm never speaking to anyone other than you three again"

Damini looked at Mykal, sadness in her brown eyes. "It's a beautiful thing to love someone unconditionally, despite the fact that they might never love you back. It is the human definition of compassion and understanding, knowing you're not who the other person wants and respecting that. But loving them anyway"

He widened his eyes, and reeled his head in as if he'd been pushed back.

Jai grinned and tipped his glass to her, "Damini has a flair for dramatic wordplay"

"Is that where you get it from?" Mykal looked down at Naira, then back at Damini "well shit, you should be a writer"

She laughed, tipping her long hair back, a hand to her chest. "Maybe in another life" she had already sorted out her job for being a wedding event planner.

Mykal shook his head in confusion "I never understand it when people say that... do both. Be both." He said while holding his hands out emphatically. "Do everything you can in this life" he said strongly pointing to the ground.

She couldn't help but smile at his sentiment, he had so much going for him he would be totally fine.

"How's the clothing thing going?" She asked with a quirk of her brow. "I love mine by the way, wear it all the time" she really did.

"Well, pretty good. Sales are up, and I'm designing a new one, with the profits I got from the sales of the other"

"That's awesome! I'm placing an early order for this new one" she said.

He laughed. "You haven't even seen it yet."

"I like supporting small businesses" she shrugged. "And entrepreneurs are very sexy" she smirked.

"If only I liked you instead of Anaisha" he smirked back.

She laughed.

The mood was lighter now.

It felt good to be home. Mykal thought, as he took a deep breath in. He felt lighter.

Their Drive…

It was 2 am on a Saturday night, and Anaisha was sitting at her desk, doing some extra credit work for Psychology. She was thinking of taking a dual degree in Psychology and Photography. The next day was the "Final Bonfire." It was a bonfire at the beach for the graduating class, a tradition upheld by the students at the school.

There was a knock on her door.

She strode over to open it and in her little doorway was her boyfriend.

An easy smile spread across her face, "Hey," she greeted him, and as usual, he bent down and greeted her with a quick kiss on the cheek. He knew her parents were asleep by now, both having to wake up for work tomorrow.

He closed the door behind him, "nice legs," he said. She was wearing denim shorts and a big t-shirt. "Nice hair," she countered. At that, he grinned. He knew she loved his hair and raked his fingers through his hair, almost unconsciously.

He went and plopped on her bed, dodging the piles of tops and jeans on her bed. Comfortable, as ever.

"You're not done?" He questioned as he watched her rapidly tap on her keyboard. Last minute - a big no. "Actually, I was doing some extra credit for Psych," she said as she pointed to the pile of tops next to his legs. He got up and handed half of them over to her.

"My girlfriend's a hard worker," he simpered with an impressed look.

"Well, not everyone is as naturally gifted as you," she sang, he only had to read something once, and he was sorted. Sometimes she wondered if he had a photographic memory.

Andries lay on the bed on his phone as Anaisha worked. There was a wonderful sense of comfort they had with each other at a young age.

"By the way, tell me when you're done. I initially came here to take you on a drive" "now? But Ries, I haven't even finished packing for the trip," her voice becoming higher.

"We'll come back, and I'll help you, promise," he said, leaping up from the bed. One hand is out, ready to help her up.

"Wait, have you finished packing?" She said, not letting in just yet.

"I have." He said with a smug smirk. "You're such a liar," she said with a laugh. Out of the pair of them, she was definitely more prepared than he.

"I swear," he said with a laugh. He actually was telling the truth. It is just that seeing her laugh always made him smile or laugh. It just made him happy. He stopped questioning about a year ago. "You're laughing," she said, pointing up at his mouth.

"I swear, call Mykal and ask him," he said, looking for his phone in his pocket. "Okay, okay, I believe you," she said, reaching over for the phone that he had left on the bed.

"Let's go." She said as he pulled her up. "But you're helping me when we get back," she said with a pointed look, but laughter laced n her voice. And he did.

Andries's SUV was parked outside, Anaisha's car was also there, and she had finally got her license, but Andries insisted on his tonight. And then they were in the car and on the road.

"Where are we going?" Anaisha said, pressing the button labelled '1' on the side, which adjusted the passenger seat to her position. When Andries first got the car, Anaisha would always have to adjust her seat because the passenger seat would either be taken up by her or Mykal, and Mykal was a lot taller. Then one day, Andries remembered how there was this setting where you could save the positioning of the seat in the car. So he changed it to hers and Mykals.

"We can drive around for a bit and then maybe the beach?" He asked, stealing a quick blue-eyed look to see her reaction.

"Okay." She answered as she connected the car to her phone to play music.

She pulled her head back, crossing her legs over each other, enjoying the music and listening to what Andries had done that day. His gravelly voice matched his unruly hair. They spoke more about the book she was reading and the growth and changes in Naira. "I really like Aki. He seems like a nice guy, a good one, you know?" he said while stopping at the white line and looking to the left and right. It was very early in the morning, and there wouldn't have been any cars around, but he was a careful driver. "When he was younger, I thought he was just a chill, sporty kind of dude, but he's proved himself worthy of Naira's friendship." Andries said, nodding to himself, his blue eyes tender, as he looked out into the road. Anaisha ruffled her hand through his hair, "you're such a cutie," she announced with the biggest smile in her voice. It was so easy to smile or laugh back then.

She loved how he saw Naira as his little sister, and it probably came from the fact that he was an only child and he had the ability to make his friends the siblings he never had. But she also liked how their lives were so intertwined. The promise of loving and caring about those she loved, making her family his. To her, it was louder than words. "Seriously, he's stuck with her throughout the years" He said how he really liked Akihoko and how he and Naira reminded him of a slightly calmer version of him and Mykal.

Andries kept one hand on the wheel and ran the other through his hair. He was speaking a lot today. Usually, out of the two of them, Anaisha vented more or was just more expressive overall. But today, it seemed that he wanted to talk. He felt it, too, that need to say what was on his mind, whether it was stupid or smart. Tonight he felt the need to take hold of precious moments. Next year, after the first semester, he and Mykal would go on tour, this was technically his second last day at the Academy till the summer, but in actuality, it was one of his last days at the Academy. And he wasn't one of those weirdos that felt like secondary school/ ages 12-19 were the greatest years of his life or anything. He hated waking up at unearthly hours, the gossiping in the halls, exams, and cramming. But he had studied hard and aced his exams, and he was excited to leave and start his actual life, but through being here, he had met his brothers, met some genuinely amazing people, and found the love of his life. He was a lucky guy.

"Wanna get some food?" He asked, turning to see her face.

"I'm down... but it's three in the morning," she said, moving to read the time on the screen in between them. "We can do a drive-thru? Or gas station?" She said, shrugging. They were nearly at the theatre, driving close to where the park was.

"I have a better idea," he said, making a vigilant U-turn.

"What is it?" She said, sitting up. "You'll see..." He said, easing up and using one hand to lightly tap her hand. Then he started breezily drumming his fingers on her hand to the beat of the song playing through the speakers.

"Andries, I hate when you do this," she said, rolling her dark eyes. "What, this?" He said, quickly looking down at his drumming fingers on her hand, feigning innocence. "I'm sorry, Aish... I'll stop." He said, taking back his hand.

She cut her eyes to him and huffed out an annoyed breath. The look says, 'you know what I mean.' And he did. She hated not knowing things and surprises, and she was a slight control freak. But he got a little kick out of it, annoying each other a little. It was healthy. It meant they were friends first, before being anything else.

Then he purposefully put on one of her favourite songs, and she leaned back and looked out the window, now drumming the palm of his hand. He could feel her rings tapping against his skin and looked over his shoulder at her silently. She ran her fingers through her head, parting it on the opposite side, the long black waves moving effortlessly. Her legs still crossed over one another, "Andries, the road!" She said, her voice confident, knowing he was watching.

With a grin, he turned his head back, eyes on the road and ran a hand through his hair, and casually said, "You know, in driving lessons, they never tell you not to drive with a beautiful girl in the passenger seat. It can be very distracting."

She rolled her eyes despite the smile on her face. OR she rolled her eyes, but he could hear the laugh in her voice.

 "You're an idiot."

"I'm just saying," he said with a shrug, "they should really tell you or at least teach you how to do it."

Silently Anaisha moved her hand to the sound dial and raised the volume. And Andries laughed. She always made him laugh unexpectedly. By doing something silently funny or saying something hilarious quietly with a straight face/deadpan.

They ended up winding around a small hill. And halted to a stop at the top. Like magic, they were at the top of the small hill. It always felt like that, like time went by too quickly when they were together. Andries pressed a button and opened the roof, he climbed up, carefully using his feet and arms to hoist himself up and Anaisha followed suit, far more nimbly than he had. They sat on the roof of the car, legs outstretched leisurely. The hill wasn't very high and had a flat top, she realized as she began tying her hair into a ponytail.

"I have to admit this is really cool," She murmured, tightening her ponytail. Her eyes softened as she looped her hand around his arm and leaned her head on his shoulder. When they first got together, they both found that they hated holding hands. It felt all weird and clammy. So they had settled on this.

Now, around them, the sky was slowly showing the small signs of sunrise. You could hear some birds chirping, and though it was still dark, there was a certain lightness and excitement in the air. The excitement of dawn and a new day is beginning. The world was waking up, lives starting again. It felt like they were at a central point in the world. The sun was rising around them.

The sun rose in front of them, an orange halo rising from the depths of the earth. She understood why some ancient religions had worshiped the sun, looking at it rising. The sky blended with hints of pink and light purple, and red. So breath-taking and beautiful. For a while, they sat in silence, in a peaceful state of no conversation. Taking in the sight of it. The only sound is chill, soft music coming from the car, the sound of the waves, and the early birds.

"Is this what it feels like to be Mykal?" She said softly with a smile. No one else was around, but it felt like you had to speak softly right now so as to not disturb the sun. Mykal was known to wake up before sunrise often. Sometimes he'd go for a walk or just open his window and watch it from his room, but he did it at least once a week. He said it made him feel grateful. And looking at it now, Anaisha knew what he meant.

Something about the sunrise was nostalgic, and oddly it was making her reminisce about her life, how she was blessed, and what her and her friends' futures would look like. She was reminded that she was growing up, and they would all go into the world soon. But she felt an odd, oxymoronic mixture of calmness and excitement. The silence brought with it was calming and the promise of a new day. It was funny how we travelled to see beautiful things when one of the most beautiful things, like watching the sunrise, everyone had but not everyone appreciated, including herself.

"You were chatty today, you know?"

"When have I ever been the silent type?" He said with a cheeky smile, blue eyes sparkling. She could see him so clearly now, in the light of dawn. His blue eyes were so big and blue, the scar on his eyebrow from when he had hit a "as a kid. A little bit of scruff was growing on his face, which meant he was trying to grow a beard. Which he nearly always failed to do and ended up shaving.

"Never," she laughed lightly, "but, one on one, your quieter" he nodded and looked at her, curiosity piquing in his intense eyes. "A good listener too," she said and kissed his nose quickly.

When people first met Mykal and Andries, they thought they were the most boisterous, loud, excitable people. But when you got to know them, especially individually, they were so different. Andries would seem intimidating with charisma, but in reality, he was understanding and thoughtful, a good listener. And one of the most non-judgmental people he knew. Mykal, on the other hand, brightened a room and made you feel like everything would be okay. He was comforting. She always admired how Reis could keep his mind open and look at other people's experiences without judgment or his pre-made thoughts clouding over him. "You judge things with a kind and understanding heart and open eyes."

He swallowed, his chest rising and those blue eyes blinking, not knowing what to do with the compliment.

"We also haven't argued at all tonight," Anaisha said, lightening the mood. He laughed at that wholeheartedly.

"You always astonish me with the things you say and just how you say them. So much intelligence in that small body."

She didn't know how to say it, but she wanted to thank Andries for taking her on drives from two in the morning to 4:30. And making it feel like only 20 minutes had passed, for taking her to watch the sunrise atop a hill.

The impulsive, 'crazy ideas' part of her was him. To make her feel unafraid to be herself.

That her ideas and words were important and noteworthy, she was glad to have grown up with him by her side. Mykal was a part of that too.

And he felt the same, and she made him feel like he belonged somewhere. He wasn't just a wayward on this planet. She would never forget this night, nor would he.

Now the sun had nearly risen all the way, and they could see someone running along the beach.

"When did you first like me?"

"I always liked you," Andries smirked. "Stop," she shoved him lightly, lovingly. "My sixteenth birthday"

She scoffed, "seriously, I was such a dick when I was fifteen. That was me at my worst" she shivered at the thought of herself at that point.

"Yeah," he laughed, "you were…, but I saw through it, I think, and I think that's when I sort of admitted it to myself" he raked a hand through his black curls. "I genuinely think I always liked you" he looked at her with those blue eyes.

"I loved you before I liked you" she swallowed.

He looked puzzled for a minute, and then understanding grew on his face. "I get what you mean." he blinked for a second, thinking, and then said softly enough for her to hear. "Same" she leaned her head on his shoulder. She thought something that made her cringe at herself and then smile because she was just so happy at that moment that she was thinking thoughts like this. She thought there couldn't be any pillow more comfortable than his shoulder. She cringed at her own thought. Being with her, he felt safe and lucky to have a girlfriend and best friend all wrapped into one… but it was also thrilling because this person wasn't the Anaisha he knew, it was a side of her he never knew existed, and until now it was a side he didn't realize how curious he was to know.

In The Summer

Who knew these would be their last few memories together? The music slowed down.

"Alright, guys, we're going to slow it down for a minute..." the musician said, grabbing the guitar being handed to him.

He was using a Grand Auditorium guitar, Mykal could tell.

"If you've come here with someone special, I hope this song makes you grab them close and spin them around" he turned to the band, and the song began. It was a love song.

Mykal stood behind, a hand in his pocket, and took a sip of his drink. His eyes lingered on Andries, who grabbed Anaisha's hand and spun her around lightly.

Naira turned her head, watching him watching them. A melancholy smile on her face.

He felt a tap on his shoulder. It was Naira. Who was looking at him with those mischievous light green eyes, some other emotion brimming inside them? She grabbed his hand and began dancing with him. He grinned, letting the music sway them.

He watched Andries and Anaisha, over Naira's shoulder...with covetous eyes. He didn't even need to hide the fact that he was basically staring. They were too enchanted with each other. His hand was on the small of her back while she rested his on his broad shoulders. Their other hands were enveloped in each other. They played with each other's fingers as they danced. Her floral dress swayed around her, carving out a space for just the two of them. And her head tipped back in laughter at something he whispered in her ear. A secret joke between only the two of them.

She whispered something to her, and he held her closer. They looked into each other's eyes, unembarrassed by the closeness they shared.

He balanced the glass between his fingers as his thoughts grew murkier.

Was he jealous of his best friend? Being able to hold Anaisha in a way that he couldn't, or was he more jealous of what they had? The way they could melt in and out of each other, go back to each other after arguments and disagreements as if they had never been without the other, and leave each other just as easily. They made it look as easy as changing seasons. Like the way, the snow fell onto the branches of a tree, but when the snow melted away, the tree just grew leaves.

Anaisha memorized his face. His unforgettable, electric blue eyes took up his whole face and melted into little crinkles in his face as he laughed. The scar on his eyebrow and look that was meant just for her shined against his dark skin. His curly dark hair was now growing out a bit.

The song was over, and Naira let go softly and clapped toward the stage. The whole stadium was in applause. Anaisha leaned her head on Andries.

Mykal looked over at Naira, a mysterious smile on his face. She was clapping, her hair falling back as her hand came up with the next song. He may not have had romantic requited love. We always crave romantic love, thinking that's everything in the world. And sometimes, we disregard our friends and family and that love that is everlasting when done right.

It became easier over time. The feelings dulled like a rainy night. One of those nights where it's absolutely pouring the entire night. But it changes from an intense monsoon that makes it feel like God is sobbing to gentle patterns that make the world seem rather magical.

Anaisha was lying down on the sofa with her feet propped on Mykal's lap. He was scrolling through his phone and showing her the different designs he had come up with. He had been working on these for a year now. His speakers were propped on the table, and suddenly the song changed to one from one of the musicals they had recently seen.

A smile spread across her face.

"Okay, I think these three for the first launch," he said, handing her his phone. She flicked through the final three designs. One was a light blueish-grey color, it was Anaisha's favorite color. On the chest was a square piece of art on it, of dark purple ocean waves on those waves was a dark outline of a boat and the figure of a boy and girl on it, it was as if they were looking into each others eyes and holding hands. Underneath, in white thick cursive paintbrush like strokes read, 'young, but forever.'

"This is cool, its my favorite color" she smiled, as her eyes lingered on the design, sharply analyzing.

"Yeah," he scratched the back of his head, "Um, there'll be an outline of waves on one of the sleeves"

She swiped her finger, the next design was a crewneck. It was plain white, but the bottom half of it melted into a gradient of colors reminiscent of when the sun rose, and there were little dark outlines of four birds flying above it, as if it had been gently dipped into the sunrise.

She smiled, as she felt her chest well up. It felt special to see little bits of his mind.

The last image had an image of the front and back of the hoodie. It was a jade green color and in the left chest corner was a bit of writing. In a small, serious, white text it read "Wear this anywhere. Wear it to the beach, to the club, or to bed". Next to it was the backside design and in a big white text, that stretched across the back in the same serious font it read, "if you're hot and funny, tap me on the shoulder."

Anaisha laughed.

Mykal smiled to himself, and scratched the back of his head. "That jade color is Ries's favorite color" he said, and she looked over at Andries's blue eyes smile.

"Your a little softie aren't you?" She grinned.

"Its a fact" he shrugged.

Then sincerity overcame her eyes, "They look amazing, Myk," she pulled her legs back, tucking them under. "Stop stressing" she placed a hand on his shoulder, shaking him lightly. He blew out a breath, stretching his arms over the sofa with a groan.

"And I'm taking the photos, so they're going to look great," she winked. "Just send it," she said with wide eyes, ready.

"Yeah," he nodded. She eyed him as he blew out another breath, "I will," he said, his voice taut "in a minute," he said as he placed his phone on the coffee table.

She eyed the phone as soon as he placed it and snatched it, leaping off the sofa in a smooth movement.

"HEY!" He said, hopping up. He was a lot taller than her, with longer limbs that were better at grabbing. "You're not going to do it. I know you!" But she was faster as she ran around the sofa toward the door. "So I'm doing it for you," she dodged as he caught up to her, trying to get out the door to her room to write and send the email.

" Anaisha, I'll tickle you," he said seriously.

"No, no, please, no," she couldn't help it. She laughed uncontrollably, trying her best to still hold the phone.

"What the-"Andries walked in, his backpack on one shoulder.

"Take the phone!" She said as she tossed it on the couch. Andries leaped over and swiftly swiped it just before Mykal could take it. He handed it over to Anaisha, who ran out with a laugh as Andries kept Mykal there.

She ran to her room and locked the door catching her breath as she typed out a professional email and sent over the designs to the vendors.

When she came back, she slammed back onto the sofa and gave the phone back gingerly to Mykal. "It's done," she smiled widely. Mykal glared at her and then began smiling, "thank you" "you're welcome" she scrunched her nose and punched his shoulder lightly.

"Whoop," Mykal leaped up from where he was sitting with a fist in the air.

Anaisha started laughing happily, and Andries grabbed Mykal's face, "you did it!" He said with excitement. "I did it!" Mykal said, holding Andries's shoulders.

Nearing, The End

This was the perfect way to end the year, Mykal thought. 'End their time at school, actually, ' he thought as he looked up at the stars.

"That one is Gemini; there's a Greek myth behind it, too," Aki said, pointing up at the sky. "Oh, my god yeah, I know the story… "Naira said softly. He was lying down, his hands resting on his chest, his head leaning toward Naira, who lay next to him. "About the two brothers, what were their names again?" She thought out loud. "It was Castor and Poly-something," she bit her lip, "I can't remember the other one's name, but the stories were sweet" she swallowed "basically, they had different fathers, but the same mom, and they were really close, and after Castor got murdered the Poly-one, asked Zeus if he could share his perpetuity with his brother, so Zeus put them both in the sky together… now they are inseparable in the constellation" she smiled. And so did everyone. It was a tragically beautiful story.

The only sound was the water ahead of them and Naira and Aki's soft conversation of constellations.

Mykal sat up, his elbows resting on his loosely crossed knees, breathing in the salty air. Calista sat by him, her eyes getting droopier as the wind picked up her hair. He nudged her knee with his and tapped his shoulder. She nodded and moved to rest her head on his shoulder, closing her eyes.

"Polydeuces! That was his name" Naira snapped her finger in the air.

The whole beach was glowing from the dichotomy of moonlight and the lights of the beach houses on the cliffs above them. Natural cool moonlight that's been watching over the world for generations. Seeing deaths and births and lives, maybe they all merged into one for the moon.

Silly people with their silly problems, not knowing that one day they would all end up as stars.

When his grandfather had died, Mykal had cried, and his mother had told him to look up at the sky and point at the brightest sky. He pointed, and then she whispered. "That's him, then" he's right up there.

Now, he didn't know what he believed. But in moments like these, he knew there was something, and he didn't know what. But something. There had to be. Otherwise, moments like these wouldn't exist. Maybe God was the moon, and we ended up as stars, only getting to see our loved ones in the nighttime. Like ghosts.

We only saw them at night because that's when our loved ones were the most vulnerable. The nighttime is when they cry and laugh, and their secrets come out. And whatever happened in the nighttime, they were up in the stars blinking for them, lighting the path for them.

And then your loved one would join you as a star up in the sky.

Talking about myths and constellations under the stars and over the sea, his heart felt full.

He knew this would be one of those gentle memories that he would look back on. One of those without a funny story or something you could tell at dinner parties, but one of those that you would always hold on to, and if you closed your eyes, you'd go right back, one of those which you told your lover, softly and gently in either the late night or early morning.

Part 2: The Breakup

Chapter 1

The Break

"Are you fucking serious?" she said, her voice between a whisper and whimper. Her voice was laced with a hint of tears coming. And her voice *broke* on the last word. Though her voice was soft, her body was shaking with the constant waves of emotion that hit her. Her body shook with the pressure of it all in large swells of betrayal and anger and sadness.

"I'm sorry," he uttered.

The same way he had a thousand times before. He said these words, the ones he had a thousand times before, in a gravelly voice, one that was ruined by a night of abandonment. His voice may have been dispassionate, but his face... was telling another story.

He turned away from her, pressing his fingers deep into his closed eyes, and tried to center himself.

"Fuck I can't do this right now" his head was heavy, and his body ached to just sit down. Next to him was the ivory love seat, the one he had helped her choose. He just wanted to close his eyes in the comfort of a room he knew so well. He was about to do just that when her hand grabbed his arm. He did not turn around.

Despite the situation, she kept her hold on his arm while she closed her bedroom door gently. "YOU can't do this right now? That's rich... you don't get to do that. Turn around." her voice was louder now.

He carried on moving to disregard what she had just said. She tugged his arm, and her voice did not grow in sound but in assertiveness.

"Andries" she was using his name, his full name. He turned. And his heart broke when he saw her face. Her face was tear-stained, and black eye makeup dried on her brown skin. Her tears created little breaks on her face. She was *breaking*. But her dark brown eyes were dry right now. Her black hair was still curled, her clothes barely crumpled. The rest of her was still in place.

"Why? Why the fuck did you have to do that?" Her voice *broke* again. The tears started streaming the second his blue eyes met hers. "I'm sorry, seriously. I don't know what I was thinking... she was just there."

"So was I!"

"You were with your friends, in the main room," he said in explanation.

"You could have found me. I wasn't on the fucking moon, you moron!" She panted. "I'm sorry, you were just... not there," he slumped.

"So, because I wasn't sitting on your fucking lap, you thought you could just get with someone else" she threw an arm out.

"We didn't even kiss-" he walked towards her.

She stepped backward, and a hand smacked against her forehead "how can you-" her voice now rose, but she stopped herself, took a deep breath in, and started again, her voice cold and eyes furious "no, you didn't, I walked in before that began. I just had to witness my boyfriend kissing another girls neck. Much fucking better, right? " her voice shook now, and her eyes were suddenly filled with tears, but they didn't fall yet. She was swearing a lot. He knew that; he knew all those little things about her.

She whooshed past him, her hair brushing his arms, and sat on the loveseat. And the tears fell now as her hands crawled up her face as she cried.

Seeing her like this, again. It was destroying him. He moved with purpose towards her and knelt before her.

"Sweetheart," he said with such a tender gentleness, his cold hands peeled her hands away from her face.

"Please don't cry, please" his voice was full of so much remorse. One would have never believed he was the same boy who did what he did. Disrespected her the way he did. He gently wiped her tears with his thumbs.

"I am so so sorry" he was the one crying now, his voice cracking, so overcome with emotion, he placed his head on her thighs.

She softened and stroked his onyx-coloured hair; despite it all, she felt the need to comfort him.

He felt her full fat tears seep into his scalp, the cold of the tears anchoring him to her.

Her breath was catching now, her sobs becoming deeper. The anger subsided, and now she felt numb. She knew what she was about to do. She breathed to get the courage, but did she really need it? This felt like something that should have been done already? They were past the point of no return. She knew it, did he?

He did not.

In between comforting strokes, she delicately kissed the crown of his head. Her lips gently brushed his hair, the tears still falling. "I cannot go through this shit again," She said, her heart resigned, but her voice still broke, reflecting the other part of her heart. The part that was tugging at her like a child to not do this. The part of her that remembered the memories and the love. But she had to do this. "I know, I know," he said while kissing the top of her thighs on which he rested his head. "I've put you through too much, and it won't happen again. I promise. I fucked up," his voice croaked. Kneeling in front of her, he looked up. His blue eyes searched hers for confirmation that she believed him. He would not put her through this again, he vowed to himself. But the devil in the back of his mind cowed down in fear that he just might.

"No, I mean I cannot. I can't do this anymore."

"I know, Aish, I'm done, I swear" his eyes stared so deeply into hers as he searched and searched for any sign of belief. But he couldn't find it.

She looked at him with tears pooling in her eyes as the memories pooled inside of her, of those blue eyes, but her dark eyes were filled with so much emotion.

Loathing, lamenting, and still loving.

She moved her eyes upward. It strained her to look away from him. Her eyes were now facing the door.

"We're done," she said softly, her voice soft enough to be a whisper. As if she could not bear to say it any louder.

Her voice was soft, but to him, those words were louder than anytime she had ever shouted at him before. Resounding in his mind. *We're done.*

113

"No, no, no, no, no," he repeated, raking his fingers through his hair. She moved up quickly, letting his head drop on the sofa, and he sat on his knees. "Please, please, I am sorry... Aish listen, listen to me. I am done, I swear... "

"*Please,*" his pleading was unbecoming and cost him his pride.

Seeing him like this pained her. She stood up, tall. He stayed on his knees, so small. Watching him break and plead pained her so much that she didn't think she could stay standing. But she kept her neck strong and held her head up.

"Go, Andries... please, just go."

She hid the pain in her voice, but it filtered through her face. She shut her eyes slowly and deeply, pressing them down as the tears poured over her face. She breathed in through her nose. As if she was afraid if she breathed through her mouth, she would not be able to stop the heavy sobs.

He got up, he was sober now. Completely and utterly and miserably so. He has raised a gentleman, and when someone said 'please, 'he listened.

He stood up, now taller than her.

He gazed completely into her dark, now dim eyes and said, "I'm so sorry." Lately, he had said it so much that they must have lost their meaning.

She watched him step away from her towards the door. They were now a meter away from each other. His hand touched the doorknob, securing himself, and he turned. And gazed at her one last time.

But he said nothing

He strode out of the room. Away from her.

Now she let herself sit on the ivory loveseat As he leaned against the door on the other side.

She took one breath through her mouth, and the sobs came

He took a breath and pushed himself off the door, slowly walking away. They both *broke at the same time.*

Chapter 2

The 1st Week

It was odd how she had now awoken to a changing world, but her room looked exactly the same. The cream-coloured curtains fly lightly from the morning breeze off her balcony.

A beam of light spread through the small gap in the curtain. She threw an arm over her eyes, shielding any form of light.

Then she inhaled some discipline threw her blanket off, and mechanically hopped down the step that led to the bathroom and the sitting area.

Her mind was blank as she brushed her teeth, the mintiness of toothpaste and the feel of cold water rousing her awake.

She stepped back up to the upper level with the bed, desk, and vanity, went over and opened her curtains, and opened the door to the balcony.

The morning cold nipped at her skin.

She held the railing and closed her eyes, and breathed in the cold morning air, letting the fresh air of the morning fill her lungs, the delicate scent of flowers from the garden mixed with the smell of salt from the beach a little further away filled her head.

She held her breath for a moment, knuckles tightening, as the cold railing sniped into her skin as she held on to the scent of flowers and freshness, something real for life support.

She opened her eyes, blinking as her eyes readjusted. The sun hadn't fully risen yet, the sky with an overlay of pink and purple. She could see the ocean bright and blue in the distance and the gardens underneath her, flowers and trees sitting serenely.

She left the balcony, keeping the door open and letting the cold air prickle the room, and went over to her vanity. She looked into the mirror that stood on her desk; she probably had it since she was about fifteen years old. Her eyes were puffy from the crying, and automatically she reached for some blush and concealer. As if this will fool anyone, she thought. Despite herself, she picked up the brush with tender fingers. She felt numb. Still.

As if she was out of her body.

All she could hear were the predictable sounds of the morning. Chirping birds and soft clicks of her own compacts and tubes, and the hazy noise of padding feet and doors shutting and opening outside.

It helped her breathe. She never thought she'd need help with that.

Her room was neat and tidy but still littered with trinkets that reflected her life. Pictures of her friends and family were tucked into the vanity mirror, and odd little jewelry dishes filled with her collection of little rings.

She stared at herself in the mirror; her golden-brown skin looked pale and dry, and her face felt smaller than usual. Her skin had cleared up, and she had lost some weight over the past few months. She had a small face and sharp features. High cheekbones, small almond eyes, but she used them so intently that they filled up her whole face and small lips, but she smiled so often that they were put to good use and a prominent nose (but her mother told her it was a sign that she was a part of the family she was, given that they all had rather large noses) and a delicate collarbone. She knew she wasn't that beautiful, but as she grew up, she just started to care less. When she was about 17, her Nani once told her, "There's just something about you, Aish, so hold your head up high and no more crying about your nose" And so she did.

She had beautiful hair, though, long and black and straight. Mindlessly, she ran a brush through it and pulled it back into a ponytail. A weekend had passed since the breakup. She hadn't left her room and had her food brought up. She couldn't face people in this state, no matter how many times her friends banged on her door.

Once she was ready, she put on her uniform, a pair of black tapered trousers and a white shirt. The violet and blue emblem on her shirt pocket stood stark against the white. She took one more look into the full-length mirror at the edge of her room, rubbed her hands along her trousers, and let her sweat evaporate into the fine fabric. She loathed having a uniform when she was younger, but as she got older, she appreciated the easiness of it, how she didn't have to bother thinking of an outfit. She cocked her head to the side as she looked at herself. She would never wear it again after this year; that was weird. She touched her stomach and noticed that she had lost weight. She had a lithe body, slim legs and arms, and was fairly short but always felt a little insecure about the fluff on her tummy. She didn't care about that as much anymore.

116

She grabbed the textbooks she needed for that day, stuffing them into her bag. Small shelves hovered above the wooden desk full of rich blue and dark red textbooks and scattered with a few novels and figurines from her travels abroad. A drawer stood tall on the left of the desk. It had not come with the room but was put there by Anaisha when she came back two summers ago. It was small, compartmentalized into two parts. Her eyes hovered over the two shiny silver handles. The top drawer had not been opened for some time now.

She took one look at her bed, wishfully aching to go under the covers and just.... cry.

But no, she had to get on with it, and so she took her steps slowly, and her slow steps led to the part of the room with the bathroom and wardrobe and a single ivory loveseat in the corner. She put her shoes on and took a look at her hands. The light of the room made her delicate gold rings glisten.

Her hands were shaking. Ignoring it, she got up and strode out of the room.

Andries lay on a couch in his father's apartment. He was hungover, and his Dad was out of town. He was landing that night. He had been staying a lot with his father's recently. 'Thank god, he's not here right now, 'he thought. Not only was he hungover, but he was also heartbroken… and not in the mood to talk.

He walked into the study. It was clean and tidy, matching the same modern interior as the rest of the apartment. His Dad always liked to read, and one of the first things he brought to his new office was a bookshelf. Looking at his father, you wouldn't think he was a lover of fiction, but looks can deceive. The bookshelf was black and wooden, letting the works of literature bring colour to the room. Andries always found the study calming, and sometimes he would do work there, at the same table as his Dad. They both worked in the same way, silent and focused. It was calming. Andries wasn't a reader like his father or Naira. They would always talk about books together on Sundays. He always found them too long. But to get his mind off whatever the hell had happened last night, his eyes lingered on the shelf as he looked for something.

He plucked a book off the shelves; its pages were old and brown. He began, *"then what, exactly, is your plan for us? He asked." PLANS.* The word screamed into his subconscious. He did have so many plans for them.

Had.

So many.

He threw the book onto the floor. Overcome with rage and guilt; disparity etched away at everything inside of him. He went back to the sofa and lay down. He touched a hand to his chest as it rose emphatically.

He fished his vape out of his pocket and inhaled. He needed something, anything to numb him even in the slightest. They weren't allowed on the premises, but he didn't care.

He was in a state of disbelief.

Though he didn't really care even when he was in a normal state, he was charismatic, one of those people that could worm himself out of just about any situation. He *was.* Ever since the incident, the one that began all this shit, he was too exhausted to be charismatic. Not just towards his teachers but to his friends and his girlfriend.

Ex-girlfriend.

But could you blame him?

He couldn't lose both of them... he just couldn't? How had he let this happen? Well, he knew how he had pushed her too far, over the edge.

It was too much for her to handle, but she was Aish. She could handle anything, and she loved him... Wasn't love enough?

Guess not.

His feelings switched from rage to guilt like a clock ticking every few seconds.

He was angry at her for making this decision, for abandoning him, but as he let the thoughts collide into him of rage and self- condemnation. Regret. At leaving her, at not paying attention to her, at not letting her envelop him in love the way he should have.

So much regret.

Over the hour, his mind kept arguing, and he ached to get out of his own body. But in a way, he was distracted from his usual darkness. He was thinking of his new loss and not *him for* once. For the first time, actually, he was distracted by another kind of depression.

His eyes drifted and shut. Yes, sleep. That is what I need, he thought. He hadn't slept at all over the weekend, just cried and raged and drank. His friends had checked on him. They tried talking to him, reasoning with him; they were fucking awesome. They even threatened to call his parents, but they didn't in the end. They would never rat out their friend. In the end, they could not get through to him. No one could. Not even Aish, though this time she wasn't there? At least they stayed, he thought. They didn't leave him as she did. But then again, he didn't put them through the same kind of hell. They told him he was pushing her too much, that he was acting cruel and unfair to her.

He didn't listen. He should have.

Was he dealing with this wrong? Yes. Was that normal for him?

Yes.

His eyes fluttered, his body ready for rest. He was ready to sleep when his eyes grazed over the clock in front of him, he would be late for his class if he did not leave now. But heartbreak was exhausting. He felt it in his body and soul.

He was glad his semester didn't start until another week.

Chapter 3

Anaisha sat in her Sociology class. The classroom was a simple four-walled rectangular classroom, but its ceiling was filled with an ornate design of rich golds and creams. The academy had a weird thing for ceilings. The floor paled in comparison, carpeted in simple grey and worn out with the stamp of footsteps over the years. It was an old, prestigious school.

Mr. Basil stood at the front of the class behind his desk. He fiddled with his laptop as he tried to connect it to the projector behind him. He looked toward the back of the class with wistful eyes, where a white floor-to-ceiling bookcase stood tall, containing books pouring with the knowledge of sociology.

He sighed as he let the kids chat for a few moments while still fiddling with the damn tablet. It was the first lesson back, and he knew the students were getting reacquainted with the routine of focus.

Unfortunately for him, on this day, he did not only face the problem of students getting reacquainted but also the ordeal of gossip and rumors that began due to the events of the holidays.

Anaisha sat with her chin resting in her hand, mindlessly tapping her fingers on the table. She sat at a table with her friends. There were three circular tables and fourteen students in the whole class, and a small student body meant that news travelled fast. She was pretty sure everyone knew about the breakup, even some of the teachers- which just embarrassed her further.

She leaned back, blowing a breath out as she fidgeted with one of the rings on her fingers, attempting to focus on the conversation her friends were having; they were trying to keep her attention. She could tell.

Asked her opinion, whispered jokes, and then looked at her to see if she laughed.

She wished she could sit alone or just leave. But that would draw too much attention. She didn't need any more today.

"By the way, we're coming to your house today after school," whispered Kiara. The sunlight beamed off her brown skin and her curly brown hair as she turned toward her friend with concern filled in those green eyes. Kiara was beautiful, the type of beautiful that could become a personality trait of its own. But, Anaisha Kiara's face was one of the faces that made her feel safe and at home.

"You don't need to. I'm fine, I swear - see," she willed herself to turn around and see her do a close-lipped smile, her movements like a controlled puppet.

"You look like you are being held at gunpoint..." Kiara said with a disbelieving smile. Then she bent her head, her green eyes soft, a consolatory hand on her shoulder "you don't need to fake it, you know, you're allowed to be upset" Anaisha ignored this.

"It is insulting that you think you're fooling us; I feel insulted," she said, dramatically placing a hand over her chest. "Your heart is on the left side of your chest." Anaisha laughed, moving her friend's arm to the left.

"Whatever, you know what I mean," she said with a wave of her long fingers.

Now, Dr.Basil decided he had let them chat for enough time and commenced his class. The hush of focus overtook the room as he began.

Anaisha loved this class.

She looked over at him and realized that the little crow's feet had begun growing on the corners of the man's eyes. He looked older. She saw how his brown hair had streaked with little grey hairs. She remembered that he had just had a new baby over the break; he looked a little like an older version of... and before she knew it, all she could see was blue eyes, curly brown hair, thin lips, a slit brow, and smoke.

Tears pooled her eyes, and with a sudden force, she raised her hand. "May I go to the bathroom?" She had to get out before her tears spilled like waterfalls.

"Yes ofc-"

With a rough push at the table. She was gone - before he could even finish. The whole room fell silent for a moment.

She briskly walked to the nearest bathroom, not wanting to drag more attention to herself. She pushed the heavy wooden door open and ran into a stall.

She pulled the toilet seat down and sat on it as the tears spilled like hard rain onto her sharp face. Uncontrollably.

She held her elbow over the bottom half of her face, hoping to stifle the wretched gasping sounds she made as her crying grew in force and sound. It was taking over her body. No, HE was taking over her body, mind, all of it... not just him because now she could see two faces, another boy with darker skin and darker hair. The tears were hot now, burning her skin.

How was she going to get through this?

For the first time, she truly just did not know.

A Few Days Later...

"So, how was the trip?" Andries asked his Dad as he pulled onto the main road. He had just picked his father up from the airport.

"Very good, very successful," his father smiled, looking at him. They had the same eyes. "But I am exhausted" he ran a hand through his hair.

"I'm sure," Andries smiled, "we don't have to go to dinner tonight if you're not up for it...." Andries said, he coughed. His voice was hoarser than usual.

"No, no, don't be silly. I'm excited" he patted his stomach, "hungry too" his father was like him, with a small appetite. They looked similar when standing together, with similar height and build. Andries liked these dinners with his Mom and Dad, and the divorce had been good for them ever since they would sit together and laugh and chat. They were always better as friends. In fact, he was pretty sure that they were each other's best friends.

They had booked a dinner at a nice, upscale restaurant. They had reached it before his mother arrived.

"She's late," Andries said, looking at the clock on his phone.

"Let her be. She's probably had a long day" his father gave him a look. Andries smirked.

"What?" His dad smiled. His son looked so much like his ex-wife when he smirked like that.

"It is just that you were never so sweet when you guys were married," Andries stretched, resting an arm over the chair.

"Thank you," he said to the waiter as he poured him a glass of water. His father shook his head, laughing lightly.

They heard heels clicking on the floor behind them, "Hi. I'm sorry I'm late," his mother chimed as she came behind her son to give him a kiss and went and hugged Nicholas, who had stood up.

"Don't worry about it, T. We haven't been here long. Also, I ordered you a drink." Nicholas said. As he sat back down, he watched her. Maybe it was the fact that his eyes were so blue that made them so readable or the fact that he was his father, but Andries could see the change in his father's face as he watched his mother. He appreciated her, watching her. Even his voice slightly changed when he spoke to her. She was wearing a knee-length brown dress, black heels obviously, and simple but expensive jewellery. Her dark hair was blown out, as it usually was. Her natural hair was like her son's, curly and unruly. She had lost some weight after her divorce and kept it off ever since.

"Do you have it?" His father asked, eyes dancing. "Of course I do," his mother smiled, her voice raspy.

"Have what?" Andries arched a brow as he took a sip of water.

"Well," his mother flipped her hair behind her shoulder, smiling excitedly, "We wanted to say how proud we are of you, Ries. Passing school with flying colors" he had gotten one of the best grades in his grade. His name was on a plaque in the reception of the school, not at the very top but high enough to warrant the pride in his mother's eyes. "And dealing with everything…."

"Let's not talk about that tonight, please," Andries said hoarsely. He knew that his parents were having lunch with them tomorrow, but he had declined the invitation. He always declined, ever since…

His mother cleared her throat, "anyway, this is a little something from both of us," she said as she handed over a dark, matte black gift bag. He opened it to a box, and it was a watch.

"We wanted to give it to you before the rest of the family arrived." His father smiled.

It was a watch, a beautiful one. With a black leather strap and silver dial. Very nice. "Thank you so much." He said, looking at both of them, "this is a lot" he laughed, lightly looking down at the watch.

"Well, we think you deserve it," his father said, blue eyes wide, and patted him on the shoulder. Andries smiled.

"Oh, also," his mother said as she took another small bag from under the table. "This is a gift from the Ricardo's. They wanted us to give it to you in case they didn't see you before you left."

It was a bracelet with a leather band and a silver clasp. He knew it must've been expensive. "I'll send them a message to thank them."

"You should," he held up a hand, silencing his mother. "I'll send them a message."

The table fell silent for a second.

"Well, let's put it on," his father said as he got up and put on the watch and the bracelet on Andries's left hand. They looked good together.

"When are they getting here, T?" Nicholas asked, regarding Andries's grandparents.

"They should be here any minute." She said as she looked down at her own overly expensive watch.

His grandparents came, and they had a lovely dinner. His mother's parents gave him a pen, one of those very expensive pens. And his father's parents gave him cash in an envelope. To be fair, he was hard to shop for.

That night, Nicholas decided to stay at their old house, now Teresa's. It had four bedrooms, so he would stay in the guest bedroom, and it made sense tonight because it was closer to the restaurant.

"Which one do you like more, this study or the one at my place?" Andries scratched his neck as he thought, "your place…." "Why?" His Dad said as he took a seat on the opposite chair.

"I don't know." He shrugged, full-bodily. Looking around, this place was older feeling, with a black leather chair that he was currently seated in. It had a long back that hugged you in. And the shelves lined along the wall were back-lit with soft, warm light, artfully, and two aesthetic leather matching chairs across him. But, there was something about his father's study that was more personal. The novels on the shelf, the coffee machine, mini-fridge, and photo frames on the desk. You could live in his father's study if you had to. It was a place of someone who loved their work and didn't want to leave it just yet. "I feel like I work better there."

His Dad grinned. "I thought you could work anywhere" "I can. I just work *better* there," he smirked.

There was a beat of comfortable silence. "What are you doing up?" It was two in the morning. "I mean, I'm jet-lagged, but you're not."

"Couldn't sleep," Andries gulped, "so I thought I'd be productive" "You don't always have to be productive,"

"Says the workaholic," Andries smirked. "Touchè, son," his father laughed.

"I just thought I'd do some pre-reading on my course," he shrugged. His Dad smiled. He was going to study Business, just as his Dad did. His father took out his laptop. The glow of the laptop lit up his face. He looked a little older but happier too. There used to be a tensity on his face that wasn't there anymore, and he looked happier. Andries's eyes flicked up as he said this out loud.

His father smiled, "you're not happy, are you?" He didn't close his laptop, but he leaned back on the chair and crossed his arms over his chest.

"Well, a lot happened… and my girlfriend broke up with me" His father's eyebrows shot up. He didn't know Andries had a girlfriend; none of the parents knew that Anaisha and Andries were dating. It would be complicated to tell them, but now that it was done. He told his Dad everything, he was leaving soon anyway, and his Dad was good at knowing what to keep to himself.

His father looked at him assentingly. "You still love her" Andries didn't say anything.

His father leaned forward, closing his laptop and leaning his elbows on the table. "Then you should fight for her. The fight only stops when your heart is no longer in it, not when it still is, "he spoke clearly, and succinctly.

The next afternoon Andries drove down to the beach. He walked along alone. It was a nice day, perfect even. This was his favourite type of day. Nature was in full swing. The waves were brushing the shore, there was a flock of seagulls flying around the sky, and sun-filled serotonin

125

beat warmth into every footstep of the people around. But, it was clement. There was still a perfect amount of breeze that made you feel cool but not cold. He hadn't been to the beach in a while. He used to be around here so often before. But before he left, he felt that he wanted to hang around there for a while.

He stopped at a little coffee spot; there was no line. He walked on and ordered his drink. Through his peripheral vision, he saw something walk past him in a flurry of black currant and jasmine scented perfume, wavy hair, and a mischievous grin that matched the glint in her green eyes. Naira. She looked like an angel, a miracle sent from God at that moment. "NAIRA!" he shouted.

The girl turned in a swoosh of hair, searching for the person calling her name. She was wearing a bikini top and shorts, sunglasses on top of her head.

"Thank you," he said as he put some cash on the counter, already jogging away from the barista. Naira turned from her friends. They all carried the same quizzical expression, he had seen two of the girls from school and the other two he didn't know.

"Ries!" She hugged him. "What's up? Are you working through the family or something?" She raised one dark eyebrow. Her skin was glowing in the sun, and her jewellery was glittering.

"No time for jokes, Nairu, look - " he gripped her arms with newfound strength. He had to say this quickly and now. Otherwise, he would lose his will. He looked deeply into her green eyes. She had bigger eyes than her cousin, but they were that same almond shape, softer though.

"I need you to do me a huge favour, tell her..." his mouth went dry. Naira knew which 'her ' he was speaking of. He knew Naira well. She was practically his little sister, and she had checked on him quite a bit after the break-up. Which she didn't need to do, but it was complicated. She shouted at him a lot... and consoled him too. He had already said bye to her before leaving. She had given him one of her heart-warming, tight hugs.

Still, he felt vulnerable being so open with her, and also the fact that her friends now had their eyes on him added to the hesitancy. Great. But, the freedom of the waves around him seeped into him too. His heart started beating like a drummer playing at a frantic speed, losing themselves in the beat. "Just tell her that I'm sorry and I am going to do better. Tell her I love her, and I will be a better man. Tell her... tell her I will become worthy of her again - please. Just tell her that."

Her mouth dropped. She was stunned. In so many years, she didn't think she had ever seen him like this before.

"PLEASE."

She blinked a few times, utterly confused.

She bit her lip. "Okay, I will" she nodded. He breathed out, relieved, and looked up to the ceiling, raking his hand through his hair.

The drummer in his heart slowed to a light tapping beat. "I could kiss you."

"Yeah, umm, maybe don't do that, that's really gross, kind of incestuous actually," she listed on her fingers, waving her free hand about, "and essentially goes against everything you just said." He ignored this and enveloped her in a great, big hug. She was short like her cousin, and so he was significantly taller than her. He ruffled her hair, which he knew she would hate.

"Ugh, Reis, stop." she tried to wriggle free, but he quickly held her head and kissed her forehead. "Thank you," he murmured against her forehead.

She rolled her eyes. "Yeah, yeah…I've got your back."

"I know you do," he kissed her forehead as he let go. She looked at him with a mixture of feelings. He could see her eyes moving over his face. A look of fondness and being impressed and confusion and compassion.

He smiled at her, "It'll be okay, I promise." She nodded. She didn't realize how much she needed to hear that. She took a breath in and put her sunglasses on her face.

He took a deep breath in, "I'll see you soon," he said as he walked backward. Now floppier and feeling happy…

She turned back to her friends, and they separated. He took some more steps forward, finally sharing some of the serotonin of the other beach-goers.

"Hey!"

Andries turned around. Naira was only a few feet away.

"Good luck and have fun! Or try!" She called out and really hoped he would. She waved with a great big smile, her gold and silver bracelets clinking around her wrist.

"I will," he shouted back, not caring who heard him. He was smiling a smile she hadn't seen in a while. She turned back around one more time to see him still standing there with that smile on his face. She missed that smile.

She hadn't seen it in a while.

Having fun, or trying

"Hey," Andries inclined his head to Inara. She had just walked into their shared dorm kitchen and put the kettle on as she leaned her hip against the counter.

"Hi, how was your day?" It was about five in the evening on a Friday.

"Good, I had a lecture earlier, but I missed it. Went to my other one, though, and now I'm doing the reading for the afternoon one." He said, tapping on the screen of his laptop. He used to do the reading before the lecture, but he found that doing it after was more helpful; otherwise, he struggled to understand the reading without a lot of contexts. Others might've disagreed, but it worked for him.

"Nice," she smiled. "I had a free morning," she said as she opened the cabinet to grab her mug. "Did you go for a walk?"

She nodded. "It's pretty cold today, though," she said, looking out the window.

Amar strolled up next to her. "Want me to warm you up?"

"Fuck off" she rolled her eyes and laughed despite herself. Then proceeded to elbow him in the ribs, knocking him off his balance. Andries sniggered.

She turned around to face Andries, who was sitting on the sofa. "Anyway, then I had a lecture, went to the library for a bit, and now I'm here" she smiled. Inara had this really unique, low, raspy voice. Like she had partied too hard the night before, but instead of it being grating it sounded gentle, and she spoke in this slow, calm way like she had all the time in the world and she was confident in the fact that the person she was speaking to was listening to her.

Julian and Ahmed walked in and slumped down on the sofa on either side of Andries. They were sweaty from basketball practice. Amar came over to sit on the other side of Julian. They had been inseparable after the first two weeks; everyone on their floor called them the 'three musketeers. They just 'clicked. 'They were in the kitchen/living room. It was an L-shaped room, the first part being the kitchen. And then, as you walked further, there were two big, grey polyester sofas. Andries sat back, his arm loosely draped behind the sofa. His laptop was balanced on his knees as everyone came in. Amar sat on one of the grey chairs on the table next to the sofas. Open books, an open packet of chips, and someone's laptop lay on the sofa. He liked the people he now called his friends, and they were a fun group: loud and loyal. Andries didn't mind sitting with them. He actually liked it. He enjoyed the constant chatter and banter. It reminded him of a time before, a time before his head hung low in clouds of woe.

"So, what are we doing tonight?" Ahmed asked. "Bar then club?" Amar said.

"Sounds good," Inara said.

"Fuck," Julian arched his neck back, letting it lay on the sofa. "I'm exhausted," he mumbled. Julian was the quietest of the three, but by no means did that mean he was quiet. Andries was happy to be in university, in a place he hadn't been in before. It didn't reek of his rue yet.

Ahmed turned his head to his friend, "Have a nap, rest up… were in for a long night" Ahmed smiled his perfect smile, but his eyes had certain mischief in them. Ahmed had a long nose and a long face. He wasn't 'perfect-looking, 'but he was tall and tanned with thick dark hair that reached the nape of his neck. All this together worked in his favor. Andries snickered to himself as he remembered when Naira had seen a picture of him. She said he was cute, and whenever he called her on a video call, she blubbered like an idiot whenever he said 'hello.'

"Ok, I'll put a text on the group," Inara said, taking her phone out of her back pocket. "And, make sure you guys have a shower before we leave, please," she said as she sent the message.

"You underestimate us, Inara. It is my natural scent that lures people in," Ahmed said as he leaned on the sofa, draping one arm behind it.

"Is that why Adela won't even look at you?" She sniped as she walked away with a little smile on her lips.

Later That Night…

"Anyone down for pool?" Amar pointed towards the forest green table across the bar. The place was nice, and it was well-worn and woodsy. Tons of colourful bottles at the bar and fun little trinkets of history, like car-number plates and cool signs, and vintage posters that lined the walls. It was artfully designed but chilled out. It was the kind of place that made you relax after a tough week. There was a fresh feel to it that made it feel like it could never grow old.

They were a fun group: loud and loyal. Andries didn't mind hanging out with them. He actually liked it. He enjoyed the constant chatter and banter. It reminded him of a time before, a time before his head hung low in clouds of woe.

Julian made a joke, and Andries clocked the look he gave to Lionel, just the flicker of his eyes, and when Lionel's normally tight-lipped smile broadened a little bit Julian's own would curve into a little half smile as he played with the silver band on his forefinger.

You know what," Frederike said with a slap of his legs as he got up. "I'll play" He was huge, all muscles and rough-hewn with dark stubble. He shared the same dark skin as his cousin Julian. But Julian was leaner and clean-shaven. Frederike was moulded in the mountains, and Julian looked like he was born in the clouds.

"I didn't know you were a bloody pool shark," Frederike said as they played.

"Why do you think I wanted to play?" Amar sniggered, he and Ahmed looked similar, but Amar had brown almond-coloured skin and large dark eyes. He was technically well-proportioned with sharper edges. He was also shorter and leaner.

The noise of laughter and pool balls slapping against each other was broken by a husky "hello boys" Ahmed looked up just as he was about to strike, and heads whipped around.

Ahmed's lips fell into his perfect smile. As he easily picked up the cue and leaned his head on it.

Lionel cocked his head, and an inviting smile played on his lips, his forest green eyes lighting up. Even Julian and Frederike began grinning.

Andries was about to turn and greet the voice, but his eyes caught the softening of Amar. "Hey, Inara," Amar breathed, his shoulders softened.

She shouldn't have looked very impressive, and her hair was simply blow-dried as it always was, and she wore skinny black jeans and a black bodysuit. But she defied that expectation. The clothes matched her dark hair and offset her fair skin. Her big grey eyes scanned the room and settled to stand next to Lionel. They were close, and she knocked her knees against his while lazily taking a seat, her eyes loitering on the red electric guitar that hung on the wall behind the pool table. Inara was stereotypically beautiful, notorious for her beauty, actually. She had thick, dark brown, almost black hair that cascaded down her back, and strong features worked perfectly together to make up her face. Her dark eyebrows arched above those big, romancing grey eyes and an upturned nose that met at a point and led down her cupid's bow to welcome full pink lips. She was voluptuous and shapely, and her curving body looked like it was carved. She was not necessarily popular in the university but beloved by a few, mostly in their little group. And to her, that was perfectly fine. It was perfect for her, actually.

Inara was followed by Adela, the chattier of the two. She had bright blonde hair and green eyes. She was very attractive and delightfully charming. But they were opposites. She was the sun, all bright and beaming, and Inara was the moon, balmy and tranquil. Each brings forth a different type of light.

Ahmed cleared his throat as they went back to the game.

They laughed and talked, the drinks loosening everyone up. Andries laughed at something Julian said and raked a hand through his hair, turning to look at some of the posters as they finished the game and settled in the booth, pulling up some more chairs. He had laughed at jokes and took a breath in, still looking at the wall. Even made some wisecracks of his own. But that spark in his eyes wasn't there anymore, or not at least in the same way that it was before.

"ok, I'm going to go to the bathroom before we leave" Adela hopped out of the booth as she hopped off the sofa, "see you guys tomorrow," she mumbled as she walked to the door. "Wanted company?" Ahmed looked up at her, he leaned an arm behind the back of his chair.

"To the bathroom?" She said slowly as she arched a brow. The boys started laughing.

"Yes?"

Adela just turned around, laughing as she sauntered away. Ahmed shook his head, a stupid smile on his face as he covered it with his hands.

Inara got up and put two hands on his shoulders as she leaned her head on his shoulder "you're hopeless," she laughed before she walked away and joined Adela.

Andries waited till he knew they were out of earshot and slid his eyes to Amar. "Do you want a tissue? Andries pointed to the side of his lip. "You're drooling" Amar shook his head as he rolled his dark eyes.

"Our Amar has a little crush, Ries," Ahmed announced as he slapped his friend on the back. "Oh really, since when?" Andries asked. "Oh, just since the moving day, really," chimed Julian. It was like they were all connected by the same tissue. Always answering for each other, it was nice to witness. But it also tugged at Andries in a way he hadn't felt before. "Oh fuck off, it's just a stupid crush" he threw his hand up, "ignore them."

The room was alive, and so were the boys. Andries was something else.

Andries was in the garden smoking. There were some other people outside who he didn't know. The music was loud but soft enough to talk, and it was nice. Andries was sitting in between Amar and Julian on the sofa. He had stopped drinking.

When he went back inside, he sat back down on the sofa, his head was spinning a bit, and he lay his head back.

"You good, Ries?" Amar asked who was sitting next to him. Andries nodded and smiled lopsidedly.

Julian turned too and put a comforting hand on his knee. "Water?" He asked with kind brown eyes.

"No," Andries said, his voice hoarse. They had saved the place in between them for him. He had been sitting there before he went outside for a smoke, and they had kept it for him.

That night after the club, they ended up at some student's house in town. It was actually nice. It was a four-bedroom house. In the small living room lay two pretty, comfortable sofas. In the center was a glass table with blooming flowers on it and an open box of pizza. There were knitting needles and a bundle of pale blue-colored yarn on it too. There were plant pots around the place and a flat screen, a little box of blankets in the corner, and a big glass door that led to the garden.

He could imagine the morning after, the residents lounging around the place with a blanket on, watching TV. The knitter, knitting.

There was a huge black matte lamp in the corner, and he thought the bulb might have been broken because there were unlit fairy lights wrapped around the whole thing.

They had some neon light machine in the corner; blue, red, and green spilled around the whole room. It was nice, actually.

The house was of some friends of Adela's and Amar's. They were a year older, and one of them was on their course.

Everyone was piled on the couch, some were drinking, and some had stopped considering they had probably had enough. The music was loud but soft enough for people to talk and laugh. He would've liked this.

Amar made a joke, and everyone laughed. He leaned back, putting an arm behind the sofa. Amar and Julian stayed in the seats next to Ries, who was pretty silent the whole time.

The room was full, and there were quite a few people in it. It seemed like more because of how small the place was. It was full, and there were a lot of people he could talk to. But one person wasn't…, and he would never be.

The threat of tears pierced Andries's eyes. It burned.

There was a drink on the table, and it was Amar's, he thought. He took a sip, and it burned.

He could never bring him to things like this, he would never know what it was like to experience so many things with him by his side.

If he could control fate, he would trade everything to just sit in a basement with Mykal strumming his guitar, talking to him. Just to hear his voice one more time.

On their way back to their place, they walked slowly. It was only a ten-minute walk. Inara was with Andries.

"You know, they say there's a reason for everything" "There is," Inara said.

He looked at her, blue eyes so oddly bright. "What? What can be the reason… for this" And truly, even though she was a believer of something, someone. She didn't question her beliefs, but she didn't know either. She didn't know what the reason was.

The next morning, Inara woke up fairly fresh, despite the night before, and hopped in the shower. Inara let herself into her room and went straight to the shower. She let the water pour over her body, her mind slipped to thoughts of the day. They were going to grab lunch today and probably just chill. Some relaxation time she didn't realize she needed. As she washed her body, she remembered a time when she felt insecure about it. She was voluptuous and shapely; her body took an obscure hourglass shape.

But, not anymore, though... she thought as she smiled to herself.

"Mummy, I wish I looked like you. Like a tiny fairy." trilled a mini Inara, staring up at her mother's sweet face into her small brown eyes.

"Oh my darling, you think I look like a fairy...thank you, my love! But I think you are going to look like a goddess." She said, propping the little girl on her lap. "You take up space in a room, and you don't blend in. What's wrong with that? There are many, many different kinds of beauty, my darling." She used her right hand to safely secure the child and the other to stroke her daughter's head. "And I think that we are so very... lucky that God blessed our little family with two types of beauty. He loves us so much that he decided to make you one kind and me, another" she smiled at her daughter, willing her to never forget this conversation. Apparently, she didn't.

She smiled to herself, lifting her head up to let the water run over her. The smell of lavenders filled the air around her.

Immediately, when she got back to her room, she connected her phone to her speakers, and music resounded. Inara brushed her hair out, flipping it over and fluffing it out. She stood back up and grabbed her phone, twirling her hair as she scrolled through her playlist. She hated when people asked her what her favourite genre was, she had a very eclectic taste, but she figured a true lover of music could find something good in any genre. She picked something urban, chill but upbeat. Perfect for the morning.

She leaned forward and looked a little further into the mirror as she put some lip balm on. Holding her own eyes for a second, then took a steadying breath as she left the bathroom and put her clothes on. She put some sweats and a tank top on and grabbed a jacket in case it got chilly.

She could hear them before she saw them; they were waiting in the lobby. All of them lived in a private accommodation hall about a fifteen-minute walk from their university.

They had walked over to a little restaurant in town. The town was mostly filled with students and wealthy, older people who had 'holiday homes 'there. The city was only a twenty, minute, sometimes thirty, depending on the traffic, bus ride away.

They sat down and ordered. Chatted and waited. Adela's food had already come. Her stomach grumbled. And Adela looked at her with a toothy smile, "Hungry, huh?"

Inara widened her eyes, "Very hungry."

"Same," Adela said as she tapped her fingers on the table. She turned her head and said something to Ahmed, which made them laugh. They were a pretty big group, and on a rectangular table, it meant that the conversation often got split into two at times. Inara sat back, crossing her legs over one another, and sipped away at her peppermint tea while listening to the conversations around her and her own thoughts. Hiding her amusement at Adela and Ahmed's conversation. It was more of a flirt-versation. Adela may have acted like she was uninterested, but Inara knew better. Adela made Ahmed a little nervous, but when he was sober, his game was better, and they were both very straightforward people, so it was fun to witness.

Andries was sipping his black coffee; he had woken up earlier today than he had in the past few months probably, he thought as he raked a hand through his hair. He sat opposite Inara.

She was sitting next to Adela, who was talking to Ahmed. He could tell Inara was listening as she sipped her drink to smiling lips. They both were. Her gaze shifted, and her grey eyes caught Andries's. She gave him a small smile. He didn't even realize he was staring. He shook his head and smiled back, angling his cup toward her and she to him. He leaned back, crossing his legs by placing one foot on his knee, wondering where his food was.

Chapter 5 - That Winter

It was December now, and before the first semester ended, they had all decided to go on the ski trip. It was a wonderful opportunity, and traveling together really only brought them closer…

He bent his head down; the whole world beneath him was covered in a blanket of white, a blanket patterned with little people whooshing downwards, leaving small creases.

He could feel the weight of the skis, heavy on his legs, gravity pulling them down. Andries sat in the middle of the ski lift, Inara on his left and Cara, their instructor, on his right.

It was fucking freezing, but he was wearing enough layers to be minimally comfortable. Inara and Cara were talking, pointing at the slopes.

Andries wasn't listening, his mind distracted. He always hated ski lifts, the height, the shakiness... but the thing was that lately, everything that used to scare him scared him less and less.

He looked to his left; trees lined the side of the mountains, they looked like evergreens. He watched the cottony snow dust the leaves... He remembered reading somewhere that 'the only person who fears nothing is the one that has nothing to lose.'

He never thought he'd be that person.

He looked at the evergreens again, the only colour in this world of white. Outlasting the other trees, which died in the winter. How lonely must they've been? The evergreens.

You know those moments when your parents tell you something about those acquaintances of theirs who lost their daughter in an accident or whose father walked out on them suddenly.

Those tragic, sad stories which shock you into submission... for a minute. You feel sad and think about that person and their loved ones... for a minute... you glimpse the fragility of life... for a minute. And then, you carry on and move on with your own life, never thinking that you'd be a character in that tragic tale.

"Andries!" Inara said.

Andries shook, waking up from his thoughts. They were meant to put the barricade up. "fuck, sorry," he said as he began helping them push it up, and then they made it to the slope, slipping off the lift and shuffling closer to the beginning of the slope.

He never thought so much before, never thought of evergreens before.

"Alright!" Cara said, her voice high and excited. She sounded like a primary school teacher who actually loved kids. Her goggles sat on her helmet. She had pretty blue eyes and soft features. She looked pretty young, just a little older than himself. "So, this is a fairly easy slope... we can start here, see how you guys feel, and then figure it out" she put two thumbs up. "Sound good?" a zealous smile on her lips.

"Sounds good," Inara said, a smile in her voice, and Andries nodded.

"Alright, Inara, right?" She said, inclining her head to Inara. "why don't you shuffle over to my right, and...

"Andries," Inara said, helping her out.

"Andries," Cara smiled at him, "come on my other side, please" They settled next to Cara and slid down.

Slowly and gently, and then they picked up the pace, angling their bodies forward. The sound of the friction between the snow and the ski's loud in their ears.

Inara was definitely better than Andries, moving with more ease and confidence. Things seemed to come easy to her. But Andries was less rusty than he had expected to be. He took an indulgent breath in. He forgot how nice skiing was, the harsh wind pushing on his face, pushing things out of his mind.

They made it down two more slopes, getting harder each time, but nothing they couldn't handle. The endorphins are in full swing now, the snow seeming brighter, and his mind seemingly tired of thinking.

They stood at the beginning of another slope. A group of kids getting ready to snowboard next to them whizzed off like it was the easiest thing in the world.

"After this one, do you guys want to head up to get some food or something to drink?" At this suggestion, Inara nodded fervently.

Cara laughed, "Fantastic" she clapped her hands together, the sound getting lost within her gloves. "This one is a bit trickier," she widened her light blue eyes, "so I want us to be in a line, and I want you guys to follow me." Andries shuffled back, letting Inara slip in between, "ladies first," he uttered as he held a hand out.

Her hair was slipping out of her helmet, her cheeks pink from the cold. "Thank you," she smirked.

And once again, they were off...

Skiing down the slope, the mountains beautiful in the distance, and this slope was barer, Andries picked up speed, shortening the gap between him and Inara. The rush of the wind made his eyes tear up; less friction, the snow softened with the sunshine. He felt his heart beat faster, the blood moves through his body, and then...

There was a thud. He had just fallen flat on his ass.

Inara stopped abruptly, sliding her skis into "pizza." She turned, her grey eyes wide, and as soon as she saw him, she burst into laughter.

"Sorry," she huffed in between breaths, "I'm sorry," she said as her eyes creased, crow's feet at the corners of her eyes as her hand touched her stomach.

He chuckled now, too, trying to push himself up.

He was unsuccessful, consistently falling back, which only made her laugh more.

Cara was already shuffling over to help him up. He grabbed her hand as she pulled him up. "Fuck, now my ass is cold," he smirked at the two of them.

"Don't worry, it'll warm up when we go indoors," she smiled.

They made their way down, all the way as the wind cooled Andries's ass even more.

Cara opened the cafe door, leading Inara and Andries in, and the warmth hit Inara wonderfully unexpectedly. She sighed as they sat down on the wooden seats. As she took her helmet off, she could already tell her hair looked like a bird's nest despite the braid she put it in.

But right now, she didn't care... her body felt exhausted and alive. The medicine of movement thrumming through her veins, and natural beauty behind her eyelids, the sounds of chatter singing in her ears.

138

Their hot chocolates came, and as she took a sip, she slowly melted. It was the most indescribable feeling coming from extreme weather to a place of comfort. And feeling the warmth go through her body. Like you got exactly what your body was craving. The drink itself was delicious, but at this moment, she would've drank hot tar as long as it was warm.

She looked around, her grey eyes sweeping around the place, nose, and cheeks all pink.

It was all woody and cozy, with big windows showing off the mountainous view, everyone around them with blood-rushed faces. "So, how did you get into becoming an instructor?" Inara asked Cara. Her voice was soft and raspy.

Cara's eyes blue eyes lit up as she told the story with enthusiasm. She explained how she had just finished university and decided to do it for the next two years.

"Make some money, have some fun" she shrugged with a smile. She took a gulp from the mug,' "it's nice because you just follow the snow, you know?" They nodded. "You get to travel around to wherever it's cold during the year, and its fun... you meet tons of new people," she said, smiling at the two of them. She was a chatty girl, Andries thought. His eyes swiveled to Inara, who looked at her with wonderstruck grey eyes.

"Sounds like a good gig," Andries said, leaning back in his chair. "It's awesome!" she nodded ardently, taking a bite of her croissant.

"What about you guys? Sorry," she dabbed a tissue on her lips with a laugh and gulped, "What are you guys? What do you study?" She asked.

Inara took her braid out, shaking her hair out. "I do architecture," she said as she rebraided her hair with a smile that didn't quite reach her eyes.

"Nice!" Cara said, with a thoughtful nod, "and you?" Cara angled her chin towards Andries.

"I want to go into business," he mumbled, eyes facing the window to his left. Inara's head turned at the sound of her name. It was Adela. Ahmed and Lionel are right behind her with their instructor. "Hey!" Ahmed said, swaggering over. He put a hand on Inara's shoulder, pointing at her hot chocolate. She nodded. He took a sip, "damn, that's good," his shoulders sagging with pure bliss. Adela pulled a chair at their table, "so, how have you guys been doing?" She said, eyes wide and interested.

"It's been so nice, I forgot how...” Inara took a breath looking out at the mountains, trying to find the words "wonderful skiing is," she said, and her effervescent smile on her face. "Like, feeling energized and at peace at the same time" she smiled. Ahmed looked at her thoughtfully. Andries realized her mouth barely moved when she spoke. "and the mountains," she sighed, her big grey eyes facing the view across her, "nothing comes close to natural beauty" a glimmer in her eyes "like *this* is our world, its" she bit her lip, shaking her head, bewitched "I can't even put it into words its... ethereal."

Adela smiled a knowing smile. She was used to her friends' way of speaking. Inara turned as she patted the chair next to her, looking up at Lionel. He sat down silently.

Andries's looked at Inara again, his eyes lingering for a minute.

He felt Ahmed come sit beside him as he and Adela explained how their lesson went. They were advanced and went on a black diamond, which they had never been on before.

Inara's eyes flickered to Andries. He leaned back as he listened to Ahmed and Adela, a crooked smile on his face, a shake of his shoulders from the light huff of a laugh. He probably didn't even realize it.

This seemed good for him, people like Adela and Ahmed. Those types of people had life thrumming through their veins. And injected it into the people around them. He needed that.

Inara took a breath in; she had always been this way. Always bringing in stray animals to nurse back to health, she had brought in a kitten at an adoption fair at the beach once and convinced her parents to keep it. Despite being an only child, her parents could be strict, but she had convinced them. Her friends often came to her for advice. She was good at it. But she remembered seeing Andries and Mykal... their friends. They were a good group. She couldn't help but feel bad for him... she was sure he must've imagined doing this with Mykal. Making these memories with him... but... alas, God had other plans.

Cara looked at her watch, "Andries, Inara... come on, team, let's go," she said, getting up. They followed suit.

As they left, zipping up their jackets. Inara held the door open and watched Andries turn his head, blue eyes looking back at Adela and Ahmed, the signs of a budding romance in existence/ sparking in between them. His arm on the back of her chair, a smile just for him. Inara could see a wish in his blue eyes as he turned and bent his head. Mumbling a 'thanks.'

Something in her chest beat beneath the beating of her heart.

"Ok, so you guys have worked pretty hard today," Cara said, helping them put their ski's on efficiently. She walked over to Inara, bending down, making sure they were locked into place "so for our last path today, we're going to do a nice, easy one," Cara said as she stood up and did the same to Ries. In front of them was a winding path of snow that looked like it had ended in a beautiful eternity.

They began on the road to a beautiful eternity...

Inara felt like she was flying, but calmly. Not like a superhero in need, but like a superhero leisurely enjoying the perks of their special powers. She could see her breath, see her life. The feel of fresh air in her lungs, her nose slightly runny, eyes watering, and her toes and fingers freezing. And she was smiling. She felt alive. Trees lined both sides of the small slow laden path they were descending on... in beautiful silence, the sky slightly pink. This was therapy, Inara thought. There was no music, but it felt like there was a song playing in her mind.

Andries felt like someone was singing him a lullaby. Like everything, it might just be alright. Not true, but right now, he didn't mind living in delusion. It felt like someone was next to him, not skiing, just moving along beside him. He let them, and he let himself feel less alone on the path.

Music was playing, and everyone was sharing their stories of the day. They were sitting with their instructors and their friends. The other tables filled with the other students that had come on the trip.

"No, no, you had to see it," Inara laughed, trying to catch her breath as she finished the story "he fell flat on his ass!" She motioned her hand downward, mimicking his fall.

Everyone laughed as Andries raked a hand through his hair. "I'm pretty sure my ass is bruised" The smell of food wafted through the air, of cheese and bread.

Ahmed indulgently inhaled, "that smells so good," he said, patting his stomach as he leaned back on his chair.

The chalet was warm, and amber lights shone across the smooth wooden table. The air felt soft and wondrous, like being inside a warm cocoon.

The food was served buffet-style. Few by few, they went up to go and serve themselves. Steam was rising from the hot dishes. Everyone seemed happily tired. It was a good feeling. That good tiredness hummed through all of them, and they looked like the kind of people you would want to hang out with, who would make you feel like one of them by making fun of you immediately. Andries still felt like life wasn't real.

The warmth of the place felt like a gift you had to relish. You'd be stupid not to.

Inara was standing in the doorway of the dining entrance, peeling her jacket off the hook. Fishing her cap and gloves from the pockets. She heard footsteps behind her,

"Hello," she said absently.

"Hi," it was a raspy voice; she turned.

She was met with blue eyes. "Andries," You really couldn't look away; even when he looked down, she wanted to move her head and follow his eyes with her own.

"Where are you going?" He noted her attire, dinner was finished, and some of them had gone out while the others had decided to sleep.

"I wanted to go for a quick walk, actually," she said, flipping her long hair out of the collar of her black jacket.

He nodded, stuffed his hands in his pockets, and walked away slowly.

He had barely made it a few steps when he turned around. "Can I join you?" He squinted and blinked, a shaky smile on his face. She blinked, caught off guard. "Sure," his shaky smile turned more charming.

Their footprints made imprints in the snow. It was still early in the night, and the town center was still fairly full. Conversation and snowflakes mingle in the air. There was even some music that came from stores they walked past.

He raked a hand through his hair. "Are you not cold?" Andries asked, turning to look at her. She seemed unbothered, her brown flowing out of the white cable knit cap.

"A little," she shrugged. "But I'm also distracted..." her eyes wandered around them, that easy smile getting wider and reaching her eyes. She had a point, Andries thought as he took in the place as well, it was a very picturesque town. Like a storybook come to life.

She looked up, and he followed her gaze. The stars were taking up the sky.

"Wow," she said under her breath. He nodded, even though no one could see. He had never seen so many stars and so bright. Throbbing with vitality and energy.

They are proud to be seen in all their sparkling zeal without any masks and trappings of smoke or pollution.

He remembered something Mykal had once said, his eyes moving towards the brightest star. She shook her head. She was stuck in ambedo for a moment "did you enjoy yourself today?"

Inara said, pulling her jacket further around herself, turning her head to look at him. "it was good," he nodded.

"That was very convincing," a cheeky smile on her lips.

He laughed, bending his head down. "No, it was a good day. Better than the last few" he shrugged.

She nodded, "and, considering my life right now. Better is good" he raked a hand through his hair.

"You must miss him," she gulped. "More so now. I bet you imagined doing all this stuff with him."

"I miss them both," he said solemnly.

She nodded, turning her head to face him, her grey eyes somber. "I was sorry to hear about you and Anaisha."

"Me too," he looked at the moon once again. It was a crescent tonight. "But," He stuttered. He should've thought about what he wanted to say, but usually, the words came to him fairly easily. She noted the shift.

"Take your time." She said, with a kind smile and a warm hand on his shoulder. They walked on in silence as she looked through the windows of stores.

"I-" he gulped, "fuck" he whispered, shaking his head.

He lingered behind her, "you know it might help if you just spit it out" He nodded silently, "works for me," she winked with a smirk. He cocked his head to the side and then barked a laugh. Her shoulders shook, "no but seriously, just say it... if you want to, that is," she said, a small smile on her lips. "I won't judge," she said softly.

Then she whirled around and held her pinkie finger out to him.

His eyes fell toward her finger, and he chuckled. He held her pinkie with his and took a breath in, he was smiling, but it was a long way down now.

"I changed," he gulped. Assessing her reaction. "A lot" Her head cocked to the side, "after Mykal-"

"I don't want to talk about it" when she said his name, he felt a hard slap across his face. He felt like he had just run into a stone wall. He felt a tsunami take him. Take him back, back to that moment.

He had been in his room. He was meant to go to Mykal's the next evening. And his cousin, but he had ditched them last minute. He was tired from the night before and had stayed in his room till noon. He was awake, sitting in his bed, studying.

He remembered the way the sunlight came through the window on his navy blue sheets. He remembered how his mother came into his room. He remembered how he had found it odd as he expected her to be working. He remembered how he didn't question it until he saw his mother's tear-stained face. He remembered how he shut his laptop and got up and asked her to tell him what had happened. He never imagined she would say what they did.

"Mykal died at 1:32 pm today."

He remembered the way the sun stayed up high, the clouds puffy and unmoving, and the cars below kept moving. The view of the city from his window looked the same. But his whole world changed in one moment.

He remembered not knowing what to do; he barely felt his mother's soft hand on his arm as he pulled him into a hug as if she could take away the grief her son felt through some sort of diffusion. He remembered hearing his mother sobbing. She held him as if she could keep him together. He had felt so still and numb and slack in her arms. His whole body was unfeeling.

It didn't seem real.

He would see Mykal tomorrow; he would see him the way he did nearly every day as he threw open his bedroom door. He would see him tomorrow *not* working like he was meant to, but instead, he would be strumming the strings of his guitar, humming. And as he heard the door fly open, he would turn around and say, "Ever heard of knocking, you prick?"

He would see him tomorrow shooing away his little sister when she asked them to 'come to see her new ballet dance'; she had a new one every day. He would see him tomorrow as he bowed his head and said 'fuck'. He would see him tomorrow as he called after her.

'Sofia, we're coming. Wait up. He would see him tomorrow as he smiled at Sofia's lit-up face. He would walk with him down the steps to the basement to watch her dance again.

This wasn't real.

He remembered what his mother softly said.

"Oh, my darling - I'm so sorry it is," in her soft voice.

He kept on repeating the whole evening - "it is not real. I'll see him again tomorrow."

He remembered when he woke up the next day and saw the black clothes hanging on the doors of his wardrobe.

He remembered the funeral barely. He remembered seeing Sofia in a little black dress, unmoving and tears spilling down her face. He remembered how she had run to him when they entered Mykal's house. He remembered how she wrapped her small arms around his waist. Crying into him, and he remembered patting her dark head. He remembered seeing Mr. and Mrs. Ricardo. He remembered how they invited him to stand with them, with their family, to receive condolences. He remembered his parents refusing them and Mr. Ricardo patting his shoulder and saying in his deep voice. "My son, Andries, has lost a brother too."

He remembered not wanting to stand with them. Not being able. But he remembered being unable to refuse them.

He remembers shaking hands and hugging people as they said 'sorry 'to him. He remembered hearing none of it. He remembered how some time in between the handshakes and the hugs, he had begun crying. The tears came silently and slowly as it all became real. Anaisha had made her way next to him. She was there the whole time, crying too.

He remembered coming back home and running into his room and locking the door. And crying.

It was real. Mykal's dead. He's gone.

I will never see him again.

I will never fight with him again. I will never laugh with him again.

I will never study in his room again. I will never smoke with him again. I will never party with him again.

I will never hear him play guitar again.

I will never see him argue with his mother again.

I will never see him go back to his mother, hug her, and apologise. I will never play cards with him and his father again.

I will never laugh at him as he danced with his sister again. He remembered when his thoughts became less selfish.

He will never fight again.

He will never calm me down again. He will never laugh again.

He will never study again. He will never sketch again.

He will never play guitar again.

He will never argue with his mother again.

He will never make up with his mother again, hug her, and apologise. He will never play cards with his father again.

He will never dance with his sister again. He will never see his parents grow old.

He will never see his sister grow up.

He will never become who he was meant to be.

He didn't remember much after that. He never went back to Mykal's home after the day of the funeral.

He took a deep breath in, stuffing a hand aggressively in his pocket and taking out a box of cigarettes. He lit one and took a puff, angling it toward her, his eyes an open question. She shook her head in a decline.

He ran a hand through his hair, and his hand was shaking.

"Are you okay?" She said, a restful hand on his shoulder. Stopping him in his tracks. He nodded. Used to the question, then said "no."

He took another smoke, "I'm not," he said, blowing out a breath.

"Take a minute" they stopped walking now, standing under a lamplight. She leaned against it patiently.

He took a deep breath, trying to get the haunting memories out of his head. Or just make the memories less haunting.

"It's just harder than I ever thought it would be," he said, looking up at the stars. His eyes shadowed in a type of pain. "I can't even imagine," she said softly, a sadness illuminated her eyes.

"Don't," he said, sucking in a breath. "Trust me."

He started walking again. She pushed herself off the lamppost and followed.

This place was possibly the coldest and warmest place she'd ever been in.

The sounds of a soft, simple life filled the air around them. Soft laughter and money chinking. Snow padding the sounds of footsteps. "It's weird," she said, eyes lingering around her, "this place feels like home." In her bones, "even though it's nothing like our actual home."

He turned to look at her. With a small smile on his lips, snowflakes began to fall.

"I know what you mean" they were speaking in hushed tones, walking in hushed footsteps.

They were from the same city. Inara went to a different school, but it was a small place, and she remembered Mykal. They were in music class together and had performed together in recitals often. Her piano and singing were accompanied by his guitar. He was ruggedly handsome. Tall and broad... With wheatish skin and big brown eyes, and curly black hair. He wore cool t-shirts and was always laughing and smiling. He was amazing at the guitar. He was an amazing person, the kind of person that made a bad day better. They had become friends over the years. They had related to their 'lazy bone 'and not being very focused. He was loved by nearly all the students and teachers even when he messed around, nice to all regardless of what was happening in his own life. Fun and funny but quiet and alone at times too. He was just a happy guy, living his life as it happened. Not worrying about the next thing or other people.

She was the one that told the rest of the group what happened when they first got to the university. There seemed to be something off about him. He was grateful, and he didn't have to talk about it himself.

The night they had all first moved in, they sat in the common area, chatting and getting to know each other.

"Andries, right?" She had said when she met him, "you're from...?"

He had looked at her, confused. She smiled, "I'm Inara," and sat next to her.

' Oh my god, yes!" He snapped his fingers as it all clicked together in his head "we follow each other on Instagram… you're *that* Inara?" She raised her eyebrows at that remark.

"He had told me about you… he thought you were gorgeous 'he smirked. She knew which 'he 'Andries was talking about.

She raised her eyebrows, pressing her lips together. Then she said something else he didn't expect.

"Anything else?" she smirked.

He laughed softly and nodded. "He said you were kind and had a beautiful voice 'he scratched his jaw, 'actually… he specifically said 'she has this distinct, unique quality to her voice… it's beautiful.'

"Oh," Inara blinked, twirling the necklace at her throat. "That was very kind of him. He was wonderful," she smiled, his face vivid in her mind...

She remembered how her father once told her to say the name of the person who floated away. He said, 'don't avoid it. It's good to say it out loud - and when you say their name. Their alive again through your voice and the identity and memory that comes with a name.

"If you don't want to do this, I get it." She said warily, looking at him from the corner of her eye. "But," he looked at her from the corner too. "Say his name." She whispered misty air in front of her.

"I'm sorry... what?" He didn't know if it was because Inara was a new friend, but he was nicer to her than the others in his life recently.

"My Dad said it," they kept walking. Slow, baby steps. "He said when you say their name. Their alive again, through your voice and the identity and memory that comes with a name"

He pressed his lips together

"It sounds silly. But it helped me" she shrugged.

He gulped; he didn't know why. If it was the way she spoke or her grey eyes that made her seem wise. But he listened. "M-" he blew a breath out. The misty air in front of him, seeing his breath. A sign of him being alive.

He took another breath in.

"You don't have to say it now... just one day" He nodded. He was trying.

And on their walk back, Andries almost felt like he could hear a score, a score of music. That sounded like hope and life. Sacred sanctity of soft, simple life. It felt homey even though it was really nothing like their home of buildings and sun and ocean.

Painkillers

Anaisha sat on her floor, angling over her knees as she tied her laces. She pushed herself up and grabbed her headphones from the desk. It was evening time, the sky was pink and purple, and she had just finished her school work. It had been a tiring day, but she didn't want to rest; she wanted to move.

She bounded out her door, down the stairs, and down the corridor, reaching outside faster than she even thought she could. She tied her hair up into a tight ponytail. She used two to make sure it would stay up and put her headphones on, and began stretching. The weather was good, and she was glad she didn't wear a jacket because soon she would be warm from sweat and blood rushing around her body. She stretched and began to walk out onto the sidewalk. She put her running playlist on, and as the music resounded in her head, she started to run. Music played and changed. She slowed down to a walk and ran again, going back and forth. She had already reached the park, and the kids were leaving, heading home. Walking past her and kindly moving out of her way.

She was breathing heavily through her nose as she reached the beach and pressed her lips together as she ran through her aching limbs. She channelled her movements through her mind, forcing herself to run to the beat. Then when it felt like she couldn't go on any longer, she slowed herself down to a walk, her ponytail swinging behind her. She closed her eyes, relishing in the floating sensation that spread through her body. Breathing in deeply through her nose, the smell of salt in all her senses and felt her body heat tingling through her. Her senses were alive.

Then she began running again, and this time it was easier. Her legs seemed to move without any effort like this was what her body was made for.

This. This moment. This feeling.

She didn't even know how far on the track she was anymore. The sweat on her temples and back was her compass, telling her that she was pretty far away. She kept moving, and the music resounded in her head.

She turned back now, and the lights on the boardwalk were turning on soft yellow bulbs. The oceans had gone from bright blue to nearly black, and stars popped up above. The world seemed lovingly sinister, like a mixed blessing. She couldn't hear her pants, the music in her ears suppressing the sound. The feeling of the ground beneath her feet created a beat.

A song came on that hit close to home, and something fiery and hedonistic filled her veins... she ran faster, kept on going even when she felt herself tiring out. If the whole town was burning, she would have run into the flames if that meant she could keep running; she was already aflame anyway.

Sweat dripped into her eyes, it stung, but she didn't care. She actually relished it. She felt like a renegade.

She reached the gate and didn't stop even there, her body expeditiously powered through and then she was at the door of her house... She stopped.

Her chest rose and fell heavily, her heart thumping in her chest, loud and clear in her ears. She savoured every breath like she was born again. Born again through heat and resilience. She felt like some sort of bad-ass renegade anti-hero. Sometimes, when she ran, it felt like she wasn't in her real life.

She stood there and stretched. Her body felt like something was running through it. Her chest rose and fell heavily. Her heart pounded rapidly as her movement slowed into a slow stretch. The sky was dark, but still, everything seemed to glimmer around her.

She would get through this shit, one way or another, she would.

Her music was so loud she didn't even hear the car that drove up her driveway. Aki strode into her lineup vision. He had said something; she took her headphones out.

"Hi," she panted, with a confused look on her face. "Sorry, I don't want to hug you. I'm all sweaty," she smiled. "Um, what are you doing here," she said, still catching her breath.

"My mom wanted me to drop off some food..." his mom loved to bake and was always sending over some baked goods.

"Oh, that's so sweet," she smiled. She opened the door, and they walked into the house to the kitchen. He put the foil container down on the counter. She felt a little weird. She looked down at her dampened clothes and ran a tight hand through her ponytail. She looked like shit.

"I'm guessing you haven't had dinner yet...." She cleared her throat. "No, not yet" it was six.

"Well, yeah, it is pretty early, but I get hungry after practice," he laughed, stuffing his hands in his pockets "me and Naira were going to grab something to eat, but she has some work she still has to get done, so she's skipping it." He rubbed a hand on his neck, "do you wanna maybe, go get dinner?" She had known Aki for ages, obviously being Naira's best friend, but they had never really hung out, just the two of them. Her brows came together for a moment, and when she realized she was doing it, she immediately stopped and plastered a smile on her face. "Sure," she nodded. "I just need to shower and change" she bit her lip.

"That's perfect. I need to drop some food off at Ricardo's, too..." her jaw tensed. He checked his watch, not noticing, "should I meet you back here in 20 minutes-ish" It was one of those electronic ones that did a bunch of other things, along with giving you the time.

"Okay, I'll see you in 20," he said with a half-smile as he walked backward and turned away. She bit her lip as she leaped up the stairs and fumbled as she opened her bedroom door.

Anaisha's hair was still slightly damp when they got into the restaurant. It was a small Japanese place, not far from her house. She had eaten here before and knew the food was good. She played with the eternity ring on her middle finger, twirling it around. She was starving, and there weren't that many customers, thank god. It was pretty early for dinner. Most people dined out later.

They ordered some water as they checked the menu. Aki had a grey hoodie on, his hair still slightly damp. He had showered quickly after practice. He smelled fresh of soap and aftershave and was leaning a long arm over the chair as his eyes strolled the menu. He had laid his phone bottom side down on the table.

A waiter came by and took their orders. When they took the menus away, he leaned an elbow on the wooden table, and they talked about their day and an array of subjects. The lights were dim in the restaurant, despite the darkness outside, but she liked it like that. She had known Aki for ages, and they were friends but not good friends. She mostly knew him as Naira's best friend. But he was lovely to talk to, funny and easy. When the food came, they carried on talking, but when they fell into silence, they were comfortable. Neither tried to fill the silence with an unnecessary conversation, and they just carried on eating until one of them wanted to say something.

"So, this might be a bit forward" He took a sip of water. She raised a brow. "But how are you?" He had tinges of pink underneath his cool beige skin.

She cocked her head to the side, "that's not forward" she leaned back slightly, "I'm good" she smiled and looked down at her plate. It was a spicy salmon roll. He shook his head, "no, I meant 'forward 'because I'm actually asking. Her eyes flickered up to his. His brows scrunched together. "I don't think I would be" he touched the rim of his ears, and they poked out. It made him look younger "if I was in that position," he looked at her with sincerity.

She gulped. "I'm feeling better." Carrying on as she rubbed her hands along her thighs, "slowly but surely. So I'm good." She shrugged with a small smile. She had a clear voice and spoke slowly and softly. Thinking of what she said before, she said them.

He looked up through kind upturned eyes. "I'm really glad to hear that," he smiled. He went back to eating, but she didn't. She stayed looking at him. For just a second longer.

"Thank you for asking."

He looked up at her through dark, upturned eyes. He nodded his eyes kind.

He didn't ask anything more, but she felt comfortable speaking to him, and he was a good listener.

She blew out a breath "sometimes I wish I could just forget about him." She admitted, looking up at the ceiling.

"Why would you want to forget him, though?" Aki cocked his head. He really was very handsome, especially unclose to his features melted together perfectly.

"Because then I wouldn't have to go through heartbreak," she said with an incredulous, wry laugh.

"Yeah, but don't you believe that everything happens for a reason," his eyebrows lifted. "I thought you were one of those people." He looked at her with intrigue in his eyes now.

"Isn't everyone?" She lifted a brow with a half-smile. "I mean, how else can you deal with life" she bit her lip. "Otherwise, it would be too... wayward. No one likes to deal with the feeling of occhiolism," she said, popping a baby potato in her mouth.

"To the rest of history, your perspective may be small and insignificant even" he shrugged. "But, at the same time to yourself and those around you, it's not insignificant at all" he leaned back, crossing his long legs to the side of the table. "It's the biggest, most important thing." He spoke calmly, with a voice like a sea breeze. "I didn't peg you as a pessimist," he smirked.

"And I didn't peg you as someone who knew what 'occhiolism' was. People surprise you." She bit back, but she was smiling as her eyes lingered on his face.

"So you used it, thinking I wouldn't know what it means?" His brows shot up. "That's so cruel," a little smirk on his lips. He had dimples. She hadn't realized it before.

She propped her head on her knuckles. "I think I like feeling a little superior sometimes. It boosts my ego." She shrugged nonchalantly.

"If I didn't know what it meant, I wouldn't have squirmed." He shook his head. "I would have just admitted that I didn't know and simply asked you what it meant." He remarked back, mirroring her indifference.

"Honesty. I like that too" her chin rested delicately on her knuckles, sharp eyes looking at him. He cleared his throat.

"So, if you *do* believe that everything happens for a reason. Then why do you want to forget him?" He leaned forward, tapping his fingers on the table. He couldn't let her off that easily. She didn't mind.

"Like I said. I don't like this pain."

"But if he was in your life for a reason, then what was the reason?" He halted his finger tapping and leaned back again, "and, obviously, you don't have to say if you don't want to, by the way..." he said with deep sensitivity in his eyes.

Her eyes softened, "it's okay. I don't mind" she smiled a half-smile.

"Well, I learned that I don't deserve a shitty relationship," she pointed her fork at him. "You don't." He said sternly.

She chewed on her bottom lip as her eyes drifted, "but before he became an ass and before Mykal's death." She gulped, blinking slowly. "He was my best friend, and he showed me that I was lovable." A wistful look twinkled in her dark eyes. "In this wonderful way that romantic and platonic at the same time" she rolled her eyes with a light laugh. Her eyes went serious again as her shoulders slumped lightly. "He loved me for who I was. He loved the good parts of me.

He adored and accepted my flaws at the same time." She played with her ring, a tender look on her face. "He taught me how to laugh unashamedly," She laughed, memories flashing behind her eyes. "He taught me how to live and enjoy every moment of life, everything it has to offer." A melancholy look in her eyes, but she was smiling happily never the less. "They both did."

She took a deep breath, lifting her chin from her knuckles and placing her hands on the table. "I guess everything does happen for a reason," she whispered more to herself than Aki.

"It does." He said softly and looked at her with awe. "I remember Ries used to laugh a lot before."

She nodded. "He said "Hi" to everyone and asked them how their day went and really wanted to know. Kind of like you," she said, her brown eyes flicking up to Aki.

"He picked the habit up from Mykal." Her sharp eyes went soft and sorrowful.

"You must miss him," He said carefully. "I do" he had a sadness in his eyes, "I can't imagine what it's like for you" his voice went low.

"He was..." an image of him slipped into her mind. She took in a shaky breath, "an unexplainable amount" she looked heavenward. "Sometimes I forget he's gone, and it feels like I can still hear his laugh. I never want to forget it" she tucked her now dry hair behind her ear. "You know when Andries and I broke up, I was actually going to call Mykal," she laughed darkly. "Imagine..." she licked her lips and pressed them together firmly. "He would've kicked Andrie's ass." This time she laughed wholeheartedly. "He would've come to my room and let me cry on his shoulder the whole night. And called Andries and shouted at him and made us work it out, probably" Her voice quivered, and a small tear escaped her eye.

He grabbed a tissue from the ox in between them and passed it to her.

"I'm so sorry I didn't mean to start crying," she pressed the tissue to her eye as she snickered under her breath.

"No. It's fine." Aki said with gentle eyes as he reached over to touch her hand. A gesture of comfort that she received. She cleared her throat, dark eyes glistening. "It does make me sad, but I actually like talking about him." She lifted on the shoulder and bit her lip. "Most of the time, people tip-toe around it...But I never want to forget him." She said with a deep force, then she leaned back on her chair and twirled the ring on her forefinger, "maybe... I don't mind the pain," she gulped, "because it's painful talking about him, but I still want to do it" she took a deep breath in, "I wish people did more often." She whispered and looked into oblivion for a moment, her eyes glazing over.

She cleared her throat and shook her head, "shit, that's a lot. I'm sorry," her voice got higher again.

"You have nothing to apologise for," he said kindly. She looked up at him. His eyes were slanted and dark, but there were actually little specks of brown in them. She hadn't taken a bite of her food in those last few minutes. She had been so engrossed in their conversation. Neither had he.

He drove up her street. The colours of all the greenery in the neighbourhood darkened in the night-time, but the rustle of the trees was omnipresent. The moon was a half-moon today, rising high and mighty.

They reached her house, and he pulled into the driveway. She turned, looking at him, rolling her shoulders, dark eyes purposeful, "thank you for tonight," she said in her clear voice.

"Anytime," his half smile popped on his lips. He knew what she meant.

She didn't realize how much she needed that, how much a conversation with another person. A person who cared about her and her thoughts were necessary. How many conversations with another person could bring her peace and understanding? She wished she had spoken to someone before. But maybe this was how it was meant to be.

Let's dance

Naira hurried to and fro from her bathroom to her long, shiny white desk, with silver legs in her black silk bathrobe. Her hair was in rollers as she brought back the mascara she wanted from her bathroom, looking into the mirror on her desk as she applied it. A halo of products surrounded the mirror, and there were two textbooks stacked atop each other and a pot of fluffy pens.

Naira's room was only a little smaller than Anaisha's. She lived in a neighbourhood not far away in a similar house with a big garden. But being in Naira's bedroom felt like getting a glimpse into a little space in her mind. She had three small shelves jutting out on the space wall above her desk and a bookshelf headboard above her bed. There were a few textbooks on them, but most of the shelves were lined with novels. Across her bed was a flat screen TV mounted to the wall. The walls were a blueish-purple, and a small chandelier hung in the centre of her room.

Anaisha sat on her bed and turned her head to smell the flowers in a vase on the side table. They were alive and blooming today. Daisies.

There was a pounding on the door.

"Come in," Naira sang in her silvery voice.

"You didn't even ask who it was" Anaisha's brows shot up.

"It's Aki," Naira said, fluffing a brush on her cheeks." who else would it be?" She swivelled around on her chair and arched a dark brow.

And low and behold, she was right.

"Naira, we're going to be so late," he said as he closed the door. He looked dashingly handsome in a simple white shirt and black trousers. His dark hair was shining, handsome features melting into each other.

"I'm nearly done," she said, touching the corner of her eye. "I swear," she swivelled around, this time looking at him with a glint in her green eyes. They really stood out against her brown skin, and the makeup only made them more alluring.

Aki just rolled his eyes as he picked up the book that sat on the white fluffy beanbag, finding a bookmark on her desk and placing it in. He grabbed her phone, put in the passcode, and chose the next song. She had these amazing speakers on her desk, called water fountain speakers, that lit up in bright blues and greens and pinks.

Anaisha's eyes lingered on the two fluffy white beanbags beside her bed. She remembered when Mykal and Andries would fight over who got to sit on it. One corner of her mouth turned up.

Anaisha hadn't even realized that Naira had gone and gotten changed in the bathroom. She walked over to the full-length, oval-shaped mirror attached to the wall outside the bathroom as she slipped on her heels and took the last roller out of her hair, shaking out the curls in her hand and turning around to face them, "okay, let's go" she cocked her head to the door.

Anaisha's eyes widened, "you look amazing, Naira!" She was wearing a gorgeous sleeveless white jumpsuit that flared at the bottom that accentuated the curves in her figure.

"Thanks," she bit her lip, grinning as she tilted her head. Naira looked a lot like her cousin. They shared the same hooked nose, but hers was less prominent, and she had these upturned mischievous green eyes that stood out against her brown skin. She had perfectly arched dark brows and defined browny pink lips. The top lip was bigger than the other, and she had big floppy ears, which she often covered with her curly hair. Her round baby face made her look younger than her cousin. In the last few years, she had gone from a forgettable face to someone quite dazzling.

Naira strutted out of the car, her arm looped through Anaisha's elbow to stop her from running away. Anaisha's steps felt slow and forced as she half-listened to the conversation Naira and Aki were having.

Tonight was the winter dance, and as they got closer to the hall, they could hear the music filter through the walls and see the glimmer of light dripping out of the door wooden doors.

Anaisha felt Naira's hand tighten around her arm, and she could feel the coolness of Naira's jewellery on her bare skin, grounding her back to reality.

Aki pushed open the doors.

Anaisha hadn't been here for some time, and she took in the room again. There was a small built stage at the back of the room with a DJ with dark shaggy hair, spinning discs, and headphones on.

Two massive black speakers were on either side, reverberating music that had pulsed through the walls. Purple and blue lights bounced off the walls, and a shiny white glossy dance floor was in the middle.

At the centre of the room was a group of people talking and behind them was the dance floor. A shiny black glossy floor that cut through the marbled floor in a smaller rectangular shape. No one was dancing yet, though.

Anaisha and Naira went up to the group of people, greeting them with hugs - even though they had only just seen each other that afternoon, lately, all the social norms people were used to stand out to Anaisha as silly and useless.

Anaisha could feel the eyes on her as she walked through the room, but she ignored them as Naira glared at people who looked on for too long.

The girls said their 'hellos 'and went back to their group of friends. The year group was obviously small, so everyone was pretty good friends, but of course, like anywhere, you meet people who you connect with a little more and make your own little family. Right now, the girls were talking to them.

Zade swaggered towards them, enveloping Anaisha in a hug, and kissed her head. She smiled and hugged him back tightly. She loved his hugs. She frowned. It felt different than before, and he had become taller and more sinewy. She grinned to herself; it was weird to see your friends growing up.

"You good?" He mumbled, looking at her directly through dark onyx eyes. She shrugged. "He's just as bad as you if that helps" he smiled. Zade and Andries spoke often. Anaisha's face fell.

Naira punched him in the shoulder and said, "Shut up, Zade!"

158

He rubbed his shoulder, "you're stronger than you look," he said, looking down at her. His dark eyes widened just for a second. She was shorter than him, even in heels. She squinted "don't mess with me."

"I don't mess with pretty girls" Anaisha's brows shot up. Naira pushed Zade away. "Shut up," she laughed as she rolled her eyes.

Zade started to smile as he caught Anaisha's eyes.

Anaisha pursed her lips, "you look very handsome, Zade," she carried on, trying to divert the conversation. He did look good. He had matured since the summer. He had cut his hair into a gradual fade and had some light stubble growing on his chin, accentuating his large eyes and lips. It suited him. He was mixed race, black and white, and he had a slight tan that was now fading.

The group sort of separated into smaller conversations as Naira spoke with the rest, and Anaisha carried on speaking to Zane, catching up.

Akihiko stood with Naira and Calista, towering over the two with a hand in his pockets, swaying to the music with a drink in his hand. From her peripheral vision, Naira saw him turn his head every few minutes. He was looking at something or someone, and she wasn't sure what. Calista's eyes drifted towards the door as a pretty girl in a short black dress walked in. Her eyes lit up. "I'll be right back," Calista simpered. Naira's eyes sparkled, "see you in a bit." This was the girl Calista had been 'talking 'to.

"You good?" She said, turning to Aki, now that they were alone.

He blinked in surprise, "yeah, why?" His hand tightened around his glass. "You just seem to be looking for someone?" She scrunched her eyebrows.

He scrunched his long nose, "no, I'm not," he said as he took a sip of his drink. "if you say so," she said inter a silvery voice as she played with her bangles.

Laughter and chatter filled the air.

Naira looked at the dance floor. It looked so sad and lonely with nobody to accompany it. No one was dancing yet.

She looked around and saw people's feet tapping to the base and swaying slightly to the music.

She motioned to Calista's drink with a little swish of her fingers, and Calista handed it over. She took a swig. Alcohol wasn't allowed on campus, but if anyone wanted any, the small rooms could cater to those wants. "I want to dance," she announced.

"I'm down," Kiara replied. They made their way to Zane and Anaisha, who were still deep in conversation.

"Come on, let's dance!" Kiara told both of them. "No one is dancing," Anaisha said.

"Well, someone has to start," Naira said, smiling and putting her hands out for both of them to hold as she dragged them onto the dance floor, walking backward and already swaying her hips to the beat.

Soon enough, the 6 of them were dancing. They were the only ones on the floor, but when you were with your friends, who cared?

The DJ looked up and saw them on the floor. He got excited, 'finally 'he thought.

They danced to the music, it was good music, and as the song died out, Naira swayed over to the DJ and whispered something in his ear. She requested a song she was sure would get people moving. He nodded at her, and she went back to dancing.

The song came on, and Naira let out a little whoop.

Like a shot, more people came on the floor as they all sang the lyrics and let themselves go.

The DJ now let down his headphones. He held one to his ear as he remixed the song spinning the discs and dancing a bit himself. Now the whole room was jumping and dancing to the music. They all let themselves go and loosen up. A feeling of euphoria melted throughout the air as people got closer and danced and danced and danced.

Anaisha danced too. She was glad she came as she watched her friends. She looked at Naira, and a smile spread across her face as she watched her. Her long, curled hair flowed around her in hues of black and dyed brown and gold as she moved her head from side to side. She looked so graceful and happy as she let her arms in the air. Anaisha could see the little tattoos on her forearm peeking through the cascade of bracelets on her left wrist. Anaisha laughed to herself as

160

she remembered how she had tried to talk her out of them, thinking they were tacky. She hadn't listened, obviously.

She watched her cousin dance around, not caring what anybody thought, and that energy was intoxicating to all those around her. She remembered a time when her little Nairu was a shy and nervous person. When anxiety had plagued her mind and decisions, she fretted over every little thing, unable to do anything. She remembered when she wouldn't be able to go to class, let alone a party. She had come so far, had grown into this young, fearless girl. At that moment, in the midst of the lights and music and laughter, she was so proud of her cousin for overcoming her demons and shutting out the voices in her head. In a year, she had grown and changed so much. It was a beautiful growth.

Anaisha had been worrying for quite a long time at quite a young age, but despite that, she was still young. There would be more to come... better and worse, and she knew that.

And tonight, though she was still followed by the grey clouds of woe swirling above her head, the rains of sadness felt more like a drizzle than a downpour, and rather than drowning in the water pooling around her, she treads. She kept her head above and just enjoyed the feeling of being able to swim.

Naira saw her watching and shimmied over to her unabashedly. They laughed as they spun each other around like when they were kids.

They danced and danced and danced. Anaisha was basically panting and went off to sit on the black leather sofas on the left of the room. She didn't realize that someone had followed her as she sat down and felt someone take a seat next to her: Akihiko. The whole room was dancing now. They were the only ones sitting.

"Hello," she said as she took her her 'ugh '- She sighed in relief. The feeling was heavenly.

"Hiii," he slurred. He was a little tipsy she could tell from the way his pink lips parted, half open. She, on the other hand, was 'dance drunk. 'And swayed to the music.

"So, how are you?" He asked, turning himself fully to face her. He had a very calm way of speaking, slow, but not boringly so. It was sort of quiet and smoky. He sounded like a sea breeze.

"I'm actually great - how are you?" She said, smiling. "I am fantastic."

"I'm sure," she said, looking at the glass tripping in his hand and the glossy sheen on his eyes.

 "You look beautiful, by the way. I didn't get to tell you that before" he looked at her through slanted black eyes that were half closed at the moment.

She giggled. "Thank you. It's Naira's," she said, motioning to her dress

"Yeah, I like the colour –" he said, touching the hair that lay on the nape of his neck. He still had his headband on, a thin, wiry one that curled around his head. He didn't mean the dress.

It was funny, and they were basically talking about nothing. But talking to Akihiko was nice. He was always chilled, but today the reservedness he usually had seemed to ebb away softly as he spoke to her. He shifted his legs and knocked her knees as he spoke to her, taking a sip of his drink, gazing down at her, and then looking around.

While they sat, he bent his head to look down at her. What he was doing was more like gazing. But she hadn't realized. He had a long face and was handsome with a long sharp nose and defined lips and thick, defined brows, but still, youth flowed through him in his looks: the sharp yet large ears and the little acne that textured across his skin and uneven hairline. He was sharp and defined, mixed in with youth. You could tell he would be dashing as he grew up. She thought he had kind eyes and an easy smile, such anthesis to Andries. It annoyed her how all her thoughts led back to him, like all the roads she drove in her mind led to the same destination.

But today, she let it go and pulled over instead of driving further.

She seemed happier today, he thought, as she laughed softly at his stupid jokes. She looked radiant today as a calm, soft sunniness poured through the clouds she was shrouded in lately. It made him happy to see her like that. He was glad she came. He realized he said that aloud. Shit - he thought. However, he lounged back, took a sip, and thought, 'nevermind.'

He pulled his arm to the back of the sofa, so his drink dangled down between his finger, tipping over but not slipping. She never noticed how tall and gangly he was before.

He saw a silhouette dance towards them, and he couldn't make out who. His vision was a bit fuzzy right now. The silhouette now came closer and spoke.

"What are you guys doing?" Naira slowed her words right now and was louder than necessary as the music reverberated around them.

"Just chatting," Anaisha replied, looking up.

"Aah, just talking, I see," she said. She couldn't help the sly smile she had in her eyes as she looked over at Aki. Anaisha didn't catch the smile as she pressed her legs, and Aki barely noticed it.

As Anaisha and Akihiko talked about nothing and laughed at their silly jokes, the rest of their little group alternated from running to the dance floor barefooted when the music was too good to refuse and standing around talking and laughing at inside jokes with the people that understood them most and the ones who were living through the same feelings and emotions.

The same sentiment ran through their veins - the pounding footsteps of youth.

Being young in all its glory: the sound of uncontrolled and unashamed loud laughter and the ease of natural, painless movement and the excitement at everything, new things and silly little things that only came with inexperience. The whole room revelled in it as it bolted around the room, sprinting and jumping at every corner. They knew that this feeling, this youth, would not last forever, so they enjoyed every moment. The experiences of age had already caught on to some of them.

So they danced to good music and laughed with close friends. Love and energy echoed throughout the room.

It was all they really needed. Well, it was all anybody really needed.

lonely without you

Andries was in the garden smoking, there were some other people outside, who he didn't know. music was loud, but soft enough to talk, and it was nice. Andries was sitting in between Amar and Julian on the sofa. He had stopped drinking.

When he went back inside, he sat back down on the sofa, his head was spinning a bit and he lay his head back.

"You good, Ries?" Amar asked, who was sitting next to him. Andries nodded, and smiled lopsidedly.

Julian turned too, and put a comforting hand on his knee.

"Water?" He asked, kind brown eyes.

"No" Andries said, his voice hoarse. They had saved the place in between them for him. He had been sitting there before he went outside for a smoke, and they had kept it for him.

That night after the club they ended up at some students house in town, It was actually nice.

It was a four bedroom house. In the small living room lay two pretty, comfortable sofa's, in the center was a glass table with blooming flowers on it and an open box of pizza. there were knitting needles and a bundle of pale blue colored yarn on it too. There were plant pots around the place and a flat screen, a little box of blankets in the corner, and a big glass door that led to garden.

He could imagine the morning after, the residents lounging around the place with a blanket on, watching TV. The knitter, knitting.

There was a matte huge black lamp in the corner, he thought the bulb may have been broken because there were unlit fairy lights wrapped around the whole thing.

They had some neon light machine in the corner, blue, red and green spilled around the whole room. It was nice, actually.

The house was of some friends of Adela's and Amar's. they were a year older, and one of them was on their course.

Everyone was piled on the couch, some were drinking and some had stopped considering they had probably had enough. The music was loud, but soft enough for people to talk and laugh, he would've liked this.

Amar made a joke, and everyone laughed. He leaned back, putting an arm behind the sofa. Amar and Julian, stayed in the seats next to Ries, who was pretty silent the whole time.

The room was full and there were quite a few people in it, it seemed like more because of how small the place was. It was full, and there were alot of people he could talk to. But one person wasn't… and he would never be.

The threat of tears pierced Andries's eyes. It burned.

There was a drink on the table, it was Amar's he thought. He took a sip, it burned.

He could never bring him to things like this, he would never know what it was like to experience so many things with him by his side.

If he could control fate, he would trade everything to just sit in a basement with Mykal strumming his guitar, talking to him. Just to hear his voice one more time.

On their way back to their place, they walked slowly. It was only a ten minute walk, Inara was with Andries.

"You know, they say there's a reason for everything"

"There is" Inara said.

He looked at her, blue eyes so oddly bright. "What? What can be the reason… for this"

And truly, even though she was a believer of something, someone. She didn't question her beliefs, but she didn't know either. She didn't know what the reason was.

The Day After the Dance

"Fuck this," Naira said to herself. She had the tendency to talk to herself when she got frustrated.

She was in her free period and trying, emphasis on 'trying 'to do her Business Studies homework. Usually, she would have called Ries to help her, but he was probably busy right now. She sat on a light brown wooden table in the library. The library, any library, really was one of her favourite places to study. She almost felt like she had escaped into another world. The labyrinth of books always inspired her. Whenever she got sick of working, she could walk around and pick up a book and get lost for a while. Sometimes, she would just stare at all the books around her, and she figured that if people could write and finish a book, she could focus on whatever she was doing. She was sitting deep in the library. It was a huge place with two levels; shelves streamed along the two floors, and in between some of the shelves were large gaps on which desks and tables were scattered.

She took a deep breath and looked down at the book, blinking at the page, and then thoughts rang through her head like an impatient person ringing a doorbell. Naira still hadn't told Anaisha what Andries had told her.

The words reverberated in her mind. She gnawed at her bottom lip.

Should she even tell her? She looked toward the stained glass windows, light and colour blending together. The library often felt like a holy place...

"Tell her *I love her,* and *I will* be a better man."

She had promised... but she knew that if she told Anaisha what he said, she would wait for him, there was no question about it.

Maybe those breaking up was a blessing... maybe she wasn't meant to tell her. She ran a heavy hand through her hair.

"Tell her... tell her I will become worthy of her again."

Even Andries didn't think Anaisha was the right person for him. They were great at one point, but... not forever. *"Please."*

But was it her decision to make? "It's just too consequential," she whispered to herself.

"Just tell her that."

She looked at the questions again, squinting.

She tried to re-focus on the questions. It was a few questions strung together on an A4 white piece of paper that they had to answer. A few lines left for an explanation.

The questions varied in depth and importance.

She couldn't concentrate. She tapped her chin. What if Andries and Anaisha were *meant to be*? Was she the one standing in between fate? But what if their fate was destined for ruins? What if she was part of their fate? Was she controlling their fate? Or was she helping them? Was it her job, or should she let them make their own mistakes?

Love wasn't meant to be fights and tears and all passion, wasn't it meant to be slow burning and honest?

She felt her breath quicken and her pulse race. The thoughts were all mushing together, taking up too much space and coming too fast. Her body knew it. Her breath quickened, and her pulse raced.

She knew how to handle this, and she had done it a thousand times. She let all the thoughts in.

1. What if they hate you?
2. What if she was standing in between their fate?
3. What if she was a part of their fate and was meant to make the decision for them?
4. What if she was wrong?
5. What if she was right?

She listened to them the way she listened to her mother lecturing her in the annoying yet loving way that she did.

Then silently, she told them.

"Okay, thank you for the opinion, but you can fuck off now."

She closed her eyes and inhaled for 6 seconds, and exhaled for 10. She lay her hand on her stomach and felt the breaths. She sang the lyrics to a song she knew, and then she opened her eyes. And she was calm.

She wasn't embarrassed to do her *exercises* in public anymore. If it made her feel better, she couldn't be asked who was watching.

She had the answer. She would make an informed decision and go with her gut. Okay. She applied the same thing to her answers, but still, it was hard.

She finished the questions. She had no more homework left for today.

She made her way over to the elevator at the corner of the second floor. With a push of a button, the lift came up, and the metal doors opened automatically. The lift was hidden in the wall, and you could really only find it if you were looking for it.

The doors opened to the first floor silently. This felt like too sacrosanct of a situation to deal with. The bottom floor was different than the first because, in the centre of the room, a slim blood-red velvet carpet slithered straight down the middle. As she walked, she resolved to make her decision before she reached the exit door. She settled on a decision as she opened the door, leading herself back into the world. OR out of the underworld.

The wind blew her hair into her face, and quickly Naira tied her hair back. She was sitting outside in the courtyard alone, ready to have her lunch. It was one of her favourite meals, and the food was usually a hit or miss at the academy. And they were specially made for her. She smiled to herself as she was about to take a bite of her fake pepperoni, avocado, lettuce, and pepper-jack cheese sandwich with multi-grain bread. It was only slightly toasted, just enough so the cheese melted but not to ruin the texture of the avocado. She was very particular.

She leaned over to take a bite and jumped up in her seat as two rough hands grabbed her shoulder. She heard the laughter and didn't bother turning.

"You dicks," she said, cleaning up the lettuce that had fallen on her lap.

Zade and Akihoko couldn't keep themselves together. Aki actually snorted. She was used to it "Sit." She commanded.

Zade sat on the opposite bench. Aki sat next to her and took a bite of her sandwich. She was happy that they finally got here. The girls were in a class while the three of them had a free period. It was the last day of the school week, and this had become their new routine, taking advantage of the free on the last day of the week.

"Sorry, practice ran late," Akihoko said as he gulped down the bite.

"I didn't know you joined the team?" She asked Zade, eyes flicking up as he sat down.

His face turned smug, "I mean, I had the charm, the looks, and then I found out that girls dig the whole sporty thing soo..." he touched the nape of his neck.

Naira cleared her throat "that's too bad," she pouted. "I have a thing for musicians, actually," she said, turning to Aki, the mischievous glint in her green eyes.

Aki raised his eyebrows, "you do" he nodded.

"Well, I've also started learning the guitar," Zade added. "Since when?" Aki asked, leaning forward on his elbows.

"Well..." He pressed his tongue against his cheek, thinking, "I decided to start about a minute ago, but I think I'll be pretty good," he said smoothly.

Naira bit her tongue, but she couldn't suppress the little laugh that came out. Aki smirked, eyes flicking between both of them as the wind picked up around them, red and yellow leaves swirling on the ground.

"What did you guys get on the Sociology test?" Naira said, taking a bite of her food.

Zade shovelled around his backpack and took out a crumpled paper, handing it to them. Naira's eyes widened. "That's amazing!" "I did so shit," she groaned, playing with the bracelet on her wrist.

"Zade, why don't you tutor her or something?" Aki said, taking another bite of Naira's sandwich.

"Oh my god, would you?" Her bracelets jangled as she grabbed his arm. Her small eyes became wider and pleading.

"Sure, I could make time." He nodded. He hoped he looked as casual as he was trying to as she smiled and squeezed his hand in thanks.

Aki smirked next to Naira and gave himself a little imaginary pat on the back.

"I got them! I got them!" Anaisha yelled as she came running toward them, closely followed by Calista and Kiara.

She squinted away from the sun as the gleam fell into her eyes. The huge bag on her shoulder was filled to the brim with books and random shit. The textbooks propped in the crook of her elbow. The flask of coffee was in her hand. Her black hair was pulled away from her face with a clip, and the glasses balanced atop her head.

The look of an overwhelming workload and a tiring day. She looked like a proper student. She looked like she was back to normal.

She basically fell down with the weight of all her stuff paired with the ecstatic feeling that was controlling her every action. "Woah! What did you get?" Zade asked, moving down the bench to make space for them.

"My tickets!" She said, waving two shiny rectangular tickets in his face excitedly.

"For a musical..." Kiara announced with a snicker. All her friends were very aware of her undying love for musicals.

"YES!" Anaisha couldn't contain the excitement, she had coveted seats and was waiting for these tickets for ages, and the show had finally come to a small town nearby the academy.

"I got them online and had to stay up till like three in the morning to get them," she said, waving the tickets around like they were a trophy.

"I didn't know people who still watched musicals even stayed up past eight," Zane laughed. "Whatever," Anaisha sang, a superiority in her voice. "You guys are missing out," her eyes glittered as she looked at her tickets. She rolled her shoulders back, with her sunny smile on her lips, "now, as you all can see, I have two tickets, and I am only one person, so who wants to join me?"

Naira stuffed her sandwich into her mouth. "It is getting colder right?" Calista said.

Kiara nodded, "I might need to go run in and get a jacket" "can I come?" Zade asked

"Oh, fuck off" Anaisha smacked her tickets on Zade's head. She rolled her eyes. "I'll just go myself," she laughed. She expected this anyway.

"Are you sure?" She said, waving around her tickets like she was giving out prize money. Aki cleared his throat, "I'll come"

Anaisha's eyes widened "you will?" She couldn't filter the excitement that bled through her voice. "Yeah, I like musicals," he nodded casually.

Naira's eyes slid to Aki "you do?" She arched a brow.

"Yeah," he shrugged. Naira's green-eyed look lingered for a moment longer.

That night, she had gone to her cousin's house for dinner and just saw Anaisha, such a broken version of the person she once was. She couldn't do it because what if Andries didn't change… what if this new, deformed version of himself was who he would be from now on? She could love him. Of course, she did… but she couldn't expect her cousin to be his partner anymore… it just felt wrong, somewhere in her heart, and she was the kind of person that led with her heart.

That was the problem of trusting people that led with their hearts. They would follow it.

Chapter 6

'Meet Inara'

Inara plunged into her bed. She stretched leisurely. Her small bed in her dorm had never felt so sumptuous. She lay on her bed and rose on her elbows, letting her hair fall down her back as she gazed at her room, letting the music surround her space. One part of the wooden shelving unit was filled with overpriced textbooks she had recently brought. She took a deep breath and swallowed. She was grateful for what she was born into. A family with enough money, where she didn't need to worry about things like how expensive a textbook was or the price of tuition. No student loans or anything like that. The other part of the shelving unit was filled with two notebooks and books with sheet music. The notebooks had the songs that she had written, which no one had heard yet. Her hair blew backward from the breeze coming through the window across her. There was also a wooden fan on the ceiling spinning around loftily, causing everything in the room to move softly and slowly. She had brought a hanging board photo display, so there were photos on the wall next to her bed, and her guitar fit in the space underneath the table. When they first moved in, she was fine… excited. But then the homesickness kicked in. So, she set about putting up pictures of her friends and family and her home and buying throw blankets and fluffy pillows. They were all white and dark blue, somewhat matching the pale-greyish blue walls. She brought lights and a good set of speakers. She put music on, and soon she felt better. The sun was bright outside, and she could see people walking around, mostly students. The sparkling sunshine glinted in her room in her eyes. A sunny day always reminded her of home.

Inara relaxed for a bit more. She had a shower and put on shorts and a hoodie. She had a sudden surge of energy and decided to go to Adela's room. Adela lived two floors below her, so she decided not to use the elevator. She didn't even realize she was still wearing her bedroom slippers.

She walked out of the elevator and reached room 1705. It was funny, all the same doors and places, but when you stepped into someone's room, it could be completely different. Adela's room was a lot messier than hers and an orange bedspread and cream-colored pillows. Her photos were in frames across her table, and two posters from the 70s were on the wall they had found in a vintage shop. She knocked on the door. There was no reply, so she let herself in, as she always did.

She screamed. BANG! She closed the door immediately and walked very quickly into the kitchen.

One of Adela's roommates was on the table studying; Mason was his name.

"Hey, Inara, what's up?" He asked her. She was panting slightly, "Are you okay?" He stood up. A second later, a half-naked Ahmed ran into the kitchen, buttoning up his pants.

"CARE TO KNOCK?"

"CARE TO LOCK THE DOOR?"

Suddenly, she turned around.

He touched her shoulder, "Inara-" she shook his hand off "your zip is open," she said, pressing her eyes shut. "Whoops," he said, turning around. The sound of the zip was awkwardly loud.

"Ohhh," Mason said, sitting back down, "I heard them all afternoon. That's when these became very useful" he pointed at the headphones around his neck.

"Hi," Adela came out in a robe. Her voice was higher and sweeter than usual,

"You guys are unbelievable" Inara threw her hands in the air, finally turning around. "Did you see anything?" A flush crept across their faces.

"barely, but I have a scarring image stored," she wagged a finger," no, stuck in my memory." The kitchen door flew open.

"I heard a scream. Are you guys okay?" Amar panted, brown eyes wide. He lived on their floor. Adela sputtered into a laugh, and soon enough, all four of them were laughing uncontrollably.

Amar stood by the door, and a line appeared between his brows.

Ahmed whispered something in his ear, and Amar burst into laughter.

"Lock your door, your animals." His eyes darted between the two of them. "Thank you!" Inara half-shouted as she threw an arm out toward Amar,

172

"Okay, were you guys done?" Inara lifted a brow "or should I come back?" She said, backing away to the door.

"What's up? Was it important" Adela asked, her features switching from laughter to concern. "No, I just wanted to chat" she stroked a hand through her hair.

"You can have her" Ahmed touched the nape of his neck, "the momentum is kind of gone anyway" he grinned.

He gave Adela a quick peck on the cheek and went over to hug Inara.

She scrunched her nose "maybe, tomorrow?" She said, sliding away. "Good call," he said, putting his head down, but he couldn't hide the grin.

Ahmed and Amar both left, shoving each other and laughing like little boys. Adela left the kitchen, and Inara followed, waving goodbye to Mason.

"Maybe...we should go to my room..." Inara's mouth twisted.

"Oh, stop being an idiot. Nothing happened. Come in," she dragged Inara to her room. "So, Ahmed, huh?" She wiggled her brows. "It's kind of a long time coming."

Adela rolled her eyes, but there was a light in them, and she couldn't help the smile that came when you heard the name of someone you liked.

"It is not a bad thing. You guys are very cute," she said in her raspy voice. Another eye roll and another smile.

"Oh my god, you really like him!" Inara said, slapping her with a pillow and a shocked face. Adela was all talk when things or people didn't matter to her, but once it did, she was as silent as a mouse.

Adela didn't answer with words but just a coy smile as she unconsciously twirled her blonde hair.

Inara's grey eyes widened "oh my god!"

"Never mind that," she said, shooing her off "tell me what's up?" She said, perking up and trying to change the subject.

"Excuse me, madam, you're going to have to give me a minute to comprehend this information." Inara couldn't help it. She let out a little squeal, which she knew would completely agonize Adela. But there was that little glow on her friend's face, and she couldn't help it. "Okay, now stop being a freak and tell me what's up?"

Inara lay down on the bed, "nothing, I'm just bored."

"Okay, let's chill. I don't have any work to do tonight anyway."

"I do, but I'm procrastinating, I had band practice all day, and I am exhausted" Inara closed her eyes for a second.

Illicit Midnight Moments

Akihoko looked at himself in center mirror, he wasn't the type of person that usually checked himself out in the center mirror of his car, but he also wasn't the type of person who felt this weird fluttery feeling in his chest and rubbed his hands along his pants. He cracked his knuckles. and couldn't help but laugh at himself.

Was this what nerves felt like? He couldn't tell if he liked it or not; there was also. He blew out a short breath. He didn't feel the "butterflies" in his stomach but in his chest.

She saw him before he saw her. She had just closed the door behind her, and checked that she had her keys when she saw him sitting in his car outside her house, one hand on the steering wheel as he checked the watch on his wrist. He was perfectly on time. On-time but never in a rush. She liked that about him. The way she felt cool and calm when she was around him.

"Hi," he breathed, as she opened his car door and sat inside. They were in the same sphere now. Breathing in the same air. He was gazing down at her as she looked up at him. She thought he smelled good. Musky and boyish. And he thought she was absolutely radiant in her dark blue dress, and glossy dark hair. Everything about her was lovely and bright to him, like watching the stars you'd look away but you didn't quite want to. He was wearing all black, a black polo shirt and black jeans. It dawned on her the way the dark clothes accentuated everything about him. His dark eyes looked darker and more slanted, and his black hair looked blacker and softer. He looked like the feeling of staying up late at night when you should be sleeping, but you just can't help it because there's something magical and alluring about the night-time, and you just don't want to miss it.

"No headband today?" She joked lightly.

He consciously touched his hair, and with a shake of his head, he laughed and drove forward. Damn, he should have said something funny back.

They sat down, the show hadn't begun yet, and chatter filled the air beneath them. They were up in the mezzanine. Below them was an array of red velvet seats. Two floors from them, small clusters of people took up the seats. Older couples sat together, some with what seemed to be their grandchildren. It was a small town, so the theatre wasn't huge, but still, it was classic and grand.

There was something atmospheric and beautiful about it. Sitting there, you felt like you had stepped through a time machine to a different decade where everything was grandiose and impressive. A magnificent crystal chandelier dripped from the ceiling in the centre. While the thick red velvet curtains swayed along the rim of the stage from the mezzanine, they could see the orchestra pit and the violinists tuning their instruments and readying themselves.

Anaisha sat and took a breath in. She felt a pang of something deep in her chest, memories, and nostalgia.

She hadn't been to a musical whilst studying at the academy with anyone else other than Mykal. She looked to her left and half accepted to see the dark, tall, rugged figure of Mykal next to her - tapping at the arm of the seat excitedly or fidgeting with his fingers, waiting for the curtains to go up.

But instead, it was Aki calmly sitting on the seat, long legs stretched out. There was a sick, twisted feeling in her stomach. She tucked her hair behind her ear, biting her lip hard.

"You okay?

"Hmm," she nodded with a close-lipped smile. This happened sometimes, she gulped, which felt tough for some reason. Tears stung her eyes.

The lights dimmed, and a voice on a speaker announced that the show was about to begin. The red velvet curtains came up, and the show began.

Anaisha quickly wiped the tear that dropped from her eye, thanking whoever was up there that it was dark now. Then she smiled to herself, willing herself to smile at the fact that she had these memories even if they would never happen again. She focused all her attention on the stage as a scene of an auction began. A man with a thick accent and perfect annunciation spoke. And suddenly, out of know where a symphony began.

It was haunting and strong, Akihoko looked over at Anaisha. Her eyes were intent on the stage as she got lost in the song.

The red-headed actor began singing, she was beautiful, and her voice was pure and wonderful. Her name was Christine. Sometime in the musical, that tune began again. The one from the beginning.

"In sleep, he sang to me."

But this time, it was a mix of orchestra and rock. It was haunting and mysterious but so compelling. Beautifully sinister.

"Sing once again with me, our strange duet."

The Phantom began to sing, and his voice was one to be reckoned with. It could have only been honed with years of training. Akihoko couldn't help but tap his feet along with the beat.

"I am the mask you wear; it's me, they hear."

He was captivated, but through his peripheral vision, he saw Anaisha mouthing the words. Of course, she knew the score. She didn't even realize she was doing it. She was on the edge of her seat, and her eyes were enchanted with the whole thing.

She watched the show the way Christine watched the Phantom, with a certain type of fascination. But unlike Christine, she wasn't afraid, and she was delighted.

"Sing, my angel of music," he commanded her. And oh, did she sing.

They were nearing the end of the musical, and the last song began. It was tense, and Aki really wasn't sure how it would end.

Akihoko felt for the Phantom, the way his fate changed him into the monster he was. So didn't that mean that he wasn't actually a monster? If it wasn't his fault?

"Pity comes too late."

176

He couldn't change. It was too much, he gave the world time, and they threw him away.

"This haunted face holds no horror for me now. It's in your soul that the true distortion lies."

Anaisha gasped, a small gasp at that line. He looked over at her quickly, and her face grew soft. Something about that lyric got to her.

Then the three voices began singing in an argument. In a culmination of the three voices singing over each other. Dark and chilling.

But then it lifted and turned into something beautiful; something about it stirred something inside him. Beautiful and tragic.

"Pitiful creature of darkness

What kind of life have you known?

God give me the courage to show you, you are not alone."

The symphony began again loud and clear as if letting the words sink in. It was evocative. And then his mind changed. He let her go.

With great power that could only come from the sadness of knowing you had to say goodbye forevermore to the one person you loved, the phantom sang.

"You alone can make my song take flight. It's over now, the music of the night."

The music swelled powerfully into a crescendo.

Small tears silently dropped from Anaisha's eyes, and she blinked tightly and let them drop. It was so poignant that she could feel the beat of her heart in her chest, and she could feel the goosebumps raise across her arms. As if her soul was so strongly touched that it couldn't contain the emotion, so it had to spread it throughout the rest of her body.

They were in a park now. It was nearby to the theatre, and the lateness meant that there was barely anyone there. Only a few other people. The leaves crunched in a satisfying nature under Akihiko's shoes. The smell of the cool night and Anaisha's jasmine perfume lingered around them. Spring was coming slowly this year. So the yellow glow of the lampposts only complimented the colours of the autumn leaves that weren't ready to leave just yet. The steady heartbeat of the midnight wind blew through the pair, invigorating them with its mysterious breeze. It made Anaisha speak with more passion, and Akihoko felt like he was in a dreamscape. They walked in the park opposite the theatre and spoke about the musical. He listened to her talk. Everything about her was shadowy and floating. Like she was made of a powerful gust of wind. The younger sister of the steady wind that blew tonight.

She spoke, not with her hands but with her eyes. It was like she told them, "you might be small, but it doesn't mean you are not mighty." Every so often, she would turn to him, and he could see them in all their glory and expression. And then, when she turned, he saw the shadow of her hooked nose. He liked that too. It made her look strong and unmistakable.

"I don't understand why the phantom didn't end up with Christine?" Aki wondered aloud.

"Some say it's because she was the first person to show him kindness and compassion," she gulped, "so he learns by example, and it causes him to find that in himself." She took a breath and intertwined her hands behind her back. "But personally, I think they weren't a good relationship. He tried to help her, but he ended up wanting to control and hurt her. And he could because he had that power over her." She took a glimpse at the night sky.

He nodded, his mouth twisted, "but that was society doing. Because of his facial abnormality, society judged him, and that" he cleared his throat "broke him. But then," he shrugged, "by showing him kindness, she does help him and kind of heals him."

"Yeah..." she spoke softly and pondered for a second.

"I guess the real act of love was when he let her go." He said in his sea-breeze way.

She thought for a second more, and his eyes flickered toward her. He could see the click in her brain. "He wanted her to live a life where she could see the light of Paris rather than live in the sewers with him. He could have kept her underground with him and kept her to himself. They already had a relationship, so she probably would have fallen in love with him. But he chose her happiness over his own. He chose her happiness over his own, even if that meant letting her go."

"A true act of love..."Aki smiled to himself for a moment. "Selflessness," he whispered. He kept walking. "In a way, it's a tragedy. The phantom has the trauma from his childhood which leads him to believe that he can only have Christine through force. When if he had been kinder

178

to her, she probably would have chosen him over Raoul because they had a deeper relationship. With the music and everything."

Her steps slowed down as her perspective opened. "Your right, he is kind of a tragic hero," she breathed out through her nose and walked over to a bench on the side. She sat down and wistfully smiled up at the crescent moon.

He followed and sat down next to her "what is it?" He nudged her with his shoulder. "Just," she looked up at him, "happy." Dark eyes are glistening.

"The show *was* fantastic."

She nodded with a little laugh, "it was. But I'm happy about the fact that I found someone who likes musicals as much as me. You don't understand. Mykal used to go with me to musicals when I watched them at the academy. It was something we did together." she smiled at the memory.

"After he died." She swallowed. It was still hard for her to say sometimes. "I didn't know if I would be able to step into this theatre again." She looked up at the sky, still. She didn't look at his face. This was hard for her to say.

He pressed his lips together. "I didn't know that," he said softly. She shrugged.

"Plus, I didn't think I would find someone who actually enjoyed watching them" she nudged him lightly with a twinkly laugh.

"Thanks for coming" her mouth turned up

"Sometimes we do things because the people we love like them. It is not unimaginable." He was looking at her with dilated pupils in those dark slanted eyes and full lips.

She bit her lips, and something in her melted, and without thinking, she tipped her head up, he bent down, and they kissed. She wrapped her arms around his neck, and he brought a hand to curve around her jaw. He was a really good kisser. He wasn't in any rush, just calm and cool, the sensation washing over them. They broke apart, and she brought her neck down to his shoulder.

With her head bent on his shoulder. He put a cool arm over her shoulders "for what it's worth. I'm glad I came. I want to see another one if you'll have me."

She muffled something into his shoulder, and he felt her head move on his shoulder. I guess that was a yes.

Red and orange leaves swirled around their feet, the night wind blowing around them and the stars shining above. The moon was watching down.

As they sat in their beautiful, warm silence, she turned and looked at him for a second.

His long nose and pointed ears and warm yellow skin and full lips and those slanted midnight-coloured eyes. She could see the slightly bumpy texture of his skin, he was still young, but somehow she could tell he would be a handsome man. A good one, a kind one. She was grateful to have someone in her life like him.

"It was a good musical." She laughed softly.

We'll be okay, won't we?

Andries entered his room now. It was Saturday morning, and he went out to a bar with some people he didn't know that well. They were on his course. Seemed nice enough but not good friends. He needed a nap. He had just been going to his lectures, coming home, maybe making some food, and heading to bed. Sometimes, he would go to the gym but not always. He'd barely spoken to his friends in a week, even though he lived with them. But he just didn't care right now. They all had the same room, but he was pretty messy. Hoodies and t-shirts are thrown on the floor. Sneakers are all over the place. The white duvet was strewn across the bed. He used to be a fairly neat person. Things had their place, but he was in a new environment, and they were leaving soon, so what was the use, he thought.

An empty water bottle lay on the wooden side tables, and on the left table, right under the lamp, was a leather notebook, untouched. A cleaning lady came once a week, and he was asleep when she knocked on his door, so he stopped knocking after a while. But Andries wasn't too bothered. He was weirdly exhausted and pummelled onto the bed. He hadn't don't laundry. He needed to change his bedsheets but couldn't be bothered. He pulled the dirty duvet on top of him and fell asleep. A little sliver of sunlight poured in through the thick curtains. Now he could have used the black-out function, but he liked the feeling of knowing that there was light outside and he wasn't alone.

180

Andries stretched in his bed, awakening every muscle in his body. His eyes still felt a little heavy as he made his way to the sink barefooted. He splashed some water on his face, and it energized him. He still had some unfinished business. He balanced his arms on the sink and stared into the mirror. It lit up on the sides, showing him every part of him. Nothing was hidden away. He stared.

He ran a hand over his now dishevelled curly brown hair. He touched the scar on his left eyebrow. He remembered how he got it, and he was playing tag with Mykal when they were about 10 years old. Their parents had told them to stop, saying someone would get hurt, and obviously, he ran straight into the grandfather clock in the dining room. He laughed to himself. He used to hate his scar, but Anaisha once told him.

'I like it, and it makes you look badass. 'He had laughed, and she carried on. 'I like the way an experience of yours is on your face, like you can *see* your story just by looking at you. And it's a good conversation starter'. It was funny how that scar was on his face, but the most painful ones, the ones that were the hardest to bear and probably most important for people to see and talk about, were invisible.

 The next evening Ries knocked on her door. "Come in," Inara said. "I need some help, actually" "Ries?" She said as she opened the door.

He was holding two mugs and held one out to her. Peppermint tea.

"Thank you," she said as she took it. He followed her into the room and sat on her bed. Her guitar was on the floor, and she picked it up and began tuning it again.

He knew she played guitar, and they could hear it echo through the walls… it was always a nostalgic sound to him. She began strumming easily, humming along as he looked at the photo frames on her bedside table and windowsill. Her parents, family, and friends. Some of the faces were familiar to him. There was even a picture of her at a recital with Mykal. She was singing on stage, behind the piano, and Mykal was playing the electric guitar. They looked fucking cool.

"I love this picture," he said with a smile. He'd said it before to her once.

"Oh, yeah, that reminds me" she put the guitar down and stood up, leaning on the table to reach a shelf that was bolted on the wall above.

She got out a little envelope. "I got this for you" she handed him the envelope. He took it slowly and edged his finger underneath the glued part. There were two photos, one copy of the one she had in the photo frame of the two of them and one of Mykal alone, on stage playing a solo on the black electric guitar.

"Oh, Inara… thank you" he looked up at her, those blue eyes poignant.

"Of course," she nodded and picked the guitar back up as she sat back down. He took a breath in as he looked at the photos again. He leaned back on her bed and drank from his cup.

"Are you drinking coffee right now?" She looked up incredulously, still playing. It was ten at night.

"I don't sleep anyway," he smirked.

She smiled, but there was a little bit of worry in her grey eyes. She stopped playing for a minute and took a sip of her own drink, "So, what's up? I've hardly seen you, not even on the weekend… " there was a little edge in her rasp, "you've ignored all my messages… I thought you just wanted to be alone for a bit" she had seen him a couple of times over the break when they went back home, but they had also been busy with their own friends and families.

He took another sip. "I just- I don't know, really" he cleared his throat and scratched the scar on his brow. "I'm back now, though," he laughed sardonically.

"Okay." She said calmly. "Just don't get lost on us again, okay? If you don't want to talk or whatever, just chill… hang out."

He nodded. He would. He felt better now anyway. But his 'better 'lately wasn't all that great.

He closed his eyes and leaned back as he listened to her play for a bit. It was a beautiful melody that she kept humming along to…

She put her guitar down after some time. "No, keep going," he said.

She shook her head, "I'm done. I have to give my fingers a break anyway," she simpered, looking down at her scarred fingertips.

182

"Oh my god! I have something to tell you, by the way," she said as she crossed her legs over one another and leaned on the chair. Even when she was excited, she spoke sort of calmly. Her voice was still soothing. She filled him in on the Adela and Ahmed situation.

"Fuck off" he was grinning now.

He leaped off the bed, opened her door, and popped her head out. "Ahmed!" He shouted, "get your ass in Inu's room."

Two minutes later, Ahmed walked in. Ducking through the doorway, he was so tall he had to duck. "What's up?" He laughed as he walked in.

"She told me."

"Oh, fuck" Ahmed started laughing and jumped on Inara's bed, essentially making it shake.

That night Adela came over too, and Amar and Julian, and they were all just hanging out, laughing and chilling. They even smoked a joint.

"Blow it out, bro... the fire alarm will go off," Adela said to Julian. Andries didn't like smoking, and it just made things worse.

It was nice, and he hadn't felt like this in this place in a long time. This feeling of being with your friends and sharing jokes and even secrets. They stayed like that the rest of the night and didn't go for dinner. Instead, they ordered in. He missed it.

When they all headed back to their own bedrooms, it was around 2 am, and Andries was smiling. The wind was picking up more ferociously, he tried to close the door of the little balcony outside his room, but it wouldn't budge. Something clicked in his head, and on impulse, he stepped outside and sat down. His room faced the forest area of the school would a little balcony in his room that faced the forest. He leaned against the glass door crossing his legs over one another, and watched the trees sway more violently. Only a full moon was visible in the sky, barely a star in sight. He was exhausted, they went diving today, and his eyes fell droopier, his head lulling. But he didn't want to go to bed.

In an instant, he woke up from a strike of lightning. He blinked, rubbing his eyes. Was he imaging it?

Thunder struck, and rain poured down.

He pushed himself up, rough hands. And he took a step out from the shaded area of the balcony, sitting down. Sitting in the rain. In the darkness, he could barely see the raindrops, but he could feel them, feel the small slaps on his skin. Feel it soak through his clothes.

He didn't know when but he had started crying, and he couldn't tell if they were tears or droplets of water on his face. OR the tears and raindrops had faded into one.

There was heat running through him now. And the rain wasn't cooling it down. It was only firing it up. Lightning struck. Thunder rumbled and the rain kept going. Harder and harder. Scarily so. No one could stop it. It was unconquerable.

Did the rain take Mykal away, with all its force and power? Who had enough power to take him away? Who was to blame? Who was stronger than the two of them that had to do this to them? "Why?" He said, banging the railing.

"How could you take him away from me?" He said, screaming up at the sky. The dark sky and the pouring drops of water kept coming, harder and harder. No answer was given.

"He was the better part of me?" shouting louder, crying harder. "Take me instead! Take me!" he sobbed, dropping to his knees. "Please," he whispered.

And the rain kept pouring. Going and going. Without any answer. Andries drowned.

The next morning. The trees looked so lush, and the whole sky was bright, blue, and beautiful. Little drops of water dripping off the leaves, remnants from the night before.

The droplets may have been a little painful for the leaves and the trees. Those little slaps of water ultimately led to the trees being more alive than ever.

Necessary, in fact.

The day had started, the sound of the train coming alive, birds chirping.

Andries was awake, his eyes still shut.

He draped an arm over his eyes, blocking out the sunlight. He had forgotten to close the curtain from the night before.

His throat felt dry and scratchy. He gulped down water at the side of his bed, eyes lingering toward the window and the little puddle on the ground from the night before.

He went to brush his teeth and have a shower.

He closed his eyes slowly, and remnants of the night before flashed in his mind.

As he opened his eyes and dried off, he actually felt a little better than the night before... a shadow lifted slightly. His vision is clearer.

There was a knock at his door.

"One minute," he called out. Grabbing a towel and wrapping it around.

"Good morning," Inara said softly as he opened the door. She was leaning against the doorway, fitted white t-shirt and sweatpants. "Breakfast?" She asked, a smirk on her face, looking at his torso

"Yeah, let me just change." He grumbled, opening the door wider to let him in.

Wordlessly she sat at the edge of the bed, leaning back on the one hand casually and looking out at the balcony, eyes noting the puddle in the room.

"You forgot to close the window last night?" She called out.

"Yeah, just knocked out," he said as he pulled a t-shirt on. Having Inara around was nice. She was like listening to relaxing music. You felt your shoulders droop and your mind less stressed. And he appreciated her willingness with him, he had barely spoken to her the past few days, and so she had given him space and time but hadn't abandoned him-' yet,' he mumbled to himself as he pulled a pair of black sweatpants on.

She turned as she heard his footsteps, running her fingers through her hair. As usual, it was effortlessly perfect. Casually blew out. "How does your hair always look good?" He smirked, running a hand through his unbrushed curls.

"Magic," she whispered, waving her fingers in the air like she was casting a spell.

She pushed herself up and gripped his shoulders lightly, leading him out the door. He couldn't help it, and a smile came on his face.

A friend was happy to have one.

"I don't know how you do it," he said, eyes drifting toward her mug of peppermint tea. They were making breakfast, scrambled eggs. He was whisking as she heated up the pan. The windows were open, and remnants of petrichor from the night before filled their senses.

She bit her lip and shrugged.

"Try it," she said, handing the mug to him.

He took a sip. None of their other friends were awake yet; it was pretty early. He barely slept, and she was an early riser.

His eyes moved upward as if deliberating to get the flavour of it.

"Oh, that's actually nice." His eyebrows shot up. "It's, like in my chest," he said, touching his chest with a delightful look on his face. She nodded with a laugh.

"I enjoy it. It tastes really..." she bit her lip, waiting for the word to come to her, "fresh and clean."

"It's a nice drink," he inclined his head, "but I need caffeine," he said, emphasising the 'need' by taking a sip of his iced Americano.

"You are a walking cliché," she sniggered.

Their conversations were interesting. Not filled with laughter and silliness all the time. But slow and steady and nice. Quiet and thoughtful. It was different, but he didn't mind it.

"Morning, people!" Ahmed said as he came into the kitchen with Julian. They had an early practice on Monday mornings, but they had showered, and his curly hair pushed back in his headband, as always. A hoodie and sweats on.

"What's up?" Andries said a loose smile as he looked over as Ahmed sat down. Quickly Andries turned his head again. Doing a double take.

His heart began beating hard, and his blue eyes flared. He gulped down the sick taste in his throat.

"Nice hoodie," he said. His voice was hoarser than usual. "Oh, thanks," he smiled, looking down at it.

"I'm just going to go to the bathroom," Andries said abruptly, pushing his chair back and stalking inside.

Adela had just walked into their kitchen as Andries zoomed past her. "What the fuck?" She said, looking at Inara. Inara looked at the others, they all shared the same confused look on their face at Andries's behaviour. She turned and looked at Ahmed, then at his hoodie. "Fuck," she swore as her hand flung to her mouth. "That's mine, right?" She said, a tenseness in her voice, grey eyes wide.

"Yeah," he turned his head slightly, squinting. They borrowed each other's stuff. She had a hoodie of his, "I'm confused," Ahmed said as he saw Inara's face.

"It's one of the Mykal's designs."

Realisation dawned on the faces around them. "Inara, I think you should..." Adela started.

"Yeah," she said, already swinging the kitchen door open...

He was right outside the side of the door, leaning against the wall, breathing heavily. "Andries," she said, placing a comforting hand on his shoulder.

His chest was rising and falling hard, his jaw clenched and blue eyes fiery.

"I just-" he raked a hand fiercely through his hair, almost pulling at it, turning around with speed.

"Fuck!" he slammed a hand on the wall. The force reverberated through his arm. Inara was silenced/paralyzed with shock, blinking rapidly.

He pulled his arm back again, his hand in a fist. His blue eyes were full of flames. She saw it now, and it was like someone had given her the power to speak again. "Andries! Stop it!"

He didn't.

Andries reeled back on his heels, catching his breath. A little blood dripping from his knuckles. "Oh my god," Inara breathed.

Ahmed, Adela and Julian tumbled out the door.

"Shit," Ahmed said, his eyes moving back and forth from the wall and Andries. He was wearing a plain white t-shirt now. Ahmed and Amar went over to Andries, who was now panting, leaning against the wall, holding his hand to his chest.

"Hey buddy, you okay?" Amar asked warily.

He nodded, pressing his lips together. His fingers really fucking hurt, but he actually did feel okay, better, actually.

"Do you want some water?" He nodded once again.

Adela went back into the kitchen to get some water.

She brought back a glass of water, handing it to Andries. "Thanks," he mumbled.

Inara snapped out of the daze she was in, gaining control of her legs.

She walked over, squatting down to him, "Andries, can I see your hand?" He showed her his hand silently.

She held it with gentle fingers.

"I think you might have fractured your knuckle." She squinted down at his hand "how can you tell?" Ahmed asked.

"His ring finger is limp," she pointed, grey eyes flickering.

She turned at the sound of footsteps. Their other floor mate Diana, who was hardly ever there… she mostly stayed over at her boyfriend's place, came out of the room.

Both, immediately rushing to Andries,

"What in the world..." She uttered, her eyes flickering to the whole scene.

Inara explained the whole situation. Diana also knew about Mykal and looked shocked but not as surprised as Inara had expected.

"I'm going to call the doctor," Diana said as she went to grab her phone.

Andries closed his eyes tighter now, the adrenaline ebbing out of his body. His hand really fucking hurt. "Chin up, Andries. It'll be fine," Adela said with reassuring eyes.

They all ushered Andries, who was cradling his hand, to the sofa in the kitchen.

About fifteen minutes later, a woman with dark skin and straight black hair, holding a duffel bag, walked into the kitchen with Diana by her side.

The Doctor came in doing everything doctors did.

She stood up with an unfortunate look in her eyes. "We're going to need to take an x-ray to make sure, but I'm quite positive that you have a fracture, Andries," she grimaced. "I'll make a call to the hospital, but I think if you can bring him in about an hour, we should be able to get the x-ray done." She took a packet of tablets out from her duffel bag and emptied two tablets into his free hand. "Take these for now. It'll help with the pain" Adela brought him a glass of water.

"I think you should take two of your friends with you to the hospital," she advised. Andries nodded and looked up at Inara.

"Would you?" She nodded, looking down at him with a little smile, but there was this sadness that lingered in her grey eyes "and Ahmed, you too."

Ahmed blinked in surprise for a second, "of course," he began, and making his way to Andries's other side.

When they got to the hospital, straight away, Andries was told to go to the third floor, where they were already waiting for him. The three of them went up the elevator in silence. They spoke to the nurse on duty, and she led them to the doctor, who took Andries in for the x-ray and a consultation, leaving Ahmed and Inara in the waiting room. Andries walked out, and Ahmed immediately stood up, scratching the back of his neck. "Andries, I'm so sorry" Ahmed began walking toward him.

"Stop" Ahmed stopped in his tracks. Despite it all, Andries laughed. "No, I meant stop apologizing" he looked up at Ahmed. "It's not your fault. Its mine. I'm sorry" he looked down at the floor. "I'm just still..." he shook his head, clearing it. "It's still fresh for me."

"I get it," Ahmed nodded. "But" he walked over to Andries, placing a hand on his shoulder, "I should have paid more attention. I'm really sorry, man."

He nodded, smiling up at Ahmed. A feeling of consolidation between them.

They were talking on the car ride back, and oddly, Andries seemed in much better spirits.

"Is it bad to say that I'm kind of glad it happened?" He asked as he leaned back on the seat. He was in the middle, pillowed in between Inara and Ahmed. Inara cut her eyes to him.

"It felt kind of" he looked out the window at this little town that he currently called home as if the word he was looking for was in a cloud.

"Cathartic?" Inara walked over and checked the time on her phone. The doctor had told him to take the painkiller every two hours.

He took it, "yes! Exactly."

"Well, that's good," Inara said, crossing her legs over one another, "just don't make a habit of punching walls, you know."

"I'll try not to," he smirked.

"She's right," Ahmed pointed at Inara "there are other ways to take your frustrations out."

"Like what?" Andries asked.

189

Ahmed shrugged, "sex."

Inara blew out a laugh, and Andries 'brows shot up. "Or... sports works too," Ahmed added with a smirk.

"I used to play tennis" Andries shrugged.

"Let's play some tennis then," he looked down at Andries's hand, "obviously after your hand has healed." He smirked. "How good of a player were you?" He asked Ries.

"I'm not going to lie," Andries straightened his neck, "I was pretty fucking good" he smiled smugly.

Ahmed started laughing, "good. It gives me a month to practice" Ahmed remembered that the doctor said that his wrist would be fine in a month, luckily. He and Inara had gone up to the doctor and asked about it when Ries went to the bathroom, just in case Ries forgot anything.

When they got back, Ahmed, Inara and Andries were chilling in his room. There was a knock on his door. Ahmed had just texted the group that all was good and that they should come to Ries's room.

There was a knock on Andries's door. "Just come in, Amar!" There was another knock. Ahmed stood up, "bro, why are you-" Ahmed stopped talking.

"Sorry, I thought you were a friend of mine" Ahmed straightened his back.

"Can I speak with Andries Adamos, please?" A tall man in jeans and a black t-shirt and braided hair that was tied back stood at his door.

" Uh, sure," Ahmed's eyebrows scrunched together, "Ries, it's for you," she said as she opened the door wider.

"Hi, I'm Eddie. I'm a 'Mental Health Counsellor 'for the school. We heard what happened today, and I wanted to have a quick chat with you if that's okay… we can speak alone if you think that would be better?" He smiled. [insert Eddie description]. - this part should become the following:

"Hi, I'm Eddie. I'm a 'Mental Health Counsellor 'for the school. We heard what happened today, and I wanted to have a quick chat with you if that's okay… we can speak alone if you

190

think that would be better?" He had dark skin and short hair and he smiled a little, but it was a kind smile. Close-lipped, yet his green eyes seemed to speak of intelligence and caring. A rare but fantastic combination.

"No," he shook his head. "It's okay... they can stay," Andries said, his ardent blue eyes flickering between the two of them. Ahmed and Inara shared a look and stood straighter, taller.

"Alright then," he smiled as he came inside. Ahmed and Inara moved up so Andries could sit on the bed, and Eddie could sit on the chair.

"So, regarding the damages. We have already emailed your parents, and they have paid for the damages." Andries's ardent blue eyes slightly flickered shut. His poor parents, he didn't want them to know about this.

"Don't worry, Andries," this man had a very comforting way of speaking, "we know of your situation. Your parents had informed us at the beginning of the year about what you went through." Eddie gulped, "what are you still going through" her shoulders melted a little. "I want to give you my sincerest condolences" he looked at him sadly.

"Thank you" Andries inclined his head.

"I am here to offer you a proposition. Due to the circumstances, if you think it may be helpful or suit you better to go home early, we can organize that," a sympathetic smile on her face.

Ahmed and Inara were silent next to him. "We can arrange for your classes to be done online and your assignments for the semester submitted via email." Andries took a deep breath in,

"Of course, you can take the week to think about it," Eddie said, holding a hand out.

"No-" he cleared his throat, "I like to make my decisions pretty quickly. If I have too much time to think about it, I get confused" he laughed lightly.

"Are you sure you don't want to speak to your parents?" Eddie asked.

Andries nodded as he raked a free hand through his hair. He loved his parents, but this was his life. He deliberated for a moment. He thought of home... his own bedroom, his mother's cooking and the dinners with his parents, conversations with his father... but there were also memories, too many of them lingering around like ghosts, and too many people who were sitting in his dorm room right now, and some who would arrive soon who he didn't want to leave yet.

"No," he shook his head. He lifted his head up. "I want to stay" he looked at them with those intense blue eyes and with a condition of conviction that he hadn't felt in a while.

"Alright then, if you need anything, this is my email," he said, handing him a business card. "I usually am very prompt with my replies, and glad you made the decision to stay" Eddie smiled as he stood up.

When he left, Inara turned and hugged Andries. She understood that it must've been hard. When she let go, she asked him a question… her raspy voice tentative.

"Can I say something, Ries?"

"Shoot," he smirked. But her face still stayed serious. Grey eyes searched his face.

"Look, it's not in your control. What happens in life, but how you react and how you handle it is.

"He is alive." She played with her pendant. "Not in the way he was before. But he's alive in the hearts and minds of his family and friends. He is alive through Anaisha and Zade and Abel, Kiara, Calista... in you.

"Naira. He's alive in Naira" Andries laughed at how similar they were.

"Yes, her too" Inara smiled. And after a pause, she carried on in a soft, calm voice that conveyed honesty and belief "in all his friends and family, in all the people that he existed beside. He stays alive with you, forever. He lives in you" what she said wasn't prophetic or anything sublime. He'd heard that rhetoric before, but maybe it was the way she said it with such sincerity. That he smiled, and despite it, all felt it might actually be true.

"He's even alive in that hoodie that Ahmed was wearing. That was Mykal's design, and a little piece of his brain is in that clothing." He could hear the smile in her voice.

When they went back in, Ahmed was just wearing a simple black t-shirt.

"Andries, I'm so sorry." He said, "I didn't realize, just woke up and threw it on" he shrugged, a helpless look on his face.

Andries nodded. "Put it back on," he said, stuffing his hands in his pocket.

"What?" Ahmed said, his eyes wary. All of them were now looking up, watching Ries.

"It's what he wanted, something that looks sick, and you can just throw on without any trouble, knowing your looking 'fly. " 'Andries laughed. "His words, not mine," scratching the back of his head.

"He worked really hard on it," Andries said, raising his chin. "He would've been so happy seeing you wear it." He took a deep breath in, "And I am too," he gulped with a nod. He stuffed one hand in his pocket, relaxing. Ahmed smiled and put the hoodie back on.

Andries looked down in surprise, and he felt his hand squeezed. Adela was sitting right next to where he was standing and was giving his hand a strengthening squeeze.

He squeezed back in a physical 'thank you. A smile on his face as he pulled back his chair gently and sat back down, settling in comfortably. Just as the door opened and the rest of their friends came through,

Mykal would have loved you guys, he thought. He didn't realize he had said it out loud until they all turned back to him. Inara was blinking rapidly, and Adela's eyes were glistening. They all slowly came around him and wrapped him in a great hug. He laughed until he felt pain in his wrist.

" Yo, guys… I still have a fractured wrist," he uttered. "Oh, shit," Amar said quickly, as they all let go, laughing.

One night, after a family dinner at Naira's home, Anaisha asked Naira if she could sleepover.

"Of course" Naira said, her green eyes surprised but happy.

They lay in bed next to each other, with only the soft light of the bedside lamp. Naira was reading and Anaisha had her hands crossed on her chest, as she stared up at the ceiling.

"You seem to be holding up a lot better than the rest of us." Anaisha whispered into the smell of flowers and vanilla and into the soft lamp light. Naira closed her book. "You're strong. It's a good thing."

Anaisha remembered hearing Naira sobbing at the funeral, horrid tears where she could barely breathe, that made her insides scrunch up.

"I don't know if it's that" she mumbled. "I still cry a lot, but I also laugh a lot... and when I'm laughing it's like I can feel him smiling, somewhere wherever he is."

Naira found Anaisha's hand and held it.

"I just... can't" she covered her face as she felt the tears burning down her face.

"Don't," Naira sat up a little and pulled her hand away from her cousin's face. "This is just part of the human existence. It's pain and happiness, and you shouldn't feel guilty for either, just feel them both wholeheartedly, and that's that."

Anaisha sort of made a laugh like sound, "that sounds like something he would say"

"I'm pretty sure he did once when I was crying" Naira said as she lay back down.

They lay in silence for a beat.

"I still see him in my dreams" she took a deep breath and smiled, ""and I know for a fact that I will see him again and I know he wouldn't want me to be wasting my time away. That would probably be the worst thing for him to have to see and I refuse to do that to him"

"Yeah, but he's not the one who's going through this." Anaisha started hiccuping slightly. "He's the one who left us" Anaisha's voice broke on that last word. Naira felt tears coming in.

Naira gulped, she felt like she couldn't get words out. She blew a deep breath out and closed her eyes, she pictured him sitting with them. He was here, he always was.

"Wherever he is, he's mourning too. He had to leave his friends and family. And, we know him well enough to know what he would say to deal with this"

Anaisha nodded, "I want to believe you and I do" she whimpered, "its just really fucking hard."

"I know" Naira said as she sat up, crossed her legs and moved Anaisha's body slightly. She felt light and limp. She moved the pillow to lean on as Anaisha lay her head on Naira's lap. Naira stroked her head gently, comforting her older cousin. They sat that way for a while.

Study Buddies

Anaisha bit her lip in concentration as she re-read the textbook, her finger following the words. Then she highlighted some of it, taking a sticky note and annotating next to certain parts, turning the words into her own.

Lately, she had actually been looking forward to studying, and it was another way for her to distract her mind. Focus on other things.

It had been really warm the last few weeks, but randomly, the weather had cooled today. It was the kind of weather where you only needed a loose jacket. They were sitting outside on the picnic-esque tables, a group study session. The only person missing was Aki. He had "sports practice."

Zade and Naira were sitting at the table across from Anaisha, Calista, and Kiara.

He was helping Naira with her Business studies assignment and then they would move on to literature. The sound of leaves and paper rustling took over the gardens, along with the soft conversation of Zade and Naira.

A brown leaf fell slowly from a tree next to them, but before it hit the ground, the wind whisked it away, and it landed on a table across.

"I fucking hate this." Naira groaned, tearing the brown leaf that just floated onto the table. "It's not that bad. Come on, just concentrate," he said, pointing at the book.

"That's the problem," she said, leaning back on her hands, "I can't concentrate on things I don't like" she looked up at the clouds.

He turned to her, deep brown eyes. "Naira." his voice sounded a bit deeper, a slight edge to it. Her eyes slid to his curiously. That was new. She took the bait.

"Okay, okay, I'll try," she said and sat up straight, eyes on the textbook. "Alright, then," a quick smile on his lips.

They began reading, and he started explaining things she was confused by. Zane was always patient, explaining it again if she didn't understand it the first time. But still, she couldn't wait to move on to literature which was her forte. At least then, she'd stop feeling like a moron.

He angled his neck, cracking it side to side.

"Oh god," she shook her head and wrinkled her nose. "Don't crack your neck; it makes my spine tingle," she said, pulling her cardigan over her shoulders.

"Does it make you tingly anywhere else?" His words fast. "You're relentless," she slapped his arm, her bracelets jingling. "Only with you," he shrugged, flipping a page.

She slid her eyes to him, intrigued.

" Anyway, it is not like you're going to be tested. You just have to maintain what you got last year" he shrugged. They had already received their university offers, and now they just had to maintain the grades in their classes during their final year.

"That's true" she blew out a breath.

She saw a tall figure languidly walking toward them, one hand in his pocket. A sports bag on his lean shoulder. He was holding what looked like a tray in his free hand.

Aki came closer, placing the coffee holder on the table. "Thought you could use it," he motioned, taking a sip from his own cup. "You're the best," Naira said, holding her hands out in praise, a childlike smile on her face.

"Is it-" she started.

"Oat milk, yes," Aki nodded, specifically for you. There was one cup with 'Naira 'written on it, made with goat milk.

He walked over to the rest, giving them their drinks. He was wearing his grey sweatshirt. "Aww, Aks, thank you," Calista said, her face melting into a dazzling smile.

"Anytime," the corner of his mouth lifted, "I'll see you guys," he saluted lightly, walking over to Zane and Naira. They all did Lit, and we're going to study together, which meant possibly listening to Naira rant about a book. Calista fiddled with her pen, leaning on the table, her eyes secretive. "Okay, am I the only one, but is Aki like, really gorgeous?"

"You are not the only one," Kiara said indifferently, her pen scribbling notes. Anaisha squinted, bending her head slightly closer to her book.

"He's severely underrated," Calista said, turning her head around. "Why hasn't he ever..."

"Oh, no, he has," Kiara said, looking up, listing off some names. Anaisha's lips twisted into a smile that she tried to hide "you've just never realized it because he's not an asshole," a wry smile on her lips. Calista rolled her eyes, "fuck off," a slight, mischievous smile on her lips.

It was the second to last class of the day and the odd, but well-understood mixture of tiredness and forced concentration mingled in the air of all the classrooms in the corridor.

There was a knock on the already open door of the classroom.

A teacher with dark hair that cascaded in voluminous curls down her back popped her head in. "Hi, I'm so sorry to interrupt,"

Anaisha had her head bent taking notes, she didn't notice, but she knew that voice, and she immediately looked up. Shit. It was Ms. Benward.

"Can I just grab Anaisha for a moment?" Ms. Benward trilled.

"Of course," her teacher said, looking at Anaisha. Her friends shared wary glances. As Anaisha got up, rubbed her hands along her pants, and strode over to the door.

"Hi," Anaisha greeted, closing the door behind her.

"How are you?" Ms. Benward said with a kind smile. Her lips were naturally very red and made redder by her pale skin. She wore a long white dress with short puffy sleeves.

"I'm okay, doing better..." she smiled, tucking her hair behind her ear.

" I haven't bothered you with photography at the beginning of this year." She held her hands together in front of her. Anaisha crossed her arms over her chest. "I thought you'd come to me..." she gulped, "but you didn't, and I think I would be a bad teacher if I didn't try to get you back." Her lips were in a straight line.

Anaisha sighed. "I-," she shook her head slowly, looking at her shoes. "Let me finish," she said, in a certain stern voice.

Anaisha looked up sharply, taking a breath in.

"There's an exhibition at the end of the year. For the students. Most of them have been working since the beginning..." she said matter-of-factly, but there was a gleam in her blue eyes,

197

"but I know you have stuff that you could exhibit. You are my most improved student Anaisha. And I know you got the offer from RISD. A small smile on her lips. "I've looked at your grades, and you're exceeding what you need... so I guess that means you're going" her blue eyes looked hopeful as she pursed her lips.

Anaisha sighed, uncrossing her arms. There was no point in lying. "I don't know. I haven't picked up a camera in," she bit her lip "sometime," she stuttered, "and I don't even know if I have it in me anymore... "She played with her ring. "I was thinking of just doing a degree in business instead."

Her lashes fluttered as she looked at the ceiling and blew a breath out. Clearing her throat, she looked at Anaisha again, "please don't waste your talent, Anaisha." His blue eyes glistened. "Your photos, they're beautiful and..." she shook her head, trying to find the words "their gentle and happy," she said earnestly. "Come to me, with the film you have... I know you have photos you haven't shown yet..."

She couldn't. She didn't even know if she could pick up a camera again "please, that's all" she held her hands up.

Anaisha nodded, gnawing at her bottom lip.

When Anaisha went back to class, she couldn't concentrate any longer. All she could think of was a bunch of things she wished she could just forget.

There's a party tonight, and you're coming

Naira was curled up on her fluffy beanbag, her eyes skimming over the words again... her fingers touching the page, and that pinnacle moment hit. It felt like she could just maybe hear her heartbeat, her breath caught, and tears stung her eyes.

"What happened?" Aki stood over her, hands in his pockets, a little smile on his face.

She looked up with wet eyelashes, in his gut clenched. She didn't even realize he had come in. "nothing," she wiped her eyes with a ringed hand. "Just this book" she rolled her eyes, the tears still there. "It's really good," she whimpered, "but sucks at the same time," she said in a half-laugh, half-cry.

His lips turned up into a tiny half-smile as he came over behind her beanbag, squatting down and putting a comforting arm around her shoulder. "Tell me about it."

And he listened like he always did. Listened and nodded as she emotionally explained a story. With so much conviction, she explained a story that wasn't true, feeling it so deeply... little tears dripping down her face. He gave her a tissue to blow her nose.

"Thanks," she sniffed.

The flowers in her vase were delphiniums, and they were still bright and a light shade of purple, but the petals looked like they were welting slightly, and the soil looked dry. Aki poured some water from his bottle into the vase.

They sat in her room; Aki wanted to watch something on the TV while Naira carried on reading her book. She was still healing internally, but the initial blow had passed.

The sky outside was bright and blue today, it was a little too hot to be outside, but the golden light from the outside illuminated the room.

Naira heard a little ping from her phone, and she grabbed it from the centre table.

Her brows shot up "there's a party tonight," she turned around to face Aki, with that glint in those mischievous green eyes, "you down?"

Aki stretched his long body as he yawned, "I'm kind of-"

"You're coming," Naira said resolutely. She texted Zade and he replied promptly with a 'why not? And an emoji.

Calista pulled into Naira's house. They were only a ten-minute drive away. She called her while still in the car, and Naira opened the door as they both slowly and silently made their way up to the stairs. It was 11:30 at night, and their parents were all asleep. It was a Wednesday night, and none of their parents would have allowed them to go to a party on a weekday. She could hear her own bracelets clang against each other as she walked, her arms swinging.

"Shut up," Calista whispered. Naira held her hand, stopping them from clanging against each other. They made it to the second door, Naira's room.

As soon as they got in, Naira shut the door, and Calista sat on the beanbag. There were several candles set up in Naira's room. A few on her windowsill and some on her side table. Her room smelt like blackcurrant perfume and vanilla candles.

"These are gorgeous," Calista commented on the new fresh white gladiolus in her vase, which was blooming beautifully. Naira smiled.

So, the plan was to sneak out, and the group knew they could successfully leave, considering they had Mykal, Andries, and Abel as their mentors. But they had never done this without at least one of them before, so Naira could feel the little nerves in her stomach as she put on her makeup, sitting on her desk. But she swallowed and focused on the routine and calmed down. Like she knew she could. Ever since this year had started, she had the tendency to do things despite being scared; sometimes, she wanted to do things because they scared her. Like she was some sort of amateur daredevil.

She put on her clothes and looked in the mirror, and music played through the speakers on her side table. She wore a tight halter top with stripes of pink and white, so light that they almost looked like paintbrush strokes, and blue jeans. Suddenly, a thought interrupted the music around her, and she popped her head into the bathroom; Calista was still doing her eye makeup in Naira's bathroom. So, Naira went over to the drawer under her desk. She retrieved the black leather notebook and flipped through to the envelope stuffed in the middle. She opened it up gently, not wanting to tear at it even in the slightest. Despite the sounds of light music (so as not to wake her parents up), all she could hear was her breathing and the sound of rustling paper. She opened her letter from Mykal and tenderly read the words he had written. As she neared the end, there was a knock at the door, and she saw the door handle move.

"Why is it locked?" Aki called out softly from the other side. "Naira, I swear if you're still getting ready, I'm going to kill you." She could feel his eyes roll from the other side of the door.

Hurriedly, she packed the letter back into the envelope, shoved the notebook back in her drawer, and strode over to the door. She grabbed him inside before he kept talking and when she knew it was safe she turned with her winsome smile, "my love, this takes time..." Motioning to herself.

A lopsided grin spread on his face "you look great," then he checked his phone, "Okay, let's get going. Everyone is already there" "not everyone," Naira said, her smile cheeky. "We have a pit stop to make," she said as she stuffed lip-gloss and some cash into her purse. Calista was still getting ready, and she already knew they would be a little late.

"What the fuck is that?" He pointed to her purse, his voice incredulous. She knew what he was talking about. It was a very small purse.

"It's not that bad... See, it fits all the necessities," she said as she pulled out the minimal amount of things she could fit in her micro bag, "cash, lip-gloss..." she rolled her eyes, waving her hands around, "and yes, my phone doesn't fit, but anyway I usually have it in my hand," she spoke quickly, justifying her purchase. "And it is just so cute" she smiled toothily, as she held up the little purple bag.

Aki rolled his eyes, and then he laughed. He couldn't help himself. "It is very cute."

They drove down to Anaisha's house and met Zade and Kiara there. Even if Anaisha didn't come, the party was in 'Whispering Waves, 'so it made sense.

Calista, who was sitting in the passenger seat, dialled her phone and told Anaisha to come outside. They could hear her refusal on the other line.

"Put it on speaker," Naira told Calista. "Anaisha, if you don't come out right now, I'll tell Mahita Masi about the time you got wasted at Andries's house."

"You wouldn't dare" even without being able to see her face, Naira knew Anaisha's eyes had turned into angry squinted slits.

Naira smirked to herself, "watch me" she chimed.

They heard the muffled sound of a defeated breath blown out, "fine, I'll be right down" and she clicked the phone off.

A few minutes later, Anaisha knocked on the car door, and Aki opened the door to let Anaisha in the car.

"I just came to tell you in person," she said as she got in, crossing her arms over her chest. She was wearing her glasses, sweatpants, and a tank top, and her hair was clipped away from her face. "I love you guys, but I am not coming tonight" Her face was deadpan.

"Come on," Naira said as she moved in her seat to face the back.

"Just come, man," Calista echoed, "hmm…." Anaisha said, cocking her head to her side as if deep in thought. "no." she said as she moved to get out of the car. "Naira, let me out" the door was locked.

Naira began, her green eyes determined. Her hands worked to create a picture. And she went off on a speech about how we were young and only lived once and didn't have much more time left, considering this was their last year. In the past, other people wouldn't have seen this part of her. The convincing and persuasive streak she held. In the end, Anaisha was not immune and ended up coming.

"You'd be a great politician, you know?" Aki said, eyes whirring on Naira whilst they waited for Anaisha. "You think?" Her voice went higher with the question. She tapped her chin. "I would be a liberal."

"Obviously"

She bit the inside of her cheek, "and I would be one of those hot politicians that everyone secretly fantasized about."

Aki snorted a laugh.

Anaisha ran up and changed. She wore the same tank top and changed her sweatpants to jeans, and she kept her hair pinned back and brought a makeup bag in the car.

Calista and Aki switched seats before they left. Naira's lights in the backseats of her car were broken, so Calista held up the flashlight on her phone as Anaisha put some makeup on. Naira blasted the music in her car as she and Aki spoke to each other, barely audible over the music. Anaisha was used to Aki and Naira whispering to themselves, she didn't mind it, though. It often reminded her of Andries, Mykal, and herself. The way they would need a few minutes to say something to only each other. Not to be inconsiderate or leave anyone out, but because it was something that was shared by only the two of them. She smiled to herself at the two of them. She was glad that her cousin had something like that in her life.

Naira whispered to Aki, "You've barely spoken since we left my room" he turned to her, his look quizzical. Apart from the 'politician thing, 'he hadn't said much, "are you okay?" Her eyes were full of concern. It was crazy how she could tell, he thought. "Yeah, I'm good," he said with a light chuckle and masking his face with a smile that said, 'how could you think that? I'm totally fine" he wasn't. Oddly, he was nervous. He normally didn't feel this, but lately, he had been feeling it more often, and he wasn't the biggest fan of the feeling.

He and Anaisha had barely spoken since their date. He was surprised, and it had gone well. At least he thought it had. And he wasn't necessarily jumping with joy when he realized that they were going to convince her to come out tonight, mostly because he didn't know what to say.

Naira looked at him once more as she took a right turn. She wished she could look at him properly, and she could tell something was off. Naira wasn't scared of eye contact. Sometimes, he thought it was the time that she had spent with Andries and his intense eye contact that had rubbed off on her. But he masked his face impenetrable, and her eyes left his face.

But, she kept one hand on the wheel as he put a long arm behind her seat, a sign of gratitude. She could tell he wasn't telling her everything, and he knew that. And he was grateful that she let him stay silent. Because she was the one person he couldn't tell, and that fucking sucked.

This house was set atop one of the hills. Anaisha could already tell which house it was, the lights seemed brighter than the rest, and the vague sound of music filled the street. Becoming louder as they reached closer to their destination.

Anaisha knew the house; they all did. It was Talia's house. The door flew open as a tall, tanned girl with dirty blonde hair and blue eyes greeted Naira and Calista, who stood before them. She gave them both a wholesomely tight hug with the air of a kind hostess. Anaisha watched them talk kindly and excitedly, complimenting each other on their outfits. Anaisha remembered how Naira had told her the two had met up for coffee last Saturday. She was from another school, 'name of the school, 'the school to which most of the kids at this party went.

One by one, they all greeted each other, and then it was her turn.

"Anaisha, hi!" Talia said with another tight hug. "How are you?" She whispered in a slightly different tone than she greeted everyone else. More softness layered her voice. "I'm good," Anaisha said with a nod as if confirming it to herself. Talia nodded and gave her another squeeze. She was a very sweet girl. She had been good friends with all of them and attended the funeral and had sent both her and Ries very kind messages after. As she brought them further into the house, Anaisha could tell her friends, and the other people around her were looking now. Their eyes were curious but pitiful. She hadn't been to anything remotely social outside of the academy for a while.

They made their way into the kitchen on which the contestable was turned into a make-shift bar. A mix of expensive alcohols, the bottles her parents had given her, and cheaper alcohols, the ones she had brought, knowing that she might need more, took over one side. The other had a couple of stacks of plastic cups and bowls of chips and popcorn.

Talia took out a couple of cups and concocted some drinks for them.

Calista coughed as she took a sip, "fuck that's strong," her face in a grimace.

"Oh, come on," Talia smacked her arm lightly, "it's not that bad," she said with a mischievous laugh.

Everyone else did end up agreeing that it was really strong, and some more cranberry juice was added on the condition that they all followed the drink with a shot after.

"So, how's Ries?" Talia asked, naturally looking at Anaisha. The music was loud, but Anaisha heard the name loud and clear. She faltered for a minute, her hand going still as she was about to take a sip. The rest of the group went silent for a minute, not knowing what to say. Anaisha's eyes slid to Naira. Naira suddenly found her drink very drinkable and sipped away quickly. They had gone out this week, and she hadn't told her...

"Is he enjoying uni?" Talia asked, popping a chip into her mouth. Instinctively Anaisha looked over at Aki, who was just blinking and sipping his drink casually.

"Mmhmm," Anaisha nodded. She really didn't know what to say.

Zade cleared his throat, saving Anaisha "he's doing okay. I spoke to him a few days ago," he said as his eyes flickered to Anaisha's. She knew they still spoke, he was one of his best friends, but they hadn't spoken about it before.

"Wait-" Talia said, pointing to Anaisha, noting the tension, her face the epitome of confusion. "Let's dance," Naira said, grabbing Talia's hand and swiftly fluttering away.

"I'm gonna join them," Zade said, finishing his Coke. "Me too," Aki said, and they trailed off.

"Are you okay?" Kiara said as she and Calista came closer, huddling around her, ready to break her fall. Calista's wide blue eyes blinked with sensitivity. Kiara bit her lip nervously.

"Yeah, of course." She said while taking a sip of her drink, "I don't care." she did. "I'm just surprised she didn't know." They both nodded fervently.

"Well, you're amazing," Kiara said with her warm smile and patted Anaisha's hair lovingly, "and shitty things have happened, god knows why," she said with a full-bodied shrug, "but, we keep going, you know," she said with a beautiful melancholy smile. All three of them nodded together, an air of sad reality around them.

Calista grabbed their hands tightly. "Why don't we do that shot? You know, before we start crying." She laughed. She didn't have the heart, to be honest with them, right now. Calista and Kiara dealt with the situation in this sadly wonderful way. With laughter and jokes mixed in with frustration. But, Anaisha just felt alone. It just didn't feel right without him. In a room full of people, she was lonely.

They laughed at how sad their lives had become, how much had changed.

So, the girls went over to the counter, took their shots, and went over to the center of the living room, where some people were dancing or just swaying and enjoying the music.

"It's our song!" Naira shouted as she grabbed hold of his shoulders from behind him. He turned his head to face her and looked down. They were always a funny duo, being at such polar opposite heights. She looked up with the biggest smile, like a child who had just won.

Everybody was used to the sly smile that accompanied the end of a lot of her sentences, but Aki knew the big toothy smile that lay underneath. She had braces when they were younger.

They both did. But Naira refused to wear her retainers because they hurt while she slept, so her teeth weren't as perfect as they once were, but it was one of the most real smiles in his life. And whenever he felt himself closing off, that smile always brought him back out.

Impulsively and instinctively, he grabbed both her hands from his shoulders and twirled her around him. She laughed without reservation, and he remembered when they constantly played this song as 12-year-olds. It was completely inappropriate with pretty rude lyrics. It was an R&B song that they had learned by heart, and whenever one of them was in a bad mood, it was usually Naira being the moodier of the two. They would put it on. Then they would lay back on his bed or her beanbags, depending on which room they were in, and listen. As they got older, he got his license before she did, and they'd drive around and blast it on full volume.

Aki could feel the dopamine rush and smile to himself. It might've been the alcohol, though. He couldn't really tell, but he felt good.

He felt a tap on his shoulder. And turned to see Anaisha. She motioned for him to bend down to her height, and he obeyed as she whispered in his ear. "Can we talk?" He nodded and followed her into the garden, a plastic cup in one hand. She led them over to one of the sunbeds at the corner of the garden, and he sat down, stretching his long legs forward and casually crossing them over one another. He had to blink a few times to actually understand his surroundings, they were outside now, and the stars and moon were so high and bright above the sprawling dark ocean. There were some wooden stairs that led down from the house right onto the beach. It really was a gorgeous home, he thought to himself.

Anaisha came over to sit next to him. "All okay?" He asked with a loose smile.

She nodded and smiled. She could hear the sound of the splashing waves under the louder sounds of music and chattering voices coming from inside. Seeing the ocean there and being outdoors in a space where she could breathe freely brought her so much ease and perspective on the matters of her life in her heart. She could feel the drinks rippling through her head, making every movement easier and slower. There were some other people outside too, smoking or talking. Some were familiar faces, but no one was important to her. Despite being slightly drunk, her back stayed pretty straight, and she looked straight forward "so, Talia clearly didn't know me and Ries were broken up." She said, speaking those words into the dark sea and sky.

"She clearly didn't..." He said, using her own words back. And he turned to face her as she followed his movement and turned her head to look at him. Leaning her chin into the crook of her palm, she said. "Do you have any thoughts or opinions on that?" Her words were gently mumbled, and her well-used gesture seemed looser than normal, but her eyes were still sharp and bright.

He scratched the light stubble on his chin and said, "I don't, actually..." with a smile that didn't completely meet his eyes and cleared his throat. She didn't move, her chin still in the crook of her palm and her sharp eyes taking in everything.

" You can tell me the truth, you know," she spoke softly. It was weird. If this was Ries, she would've had the bitterness of annoyance lacing her voice, but something about Akihoko's relaxed demeanour ebbed into her.

He chuckled softly "your good," he said, acknowledging how she could tell he was lying. "Just observant," she answered with a small smile and shrug.

"Well, the truth is..." He swallowed once again, and his eyes left her face and found their hiding place looking at the place in which the night sky met the ocean. "At first, it upset me that you didn't correct her, but then I thought that you probably have your reasons. Maybe you and Andries have some unfinished business," he said so casually and calmly. They could have been talking about the weather. "And you didn't say anything to me after we went out, so I thought that maybe you wanted nothing to do with me. So I let the thought go" she marvelled at his calmness, his sea-breeze voice, and his power to let his thoughts go or change them. "We've all been rejected, you know. I can deal with it" He touched the nape of his neck and arched his neck backward. She couldn't imagine anyone ever rejecting him, she thought, looking at his profile.

"I wasn't rejecting you," she said faster than she had intended, the words spilling out of her mouth instinctually.

"Oh..." he said slowly, then as if out of his control, he started smiling and looked back outward to the sea. Still smiling.

She followed his gaze outward and watched the ocean, and she said, "Honestly, it just caught me off guard..." The wind blew her hair in her eyes, and she tucked it behind her ears, "I literally had barely heard his name since he left. And it just..." she shook her head and let out a long breath. She really couldn't put into words how it had made her feel. Akihiko nodded sympathetically, his eyes kind. She regained her composure, once again resting her chin in her palm "also, she and Naira had met up a week ago, so I thought she would have already known." She turned her head to face him now, her chin still in her palm but her eyes on him. "And Ries and I haven't spoken since we broke up."

He nodded and leaned back on the sunbed, "I have an idea. Why don't we talk about this tomorrow? He gazed at her through his beautiful slanted eyes and said, "Let us enjoy tonight. Naira forced you here so you could just chill out and have fun, forget about everything for a while, you know?" Now he had a cool smile on his face. "I'll pick you up whenever your awake tomorrow, and we can go get some food and talk?" A question in his eyes.

"Deal." She said with a smile on her face. And she put out her hand to help him up, and they walked back into the house, letting each other's hands go as they reached the glass doors.

At first, when they went back into the house, they separated. Aki went to find Naira and ended up talking to her and some people from some other schools.

From the corner of his eye, Aki saw Zade, Anaisha, and Kiara dancing. With this sudden breeze of confidence, he walked over and put his arm on Zade's shoulder, and whispered something in his ear. Anaisha was watching him, using those intent eyes. Promptly Zane said to Kiara, "Kiara, come with me to get some water," With feigned tiredness. Kiara scrunched her brows together with concern "you okay?" She said, touching his shoulder. "Just thirsty, come" he cocked his head toward the kitchen. Zade turned and winked at Aki as they left. Anaisha's intent eyes saw that too. He came closer to her, and she smiled up as she motioned her hand for him to come closer and spoke in his ear, "we should go check if Zade's okay..." A roguish smile on her face that he couldn't see but hear. "I think he's okay, but let's go check in a few minutes?" He said and then turned and looked at her with a smile. Now he saw the roguish smile. She knew.

208

They held each other's hands as they danced, far enough apart where it still looked friendly. But if people could see into their minds and had the intelligence to infer from their captivated eyes and infatuated smiles. They would know. He wanted to pull her closer, but Naira was right there, so were others, and his wits were still about him... somewhere.

They left Naira's car at Talia's. Anaisha would pick it up the next morning, and Zade, who was sober but seemed buzzed even when he was, drove them all home. On their way back, Anaisha remembered something, she put the window down, just for a moment, and took a breath in, and she could feel the tears pool up in her eyes. Akihiko watched her from her peripheral vision, the small pause in her being, and from the corner of his eye saw that she smiled. And lightly she touched her own shoulder, gently. Almost as if someone's hand was there, someone she loves.

It was like she could hear their voices next to her, sitting in the car. Their boyish drunk laughter. The stupid remarks and jokes

It was in moments when she knew she would never forget Mykal. And Ries. Moments like this. They would always be with her, a part of her. Did that mean that she would always feel this lonely, too?

It was like hearing a song that made you cry. Or seeing a painting that brought tears to your eyes. It wasn't a hint of sadness, it was a confirmation.

A confirmation that her soul was a real thing, that they were real. Humanity was alive. It was a religious feeling. Of something touching your soul.

She smiled at the confirmation, the confirmation that those moments touched her then, and they touched her now too. Those moments were immortal.

She blinked, another truth intruding her mind. 'Did that mean that she would also be forever alone? Without Mykal. Immortally alone?'

Saturday Morning

Anaisha woke up that morning, her eyes feeling heavy, and she stretched in her bed, taking a deep breath. For a few seconds, she lay silently, blinking. Staring at the ceiling, feeling her chest rise and fall. Another day in what felt like another life.

Languidly she got up to brush her teeth and wash her face. The taste of mint and the feel of cold water signalled her brain to wake up. She came back to her bed and reached for her glasses perched on her side table, her brain barely awake, and saw her phone that lay beside it light up with a message.

One of them being from Aki,

She had completely forgotten about breakfast! Shit. But there was this sweet little flutter in her chest at his message.

She messaged him back, saying she was awake and she would come by in 25 minutes.

She sat on the edge of her bed, placing her phone back on the side table. She rubbed her eyes beneath her glasses, then raked her fingers through her hair, slowly as if touching the part of her body closest to her mind would help her make sense of her life. 'What am I doing? 'She whispered to herself. Lately, she had been an expert at putting on a mask when it came to how she was feeling. Because if people actually knew, they'd possibly try and talk or console her, and she couldn't be bothered by any of it anymore. Worse, they might worry, and she didn't want that at all.

Before she left, she told her parents she would be back by two, she knew they had a family dinner in the evening.

"Anaisha, you're not eating?" Maha Didi asked her before you left.

"No, I'm going out for breakfast today?" She said as she grabbed her car keys atop the kitchen counter.

"With who?" Her mom asked as she read the paper whilst waiting for her chai.

She sucked in air through her teeth, "my friends, ma," she rolled her eyes, "who else?" She said as she walked out.

As she drove toward his house, her thoughts were somewhere else. She was barely focused on the road, and she shouldn't have been driving. She thought of how she woke up every day, sometimes feeling normal and okay, sometimes feeling shitty, and sometimes shittier. Blinking at the ceiling. Peed and brushed and washed. Put on her makeup and clothes, did her hair, set a physical covering, and as soon as she left her bedroom door, the mask was set in place completely.

It worked out well because it wasn't like anyone was expecting her to be overly smiley or chirpy. That would have been completely impossible for her to even try to fake.

But talking and laughing and smiling, often enough. It worked. There were no witnesses. Sometimes she saw Kiara eyeing her carefully, analytically. Or Calista would randomly, silently just grab hold of Anaisha's hand. Zade's smile would falter suddenly, and then he'd shake his head and look up again. Maybe they were all wearing masks around each other.

She parked, and they walked to the cafe. The sun was out, but it was 10 am, and the sun hadn't yet hit its noon peak. Anaisha wore a short, black flow dress. She wasn't in the most talkative mood, she hadn't had a coffee yet, or maybe her head was just somewhere else today. But Aki seemed to pick up on that. He didn't question her or act awkwardly. Instead, he talked and let her stay silent.

They neared the cafe, and it was a sleek, muted atmosphere. With a sage-colored marble counter on the side of the restaurant. An assortment of pastries encased in a glass covering lying atop.

Two baristas worked behind the counter, working from the industrial coffee machines. Muted golden lights hung from the ceiling. They were turned off right now, the windows were thrown open, and the light breeze was settling in. The ceiling was like one of a greenhouse, clear glass letting the sunlight fall in. It was a beautiful little cafe, very chic. It reminded her of the new coffee shops that littered the city. But Anaisha's mind was somewhere else.

She loved coffee shops like this in the city, but when she was in the academy, at the beachside, she thought of the coffee shop in the heart of the town center. In fact, it was so compactly packed in the town center that one might have missed it. The whole cafe only consisted of the counter and a little space for customers to stand, with a single table and bench outside, so you were lucky if you got a seat. They had been going since she was 16. She would get a nice cup of milky coffee, Mykal with sugar and Andries, just black. But she swore there really was magic in those beans.

But this place was new, different, and she hadn't been before, so she felt that she should give it a try. It was lovely anyway, cozy and sleek at the same time, very nicely juxtaposed. A je ne sais quoi about it, and it served more than just coffee. It had a whole breakfast menu... lots to offer.

But Anaisha's mind was somewhere else. The coffee shop is in the heart of the town center. In fact, it was so compactly packed in the town center that one might have missed it. The whole cafe only consisted of the counter and a little space for customers to stand, with a single table and bench outside, so you were lucky if you got a seat. They had been going since she was fifteen. She would get a nice cup of milky coffee, Mykal with sugar and Andries, just black. But she swore there really was magic in those beans.

"It's in there, and I think," Anaisha said, pointing to the chest of drawers next to her bed. She turned back in her chair, biting the end of her pen as she racked her brain. She was doing some homework. Going back into the cocoon.

Aki needed a spare water bottle, he had practice soon.

Aki got up and opened the first drawer, and it was a drawer full of camera equipment. There were two/ three types of cameras inside. What looked like film... he didn't know much about photography.

Instinctually his head turned to Anaisha, she had her back straight, and chin tucked as she wrote answers avidly. You could see her sifting through her brain as she figured out the answers.

He had noticed that she had begun focusing so intently on everything she did that her mind could barely be diverted unless she was shaken out of it.

"Have you spoken to your photography teacher yet?" He asked casually, peering at the drawer.

" Ms. Benward?" Her voice went higher than usual. She blew out a breath "No. The meetings tomorrow, actually" she bit the end of her pen, turning around in her chair, "but I don't think I'm..."

"What the fuck are you doing?" Anaisha's eyes widened. She strode toward him and slammed the drawer shut. "Woah!" He held his hands up in defence, "I'm sorry?" A line formed between his brows.

"I'm sorry?" a line formed in between his brows.

She was breathing heavily and clenched her fists as she leaned on the drawers. Guarding it like a dragon.

Her breath slowed, and she mumbled, "No, I'm sorry," as she ferociously tucked her hair behind her ear.

She turned around and bent down, opening the drawer beneath it, pulling out a blue metal bottle. "Here," she said, passing him the bottle. He took it.

"That was your photography drawer," he said so softly. She nodded, tucking her hair behind her ears again.

"Anaisha, please go to that meeting, start photography again..." he leaned against the wall. "you were so good" he pursed his lip, looking at the ceiling as if her photographs were on the ceiling, "are so good" that wonderful calmness in his voice and eyes, made her feel bad and aggravated at the same time.

"You're going to be late, Aks," she said, turning back around to face her desk.

"Anaisha, come on," a little catch in the light waves of his voice, "talk to me about this," he said earnestly. She breathed in deeply, "you're going to be late" she flipped her textbook page with lightly trembling fingers.

Chapter 7

It's Friday Night

The city was alive tonight. It was a Friday night, and people were out to play. The group had never been to this club before, Inara had suggested it, and it was a good choice. The clubs in the city were different from the ones in town, which were rowdier, with music that you jumped around to, and a lot of the music was the type that you only admitted to listening to as a guilty pleasure. The city had clubs that reminded him more of home, and they were more upscale, cooler, and sleeker. A different kind of fun. The place was thronged with people, music resounding around the place, and other feelings intertwined within the notes.

Andries had decided to pace himself tonight, thinking if he got too drunk, there was a chance that it would end up pretty badly. It was too much of a gamble. He would either feel great or be depressed, as ever, and for the first time in a while, he was feeling better. He didn't feel like fucking that feeling up. He was at the bar, ordering a round for his friends.

"Ries?" He heard someone say his name, and he turned. Looking to his right and left, no one was there. Puzzled, he shook his head. He must've imagined it, and anyway, he would never have heard someone call him, it was way too loud in here anyway.

"Ries! Up here," that one was loud; that had to be real. Even his friends heard it and turned to the siren calling his name. He turned his head up, and a few steps above him was a gorgeous leggy girl with olive-brown skin and straight dark hair.

"oh my god," he said under his breath, forcing himself to move as she made her way down the stairs elegantly with the help of a man next to her.

"Hi!" He said, blinking in surprise. He couldn't help but keep the shock on his face.

She held her hands out and gave him a big hug. As his chin sat on her shoulder, he could now see his friends at the bar, now watching them.

Ahmed winked at him with a respectful nod. Then Inara whispered something in his ear, and his whole face changed. His mouth dropped, and Andries could read his lips saying, 'no way.' Inara had just informed Ahmed that that was Damini Elamin. They had talked about her when they spoke about their lives back home. They lived in a small city, and back home, possibly, every boy her age or a few years younger than her had a crush on her, or at least they had some sort of liking toward her at some point. She was sort of notorious in his class; he and Mykal were always considered 'lucky' for knowing her.

"So, how are you finding WU?" She said with a mischievous smile and a lift of her brow. She spoke like Naira, all silvery tones, but her voice was lower. He knew she had gone there. He and Mykal had both applied, not only for its prestige but also from the way she spoke of it.

He laughed, "Yeah," he said, scratching the back of his neck, a bashful look on his face. "I'm enjoying it."

"I'm jealous," she said with a laugh. She was wearing a stylish mini dress, with her hair straight and sleek.

She looked like Anaisha with her dark eyes and hair, but in other ways, their features were completely different. The differences and similarities were still stark in his mind.

"So, how have you been?" She said cocking her head to the side, her hair following the movement.

"What?" He leaned closer. It was really bloody loud. She repeated her question.

"I'm good, actually," he said, matching her volume as he raked a hand through his hair. "That's great." She smiled, even in the incandescent lights; he could see that her deep-set eyes were something else. But she didn't bring up the unsaid thing hovering in between them. It didn't feel appropriate. He was glad and grateful.

"So, how are you and my cousin?" She said with a smirk.

He stuttered for a minute, thinking she might've known. Never mind them. He got to break the news that they had broken up. Great.

" What!" She sputtered.

He nodded silently.

"Shit… I was not expecting that," she said, blinking in surprise. "me neither," he admitted, stuffing a hand in his pocket.

"Sorry, babe," she said, patting his shoulder. He knew at that moment she would be like Naira, holding no resentment toward her. She had seen him grow up and grown up with him. How could she?

"I wonder why they didn't tell us." Damini wondered out loud. She meant her and the rest of the cousins. "What?" He asked.

"I mean her and Naira, and by 'us, 'I mean the rest of the cousins" she smiled. He bit his lip silently, wondering too.

"Anyway, that's for me to wonder, not you," she laughed lightly. And changed the subject.

"Okay, I can see your friends waiting for you," she held his shoulder as she pointed toward them, giving them a little smile and waving with her fingers. They all waved back with big smiles. "Go, have fun!" He hugged her goodbye and turned around.

"Oh, and Ries, my tables up here if you want to join," she shouted, then walked back to him. She had forgotten something, she whispered in his ear, "and if you ever want to talk, I'm here." Her eyes were kind and light. She drew back "you have my number, right?" He nodded, and she smiled. "Okay, now go. I feel old seeing you here," she laughed.

They had a fun night and decided to walk around the city for a while. Inara was walking slowly next to Andries. She was a little blitzed, had a big constant smile on her face, and would randomly giggle funnily after making a joke.

She was singing a song under her breath and walking slowly on the streets.

He saw her trip and leaped over to steady her, and she laughed, "I'm okay, I'm okay" But still, he put an arm out to steady her. She didn't think she needed it, but... she did. She was a good drunk, jokey and happy, and funnily clumsy.

But still, she had that calmness about her. Self-assuredness. Regardless of how silly she may look when she tripped, it didn't bother her or embarrass her.

There were no shocking drunk revelations like she had no secrets that had to get out. Andries patted her hand with a laugh as she pointed out how "cool and magical" streetlights actually look.

They walked past a young boy, who looked to be in about his twenties, sitting cross-legged on a ratty blanket by the side of the street.

Blinking and staring into nothing. He had green eyes.

Andries turned his head back; he had seen a corner shop. "Can we go back for a minute?" He asked Inara.

She nodded with a yawn, without question, and leaned her head on his shoulder as they turned around and leaned more heavily on him now.

He walked in and brought a bottle of water, a banana, a packet of biscuits, and one of those pre-made sandwiches. He chose cheese to incase meat was an issue.

"You want anything?" He asked.

"No," she said, lifting her head from his shoulder and scrunching her nose, like a child. "You're so cute when you're drunk," he said.

"I'm always cute," she mumbled, wrinkling her nose. He laughed with a nod.

They were at the counter. "Ooh, actually, can I get a pack" she pointed to the cigarettes. "I thought you quit," Andries said, looking at her sideways.

"Yeah, but I'm drunk. So it doesn't count," she said slowly, with a slight slur but practicality in her voice. "And they're so good when you're drunk."

"How long has it been since you last had one?" He asked casually.

As the shopkeeper gave him the bill. He was an older-looking man with glasses and a checkered shirt. A small smile on his face at the conversation happening between the two young people.

Andries was opening his wallet as Inara said, "Like a year" she squinted to herself, "maybe a year and a half."

"You sure you want to ruin that now?" He said with a casual lilt in his voice, just asking the question. "I mean, a year and a half are pretty long. But it's up to you." He said as he put some cash on the counter.

"Please, keep the change," Andries said with a kind smile.

"Thank you," he replied with a smile and a little laugh at the two of them and how Andries had swindled Inara. "yeah, I'll leave it," Inara groaned. She didn't realize that Andries had already paid.

They got out, Inara once again leaning on his shoulder. And stopped at where the young man was sitting.

"Hey. I wanted to give you this..." Andries said as he handed over the plastic bag to the boy.

Inara moved to stand upright now.

The boy smiled, looking up "thank you so much," he said. "You eat cheese, right?" Andries asked.

"Love it, haven't eaten it in some time, though," he smirked. Some teeth were missing. "Well, enjoy," Andries said with a kind smile.

"That was nice, Ries," she said to him quietly.

'Ries 'hearing that in someone else's voice felt weird. But it was okay, nice actually.

He lifted his eyes to the sky, and they landed on the brightest star in the sky. "he lives in me," Andries whispered.

"He does," she uttered, a small, bittersweet smile on her face.

He looked to the side, letting Inara rest on him, the way he had for the past few weeks, her arm hooked into his.They were walking by the water, close to the hotel and the lights of the skyline twinkled against the dark, dark blue of the sky. The only natural light is the why glow of the crescent moon shining above it all. You could hear the people, their music, and their chatter.

You could see through windows. Through the slightly ajar curtains and see a peak into the lives of families chatting around a table or a single person eating their dinner, the light of a TV lighting them up.

Every person had a story, a life, a loss, and a love just like him. It dawned on him that he was feeling sonder. He felt so much less alone. He got why Mykal loved the city.

The city felt diaphanous and opaque at the same time.

Spring Break

"Where's Naira?" Her aunt said as Anaisha sat down. Her parents had forced her to come straight to her grandparent's house, and they weren't even here yet. Anaisha thought with an internal eye roll. It was only Naira's parents and her grandparents who were having a nap.

"What do you mean?" Anaisha said, taking a sip of water. "She and Aki are coming in two days" Nahla cocked her head to the side, one brow quirked. That was such a Naira look.

"I mean, they're coming together" Anaisha looked at her expectantly. "She didn't tell you?" Anaisha played with her rings. Her aunt was more chilled than her own, but still, she would have expected Naira to tell her.

"No," she stuck her tongue in her cheek.

"They're just doing this little road trip," she shrugged. Her aunt squinted suspiciously "it's only for two days, Jiji," she said, reaching for her Aunt's knee comfortingly, a small smile on her lips.

She blew a held breath out and looked up to heaven. "I used to do everything in my power to get her to leave the house and go to school, and now she won't even come back," her aunt laughed, a light wariness in her voice.

"It's fine," she said gently, "she's with Aki, and you know him. He'll keep her out of trouble," Anaisha laughed. And her aunt held her hand for her own reassurance "yeah, your right."

Naira was driving. She had recently gotten a new car, which was actually Damini's old car, an emerald green convertible. She remembered loving it when Damini drove them around toward the end of family events when the kids wanted to get out.

She had wanted to let her hair loose, feel like a heroine driving away in a getaway car. But unfortunately for her, that dream was squashed once her hair started flying in her eyes.

So instead, they were driving with the roof down, Naira's hair tied up and Aki's classic black square sunglasses, on the winding road at the edge of a cliff overlooking the sea.

Akihiko raised the music, and they both were smiling happily. They both shared a similar taste in music. And even if the music was shit, it wouldn't matter because sunshine, the sea, and the excitement of spring break were jumping at the tip of their minds. They had both passed their midterm exams with pretty high grades, above the minimum of what they needed for the university courses they would start in a couple of months.

From her peripheral vision, Naira saw a little sign for a small restaurant. "Hungry?" "I could eat." Aki shrugged,

219

"You can always eat." She laughed. At that, she expertly switched lanes and made her way up toward the stop. Oddly, driving didn't make her anxious, it actually made her feel more in control.

They walked in; you could see the marks of fingerprints on the silver handle as they walked in. A laminated menu card already sitting

"Do you think they have oat milk?"

Aki laughed, "doesn't it hurt to ask?" They took a seat in a little cubicle. The leather on the red seats was cracking, and the food was very, very average; there was also no oat milk.

But Aki and Naira were bosom buddies, and being together no matter where or when was a guaranteed good time. They either couldn't stop laughing or sat in comfortable silence, sipping their milkshakes.

Naira pulled over. She knew Aki was asleep behind his sunglasses. He had said he was "resting his eyes," but she knew better. "Aks," she said softly, pushing him gently.

"I'm awake," he mumbled, "I was just resting my eyes," he yawned. "Why have we stopped," he said, rubbing his eyes beneath his sunglasses.

"Because I have the perfect thing to wake you up," she pointed to the left, toward the sea and the cliffs.

He leaned forward, taking in what she had pointed at, a group of people was standing at the edge of the cliff in their swimsuits, and then two of them jumped.

"No way..." he said, whipping his sunglasses off.

"Yeah!" She turned to face him excitedly, a glint of mischief in her green eyes. She got out of the car. He opened his own door, jogging over to her, "no, seriously, no way." He crossed his arms, dark eyes serious. "What do you mean?" She said, already taking off her shorts.

"You're already wearing a swimsuit," his chin jutted back. She rolled her eyes, "we're driving next to the beach, silly."

"Naira, seriously. This is not a good idea," he said sternly.

"Ak's, it's fine. I'll talk to them and do it" she gestured toward the group behind them, "you don't have to if you don't want to" she shrugged, her hands on her hips.

He bit his lip, following her as she strode over to the group of people.

"Hi!" She waved at one of the girls in the group. She looked to be only a little older than the two of them.

Aki raked a hand through his hair, causing it to stick up straight. He didn't know what to say to her to stop her.

He could see Naira flipping her hair and laughing. She came back with her winsome smile and an older woman wearing a black cover-up and floppy hat along with a young man with long curly brown hair and tanned skin. "This is Mrs. Albani," she said, gesturing to the woman, and "Tenant" she pointed to the guy. "This is my friend Aki" she smiled.

He put his hand out, shaking both of their hands.

Mrs. Albani was actually really sweet; she had short manicured nails and a lot of jewelry on her wrist. She was here on a family trip, and Tenant was the cliff diving expert they were referred to.

"I'll take you guys," he gestured toward the two of them, "teach you how to do it" he nodded with serious eyes. That seemed like a dichotomy compared to his youthful smile and long curly hair. "This is usually the spot we choose for visitors, who have never done it before."

Aki nodded, feeling better as Tenant carried on speaking.

"We'd be happy for you guys to join us" Mrs. Albani smiled, that motherly smile. The type that promised safety and kindness. But she was still a stranger.

"Just a jump or two," Aki laughed nervously. "Ok, let me go grab my trunks" he grabbed Naira's hand, pulling her with him.

They moved behind some rocks as he went behind and changed. "They're still strangers Nai" he said, as he took off his sweatpants.

"Aks," he could already tell what look she was making, "we live in like the safest place ever, and Tenant is from that hotel further down… " She clicked her tongue, trying to remember the name.

221

"The Beach House" Aki said, It was a very popular resort for many visitors. He had actually gone fly boarding there once with his family. "Let's do this," he smiled, coming out from behind the rock.

It was a very popular resort for many visitors. He had actually gone fly boarding there once with his family. "Let's do this," he smiled, coming out from behind the rock.

"First, are you guys confident swimmers?" He asked, holding both hands in front of his body. They both nodded, "We grew up next to the beach, so we're good" Aki nodded seriously. "Amazing," he nodded with a smile. "No tricks," he said, slicing a hand through the air.

Tenant explained that they had to and handed them the five-finger shoes that looked like gloved socks.

Naira went first. She stood at the edge of the cliff and looked down at the turquoise blue water, waves gently ebbing beneath her. The sun makes the water glow with a pearly colour. She gulped; she could hear every breath she took, feel every beat her heart made. Pounding against her chest hard. She clenched and unclenched her fingers, her hands felt clammy. It was like her body was telling her to run away. Pounding against her chest hard. She could feel the nerves bouncing around her body as she looked down. It was scarier than she had thought it would be. She felt so fucking high up as she looked down.

But there was that loud voice in her head telling her to "fuck it and do it," So she did. She jumped.

For a second, she was flying and falling at the same time, forgetting everything she had ever said or been told.

She slammed into the water and broke into it. The feel of water rushed onto her body... Everything slowed...all the sounds and feelings of the world dissipated.

The feeling in her ears changed to something exotic in all her senses. All she could see was her limbs and blue, her hair floating around her.

Then her brain came back to her, and she kicked her legs, swimming up her head and bouncing above water. She was blinking and panting as she naturally started treading water. 'that

222

was so fast, 'she thought. It felt like she had been electrified. There was a slight sting from the salt in her eyes, but she didn't care.

She had made it. She did it.

She couldn't help but smile and laugh. It was a complete rush, and she felt completely and utterly alive.

She looked up at Aki, holding one hand on her forehead, shielding her eyes from the sun. She couldn't see him clearly, but she knew he was there.

"Come on!" She shouted, "The water's-"and before she could finish her sentence, he had jumped. She couldn't help but laugh as his head came up, pressing his nose.

"Woah!" He shouted as he treaded and swam toward her.

"Insane, right!" She swam toward him, her limbs felt shaky as they moved with a mind of their own.

They pushed themselves up as they climbed up. Her arms and legs were slightly shaking in the best way; she felt wired.

"That was amazing," she breathed as the oldest Albani daughter handed them their towels. It was cold, but the sun was out at the same time, warming their skin. It was a complete rush.

They got back in the car and put towels on the seats so they wouldn't get them wet while the wind dried their hair.

Even driving felt cooler, the endorphins or adrenaline. Whatever the fuck it is... she thought. She could feel them. They blasted the music as they drove onward.

What a way to start the little trip...

"How did you convince them to let you do it with them? And free of charge too?"

"I just asked," she shrugged. "And who can say no to me?" She winked as she tightened her hands on the wheel.

The key card clicked, and they entered the room. "This is so cute," Naira said as they walked in.

It was a small suite with two bedrooms, full of light beige, white, and pop of orange with small pillows and an orange sofa. Of course, the view of the ocean, no matter how many times she had seen it, never got old.

They sat on the sofa, waiting for the food to come. Aki was sitting on the sofa, leaning his head back, eyes closed with Naira's leg crossed over on his lap as she lay down reading a book. It had a red and pink cover.

" What made you think of doing that today?" He asked, a smile in his voice.

She lay her book on her chest, looking up at the ceiling. There were brass-hanging lights coming down from the white wall.

"I don't know," she bit her lip, "some midsummer madness, I guess," she said quietly. "It's spring," he side-eyed her with a grin.

She giggled "mid-spring madness, then" she blinked leisurely. They were both wonderfully exhausted.

There was a knock on the door.

"Finally," Naira groaned as she took her legs off Aki, who jogged over to open the door. "Hi, come in" he opened the door wider, and A waiter walked in with a round white cloth-covered table on wheels, with a margarita pizza, salad, and pasta.

"Thank you," the waiter smiled as he left "if you need anything else, just call, and the kitchen closes at midnight" The smell of food infused the air.

They sat down to eat, and she didn't know if it was the smell of pizza, but she jumped up from her seat, "oh my god! I totally forgot I packed this!" She ran over to her room, shuffled through her bags, and came out with a small plastic bag with some green stuff that looked like herbs in it.

"Wanna get high?" She raised a sly brow, taking out a fat, fudgy-looking brownie.

He scratched his jaw, "we might need more food" They ordered a plate of fries and some cookies. Naira and Aki had only been high once before, last summer. Aki brought speakers and put some music on as Naira dimmed the lights.

"I'm excited" Naira clapped her hands together like a little kid.

"Same" Aki nodded with a roguish grin. He hopped up on the centre table and put a sock over the fire alarm.

There it was, Aki thought as he leaned back on the sofa, his eyes drooping down. The music felt richer, like it was playing from inside his own head. He started smiling without really knowing why...Naira took a slice of pizza, she slumped, and patted Aki.

"That's really good," she whispered. It tasted insane. It wasn't even that warm anymore, but it tasted fucking fantastic. "Why are you whispering?"

"I don't know," she whispered back and turned back, munching on her pizza. "What were we talking about? She mumbled.

"Umm..." he licked his lips.

"This is really orange," Naira said, stroking the arm of the couch. "But it's so soft" his head lulled as it turned to face her

Naira started smiling and covered her mouth, huffing a laugh. "What?" Aki said softly.

Naira pressed her lips together, but the laugh didn't leave. She shook her head, slapping his shoulder. "It's just..." she couldn't stop laughing, oh my god. "The..." she pointed at nothing.

They had been smart and thought ahead by already setting a movie on, and so all they had to do was press one button to start it. It was a comedy.

They could not stop laughing, and Naira had so many random questions that Aki told her to write the questions down. So she began writing down her questions on her phone; she barely knew what she was writing...

"I swear I'm still high," Naira laughed as she took Aki's phone to change the song, he was driving, and she had one leg tucked under her thigh, leaning back as she slightly reclined the seat. Her thumb absently scrolled through their shared playlist called 'only for the ears of Aks and Nairu,' twisting her lips as she looked through.

A message alert from Anaisha pinged on his phone. She moved her thumb to swipe it up automatically, but her thumb lingered there for a moment as her eyes saw the word 'babe.'

She took a breath in for a moment, blinking slowly. Then she reached for the volume dial and slowly put it down. Anaisha wasn't like her or Damini; she never called her friends 'babe'.

225

"Hey, what-" Aki said, quickly looking over at her.

"What is this meant to mean?" She said in a deadly soft voice as she read out the message, "especially when it's coming from my cousin" her eyes slid over to him. Her eyes cut to him, a blade in the look. Her voice was soft, but he could see her chest rising.

Aki's knuckles tightened around the wheel.

"What, no answer?" She said, turning away from him and looking forward, her chest still rising. The blade had now moved to her throat.

"I don't want to lie to you," he breathed out.

"You already have," she shrugged in a nonchalant manner, but her chest rose, "so I wouldn't worry about that," she said, deadpan.

"Naira..."

"What song do you want to listen to? How about 'traitor?' I feel like you'd like it."

Like we said, Naira didn't get loud like Anaisha, but when she was mad, she could throw a verbal punch. Straight jabs.

"When?"

"Naira." Aki groaned, trying to look over at her whilst keeping his focus on the road. "Answer me"

"Were not even dating, I-"

"I honestly don't give a fuck what you two are. Just answer the question." She patted her lap as if she was fluffing crumbs off, "Since when?"

"When we went to the music together," he couldn't even look at her.

"Nice," she said icily, pressing her lips tightly together. Cold anger echoed through the car.

Aki tightened his hands on the wheel and gulped down, opened his mouth to speak just as she moved her hand back to the volume dial and made it louder than it was before, drowning out anything that Aki could have said and her own thoughts. She didn't look at him from that point on.

Aki tightened his hands on the wheel and swore under his breath.

He did everything he could to keep his focus on the road and not on the fact that he just majorly fucked up with his best friend.

They reached Naira's grandparent's house at lunchtime, he was supposed to have lunch at their house and then go home, but he didn't know if that was happening anymore.

He parked, and Naira silently got out of the car, slamming the door shut. That was the only real sign of fury she had shown. She went to the boot and took her bag out.

He took a deep breath, looking straight ahead. He heard his door open.

"What are you doing, staring into space? She said, standing above him, a hand on her hip, the other on her forehead shading the sun out of her eyes. "Get out." Her rings and bracelets glittering from the sunshine. He scrunching his eyebrows together, "what?"

"Aren't you coming for lunch?" She said, huffing out a breath and tapping her foot on the ground.

"I thought you might not want me to," he said slowly, wary eyes watching her.

"My family won't understand and will make the biggest commotion if you don't come," she said with a roll of her eyes "or did you want me to tell them that you and Anaisha are fucking?" She said, fixing her bag on her shoulder.

"We haven't," he started.

"I really don't care. Just come." she said, running a cool hand through her hair, shaking it out. "God, I look like shit," she said, bending down to look into the rear-view mirror.

"Feel like it too," she mumbled to herself as she straightened. Aki winced and looked down at his hands.

"Okay," he gulped. "I'm coming," he said as he got out of the car.

"Wrong cousin," Naira said, so quickly it felt like a slap. And he would've laughed if she was joking. He wished she were joking.

"I'm home!" Naira shouted as she opened the door. "And Aki's here" she had a smile on her face but looked at him with absolute loathing.

227

"Naira!" Damini said as she strode into the foyer in a black tank top and flowy white pants. She gave Naira a huge hug. A proper one, holding on to her for a few minutes. "I missed you," she said.

"Me too," Naira said and blew out a breath she didn't realize she was holding. Damini then turned to greet Aki as Naira turned to see Jai and Anaisha in front of her.

Anaisha stood a little bit ahead of Jai, beaming. But Naira angled her body around Anaisha and hugged Jai. Jai raised his eyebrows up, eyes flicking between Anaisha and Naira.

Anaisha did a double take, scrunching her eyebrows together, her mouth slightly agape. One by one, the rest of the family came in to greet her and Aki, and Naira didn't say hello to Anaisha.

Anaisha tapped Naira's shoulder, a smile on her face "hey!"

Naira popped her shoulder roughly, shaking Anaisha's hand off. "Can I just go say hi to my parents first?" she said irritably.

Anaisha drew her head back, rapidly blinking. "Of course."

"Naira," Damini said in a disapproving tone, her eyebrows scrunched together.

She went over and gave her parents a hug and then went back to stand next to Damini, "when's dinner?" She said. "I'm starving," she said, playing with her rings.

"Are you okay?" Damini asked, her wide eyes searching Naira's face.

"I'll tell you later," she said as she flipped her hair over her shoulder with a huff. Anaisha went over to Aki to say hello with a hug.

Naira glared at them.

Aki drawback as fast as possible.

"Aki," Anaisha said with a whisper drawing her head back in shock. "I'll explain later," he whispered and moved away from her.

Dinner parties can be dangerous

"Andries how are you?" Anaisha's mother said you could tell she was genuinely asking, and he was comfortable enough with her that he could be honest, well, and as honest as he could be to an adult.

228

"I wasn't great," he smiled ruefully, with a rough laugh. "But I'm better now. I'm getting better." He nodded strength in his movement.

She nodded, "understandably, nor was Anaisha. Or the rest of you kiddos…" her eyes were grave, but then she smiled, "but it's good that you have each other." She had the same nose as her daughter but with fuller lips.

He cocked his head to the side, blue eyes squinting. Suddenly he felt a hand on his arm.

"What are you two chatting about?" Anaisha said, striding towards them. She stood next to him, and he sucked in a breath. She was so close that he could smell her jasmine-scented perfume.

"Just… life," her mother said, intent eyes on her daughter. They both stood in the same way, back straight and neck tall.

"Life," Anaisha nodded, knowing what she actually meant 'and death.'

"Anyway, it's good you have each other," Mahita said, reaching over to touch Andries's arm with a comforting hand. A kind, soft smile on her face.

"Yes, we do," he said, slowly blinking, everything clicking into place. His blue eyes fell on Anaisha. She looked away hurriedly. Mahita left to go get the food.

"Anaisha, Naira," she called; Anaisha moved to go.

Something caught at her hand. She already knew whom it was from how it felt. "We need to talk." He whispered.

It still did something to her spine. She nodded quickly and pulled her hand away.

After dinner, he knew where to find her. She was at the bottom of the stairs, and he followed her silently. They came to her bedroom.

She closed her door, locking it.

"Why didn't you tell them?" Andries asked.

"In a minute," she said, pushing her hands against his chest. Her lips met his. It felt really right like this was exactly what they needed. A sense of comfort, but they had the same electricity crackling between them. A comfortable crackle.

It was like how seeing the ocean always made them feel at home, but when you saw it at high tide, it looked different, more dangerous, but it still reminded them of home.

"No, no, this is wrong," she said, drawing back from him hurriedly.

"Why? What's wrong?" He said, his head dipped, his blue eyes looking at her.

"It's just, I shouldn't be doing this," she gulped and, with great self-control, took a step back. "But why-" he said, staying still where he was.

"Because we broke up," she said quickly.

"Fair enough," he blew a breath out and raked a hand through his hair. "Just give me a minute, yeah?" He said as he sat down on the loveseat, closing his eyes and breathing deeply.

"Are you okay?" Andries said as he looked up at Anaisha. "Yeah," she answered as she tucked her hair behind her ears.

"You don't seem it," he said slowly with a knowing smile, resting his elbows on his knees, cocking his head to the side. Ready to listen.

"I just shouldn't have kissed you," she said, holding a hand to her forehead with a groan. "Was I really that bad?" He smirked.

She rolled her eyes, "shut up."

"Are you okay, Anaish?" He asked again, touching the scar on his eyebrow.

"Stop, Ries, don't treat me like I'm some sucking" she shook her head. "God, just a few hours of seeing you, and I've already lost my mind."

She blew out a breath and began again, "don't treat me like I'm some fucking" she slowed down on those last two words, "delicate flower, I'm not."

"When have I ever?" He thought aloud, and then rolled his eyes.

He had never treated her like a delicate flower, she knew that too. But she wasn't thinking straight.

"I'm fine. Naira's just mad at me."

"Why?" Immediately he looked up, sincerity unfolding in his eyes.

230

"Just- we had a stupid fight," she said, shooing his questioning look away like she was shooing off a fly, "and I really should not have kissed you," she repeated, biting her lip.

"I'm not gonna lie, Aish, I'm confused" he scratched his neck. "I mean, first you don't tell your parents that we were broken up, then you kiss me," he looked up at her, piercing her with those eyes, "and now you regret it?" She opened her mouth to talk and then closed it again, chewing at her bottom lip.

"You're not delicate." He said, looking at her chewing on her lip, but her back was still straight, "But this is" he motioned at the two of them,

"This," she mimicked his pointing, "is nothing," she said, her voice stern turning to sit on her bed. Andries's eyes flickered. Naira had never told her what he said... he didn't blame her.

"What?" Anaisha said; she caught the flicker.

He shook his head and touched the scar on his brow. "Why is it 'nothing'?" He said simply. She was surprised he didn't try and convince her, just respectfully questioned. She knew what was going through his head with just those two words.

She had kissed him, and she hadn't told her parents anything about them.

"I don't know why I just did that," she said honestly and gulped, "and as for my family, I told everyone," meaning their friends, "not to tell anyone; they didn't even know we were dating Ries. How could I explain that we just stopped being friends after one of our other friends died," she said throwing an arm into the air. Frustration radiated off her.

She sat on her bed. Hugging her knees close to her chin. Her back is bending. Closing herself. But, she was so honest in her words.

"We were meant to go through this together, you and me. Together" she repeated like the word was a memory she was trying to hold on to. "but then you abandoned me" she shook her head slowly, painfully ran one hand through her hair, and turned her face to the side, as if she couldn't face the fact herself. "No, you forced me to abandon you."

"I just couldn't deal with it, Aish; he was my brother." His voice cracked. He still is, he thought silently to himself. Always would be.

231

"He was your brother... is," she said sensitively, softly. But she had to be honest right now, bravely so. "He was also one of my best friends, Ries. I needed you too."

She laid a hand on her mouth, her words muffled as she started to cry. She hated when this happened when her crying turned into horrendous hiccups from which she couldn't get words out.

"I keep trying... to move on" she shook her head. That wasn't the right word. He waited and let her find her words. "To move… forward. Sometimes people do things that remind me of him" she ran both hands through her hair and looked down. This was the first time she was being honest, and it was difficult. "I just realize that no one will ever be able to replace him."

"Of course, no one can replace him, Aish. Why would you want someone to?" "Because," she wept, "I don't think I can do this without him."

She placed her chin on her knee. She had caught her breath now and was uttering softly. "There are even times when I feel like he's right there next to me," she smiled, a small loving smile. His breath caught at the fact that she had experienced the same thing he had. But he didn't want to interrupt her and breathed out slowly as she carried on.

"But then," a single tear slipped from her eye. "Something happens, which reminds me that he's just not there anymore, and I can do everything" she pulls at one side of her face with her fingers as if she had a headache. "To keep his memory alive, but he's just not here. He's not here to make new ones or reminisce on old ones" her breathing started to get very shallow. "And I might never hear him laugh again, joke with him again, or see him smile" her voice breaks on the last word, and she swallows the cry in her chest.

Suddenly, her hand covered her mouth, and her shoulders began to shake. Andries came over and put his arm around her. She moved to the scent of him; god, she missed him. And sobbed into his chest as he stroked her hair and let her rest on him. She vented to him.

She told him about how she had made him feel, and he apologized and explained.

She told him about how frustrating it was that Naira was mad at her. He didn't ask why she was.

She told him about how it felt to be jealous of her relationship with Damini.

232

She told him her secrets about how she had applied to the photography and business course and may not go on tour. Her tears dried.

And they made jokes and laughed.

She told him about how nervous she was about getting into the course that she had applied to. She told Andries about Naira being mad at her as her tears dried. They even just chilled.

"Do you want to watch something?" She asked, her voice hoarse from the talking and crying "we should probably go down" he laughed; he had no idea how long they'd been up here.

"Or just stay here?" She said, holding her breath, playing with her nails, looking at him through her eyelashes, her intent eyes blinking and hopeful.

"Okay, let's stay," he said with a smile. He couldn't fight that look.

She blew out a breath and started beaming. "Okay," she said, grabbing her laptop.

As they watched, they spoke.

"I need to tell you something," she gulped, raising her head from his shoulder.

"What's up?" He blinked slowly, taking in her face "what is it?" He said, laughing nervously. She took a deep breath, gaining up the courage.

"You just seem different and better," she smiled softly, "and so I think you should know..." "Thank you," his cheeks went pink as he raked a hand through his hair, "I am," he said looking at her.

"You know Aki?" She began.

He laughed, "yes, obviously" he nodded.

"Well, he and I are kind of together." She gulped "were" she squinted, "I don't really know... but we were basically seeing each other"

She usually didn't fumble when she was talking.

His face paled as he nodded, taking the information in. "right," he said as he bit his tongue. He gulped, looking towards the door for a moment. He felt like his heart might've stopped.

"I'm sorry," she whispered, a hand on his shoulder. And that brought him back to life.

He blinked, the image of Inara's calmness in his head. Took a breath in and asked a question. "Can you give me a minute?" He asked. Instinctively her head drew back; that's not what she was expecting. She nodded, then gulped. He went to the bathroom. Closed the door behind him. It was just him now. He looked in the mirror for a second.

He turned the faucet on.

Anaisha could hear it from her bedroom. She put some music on her phone. Trying to distract herself, she soon realized that wasn't really possible.

Andries splashed some water on his face, then patted his face dry. He held the towel on his cheek for a moment longer. Closing his eyes and sees both Inara and Mykal, this time in his mind's eye, the angel and the better devil out of the two.

He looked in the mirror, seeing into his own blue eyes. So, Naira had never told her about their conversation on the beach… weirdly, he wasn't mad at all. It seemed like the right decision, after all.

Why did he always seem to have self-realizations in bathroom mirrors?

He took a deep breath in, and weirdly he had one of those bittersweet smiles on his face. This was one of those moments in life, and he was going to do it right.

He came back out, delicately closing the door behind him. Raking the other hand through his hair, "so, how long have you guys been together?" He said, walking back over to where he was sitting on the bed. Sitting back down as if he had never left.

She didn't realize that she was taking in his sandalwood cologne until he had gone to the bathroom just now. As soon as he sat down, she was hit with it again. During the days, he would smell the coffee and sandalwood cologne, but at night it was just the cologne and clean clothes.

"We're not." She said, leaning back into the pillows. "Together, I mean. We've just gone on a few dates and stuff and spent time together," she said shyly.

"So you... chilling," he said, leaning back on the bed. He turned his head to the side with a sideways smile.

She couldn't help but laugh a little, "chilling," she nodded.

"Do you like him?" He asked her, still that half smile on his face.

"Yeah, he's really sweet and kind," she cocked her head to the side and played with her rings, "and he's very chilled, and we have great conversations." Her eyes flickered up to him.

"He's a very good friend," Andries added, thinking of Aki and Naira. "That he is," Anaisha said softly.

"And very handsome," Andries said, inclining his head. She smirked, "always helps."

"Loyal," he stepped slowly on that word, "that's very important," he said, looking up at her. "Very," she said slowly, as she met his eyes, "but, it's not..." she bit her lip. He knew what she wanted to say. She wanted to say 'us. 'He clicked his tongue, "never could be," he winked.

He had taken that so well. There was a little glow in her chest of pride.

"But, I really fucked up now, Ries." She put her hands over her face and dragged them down. "I feel terrible."

"Were you guys exclusive?" He asked.

"No." she shook her head and took a breath in, "but that's not the point."

"I don't even know if this really would count. You were upset, and we have... memories," she bit her lip.

"Exactly." He had goosebumps.

They held each other's eyes, the way they held on to the memories of what felt like a different lifetime.

Then she moved and leaned her head on his shoulder, a Saudade glow around her. Around them, really.

They would always have memories.

"They're going to wonder where we are…." Andries said.

"It's okay. People rarely question the grieving" she looked at him with those sharp eyes, a ghost of a smile on her lips.

But still, they got up to leave. However, Andries noticed something on her side table. "What's this?" He said, holding up a bottle of tablets.

She blew out a breath, "Sleeping pills" she tucked a lock of hair behind her ear. She'd never had trouble sleeping before, he thought. "well, I do now, okay." Did he say that out loud, he thought. No, he didn't; she just always knew what he was thinking, just by a certain blue-eyed look she could tell. "Otherwise, I would just stay up the whole night with some music on until I could hear birds chirping. They'd gone down. And everyone just thought I started waking up early. I watched the sunrise. It didn't help." She played with a lock of hair.

"I do too," he cleared his throat, "have trouble sleeping, I mean" she nodded. She understood.

That night when everyone was leaving, she hugged Andries and whispered something in his ear. Then she looked at him and smiled and walked away. She was wearing a mini blue dress that night. A deep blue.

So he did. He did come over later that night. When the whole house was asleep, and it was just the two of them, simple and quiet. It felt familiar and different as she crept outside, and they went up the stairs, careful as they took the stairs.

He changed out of his clothes to just his boxers, and she was already wearing her pyjamas. Just a simple pair of black shorts and a grey t-shirt. They spoke for a bit as they went to sleep. They didn't do anything. In reality, they both knew that was not what they were looking for. They just talked and slept in the same bed, holding each other. They just both missed their best friends. Anaisha hadn't slept that well in ages, and Andries barely slept… because he didn't want to lose one moment of these last moments he had with her like this.

When they woke up, she told him not to sneak out. "You can use the front door; I'll drop you down… they're probably gone anyway." It was a Monday, and only the kids had holidays. And anyway, in times like these, she didn't care anymore.

Chapter 8

Parental advice

"Hey, Pops," Naira said, walking in, tossing her bag on the table, and tossing herself on the couch, down beside him.

"That's a very expensive bag, you know?" He said, eyeing her over his glasses, with a smirk on his face.

Naira rolled her eyes, "sorry," she said, turning her head to look at him.

He typed a little more on his laptop and then promptly took his glasses off and closed the lid of his laptop. He sometimes worked at night, especially on a weekend night, getting ready for the next day. She wished she could be more like him. She was sure she could work just as hard as he could, but she had to find something she loved first. If only reading could be an occupation, she thought as she lay her head on her father's shoulder.

"Fun night?" He asked. The soft yellow glow of the family room made the words comforting and calm. "Yeah, it was good," the kids had dipped earlier to go grab a coffee and therefore come back home later. They sat in comfortable silence for a few minutes.

"I'm proud of you, Nairu," he said.

"For?" Naira asked with a smirk. She was used to this. Her father always showed affection easily and without hesitation, especially to his youngest daughter. She knew she was his favourite.

"Everything. The way you have dealt with your anxiety, who you are now. All of it. Everyday"

"Thanks, Dad," Naira said, smiling shyly at the TV across them. Playing with her rings, holding on to the one she got for her last birthday gift from her parents.

"I couldn't have done it without you and Mamma," she said honestly, the soft hue of the room enabling an easy honesty. They had answered her every anxious phone call, even when her Dad was in the middle of working. If he were in a meeting, he'd quickly call his wife, telling her to take over for a minute. They both booked her therapy appointments. She knew he spoke to Naila all the time, asking for updates on her progress.

Sometimes she felt like her anxiety was like a bad ex, something that brought forth pain when you remembered it, but also that feeling of relief that you were no longer together. And a certain pride and strength that you survived. And that you actually better from it. Oddly, maybe even because of it. Lighting a fire under you. Or, in her case, lighting a lightning strike.

"Family, it's a weird thing, right?" She asked.

He laughed, "Sometimes," he said. "But it's special and worth it. It means something, and if you have a good one, you should consider yourself lucky."

She mumbled something as her eyes fluttered shut.

"Go to sleep, doll," he said. He could feel her weighing into him with gentle tiredness, taking her over. She rubbed her eyes as she got up. He loved seeing her this way; it swelled him up with a nostalgic joy he couldn't quite explain. His daughter was growing up fast and slow at the same time, and then she would do small things like rub her eyes, which just reminded her that she was still his child, a baby.

She went to open the door, and just as she was about to, her father said, "Naira,"

"Hmm," she said with sleepy eyes.

"Even a good family sometimes has its problems. And even our own blood can make mistakes, and it doesn't mean you have to forgive just because they're your family. But it doesn't mean you shouldn't let them redeem themselves either," he said. She nodded.

" Sleep easy, kid," he said as he put his glasses back on. Everything would be fine. She had her parents. Everything would be fine.

Three Weeks Later

"Come in," Naira called at the knock on her door. She was curled on her grey fluffy beanbag, submerged in the chair and with a book in her hands.

Anaisha walked in with tentative footsteps.

Naira peered up, her green eyes following Anaisha like a panther. In true character, she was reading a book, "Let me just finish this page, and I'll be with you," her voice low and clear. Anaisha nodded. The novel was a lemon yellow, with block grey letters as the title.

Usually, while she was reading, she would tell her to leave and come back later, or she would finish the page and then pour out her feelings for the next minute.

She wouldn't do any of those things today, though...

Naira's eyes scanned the page as Anaisha sat on the deckchair absentmindedly, staring at the clouds.

She angled herself to her bed and grabbed her bookmark, placing it in. Her books were 'well-loved 'as she called them. Anaisha called them creased.

"What's up?" Naira said, closing her book with a curt smile.

"I thought we could talk today?" Anaisha said, tucking her hair behind her ears. Naira had told her to just leave her be during the spring break. She wanted them both to just enjoy the well-deserved break without any arguments, and they could talk again when they were back at school. Anaisha reluctantly agreed. They had never gone that long without speaking to each other.

Naira just nodded, looking at Anaisha with blank green eyes and a straight mouth.

"I want to start by saying I'm really sorry for lying to you." She looked down at Naira with sincere, soft eyes, the kind of eyes that knew they had caused pain or fucked up and would now do anything to change it. That regretful painful look. Naira just blinked and nodded.

"I... we," Anaisha said cocking her head to the side as if her mind poked her to remember, "didn't mean to hurt you at all. Ever" She said, shaking her head earnestly, "it's just that..." she blew a breath out, "after everything that happened. I didn't know how everyone would react or what they would say," she said. Turning her head and looking out the window for a moment, trouble brimming those dark eyes, she continued, "and it also just wasn't a big deal," she said with a huffed small laugh to herself, "and I didn't want it to get blown out of proportion," she said softly.

"Anyway," she shook her head again and straightened her back, "all this to say, I'm really sorry, Nairu, you're my baby cousin, and I love you, and I never meant to hurt you," her chest rising as she looked down at Naira, her hands on her lap.

Naira nodded with a little smile as she spun her bracelet around her wrist and said, "Its okay." Then she picked up her book again and started reading as Anaisha sat there, back straight, mind frazzled.

Anaisha looked around the room like one of the inanimate objects could advise her on what to do.

The best she could come up with was, "are you sure?" She said with squinted eyes.

Naira blinked her long lashes up at her slowly. "You did hurt me," Naira said, looking up at her, eyes like a wolf. "And betrayed me by going behind my back," she said, tucking her legs further under her knees. She stuck her tongue in her cheek, "but whatever, what's done is done," she shrugged as she flipped her hair off her shoulder.

"I don't want it to be a 'what's done is done situation," Anaisha said, jutting her head out, "I want us to be good" Anaisha blinked that same regretful look.

"Well, you both hurt and betrayed me, and you both know me well enough to know that that would hurt me." She looked up at the ceiling, taking a breath in, "a lot." She whispered.

"Naira-"

"Don't," Naira said, holding a calm hand up. "Like I already said, what's done is done. I know now," she lifted one shoulder up, "and it is what it is. I hope you guys make each other happy," she said blankly.

"Naira," Anaisha said, blowing out a breath in the most older cousin way possible. "You're clearly not okay, and I'm not leaving like this," she said, crossing her legs to make her point.

"Fine. Don't." Naira said and picked up her book, and started reading again.

Anaisha rolled her eyes. Naira was notorious for her stubborn nature, being the youngest. She nearly always got her way.

"Naira, please..."

Naira blew out a breath. "Fine. You want to talk, I'll talk," Naira said, her eyes turning into green slits.

"You both betrayed me by lying over the course of a couple of months." Her teeth gritted. "And you didn't need to tell everyone. You could have just had the decency to ask me how I felt about it, as your cousin and his best friend. So either you both are selfish or stupid" "selfish?" Anaisha repeated.

"I'm not done." Naira said in one motion, "Personally, I think." She shook her head, "no," she squinted, "I know that that you don't actually like him." She wiggled her finger, "no, you do like him." She said phlegmatically.

She smirked, "but not in the way that he wants or deserves," she gulped, scraping her tongue across her teeth. Sharpening her weapons, "I honestly have no idea what you're doing, if this is your way of coping after a traumatic experience or some shit like that because you are the absolute most loyal person I know, and you were in love with Ries," Anaisha's breath caught. "I saw how you guys were with each other, witnessed it first-hand..." Naira leaned back, crossing her arms. "I know you; it's not possible for you to move on yet."

Anaisha opened her mouth to speak, but Naira held her forefinger up, "one more thing," she said coldly. "You never even asked me if I would be okay with it," he voice shook slightly "he is my best friend, and you didn't even have the decency to ask me how I might feel about it."

"He's my friend too, Naira," Anaisha interrupted, slanting her eyes, in defence.

"Yes, but he is my best..." Naira said, underlining the word in the air, "friend. And you know how I am," Naira said, taking a deep breath. "He means a lot to me, and I need him." Naira said, looking down at her hands. "And if you break his heart, then what if he never wants to speak to me again?"

"Why the fuck aren't you mad at him?" Anaisha said, throwing an arm into the air.

Naira took a steadying breath, "I was mad at him! Very, actually" she looked toward the door as if someone stood there, a memory maybe. Her head whipped back to face Anaisha, "but I know you told him not to tell anyone... Aki doesn't keep secrets." Naira rolled her eyes, "it's not his thing. I'm not going to get angry at him for liking a girl, am I? And I know he would have asked me if you had let him," she spat.

"A relationship might be between two people, but this involved me too." Her green eyes glistened. "And what about Ries? How do you think he feels?"

"Ries already knows, and he was really nice."

"Are you serious?" Naira scoffed "he might seem it, but obviously he was hurt. You moved on in a few months," she said as if that wasn't obvious. "And I don't know what this is. You are too loyal and connected to him to be able to move on in a few months.

"As I said, what's done is done. I know who both of you truly are, and I just don't care. I hope you both make each other happy, and you deserve each other."

Anaisha's breaths came hard and heavy.

"Fuck off, Naira," she said, walking out the door, heat coursing through her veins as she slammed the door shut.

The next day Naira and Anaisha made up the way the family did and did.

"I'm sorry, I fucked up," Anaisha said when they were all in the common room at school; they were tucked away on a little sofa.

"I love you, you idiot," Naira said, sympathy in those green eyes. "I just want you to be happy" she smiled gently.

"I really hope no one can see us, and this is really embarrassing to be crying and saying 'love you to my cousin in the common room" Anaisha smacked her across the arm.

Inara was wearing a big leather jacket, jeans, and a small top. The brown bag slung across her shoulder, swinging as she walked from painting to painting. Inara decided she wanted to see the museum today. Andries had tagged along because he had finished all his work for the week while the rest of the group was back at the university, finishing off some assignments, and would catch a bus and meet up with them later in the evening.

She cocked her head to the side, admiring. She was always drawn to 'impressionist' art. It gave her the same feeling as seeing the sky in the nighttime, gazing at the stars.

"Impressionism, huh?" Someone snuck up behind her.

"Yeah," she said, moving on to the next one. Andries followed. "Inara is impressed by impressionism," he said.

She smirked with a roll of her eyes. "Andries is acquainted with alliteration," She grimaced, "that was bad," she admitted.

He chuckled softly, "yup, sorry to break it to you" They stared in silence for a while. Inara's eyes gracefully lingered on certain parts while Andries touched the scar on his brow, squinting.

"So, what do you like about it?" He asked, curiosity piquing in his voice.

She rolled her eyes, "you're like a child, Ries." When he was bored, it was very obvious. "You've only just figured that out now... I thought you were smarter than that, Inu" he smirked. She sighed, still appreciating the art, whilst taking care of her friend "do you remember what I told you about the sky?"

"Yeah, you said it gave you perspective," he mimicked her voice, "and that..." he clicked his fingers, racking his brain, "it made your problems seem more inconsequential." He patted himself on the back at essentially quoting her. She moved on to the next painting. He followed, "That was when I realized you were a complete weirdo, by the way."

"Well, impressionist paintings give me that same feeling, and you only figured that I was a weirdo back then... thought you were smarter than that."

It was a weekday night, and they all sat at dinner.

"What are we doing here?" Calista said, taking a sip of her drink as she looked around, her blue eyes clearly taking everything in. They were in a rooftop restaurant. It was at the very top of the building site, in the open air.

"Aki has a surprise," Anaisha said with a loving roll of her eyes and a hand on his shoulder. By now, everyone knew about the two of them. Truly, Anaisha wasn't particularly sure of how she actually felt. But she sure as hell knew that she didn't care what other people thought. And she had told Andries and her friends, and that's all that mattered.

Calista lifted her eyebrows as she took another sip.

"You never struck me as a 'surprise 'kind of guy," Kiara said, shrugging her cardigan back on her shoulder.

" He hates getting surprised." Naira said, crossing her legs and adjusting the napkin she had put on her lap. "But loves the act of surprising," she said as she opened the menu, green eyes scanning. "Exactly," Aki said, pointing to Naira and her explanation.

They ordered some starters to share, as Aki said to order the mains in a bit. Someone would be joining them. Naira scrunched her eyebrows together, "Who?"

"Maybe, that's the surprise," Aki said, leaning his elbows on the table.

Naira squinted, holding his eyes... he stared right back. Giving nothing away.

They were chatting and munching on their starters as the sky slowly darkened around them. It was coming to summer, and the sun had started setting later. Soft yellow bulbs that hung above them came on and dimmed over the restaurant.

From the corner of her eye, Naira saw a waiter pull a stool and fix a mic at the front of the restaurant.

"Oh, wow. There's live music!" Calista said, pointing, her eyes lighting up.

Slowly a tall, handsome guy hopped on the stage in a white linen shirt and jeans/pants. He went over to the waiter and helped him adjust the mic to his height.

He smiled at the waiter, touching his shoulder and thanking him. He picked up his guitar nonchalantly and put it around his neck.

Fixing the chords, he sat back on the stool, adjusting the mic, and before he started, he took a quick look at the people sitting. Then his eyes stopped for a minute, and his mouth went from shock to spreading into a small laugh himself. He touched the middle of his guitar as his face settled into a smile.

Naira had never realized this before, but Zane hardly ever got nervous. He really just didn't care. And then he started strumming. He played a beautiful Spanish guitar song as the sky darkened even more now.

The restaurant was filling up now, with more people coming in for dinner time. Naira had wondered why Aki had wanted an 'early dinner tonight, he wanted a good table.

She saw people point at Zane with an impressed nod or say things like "he's actually very good" and "how beautiful?" Cocking their heads to the side and listening for a minute.

When he finished, there was light applause and an incredibly loud over-the-top one coming from the table on the left-hand side. Zane laughed even more and said into the mic, "these aren't crazy people over there, they are just my friends," and the whole restaurant laughed lightly as Zane hopped off the stage effortlessly and came over to them. Calista was beaming as she pushed her chair back to go and give Zane a hug, "that was amazing, Zane!" Her smile looked even prettier in the restaurant sky.

"Seriously, it was great," Kiara said as he put his arm around her. He laughed, "Thanks, guys," he said, touching his chest.

"This is why I love surprises," Aki said.

Anaisha giggled, "It was a good one," she said. "You were fantastic; did you know that we were going to see you?" she said as he leaned down to hug her.

"No idea," he shrugged. "I had only just mentioned it to Aki," he said, motioning to Aki as he went around taking the empty seat next to Naira.

"I thought you only just started learning it," she said with the infamous mischievous look in her eye, a little smile on her face.

"I did. I'm just that good," he shrugged.

She laughed. And looked at him sideways, something new in her eyes as she flipped her hair over her shoulder.

She wasn't lying when she said she was into musicians. "Well, you were really good," she said.

"I'm glad you liked it," he said, rubbing his hands on his legs and smiling nervously (insert what a nervous smile looks like) at her.

She smirked down at her plate, she didn't think she'd ever seen him like this.

"Seriously though, when did you start?" She asked, her eyes softening. She knew what all of them were thinking right now. Zane reminded them of Mykal.

Zade blew a breath out and looked straight at the restaurant. "Actually, I started when I was maybe 7 or 8 and carried on. You know passed all those exams and stuff."

"How did I never know this?" Naira said, surprise on her face. Zade shrugged. "I don't know. I never really played casually or anything, and once I passed my last exam, I was so sick of it, I barely played," He said, looking at Naira now, "and I always saw Mykal play for fun, you know... enjoying it."

She nodded, remembering too.

"When he passed, I decided to start again. It just felt right, like I felt connected to him," Mykal said as he spoke with his hands, struggling for the words "to honour him." He laughed, clearly uncomfortable with what to say.

"Don't worry. I understand," she said, leaning back in her chair.

Mykal touched his chin and rested his elbow on the back of the chair as if something had clicked.

"I have to say, I get why he loved it so much now. When you're playing, it just feels like the rest of the world sort of melts away," he said, looking into the dark sky.

Naira liked musicians because talking to someone who played music was like talking to someone who she knew would understand her. Would see and feel the way she did, through emotions and words and escaping and drifting from our world. Would see and feel the way she did, through emotions and how your heart and soul felt.

"What?" Andries looked at her, eyes incredulous. "You don't think it takes intelligence to learn music?"

She clicked her tongue, "no... I know it takes intelligence, but-"

"You have the ability to do one of the things that make someone's soul flutter," he said emphatically, touching his chest.

She quirked a brow and a smile, "you sound like me."

"Don't insult me like that" he held a hand up. She shoved him in return. He laughed as he lost his balance. Regained it and carried on.

"Don't get me wrong, I'm a business person." He said with a smile, putting a hand on his chest. "But, I'm good at it, and I enjoy it."

She noted how his eyes sort of lit up at the prospect of his future.

"Of course, we need doctors, engineers, scientists to stay alive," he listed the professions off on his fingers," but we also need artists, writers, and musicians," he inclined his head to her. "To stay alive," he said looking at her with those intense blue eyes.

"In a world without doctors, we may not survive. However, in a world without musicians, we would have never lived. We wouldn't be alive no matter how long our hearts beat. I don't even know if there was a time before music."

"For god's sake, some surgeons play music in the O.R."

They were taking a stroll in the park. The squeals of children playing around them.

"It's not like I'm going to stop playing," exasperation itching into her voice. "I could never do that" her words slowed and softened as realization dawned on her.

She blinked, coming back to where she was, "I just don't think it's a career option for me" she shrugged, playing with the teardrop pendant at the base of her neck.

He grabbed her hand, dragged her to a bench across them, and urged her to sit.

He bent down in front of her, his knees on the grass, holding her hands. She could feel the bandage from his fracture against her fingers.

"Will you do something for me?"

"You're dirtying your jeans," she pointed out. He ignored this comment.

"Ok, depends on what you want me to do?" She angled her head down. He looked up at her, sapphire blue taking up her vision. "Close your eyes."

"Andries-"

"Please," he urged, blinking. He knew what he was doing. She groaned and closed her eyes.

"Okay, now think of your future." She could still hear the children and chatter around her, the rustle of the leaves.

Imagine yourself older, imagine your life if everything happened exactly how you wanted it to... there was nothing stopping you from conquering and achieving every dream you'd ever dreamt" the sounds of children softened as the wind picked up around her. Rustling her hair behind her neck. "What is your life like?" He whispered.

"I'm content, and there's bliss," she smiled unconsciously. "My parents are there. They look a bit older, but they're laughing still, and I have love; it's golden and nourishing. My friends are there" this included her friends back home and the new ones she had made this year. Her eyelids fluttered. "There's a child too. Whose laughter brings forth mirth? And there's a piano. I play it every day a little bit, and it warms my heart. I make my own music, and it makes me proud."

"You can open your eyes now," he said, letting go of her hands and dusting off his knees.

She took a deep breath in, blowing it out through her mouth. And reacquainting herself with the park they were in. "but life can't always be a dream, Andries. It's wonderful and amazing, but it's no dream," she said, getting up. "I am going to study architecture, do that and play my music for myself," she shrugged. They would have this kind of conversation more and more as the years went on. "I'm lucky I have parents that have given me a good life. I want to take that and be smart about my future," she said, pushing her long hair back.

"Your parents love you. They want you to do what makes you happy," he said, pressure in his voice.

"And I am. I practice music. I'm in the band," she shrugged, "and they're the ones that pushed me to make music… but pursuing it as a career choice," she laughed, "that's a different story" she leaned back and crossed her arms over her chest as she looked away from him, her hair fell around her face. He could hear it in her voice. It was the end of the conversation. For now, he thought.

There was an old couple sitting on the bench across from them. They were holding hands, their fingers interlinked between each other. They looked quite glamorous in their jeans, with an expensive ring and bracelet on the woman's hands. Her hair was short, curling at the nape of her neck and artfully across her forehead. He had a light jacket on and yacht shoes. Chatting to each other silently.

"Look at how cute they are..." Inara subtly pointed at them.

"Aww, they are actually..." he admitted. He turned his head as a thought flew through his mind, "you know what Naira told me once? She'd look at random people and think of their life stories or imagine something up for them," he laughed at the memory.

"No way!" She said, turning to him and touching his shoulder lightly. Even Inara's shock was still graceful and composed. "I always imagine a song that might suit them, like what the soundtrack to their life would be."

He shook his head with a laugh, "you guys are so weirdly similar but still different," he said more to himself than her.

The wind picked up a bit, and Inara wrapped her leather jacket further around herself; it was faux.

And another thought passed through him with the breeze.

"I wonder if people look at me and think, 'his best friend died recently. And he and his girlfriend broke up" pungent humour in his words.

Inara turned to look at him with gentle grey eyes. If this happened sometimes, he'd be fine.

Laughing or thinking or talking, and in a minute, he'd think about his losses. But he seemed to be less in denial or in anger about it lately. "Talk to me," she said softly, resting her elbow on the bench, facing him. He stayed looking straight.

It was as if it was just me and then an outline of Mykal. No one else mattered. All that mattered was that he wasn't there. "It's weird, you know," he said, his blue eyes squinting as he searched for the words. "Sometimes I feel like he's right next to me," he said as he touched the air to the left of him. "Like he never left." He still struggled to say he had died, she realized. "And I t-" his voice cracked for a moment, and he gulped down as if in pain. His eyes shut, and his hand still hovering on his left.

"Sorry," he said as he slowly opened his eyes.

"It's okay," Inara said, her voice as gentle as she could make it. She wanted to pat his back and physically comfort him. She touched his arm lightly and said, "Carry on."

He gulped again and, with a dry throat, carried on.

"I turn. Sometimes. I turn my head to the side, ready to say something. Something to Mykal."

Inara felt her eyes burn.

"For a few seconds, it's like I actually think he's standing there right next to me." His hand still hovered on his left.

"And then I turn my mouth open to speak to him / ready to say something to him, and he's not there."

Suddenly his hovering hand became a fist. He was holding the fist so tightly, his hand shaking as he said again.

"He's not -" he tried to say the last word, but instead, he let out a sound as he pursed his lips together. A sound came from his throat as the tears spilled down. He shoved the bottom of his hands roughly into his eyes. Willing the tears to stop. But Inara could see them drip off his chin.

"Sometimes I even dream about him. I dream of this dream where we're sitting in his room, and I'm telling him everything that's happened in my life since he left. And in the dream, it feels like he's just come back from somewhere. As he went on a really long trip." He gulped. His eyes shining and pained. A tear fell down her face, and she wiped it away. "But, in my dreams, he always comes back." "Andries-"

His tears had dried now, but his eyes still glimmered. "You were right, you know, life's no dream," he breathed in a ragged breath.

"It's not a dream," she shook her head in consolation. "And real-life fucking sucks sometimes, seriously sucks," she wiped another light tear. She gulped, "you've lost so much, so quick and at a young age. And that is fucked" she was angry at him. Then she found his hand, holding it tightly.

" But you just carry on, the way you have been. Keep moving. And life may not be as bright as when they were a part of it, but soon you'll meet people who will make it either as bright as it once was or a little dimmer. But still bright nonetheless" OR, "and life may not be as bright and bountiful as your dreams, but you will meet people, and things will happen that will either make it as bright as it once was or a little dimmer. But still bright nonetheless."

He nodded. Believing it for the first time in a long time.

"Maybe life has a dimmer. It brightens and dims as you keep living," She laughed. "Yeah, maybe there's a dimmer."

"If you had to change something about yourself, what would it be?" He asked. Without missing a beat, she said, "nothing. I'm perfect."

He smirked, "good answer."

She nodded; with a gulp, she said, "no, to be honest, I think life's too short to dwell on all the things that are wrong with you. I used to overanalyse everything about myself," she said, shaking a head, remembering how silly she used to be "my face, my body, and the way I talked, the things I said. I think girls are conditioned to feel that way... insecure." She took a shaky breath in.

He turned his head sideways, wondering what earth she could have found ugly in herself. She was possibly the most beautiful person he had ever seen.

"But then I thought, I just need to stop giving a fuck. If I fuck up, I apologize with sincerity and humility, learn from it, and move on. And when it comes to the external, if I care enough about it, I'll go change it, and if I don't, just let myself be and carry on with a smile."

"What did he teach you before..."

"It all went tits up?" He smirked, picking a flower from the field.

Andries slowed down his movement, laying down in the field. Closing his eyes up at the sun, laying an arm over his eyes.

And in a soft raspy voice, he said, "he showed me how to have a brother, how to be loved by someone who doesn't need to love me.

Has no duty to it."

That night they went to a bar with live music. The doorman opened the door. It was a whole world in there, chairs pulled up to tables, too many people sitting at one table. Laughter filled the

251

air, and smoke lingered in air. Three chandeliers hung from the air, juxtaposing the simple wooden floor. A wooden bar on the side, with two bartenders, a male, and a female in black shirts, expertly making drinks. Neon signs and vintage posters plastered the brick walls.

There was no host, and you just found a table. They played by the 'no-rules 'rule of the place and scrounged together two tables and a bunch of chairs.

Inara laughed, a look in her eye, "you know what, fuck it, why not?" She got up, sipping the last of her drink. Raising her hand and walking over to the small stage.

"We have a volunteer, this pretty girl named... what's your name, darling?"

Inara moved toward the mic, "I'm Inara," she said. The group whooped from the table. Inara blushed.

"And what are you doing for us tonight, Inara?" "I'm playing the piano," she smiled.

"Alright! Can we get a round of applause for... Inara. Take it away," he said, bouncing off the stage as she walked over to the piano. Luckily, they were sitting in a spot where they could see her fully.

She began playing a tune, talking into the microphone. "So, as the night is coming to an end,

I'm going to leave you with a song that hopefully conjures up some memories and makes you feel something before going to bed tonight," Her deep voice reverberating around the place. The glow of the chandeliers above her. She wasn't nervous. She was used to playing to people in recitals and things, and this was a nice piano.

"And please, forgive me if I'm a bit rusty... I haven't played in a few weeks."

It was one of those situations where someone is quite modest about their skills because they're actually so good that they really don't need to big up their skills because there is already that much innate confidence within them.

Andries had heard her play before with their band, but not like this. Not solo, just singing and playing. It was different, somehow. The way the spotlight highlighted her. Inara had a beautiful voice that accompanied the piano so well. And she was amazing at the guitar, but you could tell that the piano was different to her. She was so good that a light hush actually spread around the place. She had a voice that worked in small places like this, and it felt like she was singing just for you. Even the bartenders stopped pouring and cleaning their glasses; one of them actually leaned on the counter, watching her play and sing.

Her eyes were whirring around the keys and even closed at times, knowing it by touch.

And then the music changed, almost like a different song altogether. Her fingers moved faster, in a more complicated way. And her voice... it was like she sang regardless of how she sounded, spreading the message of music and the lyrics. It was a sad song, but it was about pain, not being forever so that it would get better but in a real way. A song about slowly healing.

Listening to her felt like listening to a song that you knew you would replay again before it finished, just listening to the bridge again or feeling that key change.

Even before he finished, he knew her as her friend. It felt like a duty almost to make her follow this dream that you could almost see.

Aki was practically walking with a spring in his step. Or, at least, his version of a spring in his step, which was one hand in his pocket and one around Anaisha's shoulders, omg strides, and a gorgeous smile on his face.

"Naira and I came here once, and they have the best hazelnut lattes."

" Hazelnut lattes..." Anaisha repeated, looking up at him, her voice masked in intrigue. All she really wanted was a normal coffee, the way she liked it. She didn't realize when this had become their thing, trying out the swanky new coffee shops in town.

Anaisha turned her head to the side, he had some stubble growing, and god, he looked beautiful. With those deep-set almond-shaped eyes, full lips, and clean nose. Even his side profile looked handsome. That was a hard feat to achieve.

It was a nice day, still breezy as always, but the sun seemed to have at least a little bit of power today, giving them some warmth. They reached the cafe, and as usual, Aki opened it for her. "Thanks," she said, striding inside. He was always doing things like that, polite, gentlemanly things. Like opening doors and so punctual and complementation, he even brought her flowers randomly.

It was very cool. The whole place was white and with these light brown wooden benches, which looked cool but somewhat uncomfortable. The walls were lined with great, big glass windows. Letting in the moments the sun was unafraid to show its face. They were led up the stairs to the second floor. The stairs had no railing, it was just a flying staircase. And Anaisha felt off-kilter as she walked up. They sat down across from each other.

The waiter asked them what they wanted as she popped down the menu.

It was a food menu, Anaisha read confusedly, thinking this was a coffee shop. "I thought you made coffee?" She asked the waiter. He flipped the menu for her. "Right, sorry," she grinned.

"There was some normal coffee, but clearly, they specialized in 'coffee with a spin, 'as Anaisha called it. With pistachio, rose, and hazelnut lattes. There was even a birthday cake and coffee.

"I'll get the hazelnut latte," Aki said, looking over at her. She knew he was hoping that she would get it too, but he wouldn't order for her. Not his style.

"Same..." she said, handing the menu back. They got their hazelnut lattes.

Anaisha took a sip. It was delicious, but something felt wrong.

"How good is that?" Aki asked, looking at her with anticipating eyes.

She nodded as she took another sip. Her eyes raked the place/territory. All clean cut lines and smoothed out wood, her fingers tightened around the bench she was sitting on.

She turned to look around her, and there was a woman with curled hair and manicured nails typing away at her laptop. Eating a smoothie bowl and cappuccino, which was tinged pink.

She shook her head, her nails were manicured, too, and she loved smoothie bowls too. Then there was a man leaning back casually in a cashmere sweater, having a soft conversation on his phone, lightly pinching the bridge of his nose.

"I can't," Anaisha said, slamming her hands down beside her hips. "What?"

She gulped and looked up with scorching eyes. "I just want a normal fucking coffee, Aki. You know, with milk and maybe some sugar," she said, looking up and waving her hands about, "maybe stevia, instead of sugar," she lifted her hands up in exasperation. "But not hazelnut lattes and places that serve a whole fucking menu of food along with the coffee."

"We can change it to a normal coffee" Aki shrugged, eyes moving, taking her reaction in. He hurriedly tried calling the waiter.

"No, no, it's not that," she said, reaching over to put his arm down. "It's just that..." she didn't even know what she was trying to say.

Her thoughts were moving at 100 miles a minute. She held on to his arm, catching her breath. This place was just too clean and white, and the walls felt like they were caving in despite the big windows.

She grabbed the purse that sat beside her on the smooth wood bench. "I have to go. I'm sorry," and she grabbed the hazelnut latte with her other hand.

Aki's mouth was agape. He stuttered. "I thought you didn't like the hazelnut latte."

She was already standing, and her purse flailed up in her hand, "of course I like the hazelnut latte! It's fucking delicious!"

And then she walked out. Bounding down the stairs, and as she walked outside, she took a deep breath. Felt like she could breathe again.

After Mykal's Funeral, Anaisha went For a Run

She preferred running at night. It felt like she could just melt away into the darkness. The daytime meant that the problems would follow her after the run, but when you ran in the night, they melted away, and then you went to sleep, and for a few hours, there was no time to think about the sad things.

She loved running; it was the closest thing to drugs.

Anaisha had always liked to run on the treadmill as a workout. But she had never done it as therapy.

It was the night of the funeral. She had come home late that night. Stayed out with Andries and her friends for a bit, remembering and smiling and crying. All kinds of fused together.

She parked her car in the driveway. Her fingers tightened around the wheel for a minute as her chest rose. She faced the door of her home, her eyes burned.

She made a quick decision and took a quick breath in as she hurriedly turned the car off, took out the key, tucked her hair behind her ears, and silently but speedily got in the house.

She thought her parents would be asleep; it was midnight. But she could see the family room light on.

"Anaisha?" her mother called.

Anaisha padded toward the room. She opened the door completely.

Her mother had her glasses on and was reading a book as her Dad massaged her feet. Her mother yawned, and so did her Dad. It was late for them, and sweet of them to stay up. "Hey, thanks for staying up," she said softly.

Her parents looked at her, their eyes were soft, sad, and sympathetic... her Dad opened his mouth, about to say something.

And before he could, she announced, "I'm going for a run." with a small smile. Her Mum blinked in surprise.

Her Dad looked at his wife and then turned to Anaisha and said, "It's late, Jaan," her Dad said, clearly choosing his words carefully.

But he didn't say no. This was a sensitive day.

Anaisha shrugged and made her way out, saying nothing else. She felt like if she spoke, she might cry.

That was one of the good things about your best friend dying; everyone sorts of let you do what you want.

She went up to her room. The comfortable silence of being in your bedroom... where the silence is not scary but more of a silent song. Without any actual thought, she went to her closet and grabbed everything she needed. Sports bra, jacket, shorts, sneakers, and headphones.

Then she went up the stairs. Opened the door of her room, in the comfortable silence and feel of your own bedroom. She closed the door and strode to the closet. Without any actual thought, instinctually, she grabbed whatever she needed, ticking the things off in her mind.

Slipping off her clothes and leaving them in a pile on the floor, she wanted to burn those clothes. She pulled a sports bra over her head, pulled on shorts, slipped into her sneakers, and tied them up. She grabbed a sports jacket from a hanger, zipped it up, and grabbed a hair tie that was on the side table. Pulling her hair back. And got her headphones.

She bounded down the stairs, quick steps. And as soon as she closed the door. She hit the pavement, and she just went for it.

She didn't know how long she ran for, possibly six or seven kilometres. Running most of it and walking when her body betrayed her. Her heart beat fast, and it hurt to breathe, but then it was like something clicked, and she felt so alive and distracted at the same time. It felt like an amazing key change in a song. Obviously just the release of serotonin, and it was fantastic. And her thoughts just dissipated into the night air, and either her thoughts just dissipated into the night air and if any thought snuck in. She just ran away from it, literally. Every thought of sadness or rfunning in the night felt like maybe if you made it far enough... you could truly just run away.

If she hadn't run that night, she probably would've cried or screamed at the sky. That probably would've been better in the long run. But she never said she was a long-distance runner, more interval based.

And often, things like this could only be dealt with on an interval level.

And right now, she didn't want to deal with the pain; it was easier to suppress. She felt wired, like she might scream or cry or laugh, anything other than break.

Anaisha had just hopped out of the shower, drying her hair with a towel. She had gone for a run after leaving Aki. She looked in the mirror. Sharp dark eyes looked back at her.

"What are you doing?" She asked herself as she bit her lip. There was a knock at her door.

"One minute," she called out, yanking a robe on, still drying her hair. She opened it tentatively. It was Aki.

"Hi," she breathed. His hair was pushed back with a headband. She looked up; he was always taller than she remembered.

He looked down at her robe and wet hair. She stopped drying it. "I went for a run." She gulped.

He nodded. She could smell him, musk, and powder.

"Can I come in?" He asked, his voice sounding more serious than she had ever heard it. "Maha, let me up," he said.

She nodded, blinking. Turning to make room for him to enter. He didn't sit on the bed like he usually did, instead stayed standing with his hands in his pockets.

"What happened back there?" He asked, his soft sea-breeze voice softening her. "It wasn't about the hazelnut latte..." she began playing with her fingers.

257

"I figured that much" he cocked his head to the side. A strained smile spread across her lips. "I think it was just too much" she played with the rings on her left hand. "Like when I left, I felt... relieved" his shoulders sagged, and she sucked in a breath noting it.

"And I was finding non-existent faults in the place," she looked up at him, earnest eyes. "Even though it was lovely."

"Right..." he nodded. He held his chin up, "were you finding faults in me?" "No, no," she shook her head, asking her to believe him with her eyes.

"In our situation then?" He leaned against her wall. She appreciated him saying what she couldn't, making her feel a little less shit about herself.

She nodded silently.

"you're going to make me do this?" He asked calmly.

"I'll feel like too much of an idiot if I do it myself" she looked up at him with sharp, sympathetic eyes.

He nodded resolutely. Pushing himself effortlessly off the wall. Took a breath in, "let's halt this," he pointed between the two of them, with long nimble fingers. "take a break."

"Aki," she stood up. He was already backing away.

"You don't have to say anything," a sober, complicated smile on his face. "We're good," he nodded as he turned and walked out.

She sat down, taking a deep breath. No tears came; she just put some music on. Blaming her heart for being the stupidest part of her.

It was nighttime in the school. It felt so weird being in classrooms at night, sort of transgressive, in a way. It was the last week of their final year, and they were only a couple of days away from graduation.

Two classrooms were taken up for this exhibition. She was in the first classroom.

"Yes, I focus on lifestyle portrait photography," she nodded. Anaisha's photographs were on a white rolling board next to her; she stood next to them with a beaming smile, gesturing to them as she explained the photographs and inspiration to the people that came to see them. It was groups of parents, families, and friends of the students and teachers. The whole room was filled with chatter and expansive bags and watches and 'oohs and aahs.'

She saw her parents walk in and waved lightly toward them as she carried on explaining her photographs to strangers. She saw the look that came over people as they looked at her photos. Their heads angled, and then a small smile spread on their lips as their shoulders softened.

"Anaisha, they are wonderful," her mother said, giving her a hug. "Thanks, mamma," she said, letting go.

"They are really excellent," her father beamed as he put a strong arm around his youngest daughter.

"Amazing!" her sister appeared in front of her, smiling.

Anaisha squealed, grabbing her sister into a tight hug, "I thought you couldn't come," she muffled into her shoulder. "I lied," Ishaani gasped with a laugh.

Calista, Kiara, and Zade were already there, looking around at other students' work.

From her peripheral vision, she saw a girl with curly dyed hair and vivid green eyes saying something to a tall guy with jet black hair, and a half smile, who bent down to hear her. Anaisha blinked in surprise.

A few minutes later, the duo walked over to her.

"This is so good!" Naira clapped her hands lightly together, holding them together as she gazed at the photos standing with her family. Her uncle put an arm around her shoulders. Naira leaned in, "I can't wait till Dad sees these," she said to him.

"He's going to love it," he said, pride in every movement.

" Thank you for coming," Anaisha said to both of them, but mostly to Aki. He was wearing a headband and his uniform. He looked older than at the beginning of the year, shoulders broader, and jawline sharper.

"Of course I-" he cleared his throat, "we were going to come" he smiled his half-smile. Anaisha laughed softly, intent eyes looking at his beautiful slanted ones. How did she get so lucky? To have the best ex.

Zade came up next to Aki, "you made it" he smacked his back. He smirked, "I'm not surprised" Calista and Kiara came up next to him, and all three went over to greet Anaisha's parents.

"We're going to miss her when she doesn't come on Tour with us," Calista pouted, her wavy brown hair tied back, showing off the sadness in her blue eyes. Anaisha was going to go on a four-year dual degree, studying business and photography.

Selena came up to them, her dark hair in a heavy side part, glamorously curled and placed on the side of her head.

She bumped a hip against Mahita, "you must be so proud," she smiled, proud herself. "Marco wanted to come, darling, but he had a really important meeting," she said, looking at Anaisha with the same eyes as her son.

"Of course, tell him it's totally fine," Anaisha said with a heavy smile. She nodded as all three ladies gazed up at the photos.

A photo was blown up of Andries and Mykal. The photo she had taken on her birthday.

There was a photo of Naira reading on her beanbag and a photograph of Damini talking to Mykal in a garden.

Aki and Naira sat together in the common room, her head on his lap as she read and he slept. A picture of him and Zade throwing a ball.

An old photo of Zade and Abel together.

Calista and Naira and Kiara, laughing together at a restaurant.

A photo of Naira lighting candles in her room.

There were pictures of her family too. So many beautiful moments of life are forever captured. And a shot of Mykal strumming his guitar in his bedroom, wearing one of the hoodies he had designed.

Home is always home

Andries drove to meet Inara at the beach, driving around this part of town put an odd feeling in his chest.

It was melancholic and monumental.

It made him feel older, somehow. it consolidated the face that he drove through these parts less and less. There had been a time when he was in this place nearly everyday...

It consolidated the fact that he had moved away from home.

Every tree, every sign and building reminded him of a life he had once lived,

Reminded him of his old life, he was the kind of person that could now say 'old me 'and 'new me'.

'I think, its making me feel like I'm growing up'.

His heart felt sort of heavy, sad and happy at the same time. In that way that only humans could feel. Kind of ambivalent, as he parked his car and got out of the car. He took a deep breath in of the salty, fresh air. He could see a dark haired girl sitting on a towel, holding her knees to her chest. He missed the sand, the wind and the ocean, he missed the beach.

"I have lunch tomorrow at Mykal's house," Andries gulped, the wind pushing up his curly black hair as they walked on the beach. "That sounds lovely" she looked over at him, grey eyes blinking as the sun was setting. The night brings its coolness.

"I don't know if I can do it," he admitted, carrying on the sandy path.

A flock of seagulls flew a little bit away, their sounds echoing around this portion of the sky. "Why not?" She held her shoes in her hands, her flowing pants touching the sane; she had just come from dinner.

His eyes cut to her. His blue eyes were incredulous. Sometimes Andries looked like he belonged in the ocean, with those blue eyes. But they were an electric colour. He could belong in the sky or the sea.

"Say it," she pushed "why not?" She repeated the sound of the waves making this conversation easier.

"It might be awkward," he gulped, "and I don't know if I can go into that house knowing he'll never enter again... I've accepted that he's gone. I know" he nodded, wistful eyes and a rueful smile "but if I don't go, in a small way I can live in delusion. That he may not be with me, but he's in that house. In his room." His smile turned helpless as the waves touched his feet.

She blinked slowly, looking down at the footprints they made in the sand.

She remembered the footprints they made in the snow. He was so different then, and she was too. In the snow.

"Do you remember the mountains...?" She felt him nod next to her.

"You were so different, Ries," she sat down on the sand, looking out at the ocean and the setting sun. The wash of colours against the sky.

Her dark hair flew back elegantly.

"You may not see it, but it is clear as pink in the sky today," a pink streak brushed against the purples and blues above them. "Even if you can't go tomorrow. It's not a failure; you've already made it," she said in her husky voice.

"I want to go" he took a deep breath in, sitting down next to her. He raked a hand through his hair. "I just don't know if I can" he looked out toward the ocean.

She turned her head. He had put on some weight and had a tan on his skin. His curly brown hair looked more perfectly dishevelled as it picked up with the wind.

She spun circles with her finger in the sand. "You want to know what I think?" He would miss her raspy voice when he left for university, and he was going to go and study business. And for the first time in his life, he had a dream. He would open a clothing business, selling very specific outerwear.

"Always"

Crows 'feet imprinted at the corner of her eyes when she smiled at that.

"I think life's too short to dwell on all the things you cannot do" He nodded. She pressed her red lips together, "If you really feel like you should do this, then push yourself..." She stroked her hair unconsciously, "Call me tomorrow morning, and we'll do it together. But if you really don't think you can, then let it go" she looked out at the ocean as she touched the diamond teardrop on her chest "they know you love them and him. That's enough."

He breathed in the salty air, the calmness that inevitably came with the ocean. "Thank you he said, his voice ebbing with the waves.

"You don't need to," she said, shaking her head as she touched his arm.

262

"No," he took a breath, "I was in a ghost town, all alone. And then you drove into it, peeking around, curious... thank you" She played with her pendant, a slow trickle of tears moving down her beautiful face as salty as the air around them.

2 years later - You're here

Talking to him felt like reading a story from your childhood or hearing a song that you had once loved...one that you hadn't heard in a while and was slowly remembering just how good it was.

Two adults came out, holding hands and talking softly to one another. The woman looked up at the man with a laugh, pushing him lightly. He had a cheeky smile on his lips as he looked at her adoringly.

"Oh my!" the woman exclaimed as a hand fluttered to her chest. Andries and Anaisha looked up in surprise.

Anaisha blinked rapidly as she sighed and quickly got up. Andries grinned; putting his hands in his pockets as he slowly strode over. "Hello, son," Mr. Ricard said, patting Andries on the back. He was only a little shorter than his deceased son was. Mr.Ricard hugged Anaisha.

"Hi, sweetheart," Mrs. Ricard said in her soft-spoken way as she hugged Anaisha. "It's been so long," she said, holding her hands. She gifted you with one of those long, heart-warming hugs that made you feel safe. Just like her son. "Too long," Anaisha smiled, eyes glittering.

"We should all go for lunch," Mr. Ricard said, with a benevolent smile. "We should," Andries said, with a beautiful half-smile.

"I would love that" Anaisha smiled wide as her hands came together behind her, as she let go of Mrs. Ricard.

Andries made a joke, and Mr. Ricard tipped his head back, laughing while clapping his hands a single time. Just like his son.

They all shared that smile that looks that only people who had experienced loss or any type of heartache had. A kind, beautiful smile, because though they had lost and been hurt... only those who had lost could appreciate life and happiness in that special way.

They both looked up, and like some cosmic miracle, one star in the sky shone brighter than all the rest. Anaisha and Andries locked eyes. Anaisha touched the necklace at the base of her throat, and the bracelet on Andries's wrist felt heavier.

There was another soul with them.

They both felt it.

Lightning Source UK Ltd.
Milton Keynes UK
UKHW050715060223
416538UK00013B/869